Anne Marsh writes se[...]
paranormal romances, [...]
enjoy one more alpha [...]
romance after getting [...]
technical writer—and quickly decided happily-
ever-afters trumped software manuals. She lives in
North Carolina with her two kids and five cats.

New York Times bestselling author **Lauren Hawkeye**
never imagined that she'd wind up telling stories for
a living…though she's the only one who's surprised.
She lives in the Rocky Mountains of Alberta, Canada,
with her husband, two young sons, a pit bull and
two idiot cats. In her non-existent spare time Lauren
partakes in far too many hobbies! She loves to
hear from her readers through email, Facebook and
Instagram! Sign up for Lauren's newsletter here:
eepurl.com/OeF7r.

If you liked
Hold Me and *Skin Deep*
why not try

With the Lights On by Jackie Ashenden
Give Me More by A.C. Arthur

Also by Anne Marsh

Ruled
Inked
Her Intern
Hot Boss
Hookup
Have Me

Also by Lauren Hawkeye

Sweet Temptation
Between the Lines
Playing Dirty

Discover more at millsandboon.co.uk

HOLD ME

ANNE MARSH

SKIN DEEP

LAUREN HAWKEYE

MILLS & BOON

First Published in Great Britain 2021
by Mills & Boon, an imprint of HarperCollins*Publishers*
1 London Bridge Street, London, SE1 9GF

Hold Me © 2021 Anne Marsh

Skin Deep © 2021 Lauren Hawkeye

ISBN: 978-0-263-29796-6

MIX
Paper from
responsible sources
FSC **FSC® C007454**
www.fsc.org

Printed and bound in Spain
by CPI, Barcelona

HOLD ME

ANNE MARSH

MILLS & BOON

CHAPTER ONE

Peony

"HE'S A BASTARD. A really hot, completely insufferable, prick. He always fires half of the staff on his first day." Hotly's newest software engineer, Josie, slaps her palm on my desk, making my Melvil Dewey bobblehead dance.

I straighten the stack of books on my desk. They're for show as Hotly's archive consists mostly of television footage, but a book-less librarian would be like Barbie without her awesome shoe collection.

I should discourage Josie's highly inappropriate work gossip, but the whole company's been at DEFCON 2 since notice of the sale started circulating this morning. Startups get sold or close down constantly in San Francisco, but everyone's twitching, wondering how it will affect them. I've quit or been fired so many times that I can't bring myself to care.

Instead, I worry about Josie. "Are you hiding out here? So that our new boss can't find you?"

Josie nods. "You work in the basement," she says. "I figure he'll start at the top of the building. Do you think he fires us in person or does he have people to do that?"

"People." I say this with confidence because I've always been fired by a random Human Resources person; CEO spottings have been rarer than the dodo bird in my work life. I can't imagine the new owner of our internet television channel will bother coming down to the corporate library.

"Maybe it would be better if he did it himself." Josie looks agonized. "He's hot and loaded. When will we ever get the chance to meet a guy like that again?"

"You make him sound like a baked potato with bacon and cheese. I don't think this is a dating opportunity."

"Dating opportunities have been limited." Josie waves her hands as if fresh air will make everything clearer. "When is the last time you had a date? Or a second date?"

"Three months." Although it was more than just a date. I hate that I can't stop thinking about the guy I met over the summer. I'd feel even guiltier about ending it with him except that, eventually, I'd have screwed it up and then he'd have been the one to walk away. It's always better to leave first.

Josie bounces back from a dejected slump. "If we're still gainfully employed tonight, I'll buy you a drink and we'll work on your dating plan."

"You're on," I say.

Since Josie's only been my fellow employee for two weeks, she has legitimate grounds for her continued-employment concerns. Last in, first out is practically a workplace rule. Plus, rents in San Francisco are brutal and she shares a one-bedroom apartment with three other girls.

Since I've been working for Hotly.com for almost three months, I'm practically an old hand. As my family would tell you, this is a record for me. I'm a temp, so I bounce from job to job like a pollen-seeking bee. Except, in my case, I'm looking for a paycheck and some ephemeral something else. I'm currently organizing four years of internet broad-casts, along with a ton of scripts, props, contracts and other ephemera so that people can instantly put their hands on what they want.

I spent the first two weeks on the job sorting through about a thousand boxes and organizing backup tapes. It was like a treasure hunt—so much fun but also super dusty. So I've adopted the engi-neering wardrobe of blue jeans and an old button-down. Since it's Friday—always the most popular day to fire staff—I'm also wearing a bright orange T-shirt with Hotly scrawled across my boobs. The girls are generously sized, so the letters have to really stretch to cover my real estate.

Josie twitches as the silence drags on. "Do you think he can possibly be as hot as they say?"

"Google is your friend." I push my phone toward her. This is not the sort of search that should happen on the company network.

"What if he *is*?" Josie chews on her bottom lip. "Wouldn't that make it really awkward working with him? Like, I'm supposed to say 'yes, sir' to whatever he asks. It's a bad BDSM plot waiting to happen."

"I don't think we're supposed to tie people up during company meetings."

Naturally my head decides now would be a great time to start a porn strip starring the hot boss and the naughty employee. I blame my recent lack of non-solo orgasms.

The important question is whether I want to be the boss or the employee.

Women's rights win, and I mentally flip the script in my head so that I play hot, bossy boss and Josie's unknown suit is my very bad secretary.

If in my head he looks a lot like my last hookup, it's just because I lack imagination and Jax Valentine had an amazing pair of shoulders. He was a big, bad-ass, scruffy surfer built on Goliath-like lines. A long-haired, inked-up giant with a soft spot for making me happy, particularly in bed. Really, I'm not sure why I ran off.

Okay. So I totally know why I did—I'm Ms. Anti-Commitment. I've had six different mailing addresses in the last four years and ten different jobs.

Josie pokes me. "Are you even listening or are you trying to telepathically update your résumé on LinkedIn?"

I grin at her. "How could I not be listening? Please describe our potentially hot new boss in intimate detail."

This is me living vicariously because getting it on with my boss is firmly on my Do Not Do list. Or at least my Do Not Do Again list, which is longer than I'd admit out loud. Still, banging the boss is a fun fantasy and I sort of wish that Jax and I were still a thing so I could tease him into playing with me.

Come into my office, Mr. Valentine.

Shut the door.

Explain these mistakes in my spreadsheet. Are you trying to get into trouble?

In my head, we lean over a computer screen, our shoulders brushing as I point out his errors. He's very apologetic, of course, and wants to know how he can make up this bad behavior to me, which leads to a discussion of extra credit projects.

Jax never had a submissive side—I took that part

when we role-played—so maybe he wouldn't be into me taking charge. Eh. This is my fantasy, so secretary he is.

"I want to see his suit," Josie says wistfully. Apparently, our new boss has already made a big impression without getting naked. "I read online that he gets them hand-tailored. He flies to *London* in his private jet just to go shopping."

"Glamorous if environmentally shortsighted," I agree.

Josie thunks her head down on my desk and Melvil goes wild once again. "Do you think we can bribe him with sexual favors?"

"Ménage is a lot of work. I'm not sure our big bastard boss would be worth the effort." Josie's mouth drops open, so I barrel ahead as she clearly isn't going to contribute to this conversation. As it's highly probable I'll get fired today, I don't filter.

"You don't agree? It's all the logistics that bother me. You have to figure out where to fit together multiple sets of arms and legs. Unless you were envisioning something more like a spectator sport?"

Josie squeaks. Possibly, she's having a stroke. Or mouthing the word *boss*.

Shoot. Me.

"Ladies." The dry voice that comes from behind us is deliciously rough and confident. If cavemen or victorious Roman legionnaires could speak, they'd sound like this. Does that make any sense? Absolutely not, but I blame my mental twaddle on the inescapable truth that the voice is also—unfortunately—very familiar.

That has to be a sex-deprived hallucination.

I mean, I've never had one, but the Victorians were certain lack of orgasms led to hysteria and delusions. And there's no way my new boss actually sounds exactly like my summer fling. He definitely hasn't talked dirty to me.

Or issued dirty commands.

Or done dirty, dirty things while he was inside me.

It's just the mother of all coincidences. I should have asked Josie more questions. Sadly, she's spent so much time explaining why he's imminently datable/beddable that I neglected to ask his name.

I don't want to turn around, but certain mature behaviors are expected of adults and crawling under my desk isn't really a viable option.

Reluctantly, I swivel in my chair.

The man watching me from the library door is a scary, hot bastard, all right. For a moment, I think I'm mistaken and that he's not my Jax. He's someone else's Jax—a giant of a man in an expensive suit, crisp white dress shirt and dark blue tie. His thick, shoulder-length hair has been pulled back in a club that just brushes the top of his collar; the archive's crappy canned lighting makes it look blue-black. Stubble roughens a jaw that's sporting a faded yellow bruise as if someone popped him, which is impossible. He looks exactly like what the office gossip claims he is—a ruthless billionaire who not only owns us lock, stock, and barrel, but isn't particularly happy with his purchase and is considering a refund.

This can't be the man I played dirty pirates with.

One of the studio VPs scoots out of Jax's shadow. "Peony, this is—"

"Jax Valentine," I say.

"Your big bastard boss," he growls as he steps into the library. He follows this up with a snarled, "Out."

While I'm not sure he means me, carpe diem, right? I bounce out of my seat, almost colliding with Josie, who's making her own mad dash for the door. She scoots around Jax and then hightails it into the stairwell, followed by the studio VP and the rest of the power entourage. Jax promptly shifts until he's blocking the door. A muscle in his jaw flexes.

Is he going to tell them we've hooked up and that I broke up with him? God, if I'd known he'd be my boss someday, I wouldn't have gone near him, let alone dropped my panties.

He reaches behind him and shuts the door. Firmly.

I go back to my desk and start packing up.

"So, you're a billionaire," I say too brightly. "And a businessman. I'm not sure how this didn't come up in conversation before, but it's going to take me some time to process that you're not a normal person like the rest of us."

There's a moment of tense silence during which I shove the bobblehead Dewey into my purse.

"Peony." He really, really doesn't sound happy.

"I'll email my letter of resignation by the end of the day." I sweep my phone into my purse then drop down into my chair so I can turn my drawers inside out. "Or I can send it from the train. If the WiFi is working and I'm not stuck in a tunnel. Either way, you'll have it and—"

"Firefly." He pinches the bridge of his nose. "You quit too much."

He's not wrong, but I'm smart enough not to agree.

"You ran out on me," he says more gently. "You left a goddamned Post-it note on my kitchen counter. Then you changed your number and moved. I couldn't get in touch with you."

"I didn't think you'd care. We were just a summer thing. Why would you want to talk with me?"

"We still had things to say to each other. *I* had things to say since I didn't get to write a note of my own. Finding you here is a surprise." He comes over and leans against the edge of my desk. Brown eyes the color of chocolate examine my face. I let him look. It's not as if I can stop him.

His knees bump mine.

"So you're not a superstalker. Good to know." I

reach out and tap the encroaching knees. "You're in my personal space, big guy. Pretty sure that's an HR violation."

"Am I doing anything you don't want me to do, Firefly?" His voice is low and confident. The way he says my nickname—part groan, part greedy whisper—is familiar. He knows things about me. He learned all my tells during our summer, so I'm certain he's caught the hitch in my breathing.

Touching him is a mistake. The simple contact of my fingers lightly brushing his knees reminds me of how hard and warm he is. When I'm with him, I feel safe. I stroke the soft fabric of his suit pants over and over.

You can't sleep with your boss.

Remember what happened last time. And the time before that!

Jax and I had only been together anyhow because we'd met at a Napa Valley sex party where he rescued me from my then-boss. Apparently, boss dating was about to become a pattern and I just hadn't known it. Stupidly, I'd thought attending the exclusive event would be fun or glamorous. I'd never done something like that before, so when the invitation had mysteriously arrived, I'd thought *Be bold!* And I'd gone.

It turns out that sex parties are highly overrated. They're also disproportionately full of assholes who don't understand simple concepts like *no* and *fuck off.*

"Peony. I can't do this." Jax makes a rough sound. I remove my fingers from his knee. God, where is my *brain*? "We need to talk."

"I don't particularly want to."

"You have two choices." His face is tight and controlled as he leans down so I look him in the eye. I have no problem believing that this man dismantles companies for fun. "We talk now or you can meet me after work tonight for dinner."

"Pass."

"Choose." His voice has that note of command again. A note I've only heard before in bed.

"Do you have an evil twin?"

"Pick, or I'll start our conversation now."

"What can you possibly want to talk about?"

He looks me in the eye. "Our marriage."

"That was a game."

"No." His mouth softens. "You thought it was. Fuck, I thought it was. But it turns out we're married for real."

"What?"

"I got a wedding certificate in the mail from the fine state of California." He shrugs broad shoulders. "It seems that we're married."

I'm married to Jax Valentine.

I'm the boss's *wife*.

CHAPTER TWO

Four Months Earlier...

Peony

As far as parties go, tonight's is a bust. I can accept the ridiculous over-the-top circus theme and the hundreds of people dressed as sexy acrobats or ringmasters is absolutely fun. I freaking love sexy role-playing and see no reason to limit it to Halloween. I'm even willing to overlook that most of us couldn't do a backbend to save our lives—making the sex acts being performed under the big top more aspirational than DIY demonstrations. It's the guy putting the moves on me who is the deal killer. Each time I take a step away from him, he moves closer, as if my showing up at a sex party is all the consent he needs.

What takes the crap cake? He's not even a stranger. Seven hours ago, I said goodbye to him at the of-fice because that's what you do when you're clocking out for the week and your boss is still hanging around. When Mr. Martin—clearly my about-to-be-*ex*-boss—mentioned he'd see me around, I didn't realize he'd meant tonight. Or that he was the reason I'd gotten an invitation to this swank party in the first place. Invitations to sex parties at a California billionaire's place in Napa Valley have been few in number—I'm a total sex party virgin—so of course I'd seized the chance to legitimately visit a ten-thousand-square-foot faux château. The fountains are awesome and I'd kill to swim in the pools, but the public sex acts make Marie Antoinette's real French court seem tame.

"I'm really happy to see you tonight, Peony. I thought you'd like this." Mr. Martin—"Call me Bob"—braces an arm beside my head and leans in far too close. This is not the first time I've encountered his lack of personal boundaries, but I've dismissed his previous transgressions as accidental. Apparently, I've been too charitable. Peony 2.0 needs to work on that character flaw.

Should I lie and chirp back that I'm thrilled to see him? Because I'm totally not. He's swapped his circumspect, weekday suit for crotch-hugging khakis and a white linen shirt. The top buttons are undone, revealing a tuft of blond chest hair I'd rather not know exists. His own "happiness" is also apparent, straining against the front of his pants.

I look him in the eye. "I'm not okay with this. Please move."

Please is the wrong word choice. I've dealt with bad boss scenarios before and you can't give them a hint of wiggle room. I could knee him in the balls or make a scene, but I hesitate because I'm supposed to be turning over a new, responsible leaf. If I hit him, I could end up facing an assault charge and then I'll have to put plans for Peony 2.0 on hold because Mr. Martin strikes me as the kind of guy who holds a grudge.

The last thing I want is to piss off my employer *and* hand him ammo to use against me. I've stood up to assholes before and it's a lot of work. Also, my rent's due in four days, making any indignant walking away from my job a luxury I can't afford, at least for the rest of the week. So as much as I'd like to take him on, I mostly just want to get out of here…possibly via the open bar. My decision to come here wasn't a good one, but I won't apologize for compounding it with alcohol.

Mr. Martin leers at me. *Ugh.* "I've been fantasizing about doing this for weeks," he announces.

And then, before I can repeat my no and remove myself, he swoops right in for a kiss. So much for using my words.

I twist, trying to slide down the faux Grecian column he's backed me into. There's an unwelcome flash of chest hair as I sink down and, for a moment, my escape plan looks successful. He can't kiss me, or at least his mouth is limited to rooting around the top of my head. I lurch-angle myself to the right, seeking freedom, and am hit by a wave of cologne—he's man-sprayed his happy trail—and then his hands catch my shoulders, stopping my retreat at a really awkward and unpleasant vantage point.

I'm facing his belt buckle *and* his hard-on.

And while I'm here at a sex party by choice, I assumed my choices also extended to who I got up close and personal with.

Mr. Martin chokes something out—the bastard sounds excited—and then one hand fists my hair while the other goes to his belt buckle. Yuck, yuck, YUCK. I shoot upright, palms smacking his chest. He doesn't let go, as the pain in my scalp attests.

"What part of no don't you understand?"

Not that he's listening.

Nope, he goes in for the kiss again.

The next handful of seconds are unpleasant. We grapple, my hands slapping his. The good news is that I can sleep in on Monday because there's no way I'm working for this guy. The bad news is that I just want to go home because all the magic's been sucked out of what was supposed to be a fantasy night where I attended a glamorous, sexy party and pretended to be someone fun. I'm grossed out and angry, and all the alcoholic flavors of ice cream in the world aren't going to erase this memory—

Martin the Asshole flies backward. I make an embarrassingly high-pitched squeaking sound as big, sure hands lift me and set me down to one side. I wish I could say I take advantage of Martin's removal to punch him, but I just stumble to the side and stare because I'm tired and this night is turning into an unending parade of sucky moments and, while I'm really big on handling my own shit now—

I have a rescuer.

Or possibly my own pet caveman-slash-berserker.

"Excuse me," he growls, ridiculously polite for a caveman.

Really, I just expect him to start smashing because the man standing there with Martin in a headlock is a very, *very* large man. He massively exceeds six feet tall and is built like a hockey player or linebacker, a mountain of pissed-off, cold-eyed, muscles-on-muscles man. He's dressed for the party in expensive-looking black dress pants, the dress shirt open at his throat. No jacket or circus-themed costume for him. Rolled up sleeves reveal powerful, inked forearms.

He's not pretty, not the way Martin is. Martin's smooth and polished, like a cheap souvenir rock that's been run through a tumbler and come out with a slick sheen. This guy is something else, someone you can't help but look at—partly because he's a big, beautiful animal of a man, but also because he's an apex predator who's just marched into a dog park full of poodles and mini schnauzers and the only foreseeable outcome is carnage. Dark hair tumbles around his face, past his stubble-roughened jaw, the mouth pulled into a frown. I should stop staring at him and get the hell out of here, but tonight's alcohol is catching up with me and I'm tired.

Tired of starting over, tired of having to do everything for myself, tired of learning—yet again—that there's no fairy-tale ending to my evening and that Prince Charming has not invited me to his ball, so I'm stuck with Prince Dick, his evil cousin. Whatever magic I'd hoped for tonight, I'm going to have to make do with my vibrator, a bag of Cheetos, and a really good book.

Caveman Guy slams Martin into the Grecian column I've just vacated. It's more real than I've given the billionaire party owner credit for because the stone doesn't give at all. Martin groans, but Caveman has discovered the power of speech and he has a lot to say.

"What the actual fuck? Even I heard her say no. You have to listen to that. You have to ask for her yes." His voice is a rough, low rasp. One arm twists Martin's shoulders and hands into a painful-looking pretzel, while the other makes itself at home on his throat. When he leans in, Martin turns a puce color.

Go, caveman. I can be independent tomorrow—tonight I'm outsourcing.

Sensing danger, Martin starts babbling the usual predictable crap about how I'm totally okay with his going "a little alpha" and that rough sex and some dominance will get me going. He concludes this bullshit explanation by pointing out that I'd come to this party, after all, so clearly I was "into it."

"You're here." Caveman steps into Martin, herding him up against the column. He removes his big hand from Martin's throat and braces his arm beside my boss's head. They're thigh to thigh, bodies touching, and Caveman completely, one-hundred-percent outmuscles Martin. It's the same position Martin put me in a few minutes ago, and Martin's expression makes it clear he's not finding it any sexier than I did.

"Back off, man." Martin shoves, trying to free himself.

Caveman makes a dismissive sound. Martin's efforts don't even seem to register, although that's likely because Caveman's built like a mountain and he's busy making a point. "You're here," he repeats.

"I have an invitation."

"So you want this." Caveman trails his fingers down Martin's freaking throat and then lowers his head until his mouth is brushing the man's cheek.

Holy shit. I've never got the whole eye-for-an-eye thing before. I do now. Martin is an asshole and watching him get a taste of his own chauvinistic medicine is delightful.

Martin sputters an obscenity, but Caveman just talks over him and fondles his cheek. "How does it feel? Being held down? Do you like it as much as she did?"

Martin lets loose a torrent of profanity, still trying to figure out how to make Caveman move. It's a losing battle.

"Did you hear her say yes?" Caveman repeats.

"No," Martin mutters. His belligerent gaze slides toward me. I'm so looking for a new job.

"Apologize," my rescuer snaps. Then he looks at me. "How do you want your apology?"

I pause in my Monday prognostications because he sounds so casual, as if he's asking me if I want fries with that. "What?"

"On his knees? With words? You want him to itemize what he fucked up or just give you the executive summary? I can tattoo it on his dick, if that works."

I clap vigorously. "Is that even possible? Do you think there's enough real estate? Because I'm tempted."

"Tell me what you want and it's yours."

My rescuer has a cold air of command about him. It's less caveman and more medieval king, I decide. I can totally imagine him going all Henry the Eighth on Martin's ass. Martin just glares. I don't think he gets the whole apology concept.

Right. I let go of my making-the-rent fantasy. "This is going to make things really awkward on Monday."

"You know him?" Caveman removes his angry stare from Martin and redirects it at me. His eyes are dark, intense, framed by fine lines that might come from laughter or sun and promise he has a happy side. He's not an iceberg-dwelling Viking. Or, at least, not entirely.

The anger banks while he examines my face, as if it's something he can just take on or off like a shirt or a costume.

Focus. He asked a question.

"Not in the biblical sense," I say judiciously. "He's my boss. *Was* my boss." So much for Peony 2.0 and her grand plans for fiscal prudence and financial independence and a little house of her own. I tear my gaze away from Caveman and redirect it to Martin. "I quit."

Whatever Martin says is inaudible because Caveman's reapplied his arm to Martin's throat.

"Uh." Because my brain's clearly checked out for the night, or has possibly suffered irreversible cell loss from the testosterone filling the air, I take a step toward Caveman rather than away, and tug on his arm. "I really don't think you should kill him. Momentary satisfaction versus long-term consequences, right?" Caveman regards me silently. I can't tell what he's thinking, so I babble on. "It's like cake. One slice is great, two can be excused by a really shitty week, but the whole cake is going to go straight to my belly and then I'll be regretting it when it's swimsuit season, and since this is California, it's *always* swimsuit season."

There's a pause broken only by Martin's muffled sounds. Caveman nods finally. "So don't kill him."

"Sadly, no." I pat his arm and discover a new, shallower side of myself. Holy shit, he feels amazing. The biceps hiding beneath that dress shirt are rock-hard. The man could probably bench press a small car with me sitting in the driver's seat.

I whip my hand away as what's obviously a security team moves toward us. From the looks of the weapons they're openly carrying, they're not just for show.

"Where were the armed guards before?" Because I was lucky, but what if someone else at this party isn't as lucky? Assholes are everywhere and I doubt Martin's the only one of his kind here.

Caveman slants them a cold, pissed-off glare. He's apparently got an endless supply of them. "I'll find out."

Wow. I think he means it. Maybe he's the head of security?

Whatever he is, the security guys surround us, taking over Martin-restraint duties. I can't help but notice that their questions are all directed at Caveman. They call him *sir* a lot and one guy does a head-bob thing that could even be mistaken for a bow.

Caveman looks at Martin. "Apologize."

Martin clearly recognizes the apex predator because he sucks in a deep breath. Pauses. Inhales again. "Sorry."

As apologies go, it's neither satisfying nor detailed, but I'll take it. In record time, they march Martin away to be unceremoniously booted off the property. I don't think he'll be getting another party invitation. I can feel totally inappropriate laughter bubbling up, but it's laugh or cry, and I hate crying, so it's Inappropriate Laughter for two hundred dollars, Alex.

"What?" Caveman makes another one of those growly snappish sounds.

"Are you the king of Silicon Valley?"

The corners of his mouth tug up ever so slightly. "What do you think?"

"I think my brain's gone offline," I confide. "This whole night is just surreal. I don't know if I should have been recording that on my phone, running, or applauding. I should *not* have come here. I'm supposed to be releasing Peony 2.0, but now she's going to need a bug-fix release straight away."

This strikes me as so ridiculously funny that I give in and laugh until I have to sit down.

Caveman sinks down into a crouch next to me.

"Maybe you should think of tonight as a test run and just do whatever you want to do. See how the new Peony holds up."

"You're not going to judge me for being at a sex party?"

The corners of his mouth curve up even further and he tips his head at me.

"I'm here, too," he points out.

CHAPTER THREE

Jax

OKAY, SO MAYBE I overreacted, but I don't like bullies and parties like this one attract more assholes than shit does flies. Since punching this particular bully is now impossible thanks to his forcible removal, I make a mental note to talk to Liam Masterson about his guest list. Even if he wasn't my best friend, he'd make sure the asshole never sets foot on his property again. There's a moment of silence—or as near silent as you can get at a raging sex party, which is to say not silent at all—while my companion and I stare at each other.

I'd spotted her earlier because she's hard to overlook. Not because she's gorgeous—although she is—but because she has a spark to her that lights up the place. She looked like she was torn between having fun and laughing at the ridiculous, over-the-top sex party where most people were dressed up like a circus act.

She's also one-hundred-percent into tonight's theme, which I fucking love even though the whole circus thing isn't my kink. Her costume looks vintage and, for a moment, I imagine her picking it out from one of those used clothing stores that line the Haight in San Francisco or maybe Berkeley, where my sister and I grew up across the Bay. The color's pretty—somewhere between pink and red—although I'm not clear on whether it's a dress or a sequined bathing suit with a tulle skirt. She looks amazing. The fabric hugs her curves, the perfect frame for her sun-kissed skin. She has freckles and it takes me a little too long to stop staring at them because my small head thinks we should kiss from one to the other, draw a line with our tongue and—

Yeah. I'm officially an asshole because I'm *rescuing* her. Not picking her up. Not playing sex games with her. I should be reassuring her because she probably feels either out of her league or out of control after what that bastard tried to pull. Parties should be about having fun, and that goes double for sex.

Sex should always be fun. My favorite kink is role-playing. Playing games in bed, having the chance to become someone different for a night, is the best. Most nights, it's easy enough to find someone who'll be the bad girl to my good cop, the hitchhiker to my biker, the duchess to my gardener. Rescuing damsels in distress is not something I do when it doesn't come with a side of sex. I never rescue *for real*. But I've gone and done it, and I have no idea how to extract myself now that the scene's played out.

Pretend it's the morning after. Or post-orgasm anyhow. So I'll check in, maybe walk her to the front door, and then I'll resume my mission to get laid. This is just a blip in my night.

"Are you okay?" My voice sounds gruff, even to my own ears. Circus Girl flinches but she doesn't look away. We're locked in a death stare, her gray eyes holding mine. They're rapidly acquiring a suspiciously wet sheen, as if when she blinks, she's going to cry, which means I really need to roll on out of here. I'm no good with crying girls, so someone else is going to have to pick up her pieces. My sister claims this is a character flaw I should work on, but I don't come with emotional radar and it's not something my money can buy. I defend, I protect, and I boss the fuck out of people for their own good. This works in the bedroom as well as the boardroom, so I see no point in changing.

Circus Girl makes a face that twists her pretty mouth up. "Other than being unemployed yet again? Yeah."

I could fix that, but handing out jobs tends to make people think there are strings attached. Worse, sometimes they want the strings, and bosses in bedrooms get messy. So I hesitate, not sure what to say.

Circus Girl barrels on, undeterred by my silence. "I'm Peony."

She shoves her hand at me and I take it automatically. My fingers dwarf hers and I actually wonder for a second if I could accidentally break her just by holding her hand. That moment of stupidity has to be why I raise the back of her hand to my lips like a prince or a royal fool. I don't miss the way her breath catches when my lips brush her fingers.

"Jax Valentine." I stroke my thumb over the back of her fingers and force myself to let go. I'm not the same kind of asshole as her ex-boss.

I wait for her to realize who I am. It'll change things between us, and I'm almost irritated anticipating it. As one of Silicon Valley's hottest billionaire bachelors, these parties are full of guests who'd like to get a piece of me. It's strangely impersonal, as if my dick or my head is merely an accessory to my money.

"Well, Mr. Valentine, what brings you here tonight?"

I lean in, closing the distance between us. "Sex, of course."

She worries her bottom lip with her teeth, as if my statement requires great thought. But there's not all that much to think about, is there? The whole point of a sex party is to have casual sex with strangers. It's like picking a movie: seen that one, am I in the mood for dark angst, something rough, something hot and sweet and fun? I run my thumb over her bottom lip, trying to convince myself it doesn't matter if she turns me down. As if this is totally casual and completely impersonal.

All I can think about is touching her.

The corner of her mouth curves up beneath my thumb, and I need to know what she's thinking. Peony makes me curious. I'd been close to her when I removed her from Martin's hold, but this feels different. We're two people—two consenting adults—at a sex party together. My shoulder brushes hers and she relaxes against me.

"Giving, receiving or policing?" Gray eyes laugh at me. No, *with* me, inviting me to play.

I tug gently on her hair. "Policing?"

She nods, ponytails bouncing on her shoulders. "When you came over here, I thought you looked like security and maybe I was in trouble."

She *had* been in trouble, all right, but I don't think that's what she means.

"Your ex-boss needs to understand that no means no. You okay?"

I'm good at punching assholes and I'm even better at running them out of Silicon Valley, but I really hope she's fine. I suck at the emotional comfort and moral support shit.

"I don't want to think about Martin right now," she says, as if she can read my mind. "Let's pretend it didn't happen."

"We could absolutely pretend something else," I hear myself offer.

She hesitates, and I want to pull her into me, wrap my arms around her and make promises. *We'll do whatever you want.*

She bites her lower lip again. "Are you...the good cop?"

I rub my thumb over the soft skin. "I'd love to be."

She peeps up at me through ridiculously long lashes. "Well, Officer, I may have been a very bad girl."

Thank *fuck.*

I flow to my feet, tugging her with me. Exhibitionism's not really my thing, although I'd be willing to give it a go if it's hers. There's a pool cabana tucked away nearby and, conveniently, I know Liam's passcode. She lets me steer her away from the party, into the shadows and down a gravel path made from some expensive stone Liam's imported from France in the name of authenticity.

Fortunately, Peony's red sneakers are more sensible than most of the footwear I've spotted here. Gravel and hooker heels are a poor combination. Her fingers curl trustingly into mine, stroking my palm. She doesn't say anything—she just holds on.

The cabana is right where I remember it, a small, vine-and-moonflower covered structure tucked away in the shadows. If I get bonus points for romance, I'd like to cash them in for a blow job because Peony on her knees...

While I punch the passcode into the number pad on the door, Peony watches me. Part of me is afraid that if I take too long, she'll change her mind about playing a game with me.

"Do you know the owner?"

I don't want to tell her the truth—that Liam is my best friend—because money changes things. Founder hounders chasing start-up entrepreneurs, gold diggers, desperate people, people who just want to dream a little on someone else's dime—everyone wants money from me.

"I know his passcode." It's the truth, even if it's not the whole truth. "He gave it to me."

I open the door, but there's something she needs to understand before we do this. "If you want to stop at any point, say *stop*."

She brushes past me. "No safe word?"

I follow her inside. "I don't play that kind of game. You say stop, I stop. You're always safe with me."

She nods. "Okay, and ditto."

It's cute that she wants to protect me. "Firefly, you can't do something I won't enjoy."

She is a little firefly, all unexpected sparkle in the night. If I take my eyes off her, it feels as if she'll flash away into the dark, and I don't want that.

Her mouth twists but then relaxes into a smile. "Promise?"

I flick the lock shut. I don't want anyone interrupting us, so I also leave the lights off. God bless French doors because I can see fine. "I promise."

The pool cabana is much more predictable than the rest of Liam's estate. White and beachy, there's a small, open kitchen for drinks and snacks on our left and a bathroom to our right. The rest is open space occupied by two large couches, an army of decorative pillows and those round ottoman things that I never know if they're for my feet, my ass, or my drink. Knowing Liam, the stuff hanging on the walls is either priceless French crap or crayon scribbles from one of his employees' kids that he'll pretend is sourced from a hoity-toity San Francisco gallery just to make fun of his own pretensions.

"Wow." Peony turns in a circle. "Being a billionaire has its perks. Have you seen the guy who owns this place tonight? Do you think he looks like a normal person or is he polished up pretty like his art?" She giggles. "It's like trying to spot an octopus in the wild. He's probably camouflaged and lurking in plain sight, but I'll never spot him."

This is not the time to confess that I'm also a member of that club. "So you think he's camouflaged?"

She twinkles at me. "If he's smart, he is. He's a hot topic in the ladies' room."

"Billionaires don't do it for me." I pull her to me. Slowly, so she can let me know if I don't get it right. It's like easing into the pool one inch at a time when you're hot, teasing your skin with all that water.

"What's your favorite game?" She whispers the words against my mouth. Her lips part on a smile.

"Ladies first."

"No." She swallows, the sound loud in our quiet hiding place. The fingers she runs down my throat tremble slightly. I don't think she's scared, though. I'm a lucky bastard because I think she's just as turned on as I am. "Let's do yours first."

My mouth goes dry. I really hope I didn't misunderstand her before. "I could be here because I'm a cop. A bodyguard. Maybe you're not supposed to be here."

She nods. "Good cop, bad girl. The cop and the criminal."

She talks too much, putting labels on everything. It's so freaking cute.

"The bodyguard and the trespasser. Do you want to play?"

Her breath catches audibly. "Yes."

"I think you like breaking the rules."

She grins, the smile breaking across her face. "You're an excellent guesser, Mr. Valentine."

Her eyes are darker than I realized, a gray-blue, the color of the Pacific Ocean when it's stormy. A color I could fall into. It's easy to imagine her as an ocean girl, a surfer, someone who lives and plays by a wilder, freer set of rules. Someone who's willing to play my favorite game.

I toss the excess pillows to the floor, then gently push her down onto the closest sofa. I keep one hand pressed lightly against her shoulder. We're just playing, but my heartbeat picks up like I've just run a marathon after a month of couch time.

I frown down at her. "Do you know why I pulled you over?"

She bites her lip as she looks up at me with wide eyes. "Was I going too fast, sir? On your private property? I know I'm not supposed to be here, but I just wanted a little peek."

Fuck me, she's amazing.

"Step out of the car."

She pouts, her lips drawing up deliciously. "I can be good. Can't you just check my license? Let me off with a warning? I could—"

She trails her fingers down her throat to the sweet hollow beneath her breasts.

"Out."

She shivers visibly at the hard note in my voice, her nipples puckering beneath the sequined fabric.

Wrapping a hand around her wrist, I pull her to her feet and point toward the wall. The skin I touch is soft, her pulse beating an urgent rhythm beneath my fingertips. I let go.

"Up against the wall. You've earned yourself a search."

When she hesitates, I give her a stern look. "Now."

She meets my eyes then makes her way over to the wall, dragging her feet. Her face is adorably pouty. The urge to kiss her and move straight to the sex is almost unbearable, but I restrain myself.

Once she's facing the wall, I move up behind her. "Naughty girls get put in the corner, don't they?"

She snaps something uncomplimentary and I grin.

"Left hand here." I tap the wall.

She slaps her left hand against the spot I've indicated. "I don't think this is necessary."

"Sir." I trail a finger down her spine. "You call me sir."

"You're not the boss of me," she grumbles.

But she moves her right hand into position without my telling her to. Her legs are squeezed together.

I insert my leg between hers. "Legs apart."

Her defiant "Make me" has my dick hard.

"Let's strip you down." I pull her dress up and over her head. She helps me slide it free of her arms. I press her palms back against the wall and toss the dress away. We don't need clothes between us.

"Let's see what you're hiding from me." I run my hands down her arms and she gasps and jumps. "Hold still or I'll use the handcuffs. Tie you up so you have to take whatever I do."

She shudders, muttering something. Such a bad girl.

"It's not nice to accuse someone of being a tease."

I drop down into a crouch and run my hands up her legs. She's toed her cute little sneakers off at some point, which leaves her with just a thong. It's a cheerful little scrap of yellow nylon that hides nothing. I have a thing for panties. They're like a bow on a present someone's picked out just for me.

I make a stern sound. "Wider."

I help her ease her legs wider, angling my shoulders between them. My fingers stroke over the fabric covering her pussy.

"Sir—" Her breath catches. "Is this necessary?"

"Shh," I tell her. "This isn't up for discussion."

I run my hand down the outside of her thong, firm enough that she can't mistake what I'm doing. She's holding her breath now, focused completely on what I'm doing to her or on our game. Probably both. She's hot and damp, pushing herself into my hand. I caress her with my fingers, then push deeper into the slick folds. I can feel the little heartbeat starting in her clit.

She rises up onto tiptoe. "Are you done? Can I go now?"

"Stand still." I rise with her, dragging my hands over her ribs to cup her breasts. "You could be hiding something from me."

"I wouldn't," she whispers.

"You can't," I correct her. "But I'm going to push your panties down and find out. Is there anything you want to tell me?"

She shakes her head. "Do it, sir."

I drag her thong down to her thighs and then I push two fingers into her, finding her clit with my thumb. She groans and I listen, but it's not *stop* that she's saying. We're good. She drops her head against the wall as I work her with my fingers. I can feel her trying not to come, but she's not the one in charge of her body right now. She's let me borrow control and I plan to make the most of it.

"I need to see for myself," I growl against her ear.

She nods frantically as I drop to my knees and bury my face in her pussy. I suck on her clit, still working her with the fingers of one hand. I use the other to hold her up so she can let go and just feel. Peony isn't a screamer, but she whisper moans, little half-formed words falling from her mouth because, apparently, she can't not give feedback. *Yes...wow... do that again... you're so—*

I drink it up. She feels amazing and tastes even better. I love hearing how I make her feel.

Even when she comes, she's quiet. She stiffens and then jerks a couple of times, her body bucking against my mouth, not sure if it wants to press closer or to get away. She can choose whatever makes her happiest. I kiss her down, pressing my tongue against her carefully, holding her close. I've got her. It's safe to let go.

Even if I don't want to let her go. I freeze. I'm so *screwed*. This is a sex party hookup. It's not like we're on a date.

Or a couple.

Or two people with a future longer than a handful of hours.

Unless…

CHAPTER FOUR

Peony

"WHAT DO I WANT?"

At least that's what I think I say. It might come out more *guh* and *whaIwan*. My voice sounds dazed, probably because my new friend Jax has just made me come hard enough to see stars. The happy supernova exploding in my vagina is not helping my speaking abilities any.

Not only is the man supremely talented in the dirty role play and sexy orgasm-giving department, but he's good at logistics, too. Somehow between when I squeezed my eyes shut, enjoying the amazing personal fireworks show, and now, he's scooped me up and carried me over to one of the couches. I'm draped over the top of him and he's staring up at me as if my answer is the most important thing in the world. His undivided attention is almost as sexy as his mouth.

"No judging." He nods, holding up his pinky finger. As if it's that simple—tell him who to be and he'll do it. And maybe he would. Maybe I could ask my sexy good cop stranger for my strangest, most personal fantasies. The thing is, he's already done my favorite: strangers in the night. When I tell him this, though, he gives me a slow, wicked smile.

"Did we pick each other up at the bar? Or did we hook up online?"

I make a face. "Don't be predictable. Maybe it was on the beach, so I've already seen you mostly naked and wet. I know exactly what I'm getting. Maybe we're in Thailand on this gorgeous stretch of beach and there are palm trees and water so clear we can see the fish." I wave a hand, trying to paint the picture I see in my head for him. "We're not there for a hookup but there's sexual tension we both feel, we're looking at each other, imagining things—"

He mock frowns. "You do a lot of thinking, Firefly."

I grin at him and give a little wiggle. Geez. His dick is rock-hard beneath me. "It's one of those skills required for gainful employment. Don't tell me you're actually a trust fund baby or a boy toy."

He rests his arms on the edge of the couch. "Rich asshole isn't one of your secret fantasies?"

"Not really, although I'm not averse to playing English duke." I slide my hand down his chest, exploring his delicious muscles. Unfortunately, good cops leave their clothes on, so my mission of discovery isn't as detailed as I would like. "And I'm quite sure I couldn't afford to keep you."

This earns me another half smile. "Do I look expensive?"

"It's more I'm that broke," I confide, tracing the upturned corner of his mouth with my finger. Ugh. *Overshare.* His fake frowny face draws into more genuine lines, so it's time for a topic change. "But it's still my turn to pick."

"I'm happy to pick for you." He's teasing, but I think he'd be more than happy to revert to his caveman persona and make the choice for us. It would probably be a good one, too, but...

"Shh." I tap my fingers against his beautiful mouth. "Don't rush me. This is the golden ticket of sexual fantasies, so I need to ask for the best scene. I don't want to rub the magic lamp and then waste a wish asking the genie for a pizza."

He slants me a look. "Do we each get three turns?"

God. "That would be a *lot* of sex to fit in one night."

A wicked smirk lights up his face, warning me that epic bad pun-ness is headed my way. "I'm up for it if you are."

Right. This is a one-night deal. It has to be because tomorrow—no, later *today*—I become Peony 2.0, the new, responsible, career-mind, settled-down best version of me. He's my Fat Tuesday before a lifetime of Lent, so I need to make him count.

His monster size raises the possibility of Viking raider, but I'm not in the mood for quick, hard sex. Making my past-due bill up to my landlord, stern boss and the screwed-up employee—too close to home—bad boy rebel and the country club sweetheart, or…

"Virgin bride." The words pop out of my mouth.

Wow. I'm not totally sure where that came from. It's not like I've fantasized much about finding The One. Weddings mean settling down and writing *The End* and *They lived happily ever after* to the story and I'm more of a Choose Your Own Adventure gal. But…

Right now, that's what I want.

He runs his hands down my arms, his fingers tangling with mine. "Okay. Tell me the rules. Tell me what makes you hot about a wedding night. What do you like? Am I a virgin, too, or do I take charge? Do we know what we're doing or is one of us surprised?"

It's like ordering from the menu at the fast-food drive-through. So many choices that you'll regret later but that you're greedy for now.

"Peony?"

"You talk too much, Jax."

His big fingers caress my jaw, skin callused and a little rough. Maybe he's a lumberjack or a firefighter on the weekdays?

He snorts. "First time I've been accused of that. Tell me how you want to play the next scene."

"We're high school sweethearts." I place a kiss on his jaw. "And we've both been waiting for the main event. Lots of petting, lots of kissing."

He smirks. "Have we had anal?"

"No." I mock frown, poking him in the chest.

If I'm totally honest, what I really want is the illusion of feeling cherished, loved, having someone who will take care of me no matter how much work I am, because he loves me. That's way too much to ask from a scene, however.

He thinks for a moment and then stands. I'd sort of forgotten temporarily just how bear-size he is. He's a big, protective, mountain of a man and I'm staking a temporary claim to him for tonight only.

He holds his hand out to me, regarding me with a strong, warm gaze. "Come on. Let's find your clothes."

I let him pull me to my feet. "Where are we going?"

"We're eloping, Firefly. We're gonna go to the chapel and get married so I can have my wicked way with you."

Twenty minutes later, we're fully clothed and standing in front of a guy dressed up like a ringmaster. Someone's pinned a length of white tulle into my hair in keeping with the spirit of things. My "veil" has sequins that catch the lights of the big top and I keep turning my head to see the sparkle. I've even got a bouquet, stolen from the grapevines that surround the tent. Even if I never get married for real, at least I have this memory.

Jax takes my hands, turning me to face him as he repeats the vows the ringmaster dude rattles off. His dark eyes watch my face so carefully that it's hard to remember that this is pretend. The man deserves the biggest acting prize of them all.

My insides twist, my voice coming out in a nervous squeak when I parrot my *I do*s. Jax's thumb rubs the back of my hand and I focus on that small, delicious motion. It feels almost too real.

When the ringmaster announces that Jax may kiss the bride, Jax's face lights up as if he really has been waiting months for this moment. He cups my face with his hands, tilting my mouth up.

"My Firefly," he whispers. "Here you are."

His lips touch mine and I forget about our audience. There's just me and him and a magical, electric heat that starts where we touch and fills me up.

His mouth is curious, and warm.

So confident.

And yet somehow it asks questions. *May I? Do you like this? Do I? What do you taste like?* His lips brush mine, retreat, come back and press a little deeper, his tongue sliding along the seam of my lips. *Knock, knock. Let me in.*

We've never kissed, not mouth on mouth. For a second, I panic because it's too intimate, but Jax strokes the sides of my face with his big, warm hands, keeping me safe and grounded. His eyes drift closed as he kisses me deeper and I moan softly into his mouth. *There you are. Hi.* I like watching him kiss me, long lashes brushing sun-tanned skin, the hard lines of his face relaxing. He likes this, too.

The applause makes us break apart. The ring-master presents us to the audience with a flourish and then we make a pretense of scribbling our names on the back of what looks like a Walmart receipt—our wedding "certificate."

When Jax sweeps me into his arms, I grin up at him, as dizzyingly happy as any new bride.

"Where are we going?"

"Wedding night," he says gruffly.

I thread my arms around his neck, dipping my head back to look at the night—no, *dawn*—sky as he carries me out of the big top. "So we're skipping our wedding reception, the cake, the first dance, the endless parade of relatives whose names we can't remember but who give lovely, large presents, and we're going straight for the sex?"

His thumb caresses my cheek. "I can't wait to have you all to myself."

"That sounds like a plan."

I rest my head against his shoulder and listen to the sound of his boots on the walkway. Our billionaire host's garden is a decadent expanse of plants and terra-cotta statuary, a sweep of broad steps leading up to the ginormous mansion. I guess there's something to be said for being rich, after all.

Jax carries me inside as if he owns the place, his boots hitting the stairs hard and loud. I'm tucked into his arms, my head against his shoulder. He has one hand curved against my head, his fingers stroking my hair, petting me gently. It's the perfect touch. His arms are solid, heavy muscle. He doesn't seem like the kind of guy who would spend hours inside a gym, exercising just to tick a box on the health list. I don't think he's vain, either. Maybe he just admires strength or pushing himself. Maybe he has a really physical job or plays football.

He pushes open a door and steps through it. The click of a lock follows, but then he hesitates, setting me down. His fingers guide mine to the door, showing me the lock and how to undo it. Reminding me that I can leave anytime I want to.

"Got it?" He straightens and strides across what looks like a guest room.

"Yes." I press a kiss against his shoulder as he knocks a pair of decorative pillows off the bed and yanks the covers back.

The sweet, dark look in his eyes almost makes me forget I'm the blushing virgin bride who can't wait to have her way with her groom. What would that girl do now that she could do anything? It's the

Christmas morning of sex, when nothing's been un-wrapped yet and everything is still possible.

"Come here." Jax sits on the side of the bed, spreading his legs. When I hesitate, he says, "Baby girl, we're married now."

"We are. You make a good point." I step in be-tween his spread legs—or try to. His hands settle on my waist, lifting me to straddle his thighs.

I settle my hands on his broad shoulders, my fingers stroking back and forth and then slipping underneath the fabric. There's something about the heat of his skin, the scent of him, all cedar and starch and man. It does feel as if we've been wait-ing for each other for years…like I know him and will get to know him even better in the next few hours, and it will be magical and sexy and special.

Giving in to temptation, I lean forward and press my mouth against his throat, and then lower, where my fingers have made inroads beneath his shirt. His big hands gently work my veil free, setting it on the bedside table.

He fists my hair carefully, tugging my head back so he can see my face. His eyes drop to my mouth. "Kiss me, baby girl."

"Where?" I whisper back. Because if he were my high school sweetheart, if I'd been waiting for this night, I think I might have cheated, just a little.

"I'm the kind of girl who sticks her fingers in the frosting when no one's looking," I say apolo-

ANNE MARSH 53

getically. "I think I may have kissed you before. Somewhere dirty."

"On my mouth," he agrees. "And you always loved kissing my nipples because then you could show me what you liked best."

"And then I'd kiss you lower."

"Yeah." His eyes darken. "I loved when you did that."

"But no sex."

"No sex," he says, and he wraps a hand around the back of my neck, pulling me in. "No sex until tonight because we agreed we'd wait until we were married."

"You listened to me." I press my fingertips against his beautiful mouth. "That's how I knew I wanted to keep you."

"As if I'd have let you get away from me," he replies. He leans in, pulling me to him, and it's the perfect second kiss. The kiss under the big top was for everyone else and this one is just for us. His mouth moves over mine; soft and knowing, tasting and nibbling. I part my lips for him, already anticipating how he'll take our kiss deeper, his tongue pushing inside my mouth the same way he'll push himself into me later.

He doesn't disappoint. His tongue licks the corner of my mouth playfully, and then he sweeps inside. I've never been a huge fan of tongue kisses, but everything is different with Jax. His tongue traces mine, his teeth nip at my lower lip, the bright sting making me tighten lower.

His hands cup my head, strong and sure, cradling me. It feels so good. Heat races through my body and I press against him. His thighs tighten underneath me. I'm safe. It's so very safe to let go.

"We don't need this." He nudges the straps of my dress down. His mouth follows his fingers, planting small kisses against the skin he uncovers. "You never have to hide from me, baby girl."

"I don't know what to do." I hold on to his shoulders.

Dark lashes sweep up. "You don't have to do anything. I'll do it all. Just let me love you."

He strips off my dress and lays me back on the bed. I never did find my thong in the pool house, so now I'm completely bare before him. I'm not sure I've done this before. I wrap an arm around myself, covering my breasts, my palm cupping my pussy.

Jax sucks in a breath as he stares down at me. "You're the sexiest woman I've ever seen."

"I'm the only one you've seen," I remind him.

He flashes me a wicked grin. "Doesn't make it any less true. I'm a lucky bastard to have you."

He strips off his clothes with ruthless efficiency. Boots, shirt, pants. I could look at him all night. Dark ink covers both his arms and his chest is all corded muscle. Lower…he's big and strong and present. He belongs to me and only me tonight, and I feel powerful and sexy.

If I were the girl I'm pretending to be, I could love him. I would. I want to curl up in this bed and not leave. Let him love me back, press me deep into the mattress and take me in the simplest, most primitive of ways. Him on me, in me. No fancy games or tricks. No comparisons. Just *yes* and *Do you like this?*

He drops down on top of me, holding himself up on his arms so that I'm not flattened beneath his weight. Instead, I'm surrounded by hot, aroused man. He gently lifts my arm away from my ribs and presses a kiss against my palm.

"Did you mind waiting?" I stroke the hand he freed over his shoulder and down his back. The muscles flex.

"You're always worth waiting for, baby girl. I'd wait forever."

He kisses his way down my body until he reaches my hand.

"We haven't done this before, but I want to." He traces the seam between my ring finger and middle finger with his tongue before pushing gently inward. I let him do it and I don't move my fingers from where he's put them.

"May I kiss you here?" He blows gently, his breath teasing my clit.

"I don't know. You shouldn't."

His tongue presses between my fingers again, licking a slightly deeper path.

"If you'd enjoy it, I should. Let's try it, baby girl."

His tongue teases me, grazing my slick folds, tasting and retreating. He's sweet but, oh my God, he's in charge. When he shifts my hand up, I don't protest. Not even when he puts my fingers on my clit.

"Show me what you like best," he orders. "So I can give it to you every day."

I remind myself that this is just a game we're playing but I want to tell him *yes* and *please* and *Can every day start now?*

Instead, I do what's he ordered me to do. I trace the soft, wet skin around my clit. Slowly, gently. Because that's what I've asked for tonight, the fantasy that we have feelings for each other and that this isn't just about getting off.

He's watching—

I'm—

He ducks his head and then I feel his mouth on me, echoing the little movements I make with my fingers but lower. His fingers tangle with mine and I flush. He knows exactly how he's making me feel. I don't even know what to do next, where I want to move my fingers. It never takes me long to come alone but tonight I spin it out in drowsy, slow strokes, in no hurry to finish. I watch his dark head move as he kisses me down there, his hair spilling across his shoulders and my thighs.

I don't want this to be over.

But I can't hold back the orgasm that's building in me. It tears out of me, a hard, greedy heartbeat between my legs, and he groans something. *Baby girl.* It's not my name, it's not really me, but it's who I'm pretending to be. It's part of our game, I remind myself.

I push my fingers into his hair, holding on, pulling on thick, glossy strands as he undoes me. Part of me wants to hurt him, to make him feel this moment in his skin the way I do. I don't know what we're doing or who we are. I—

His hands are busy, smoothing on a condom, moving me. He slides up my body until we're face to face and his penis is right there where he was a moment before. I wrap my arms around his body. It feels as if my fingers shouldn't meet, but they do.

"May I?" His voice is tight, his eyes warm as he captures my gaze with his.

"Yes," I tell him. Yes, yes, yes and yes some more. Always yes.

His hands move over me, touching, stroking, stoking the fire in me again. "You're so beautiful."

He's the sweetest liar, but he makes me feel like it's the truth.

"So are you," I blurt out.

He grins and pushes inside me.

I wrap my arms around his waist and hold on.

He cups my head with his big hands, his forehead resting against mine, as he gives it to me long and slow and sweet. And then he opens me up, making room for himself deep inside my body, pushing deeper and deeper. It's good.

"Still yes?" he asks. He pauses, too, searching my face for something. Permission. Ecstasy. Not a road map, that's for certain. He knows exactly where and how to touch me.

I pull him back to me, forgetting I'm his virgin bride. "Don't stop. Don't, don't."

He laughs, a dark, rough sound, and then he's pushing the hard length of his dick back inside me. Out and then in. He sets a fast rhythm that has me tensing and moaning. I don't want to come too fast. This needs to last. I need—

I grab his butt, squeezing and moving against him, then we're both groaning, grabbing at each other, our arms wrapped around one another. It's over too fast. He groans, hips jerking hard one last time. I come, squeezing him tight.

"A picture-perfect finish." I bite his shoulder lightly. I want to leave my mark on him.

His laugh is satisfied. "Now what would you like to do?"

Later, I'll be embarrassed that I asked for this. I'll tell myself it's not as kinky as his dirty cop and that he enjoyed telling me what to do. I'll tell myself it's just a memory, a good one. But right now, I'm not ready to be done.

"Hold me?"

I think there might be other words and sounds that fall from my mouth. I might mumble about *strong* and *more later* and *fucking ruined*. His laughter tickles my ear as he rolls onto his side, pulling me against him.

You're the best playdate ever, Peony.

I know we're drunk, that this is a hookup—a sexy game with a perfect stranger who can never be my husband, but I almost forget that this isn't real. I relax into his side and pretend a little longer.

CHAPTER FIVE

Jax

I LIKE MY life just fine as it is: billion dollars in the bank, owner and CEO of my own company, casual playdates. One party and one Peony later, and I'm off-kilter. I kind of don't mind—at least not as much as I should—but maybe that's because playing with Peony is so much fun.

I'm definitely not ready to be done with her, so I wrap my arms around her, pulling her closer after we finish her scene. It's just aftercare, me looking after her, making sure she feels safe. That's all. I run my thumb down the soft line of her shoulder. Maybe I put too much of myself into our game. I'm not sure. Whoever Peony's played with before is simply competition, and I always win when I play. I'm not going to tell her this, though. The few friends and family in my life remind me on a regular basis that my competitive side scares nice people away.

I glance down at her, looking for my cue. Her eyes have drifted shut, the lashes tickling my skin. Her breathing comes soft and easy, a steady in and out like the ocean. She's asleep, half sprawled on top of me, her leg thrown over mine. I've never needed much sleep myself and with the post-sex adrenaline humming through my veins, there's not a chance I crash.

The party sounds outside are winding down and the light's got a hazy, predawn quality to it even here in the darkened room. The night is over. I know what comes next. I slip away, or she does, or we kiss goodbye and tell each other that it was fun or amazing. Maybe we exchange phone numbers, even though I rarely use them. I prefer my stranger fantasy. Plus, it's easier. My money changes things. Peony will become a memory, one I come to in the middle of the night or in the shower, her flushed, bare skin, the silky curve of her thigh, the freckles on her ass, her chest and behind her ear.

She mumbles something into my chest, a word sigh, a grumble as she stretches. Man, she's cute, which would be reason enough to wake her up for more sex, except it's late or super early and, either way, we can't stay here forever.

When she shifts restlessly, I seize the chance to ease off the bed. I need clothes. My shirt's a lost cause because Peony's wearing it, half the buttons mismatched, the other half undone. First she was hot and then she was cold and this way, stealing my things, was just right. She also said perfection was boring—Peony talks a lot once she gets started—and then she fell asleep before I could sort out her button situation.

I reacquaint myself with the rest of my clothes and rejoin the pants-wearing world. Peony sleeps like the dead now that she's got the whole bed to herself, her body star-fished in the center. It's too freaking cute.

A quick check of my messages on my phone reveals nothing that can't wait until later. It's Saturday and no one needs me.

It's six in the morning. The sun's not quite all the way up—and there's zero reason I can't do what I want.

I add *Bad for my impulse control* to the list of reasons why Peony is dangerous, consider that argument for a full second, and give up. I'm not sure there's any point in resisting. She's like the Borg of sexual fantasies: resistance is futile.

I crouch beside her. *Still time to run!* my brain points out oh so helpfully. *We can achieve warp speed, find a convenient wormhole, and vanish. Nothing has to change.*

My brain makes a good point. If there's one thing I've learned, it's that you cut and run. And if you're not going to do that, you play with people in your own income bracket. Somehow, I don't think Peony's a billionaire. Not if she worked for that asshole I had escorted off the property last night, not if she's worried about making her rent.

"Sleeping beauty." I lean in and brush a kiss over her mouth. "You gotta wake up for me, Firefly."

It takes a half dozen kisses before Peony's eyes blink slowly open.

I back off just in case she's feeling the aftereffects of last night's alcohol. Also because I'm a big bastard and probably scary-looking. What was fine with her last night needs confirmation this morning.

I have a reputation in the business world for dismantling shit. I buy a company, I swoop in, and I ruthlessly prune away the crap that's keeping it from earning its shareholders a fortune. It's community service, if you look at it from my point of view, or at least one of those makeover TV shows where a ruggedly good-looking contractor knocks down walls and what was a dated flophouse turns into modern chic. It's just that if you're the wall, you're not happy about the process.

Fortunately, Peony isn't unhappy at all. She focuses on me, mumbling a sleepy, "Hey."

"Come on." I drop another kiss on her pretty mouth, tempted to stay where we are. The problem is that I can already here Liam's cleaning crew moving around outside. Before too long, someone will discover our hiding place, and while I can kick them out, I'll have to be honest about who I am. It feels good to be just Jax, someone's hot hookup and partner in crime. Peony's here because she wants me, not the billionaire, the bachelor topping San Francisco's Hottest Men list, or the financial Prince Charming who can rain BMWs and diamonds on his temporary princess. She just wants me, and I don't want that to change.

She sits up, pulling my shirt around her like a blanket. Pink stains her cheeks.

"Are they kicking us out?" She yawns with jaw-cracking force as she scrubs at her eyes with her hands.

"Better. I hear pancakes calling my name, the siren lure of syrup." I playfully mime cupping my ear, as if it's totally reasonable to listen for a stack of anthropomorphic pancakes.

"Sir Jax and his noble quest." She laughs, a belly giggle that has her slapping her hand over her mouth. "I will ride with thee."

"You're a nut." I tug her to her feet and toss her acrobat dress at her. It's somewhat the worse for wear, but only thing Liam stocks for his guests are string bikinis, condoms and towels.

She wriggles back into the dress without a com-plaint and then we both raid the bathroom for a lit-tle oral hygiene, teasing one another as if we really have known each other for years.

Ten minutes later, we're standing in the six-car garage behind the main house. I parked my bike here so I could escape without being at the mercy of the valet parkers.

My bike's not the flashiest, nor is it the most expensive ride. What it is, is a big, powerful beast. It eats up the road effortlessly and I can make it fly. Peony gravitates to it like a moon to a planet.

"Is this yours?" She's already running her hand down the seat, her fingers roaming over the leather. "Because if not, I might be tempted to commit my first felony."

"All mine," I confirm.

She grins at me before returning her attention to the bike. "In case you haven't noticed, I just fell in love with your bike."

"You believe in love at first sight?" I tip my head at the bike.

"Of course not," she says. "Who does?"

I don't think I do, either. Not really. I take a step toward the bike, my brain screaming at me to straddle it, to drive away and abandon the whole breakfast idea, but Peony's right there. She gives the bike a covetous glance—part lust, part greed—and I still want her.

"Can I drive?" Peony's practically bouncing in place, she's so excited. It's distracting because it makes me think about cheerleaders, and Cheerleader and the Football Player is always fun.

I'm not sure how I feel about her driving, though. Frankly, I drive in all areas of my life and I like it that way. But she looks so eager, that I hate to tell her no.

"You have an M1 license?"

She gooses my side. "I took the road test with a friend's bike a year ago. I was supposed to be getting my own, but then plans changed." She waves a hand. "Okay. So more accurately, I changed jobs again and owning my own bike had to wait. I'm a public transit and Lyft girl at the moment. But I *meant* to get a bike and I'm fully licensed and trained.

"Trust me?" She pats my bike, running her hand over the leather seat. "I'll be gentle, I promise. If you want, we can even drive a few loops around this place so you can road test me, but you'll like it if you let me drive. Swear to God."

"Right." I slide an arm around her waist, tugging her back against me so I can brush a kiss on the top of her head. "Because we all know which part you play in the Good Cop, Bad Girl game."

She just grins at me. "You had a good time."

"I did." Because I'm Good Cop, I try not to remember the details about that good time because my dick's already making it clear that he'd like to do it again.

"Gimme," she says, holding out her palm. "Pretty please with a cherry on top."

I hand her the keys with a groan. "How did you get here if you didn't drive?"

While she makes porn noises over my bike, I

rummage around in one of the big metal storage cabinets lining the garage.

"Peony? Are you going to answer the question?"

"Lyft. I was going to call for a pickup when I got bored." She sticks her tongue out at me. "Obviously, I'm not bored yet. Why are you ransacking our host's shit?"

I thrust a pair of coveralls at her. "Put these on."

She takes them automatically. "Are we playing Dirty Mechanic and the Pit Stop now?"

"You shouldn't ride in just that dress. Your legs might get all chewed up."

She bites her bottom lip, which is freaking adorable. "Shouldn't we ask before we just take stuff?"

"Let me repeat what a very sexy someone just said. 'Trust me.' It's fine."

Liam's my best friend, he's a billionaire, and I'm about ninety-nine-percent certain he has no idea what's in his garage cabinets anyhow. As long as we don't nick his Veyron, it's all good.

"We should at least leave a note," she says. "Not that I think a billionaire is going to sweat the loss of a pair of used coveralls, but it's the principle of the thing. You have to treat people the way you want to be treated, and I'd be pissed if someone just helped herself to my stuff, even if it was a transportation emergency.

"I'll leave a note," she decides. "And I'll wash them and return them. That should be okay, right?"

"Bake him a plate of brownies if you must," I groan. "But let's ride?"

"Do billionaires eat brownies? If I put them on a tinfoil plate, would the foil have to be gold?"

"Billionaires love brownies. Get dressed." I mock growl at her, aiming a playful smack at her butt.

"How many billionaires do you know?" She shakes out the coveralls and unzips them.

"You got a thing about people with money?" I take the coveralls from her and hold them up so she can step in.

"Money turns people into assholes." She goes to work on the zipper, but it's stuck at crotch level and not budging. "You think Mother Teresa or the Pope would be the same with a billion dollars in the bank?"

I grunt and take over the zipper. Then, for good measure, I put her into my jacket and a helmet. I won't let her crash, but there's no upside to taking chances, either. I don't like the thought of Peony getting hurt.

"Note," she reminds me when I go to get on the bike.

Right.

We're pretending we're moral, upstanding party guests who are totally not absconding with forty bucks' worth of protective gear. We leave a quick IOU scrawled on the back of a gas receipt I fish out of my jacket pocket.

"You're really sure this is okay, to borrow this?" She smooths a hand down the coveralls, molding the practical, navy-blue cotton against her curves. I'm tempted to yank the zipper back down and bend her over my bike. The problem is that I find her equally sexy all zipped up, nibbling nervously on her lower lip. I'm not sure there's any way I wouldn't be attracted to her, and then she straddles my bike, her legs hugging the sides.

"Promise," I say, swinging up behind her on the bike. I can't remember the last time I rode like this and let someone else drive. I generally insist on being in charge.

And yet here I am, wrapping my arms around her waist, my legs bracing hers. I keep my hands PG. She wants to ride, so we'll do that.

This is where I should tell her that Liam's a great guy and I've known him since he was a teenage asshole. But that's going to lead to the next question, which is how I met him and are we still friends. I don't think Peony's going to ask to meet him or suddenly express an interest in his money, but I like being just Jax, her fuck buddy and playmate. I'm not a billionaire businessman who makes and breaks companies. Here in this garage, I'm just her very good time and she's just the girl I'm interested in.

CHAPTER SIX

Peony

"SIX IMPOSSIBLE THINGS. Go!" I have to speak a little louder than is strictly sexy because the waves slapping at the wet sand a few feet from us have drowned out more than one of my questions.

"Am I supposed to believe them?" Jax is smiling, his voice a rough growl that sends delicious little flutters through my stomach. And lower.

"A man who reads." I feign a clap for him because, honestly, a guy who knows his *Alice in Wonderland* deserves some positive affirmation.

"Yeah, I do." Jax leans back on one arm. His other arm's wrapped around me. It's like cozying up to a really sexy Rock of Gibraltar. I've had him completely naked and I still can't believe the man's size, both in the biceps department and in more personal areas south of the belt border. I realize I'm not making any sense, but the man has magic, brain-frying skills. I want to be confident and sure around him, but I'm still a work in progress and Jax...

Well, he's kind of overachieving in the life skills department.

"Waiting," I prompt him.

"Ganghkar Puensum. Muchu Chhish. Sauyr Zhotasy. Tongshanjiabu. Chamar South. Sanglung." He's watching me as he talks now, not the ocean. My stomach clenches a little, or maybe that's just the gibberish he's spewing.

"You're impossible to understand."

"Really tall, unclimbed mountain peaks." He shrugs. "At least, no one's proved they've climbed them."

"You climb?" The closest I've come to mountain climbing ever is when I worked temporarily in an office on the tenth floor that had a perpetually broken elevator. Also, I once took the stairs to the galleries above Westminster Abbey, which was a hundred and eight steps of gargoyle- and view-infused goodness.

"Yeah," he admits. And then, of course, he freaking stops when I'd like him to elaborate and add a few details to the picture of him I'm building in my head. I know now that he has a playful side, that he loves dirty sex, that he has a mouth on him, and that he owns the best motorcycle in the world. He also refused to let me pay for my own pancakes, and my body lights up like a Tilt-A-Whirl when he's near.

"Details." I poke his ribs. "Give it up."

"It's rock climbing," he protests. "Quite straight-forward. I see a big pile of them. I climb them."

I make a face at him. "Do you just climb rocks in California or are you an equal-opportunity climber who scales things in all fifty states? God, I'll bet you've done it on all of the continents, haven't you?"

He gives a bark of laughter. "I'm all for doing it."

"I married a creep," I say, laughing.

He's the kind of hot that makes me want to throw caution to the wind and ask him out on a second one-night hookup. Not pretty, not a crème brûlée kind of man, but more like a dark, brooding, unex-pectedly sweet-sticky toffee cake. Looking at him makes me think about getting naked with him again, which has to go on my own list of impossibilities.

"Now, let's do yours."

"Well, this week my list includes paying my rent, finding a new job that I love, and running a half marathon."

"That's three." His thumb strokes the back of my hand.

"Such a stickler for a total cheater. Are you an ac-countant?" I blurt the question out without thinking. I don't like personal questions, so why would he?

"What if I work for the IRS? I could be the tax guy."

Somehow, I don't think he is. "With that tan? And your love of scaling tall objects? Impossible," I scoff.

"Three more impossible things," he orders. "Come on."

"Flying. Cupcakes that are a diet food. Free trips to Bora Bora."

He frowns. "I'm not sure any of those are completely impossible. I may need to assess a penalty."

We've been hanging out at the bottom of a huge sand dune for the last hour, having what's turned into a sunrise beach picnic. This is my favorite time of day, when everything goes from dark to a shimmering gray and then you blink and sunlight's slipping up over the horizon. Everything looks different and new, as if I could do anything, go anywhere. Usually I just end up going to work or to bed, but the possibility is there.

Jax hasn't said he needs to get going, nor has he suggested dropping me anywhere. Maybe he doesn't have mad weekend plans, or maybe he's just enjoying the beach. Strangely, it doesn't feel awkward and it's certainly a pretty beach. Scrubby, sea-hardy plants carpet the hills wrapped around the sandy bits and an enormous pile of rocks jut up on one end. They could pass as a mini mountain and I briefly consider climbing on them, but they look wet from the tide and neither my circus costume nor the too large coveralls are really rock climbing gear.

"I wish I had wings," I blurt.

"Where would you fly?" he prompts. "Or are your feathers purely decorative?"

Bora Bora does sound attractive, but…

I point to the rocks. "I'd fly up there."

He nods, eyeing the rock face. "I'm warning you right now that there's going to be an abundance of bird shit and other unhygienic stuff."

I believe him. The beach isn't flat. There's a vast pool of leftover ocean trapped behind us like a mini pond. Jax carried me piggyback over it. I've probably overstayed my welcome with him and he's trying to figure out how to dump the crazy girl, but… it's nice.

He's nice.

On the other hand, I'd kill for a mattress, a pillow, and a nice light-blocking eye mask right now. The sun's fully up and I yawn, my jaw cracking. Maybe it's time for some solo bedtime action with my pillow.

"I should get back." It's better if I end this thing now, rather than wait for him to make up an excuse to leave.

"I'll give you a lift." Jax rises to his feet.

I'm not sure more time with this man is wise. "I could live in Timbuktu. Or Florida. I can just call for a Lyft."

He holds his hand down to me. "Service out here is going to suck."

"So I'll wait. It's a beach, not the antechamber of hell."

"Or we could ride together."

"You don't even know where I live."

"I was being a gentleman. You can tell me and then I'll take you. Or tell me somewhere close enough."

I hate strings and commitments. It's one of the many reasons why I've bounced from job to job since graduating from college, and it's certainly why my relationships have all been quick sprints rather than marathons. Hooking up with Jax was supposed to be fun and quick, so him knowing where I live or being concerned about my getting home safely throws me off-kilter. He has a penis, so I also don't get why he's not perfectly happy to have some meaningless sex and then for me to run right out of his life.

He goes in for the kill. "A Lyft will cost a fortune. Prices will be surging."

He can't know that without checking the phone app, but he's probably right. Given my newly unemployed state—along with my perpetually broke one—I decide to give in.

"Okay. If you really don't mind."

He just shakes his head. I get the feeling Jax usually gets his way.

I'm used to taking care of my business myself. Not having a car sucks, but I've got it handled. On the other hand, a quick check of my phone while Jax made a trash run just confirmed that he was right about the lack of rideshare opportunities. I might also have to stop and sell a kidney to cover the ride.

I consider giving Jax an address that will put me within walking distance of my place, but I'm exhausted. Plus, if he were a serial killer, he's already had ample opportunity to murder me. I don't want to be stupid, but I've slept with him, he's been inside me, and we're pretty much alone on this gorgeous, windswept beach, so I think I'm safe.

Jax drives this time, and I don't protest. My late night's definitely catching up with me. We ride over the Golden Gate Bridge, which is thronged with early morning walkers, and then pick our way through San Francisco. The usual cacophony of car horns, construction equipment and sirens makes it too loud—and hazardous—for conversation, so I just rest my head against his shoulder and watch the world slip by. Jax drives with easy confidence, handling his beast of a bike effortlessly.

My rental place is on a beach on the western side of the city. It's a nice stretch of sand with some amazing wave action. The water's the stormy dark blue of the Pacific, colder than an ice bath, and the beach is pleasantly breezy on a good day. On a bad day, it's like living in the middle of my own personal typhoon.

I'm currently staying in the third camper in a long line of beat-up RVs shoehorned into a narrow strip of space between the main road and the beach.

The rent is so cheap that I have my doubts about the legality of the parking job, but I've kept those suspicions to myself. There's less doubt about the roofing job. My RV has a blue tarp fastened over the original roof, which has long since sprung a handful of leaks. I direct him to the end of the row and he pulls into an empty parking space.

I hop off the bike before he's even killed the engine. "Thanks! Enjoy the rest of your weekend."

The queen of awkward small talk, that's me.

"Hang on, Firefly." He double-checks his phone, frowning. Looks at the row of dilapidated, tarp-covered campers. "Something's not right."

Yeah. Not wanting to wait for the Judgment Train to pull into the station, I grin like a demented chipmunk and start shimmying out of his jacket. "We're good! That's me."

He scrubs a hand over the back of his head while he eyes the ancient RV I'm pointing at. Whatever. I blame his unimpressed state on our night at the faux French palace in Napa. It's hard for my real-people place to compete with the lifestyles of the rich and almost-famous, after all. I mean, he could know a dozen billionaires. Maybe he has their house keys and waters their plants while they swan around the world in their environment-destroying private jets?

He puts the kickstand down, killing the bike's engine. "You live in a camper?"

"It's affordable beachfront real estate, which is a miracle in San Francisco."

He mutters something under his breath. It's not complimentary. And sure, the campers themselves are more than a little rough around the edges. They've got a lot of miles on them and, when it rains, I'm super grateful for the tarp stretched over mine. I love the sound of raindrops, but not when they're hitting my bedroom floor. Still, I get to go to the beach whenever I want.

I've lived in a lot of places in the last ten years, but this is one of my favorites. The camper's small and the solar-heated shower is an interesting challenge, but I have the run of the entire beach.

"Is it even legal?"

"You bet." Honestly, I have no clue, but I learned early that if you say it with confidence, people don't doubt as much.

Jax just shakes his gorgeous head and gets off the bike. This was not how I envisioned the end of our night together. He's supposed to pull up, I hop off, and then he gets gone from my life and I can get on with figuring out how I'm going to handle Monday and its four professional companions: Tuesday, Wednesday, Thursday and Friday. He strides around the bike, cupping my elbow with his hand like we're some kind of geriatric couple headed for the opera.

I give my elbow a shake, but the man sticks like a burr. "What are you doing?"

"Walking my date to the door." He's smiling, but his voice is firm. He's not going to budge on this.

Up close, my camper doesn't look any better. There's a streak of something green-black running down one side and the screen's mostly popped out of the window closest to the door. It's like a half-opened tin can. But it's mine. I get to live here alone, on my own terms, and I'm completely self-supporting. Or I was, until Martin the Asshole made his asshole moves. It'll be okay, or that's what I tell myself as I fish around in my purse for my keys. I'm really good at coming up with new plans.

The door pops open easily, making me wonder for the umpteenth time if the lock is more decorative than functional. A quick visual check of the tiny space inside seems good, though—no one's cleaned out my stuff while I've been partying at a billionaire's house.

Jax snags my wrist, clearly anticipating my next move, which is to hide inside and shut the door on him.

His fingers tighten gently, pinning me on the spot. I don't like it when people hold on to me, but this feels different somehow. Maybe it's all the hot sex. Maybe he's fucked the imagination right out of me and that's why I can't think of the many reasons why walking away from Jax—or running or hiding—is so important.

"Peony." His voice is a deep, luscious growl. It also packs a whole lot of judging into my name.

"It's cheap and it has an ocean view." I sound defensive and we both know it.

"You worried about money, Firefly?"

"Hello? Got propositioned by my boss last night—the odds of my having a job on Monday are slim." Crap. Why did I say that? Why do I always worry and overshare? I force my hands to untwist and relax by my sides. *Nothing to see here. Everything's under control.*

The furrow between his brows deepens until he's sporting a Grand Canyon-worthy chasm of pissed off. "He's lucky you don't sue his ass."

Yeah. Been there, done that, got the souvenir T-shirt.

"I'm not convinced this place is safe." He sounds like he's about to march over to the nonexistent property manager's office and lay into someone.

"Fortunately for you, you don't live here, cupcake. I do."

"Cupcake?" He gives me a dark look.

"You seem to have christened me *Firefly*," I mock. "I'm just returning the favor."

"This is not an apartment," he bites out. "Or a condo, a house, or any other kind of normal living arrangement."

Honestly, it's San Francisco. Tons of people live in their cars or other makeshift places, and I've got it good in comparison with them.

"Uh-uh." I press a finger against his gorgeous mouth. "This is what I can afford. Fuck, it's my choice. I'm not rich and even if I were, I'd rather be down here on the beach with the real people."

He huffs out an offended breath. "No rich people allowed. I'll make you a sign. You can yell at them to keep off the grass."

Heh.

When I slide off his jacket and hand it back, he rummages inside it and produces a little square of cardboard and a pen. Then he scribbles out a name on it and scrawls *Jax* and a number.

"This is mine." He taps the written string of digits and pushes it into my hand. "If you need another rescue, call me."

I turn the card over in my hand. Its original owner appears to have been a software developer. "If you're going into the rescue business, you should get your own cards. Don't be a cheapskate about it."

"I'm just up the beach." He points toward a distant bluff where there is a smattering of cottages and oceanfront housing that does not involve campers or tarps. "I surf there."

"You surf?" I'm embarrassed at how breathless I sound. At least I keep my eyes on his face this time.

"Yeah." He pulls me into his arms. It feels more

comfortable than I expect it to, although there's absolutely nothing *comfortable* about the kiss that follows. He kisses me hungrily, his mouth devouring mine, until I'm clinging to him.

"Firefly?" His mouth brushes my ear and I swallow a moan.

"Yeah?"

"There's another option. You could just call. Because you want to."

I'm still processing that when he drops a last kiss on my mouth and leaves.

CHAPTER SEVEN

Peony

WHEN GOD CLOSES a door, he opens a window. Everything happens for a reason. Make lemons into lemonade. Okay so that last one was supposed to be a directive for me and not God, but seeing as how He's the expert on turning water into wine, I could use His expertise.

By Monday morning, I've fired off a formal email to Human Resources, officially giving notice. Friday night had already established that there was no way I could continue working with Mr. "Call me Bob" Martin, but I figure I should at least quit by the rules. Obviously, I'm not particularly good at rules, but I'm supposed to be getting better. Mostly, I just keep thinking about Jax and how he felt when he was on me. *In* me. Doing all those dirty things with me.

While I wait to be magically reborn as Peony 2.0, I take my coffee outside on the beach. I also bring my laptop so I can pretend I'm doing something constructive and adultish. Sitting on an old towel, I scroll through Craigslist and find a couple of possibilities, including an opening for an archivist at a digital television station in San Francisco. Fingers crossed that they're hiring quickly. I put out feelers to some temp agencies before I flop back on my towel and meditate on other ways to make money quickly that stop short of naked dancing in a sex club or outright prostitution.

Unfortunately, my brain doesn't want to be productive. It just wants to think about Jax when I've vowed to never, ever, think of the man again.

Or kissing Jax.

Definitely not about having sex with him.

It's just that he's super talented with his fingers, his mouth, and his dick. Probably with other parts of his anatomy, too, which I'll never discover now that we've parted ways for good. My imagination goes to work—at least part of me is working, right?—imagining all the undiscovered ways Jax could be good in bed. He's creative, but he's also not afraid to ask for what he wants—or to listen to what I want. He even let me drive his bike.

Eventually, I give up on maturity and retreat to my RV, where I jill off frantically to my memories of Jax. It's not as good as the real thing, but it takes the edge off.

I have to be quiet because RV walls are thin and

I've already learned way too much about my neighbors' sexual habits. Eventually, I'll move into an apartment like a normal adult, but right now this is cheap. I have a loft bed over the driver's compartment, kind of like one of those shelves in a U-Haul, plus a miniature solar-heated shower and a composting toilet that I'd happily trade in for a fully plumbed model. Most of the rest of the space is taken up by a built-in table, squashy sofa, my favorite pillows, and the three succulents who sublease the windowsill. I've named them Fred, Frank and Fancy. Frank is currently raising two offspring and may merit a move to a larger pot to support his progeny.

I could call Jax. He'd probably hook up with me again unless he's already moved on to someone else or has one of those stupid "no repeat guests" personal rules. It's not like we made any real commitment to each other, fake marriage notwithstanding. But as much as I hate the idea of him kissing someone else, I don't call. I'm not sure how well I can do casual sex with him.

Wednesday after my big weekend, I jolt awake to a surprising email from HR. My phone's buzzing under my pillow like a vibrator gone mad and sun's pouring through the window. I've overslept, and my mouth is gritty and I feel almost nauseous from too much sleep. When I check the phone, I learn that my last gig is "pleased" to offer me an exit package that includes a month's salary and three months of paid health insurance. Mr. Martin is no longer with the company, my chipper correspondent explains, but if I need a job reference, I can contact her.

Rescued from immediate penury, I go outside and putter around the beach. I do way too much staring at the waves and the tiny dots of surfers up near the bend, looking for Jax. I spot multiple lumberjack-size men in black wetsuits, but all of them are false positives. I'd stalk the beach longer, but I'm starting to feel like a pervert.

Eventually, I wander back to my camper, where I discover a missed message on my phone. It's just raining good news: I have a job interview to be the one and only corporate archivist at Hotly. God's clearly listening, so I make a quick pitch for seeing Jax again.

There has to be someone permanent in my life. A friend. Someone I can call and who will come over for tea. It's just that I'm new to San Francisco and haven't put down roots yet. I met a couple of girls who seemed fun at my last job, but then I bailed out of there without a word and so those potential friends haven't happened. Jax isn't my friend, more of a brief fuck buddy, but it doesn't hurt to see if he's around and maybe up for company. I thumb through my photos to find the picture I took of his card.

"Don't do anything stupid, Peony. Think it through," I tell myself. I'm the queen of rushing in. Do I text him something flirty? If I do, am I asking him for sex? Do I want sex with Jax? Honestly, I'm tired and role-playing is a lot of work sometimes. I sort of just want someone to hold me and tell me everything's going to be okay. That I don't have to hold it all together on my own and pretend my life's totally Instagram-worthy. I can practically hear my sister snort.

I Google quickly for some Cosmo-worthy opening texts, but the internet fails me today. I'm not above a little plagiarism, but none of them feel right. They're all me pretending to be someone hotter, sexier and way more fun. Today I just feel quiet.

Hey, I text. Are you at the beach today?

As texts go, it's not inspired.

A drop of water splatters on my phone screen. Crap. I wipe it off with my shirt because I'm classy like that. It's probably an editorial comment from the Big Guy Upstairs. If, you know, God took an interest in my pickup lines. Water inside the camper means water outside, so…rain.

I lean over and poke a finger through the Venetian blinds to confirm the weather. A drizzling gray mist shrouds the beach, the sand and waves obscured by fog. Rain spots the pavement and the sand.

Rain almost never happens in San Francisco. Sun, yes. Morning fog, absolutely. Wildfire smoke and unrelated smog? You betcha. As I wait for Jax to respond, the rain picks up its tempo. My tarp's not quite up to the job because new drops sneak inside to join me.

There's probably a metaphor in that. My life's a leaky mess that's patched together with a twenty-dollar sheet of plastic.

It takes him way too long to respond—Do you want to hang out?—long enough that I've grown at least two complexes.

Men should come with secret decoder rings. I can't tell if he wants to meet up—and if that would be a purely platonic, sure-we-can-share-the-beach meet-up or an invitation to have kinky sex. I debate texting my sister a screenshot and asking for her opinion, but she's been married ten years. Her dating/hook-up radar is permanently rusted.

I'm still trying to decipher his text when he adds, Incentive?

His text is followed by a photo of a taco truck. From the angle of his shot, he's in the water. I decide that's a decent reason for the delay in his response.

Since someone should be looking out for his poor at-risk phone, I text back.

Who takes their phone in the water?

This time his response is gratifyingly quick.

I'll buy you dinner and we can discuss.

I suppose if I can have sex with him, I can eat with him. My stomach gives a protesting lurch. What if I'm not what he remembers? What if my everyday self is too weird, too boring, too unsexy? Tacos aren't a four-course meal, so I guess neither of us would be trapped in awkward date hell. It could be okay.

What if *he's* different?

I've got an indoor shower, so I text.

Rain + holes in roof = free rain shower!

He responds almost instantly.

Are you all right? You call your landlord? I can come over there and MacGyver things.

He hasn't changed.

I totally remember that endearingly overprotective streak. It must be hardwired into him.

Another splash from above interrupts my train of thought. Shoot. I'm breaking out the towels.

It's NBD but I need a change of scenery, so those tacos sound good.

There's a slightly longer pause this time, but then he responds.

I can come down and take a look. Be there in ten?

I try to imagine how that would go. He comes charging down here and goes all white knight on my leaky roof and then...what? We either sit and stare at each other, knees bumping in my teeny camper or we have sex on my really small bed or... I guess we go for a really awkward, not-romantic beach walk.

I vote tacos, I text.

Coming ashore, he responds. See you soon.

I guess we have a date/not-date then. Just tacos. On the beach. Something fun and uncomplicated. We were great together before, but I feel like I'm asking for something different. That I'm winging this in a way I haven't before.

I grab my favorite red-white-and-blue kimono and wander up the beach with a precautionary umbrella, trying to stretch the walk out so I don't look too eager. It's mostly beige-colored sand, seagulls, and the odd cigarette butt, although at least the rain stops after a few minutes and I can fold up my umbrella. There are palm trees where the sand meets the road, sure, but it's not particularly balmy or bikini-studded. Still, it has a wild beauty of its own. I gaze out over the dark water, checking the waves that are rolling in hard. A handful of surfers fly toward the shore.

When I reach the bend in the beach that I've mentally labeled *Jax's spot*, I spot Jax immediately. He's straddling a board maybe a hundred yards out, deep in conversation with another surfer. They look relaxed and happy. Although I know he wouldn't have told me to come up here just to be polite, I can't help but wonder if I'm interrupting his fun. Is he really ready to be done with the water?

As soon as he sees me, he slides off the board and into the water, wading toward the beach with determined strides. Memories of our playdate tease me. He's so big. So strong, so determined to look out for me. So sure he knows what's right and what's best and how the plan should unfold. And yet the man also knows how to take turns in bed, and he's both dirty and creative.

My stomach twists. What do I do now that I'm here? Do I hug him? Kiss his cheek European style? Pretend I've never touched or held his penis? Handshaking seems weirdly formal after he's had his face between my legs. And yet…it's not as if I'm going to drag him back to my camper for quickie sex. Okay. So I totally want to do that but I'm refraining. I rock back on my heels, thinking furiously and getting nowhere.

He gives me that head tip guys do, but then a smile tugs the corner of his mouth up. "I'd be more friendly, but I'm gonna get you all wet."

There's an awkward pause while we both consider the dirty pun. He winces. "That sounded bad."

"Awesome! Now I don't have to worry about being the person who says something awkward."

"Yeah. I've got it covered." He grins wryly. "Don't tell the world, 'kay?"

"Our little secret." I mime locking my mouth with a key.

He sets his board on the sand and then proceeds to tug down the zipper on his wetsuit. His sun-tanned, inked-up chest is all muscled lines and teasing patterns. I barely resist the urge to lick him. He shoves the unzipped suit down to his waist.

My stomach growls and he holds his hand out to me. "Come on."

I let him pull me forward. His fingers are strong and callused, shockingly warm for someone who's been frolicking around in the Pacific.

The taco truck turns out to be a white van with a window on one side for taking orders and passing out the goods. Oye Taco Taco is painted on the front hood, while the menu's listed on the side in red and yellow letters decorated with a big chili pepper. We order Tacos al Pastor and a pair of beers that the proprietor fishes out of a plastic cooler. They're icy cold, the condensation dripping down their sides, and they're gone long before the food is ready.

When we collect our tacos, however, there's not a single empty table in the handful of plastic patio furniture that's doubling as restaurant seating. Jax scouts around, but it would take superpowers or the ultimate miracle to find a free spot. Everything's taken and no one is budging.

He makes a second and then a third scan, but there's still no miraculous freeing-up of chairs.

"Okay, change of plans," he says. "Don't take this the wrong way, but why don't we head back to my place and eat there? Just food, no kinky stuff. I promise."

I'm not sure how I feel about his promise, but I do know that I'm starving. My stomach growls loudly and he grins.

"Do you own a table?" A girl's got to have standards.

"I have both a table and a kitchen counter. Although in the spirit of full disclosure, I should note that the table is on my balcony and is not particularly large. However, I own not one but *two* chairs."

"Sold," I say.

CHAPTER EIGHT

Peony

I'D HAVE PEGGED Jax for a bachelor boy with an apartment, a leather couch and a massive flat-screen television. The kind of inexpensive place accessorized by roommates and a pile of sports gear, bike parts and maybe a basket of unfolded laundry. *Definitely* a 24-pack of beer.

Instead, he stops just across the road from the beach in front of a two-story, cherry-red cottage with white trim, a second-floor Romeo and Juliet balcony, and a dark, shingled roof that shows zero signs of leakage. A French door leads inside from the postage-stamp-size front yard filled with white hydrangeas, and there's a cutesy wood sign over the door: Our Little Secret.

Like so many San Francisco properties, the house seems like a real estate afterthought, shoe-horned between two other, larger places. A tiny alley on the left hosts his bike, while another, equally narrow alley on the right leads behind the house. When Jax pops the gate and props his surfboard against the fence, I catch a glimpse of a fire pit and green Adirondack chairs.

Oh—

He shoves the wetsuit down his legs. It's not as if I haven't seen him naked before. We had sex in that pool house and then again in the billionaire's spare bedroom. It's just that we were totally planning on doing each other then and getting naked was part of our scene and—

I'm staring.

Anyone with hormones would.

"You're gorgeous. I mean. You—" I wrap my arms around myself because it's that or jump him in his yard and it's not quite dark enough for that. That is also good because I can see all of him clearly and there's a whole lot to look at.

He's still built like a giant absolutely everywhere. His big, inked arms flex as he shakes out the wetsuit and then tosses it into a trough-like vat. The suit lands with a splash and then he bends over—oh yes—swiping a towel from the cottage's tiny back porch. He wraps the towel around his lean hips and...

"Such a waste." I stare at what he's covered up. Despite his afternoon in the very cold Pacific and a damp walk back in what amounts to a giant latex condom, he's erect. Impressively so. When I drag my gaze back up to his face, his eyes laugh at me.

"You're good for my ego, Peony."

"I'm honest," I counter. "And you probably have the happiest neighbors in the city."

He laughs some more and then brushes past me, his hand capturing mine. "Let's get you inside."

"Is this what the Beast said to Beauty? Do you have a dungeon inside?"

That sound? It's my brain short-circuiting and all rational conversation going up in smoke. Flames. Something totally incendiary and one-hundred-percent immature. It's just that this big, rough, way-too-gorgeous man makes me want to press up against him. Lick the lines of his muscles. Taste him right now because what if I don't get the chance to do it later?

He's addictive. That has to be it.

He's also practical and efficient because he tugs me gently toward the front of the house and onto the porch. He flips up his doormat, on which a pair of honey bees fornicate or gambol or do whatever it is that bees do. There's a key underneath. I toss my umbrella onto the porch and refrain from pointing out how desperately insecure his key storage solution is.

"Are you sure you live here?" I tilt my head back, trying to take it all in.

Our Little Secret is oceanfront and it's not a card-board box. That's a huge win in the game of adulting. I don't know anyone who could afford to rent a place like this.

I'm officially in love. It's the cutest thing ever.

"We're one hundred percent not breaking and entering." He waves his key in front of me. "Yes, I live here."

He unlocks the door and holds it open for me. The inside is as unexpected as the outside. A white brick fireplace anchors the big open space and there are loads of windows. A tiny open galley kitchen leads to the backyard and stairs head up to the second floor. Another surfboard leans against the wall, and the only furniture is a desk sporting an impressive pile of hardware, and a couch.

I can't help myself. I prowl around his space like a stray cat let inside from the yard. The ocean's a bright slice of blue through the front windows, so close I almost feel like I can touch it. No curtains cover the glass, but the space feels cozy and safe.

I run a hand over the back of his couch. It's white, covered in a drapey, lacey throw and positively snowed under a mountain of equally white pillows.

"Came with the house." The corners of his mouth lift.

Mmm-hmm. I run a hand over the stack of laptops and hardware bits on the desk. "Are you hacking into the Pentagon's mainframe?"

Possibly, my knowledge of hacking comes almost entirely from *WarGames* and *The Matrix*. I'm not sure it's an accurate representation of the skills required, but Jax would rock those long, black coats the heroes of *The Matrix* wear. I'd happily watch him storming around in shit-kicker boots.

He runs a hand over his hair. "Surfing doesn't pay the bills."

"I feel your pain. I was crushed to realize that no one was going to pay me to travel the world and stay in amazing resorts."

"I'm in tech." He volunteers this cautiously, as if he expects a reaction from me, but computers seem like a perfectly benign way to make a living. Unless, you know, he's hacking into people's stuff and holding it for ransom or something.

"Do you like it?" I can't quite wrap my head around him spending hours bent over a laptop, pounding out lines of code or whatever it is engineers do.

He gives me a look I can't interpret. "I'm good at it. I make money."

"Sweet, filthy lucre." I mime kissing an invisible person. "We all do what we have to do. I myself am wallpapering San Francisco with my résumé. I have an interview with a startup."

He nods. "You could be the new Google employee number fourteen."

"How often do you really think it happens?"

"A stock IPO that makes the employees millionaires over night?" He shrugs and heads for the kitchen with our tacos. "I've seen it happen more than once."

I'm twenty-six years old. I've worked a dozen jobs in the last three years and none of them has made anyone rich, let alone made me financially solvent. "So you've worked places where everyone wakes up some random Friday morning a millionaire and buys an island in Fiji?"

"Millionaire, yes. Island, no. There are only three hundred islands in Fiji. Most of them aren't for sale. Also, there's nothing random about an IPO that explodes."

"That's a lot of millionaires."

He pops the door on the fridge and frowns. "I should have gone to the store."

I peek around him. Mostly this is an excuse to cuddle up against his back because I'm freezing and he's warm, but I'm also curious. He's definitely got the whole bachelor-fridge thing happening. There's a pile of random condiment packages, a Chinese take-out carton, and some weird energy drinks.

He shuts the door and leans back against the kitchen counter. His hands find my hips, his thumbs stroking my hipbones. "Tap water or bourbon?"

"Definitely the bourbon."

He snags the bottle from the counter, but then pours us both big glasses of water anyhow—to fight off the evils of dehydration, I guess.

"Sofa or balcony?" He makes a face. "The chairs are on the balcony, if that matters to you."

We decide to take our haul to the balcony. I follow him up the stairs and through the second-floor bedroom. Like the downstairs, there's just the one, big room that's mostly unfurnished. He does have a big platform bed with a white duvet and a striped throw that's been folded back into near surgical thirds. The floor is a really cool bleached pine and the walls are a soft almost-white. Maybe it's the almost total lack of color that makes it seem so sterile. Or maybe he moves around a lot, like I do.

"It's like a blizzard threw up in here."

Of course I blurt it out. I couldn't possibly keep my uncomplimentary thoughts to myself.

He flashes a grin at me. "Tell me what your favorite color is."

"Rainbow. Why settle for one?"

He's silent for a moment as he undoes the latch securing the porch doors. "Wouldn't that be ombré?"

"A Scrabble-worthy word." How unfair is it that he's both hot and well-read? "Feel free to ombré your bedroom, big guy."

His porch—which is more of a precarious perch over his front yard—has an amazing view of the ocean. What's even better is that I can smell the sea and the sand, but we're high enough that there's none of the noisome bits that makes San Francisco a little too gritty sometimes. A pair of seagulls duke it out on the sand. There's a breeze, too, cool and salty, and the drizzling rain has stopped.

Jax briefly disappears inside the bathroom that's tucked off the bedroom and comes back in jeans, much to my disappointment. We work our way through the bag of tacos. He's ordered enough for two Jax-size people, so it takes a while. While we eat, we watch the world go by on the street between the cottage and the beach. Mostly, this consists of judging the parallel parking attempts happening on the narrow, car-packed street, but there are also pauses that neither of us tries to fill up with small talk. It's strangely relaxing.

After I've achieved a six-month food baby, I wander back inside his bedroom, because I'm nosy. Jax follows me, depositing the remains of our dinner picnic in his trash. He's almost preternaturally neat, so it's a good thing he's never actually seen inside my RV. I'm most definitely not neat when it comes to my personal stuff, despite being practically a professional organizer at work.

The rainbow throw demands attention. Each side forms a perfect line. It doesn't seem like something he would have chosen since the rest of the place is the color of tofu and rice, but it's impossibly soft and I'm tempted to strip down to my skin and wrap myself up in it. If cashmere and kittens had a baby, this blanket would be it. When I straighten, I collide with a hard, male chest.

His arms come around me, steadying me. "It was a gift from my sister."

"You have sisters?" I twist around so I can see his face.

"One. She lives up in Napa." His finger skims my cheek. "She's an organic honey farmer."

He makes a face as he says this, as if he can't quite believe the words coming from his mouth.

I giggle. "That's not the most common occupation."

"What's the weirdest thing you've ever done for money?"

Given my extensive job history, there are so many candidates. I think for a moment. "I've been a professional stand-in-liner. And I trimmed mouse toe nails in a university lab for a week. What about you?"

His mouth replaces his finger, finding my throat. "I was Chief Listening Officer for a friend's company. I was supposed to report back about everything people said online and on social media. And I did some ethical hacking for a sex toy site. You wouldn't believe the amount of fraud that happens on those sites."

"So you used your computer skills for good instead of evil? I don't have to worry about the Pentagon busting down your door while we're having a moment?" I tilt my head to give him better access. He takes the hint, his mouth moving across my skin.

"You are entirely safe with me."

"Somehow I doubt that."

"Let me restate. You're as safe as you'd like to be."

"So I'm at total risk of losing my panties." I happy sigh, wriggling out of my kimono. Getting a head start on losing my clothes seems desirable. "Awesome."

"I like how you think." He grins at me and there's one of those weird moments where you and another person are sort of sharing a brain. I can practically see myself through his eyes as he moves his mouth to cover mine.

At first we kiss as if we're not in any rush. His lips press against mine, warm and gentle. His hands settle loosely on my hips, his thumbs working beneath the edge of my top and smoothing over my skin. My mouth parts, and he deepens the kiss because we've both been waiting for this since I met him on the beach. I want him.

He makes a rough sound when I glide my tongue along his, tasting, teasing. I'm not always a fan of wet kisses. They're kind of gross and I don't like the sounds. But somehow it feels right with Jax—a little funny but mostly raw and honest in a way I can't usually be. He needs this and so do I. His big hands make short work of my shorts and panties. When he tears his mouth away from mine to whisk the top over my head, I hear my own greedy sex sounds.

"This okay?" His voice is hoarse and gravelly. He needs me, too.

He likes to play.

"Don't stop. Tell me how you want to play this."

He groans something. "We could do yours again. Wedding night. Tell me what you want. Or I could choose for you."

Oh. I like that. I'm tired and I don't want to have to think.

"You choose."

He grunts something, but I'm not really paying attention. I'm too busy getting my hands all over his big, warm body. He strips off his jeans, finds a condom, and then gently tumbles me backward onto his bed, going in for another kiss. I have just enough brain cells left to toe his sister's throw off the end of the bed. There's no way I want to get sex stuff on it.

And then we're tangled up together, Jax pressing me down into the mattress while he braces his arms on either side of my head. There's more kissing and hands going everywhere. I wrap my legs around his waist, trying to put him where I want him. He gives a dark laugh, running his hands down my sides then to my pussy.

His fingers… God…the man is freaking diabolical.

He's saying stuff, too. Dirty words, filthy promises. *All you have to do is lie there and let me touch you. Open your legs. You can come again for me.*

I wrap myself around him, essentially turning myself into a horny human octopus while he skillfully reduces me to a happy, orgasmic puddle. It's stupid, but I pretend to myself that Jax is just my boyfriend and that we're having regular, routine comfort sex, the kind you have when you're tired and horny and the tired wins out over sexual gymnastics. The mac and cheese of sexy times.

He finally gets inside me, his thighs pushing me wide. "You love this. You're so wet."

I am. I wriggle against him and succeed in getting his dick lined up with where I need it. He pushes inside me and I make a mewling sound I'll be embarrassed about later. Right now, I'm too tired and too turned on to care. He shifts, pumping in and out of me, and I explode. He feels so good. I mumble incoherently into his shoulder while he moves faster and faster until he finishes, making rough sounds of his own. I'm boneless and relaxed when he pulls out and almost asleep when he rolls me into his side so he can hold me.

Despite the amazing sex and being six kinds of exhausted thanks to my crappy RV and its lack of weather resistance, I jolt awake. Jax sprawls next to me on the bed, sound asleep. At some point, we've moved apart, but our arms and legs still touch. My mind immediately starts buzzing, going a million miles a minute. When I fish my phone out of the shorts I lost beside the bed, it's five in the morning.

Would leaving now be weird?

For a while, I watch the outline of him sleep. He breathes deeply and evenly on his front, as solid asleep as he is awake. He's rough around the edges and blunt, but I like his no-holds-barred approach to living, and he's got to be the hottest guy I've ever seen in real life. Also, now that I've seen him naked again, I realize my memory omitted a few key points from our first night. Points like the curve of his bare shoulder, the dark ink on the forearm shoved over his pillow, the muscled sweep of his back down to a pair of delicious man dimples above his tight ass.

The room grows slowly lighter. I need a bathroom, plus I sort of want to ransack his beach cottage and see what I can learn about him. Slipping out of bed, I pad over to the bathroom, shutting the door carefully behind me before I turn the light on. I don't want to wake him up.

After I take care of business and wash my hands, I indulge my curiosity. Like me, I don't think he's been here long. He has matching, pristine white towels, no old stashes of toiletries or hotel freebies or even half-used stuff. Just the basics for the most part.

I should really, probably, almost certainly go now. After switching off the light, I use my phone's light to find the rest of my clothing. No way I walk home pantless.

I'm tiptoeing toward the stairs when I hear rustling sounds from the bed. I've woken Prince Charming, after all.

"You don't have to run off, Firefly. You could stay."

"Uh, yeah, that's not—"

A good idea.

Or smart.

"Wait a minute."

He mutters something and I hear him stand, followed by the sound of jeans sliding up. I wait for him, even though that's not smart, either. The longer I stay, the harder it is to go at all.

He ushers me down the stairs, his palm burning against the small of my back. When I keep moving toward the door, he tugs me back against him, curling his finger in a belt loop. "Stay."

"I need to go. This is all—" I wave a hand around his house. "I don't usually…"

I pull slightly against his hold. I don't do casual overnights and anything that smacks of a long-term relationship has never worked for me. I don't finish my sentences, though. What would I say? *I don't usually, but for you I might make an exception?* That he makes me rethink what I want, and that scares me?

I give in to impulse. "Can I come over and play tomorrow?"

His eyes darken.

"Yeah."

CHAPTER NINE

Jax

INDEPENDENCE IS HIGHLY OVERRATED, especially when you can outsource to someone better qualified to handle your problems. So, although Peony insists on heading out alone after our taco fest and sexcapade, I insist on going with her. For as long as I can remember, I've been a stubborn bastard. I'm a big guy, too, so I'm perfect for beach defense. It irritates me that she won't let me look after her, despite my obvious qualifications. It's dark, the beach is lonely, and her rental is in a bad area, probably thanks to her neighbors. She's not walking home alone.

We're halfway down the beach before she thaws enough to start talking to me again, her shoulder bumping my arm companionably as she comments on the weather, the stars, the traffic, a random dog dashing across the sand, and a dozen other things I can't be bothered to notice.

All my attention is focused on her.

She has a great voice. It's low and husky, a cheerful murmur that I can't find any comparison for. Maybe it's the animation with which she delivers her words, or her seemingly genuine interest in the stuff she's sharing. I like listening to her.

When there's a break in the flow of words, I reach for her hand, threading her fingers through mine. She has the long, slender fingers of an artist. Mine are stronger, bigger, and way blunter in comparison—the hands of a boxer or a brute.

She doesn't seem to mind.

She swings our hands where they're connected. "Are we pretending to be boyfriend-girlfriend?"

Sometimes I get tired of pretending. This is only the second time I've seen her, I remind myself. It's not like we have an actual relationship. So far we've just had sex and two meals. Pancakes and tacos, not even a real dinner in a restaurant or at a table. My favorite restaurant wouldn't let her in dressed like she is, or at least they wouldn't until I forced the issue. She's wearing a ragged pair of denim Bermuda shorts paired with a tank top that cups her tits. A patchwork kimono flares out behind her in the ocean breeze. She's twisted her hair up on top of her head in a messy swirl, little strands escaping here and there.

I'm used to the women who come to Liam's parties, usually looking to hook up with a wealthy techie. I stopped believing they were interested in more than my money or my dick years ago. To be fair, I wasn't looking for more than sex from them, either. There's something exciting about whatever this is with Peony. She's here for the sex, but I think she's also here for me.

There's a gust of wind that plucks at her kimono, dragging the folds through the water that creeps in, washing over our feet. I have our shoes in my right hand, the one that's not holding on to Peony. I get the feeling she'd sprint away from me if I let go for even an instant. She's not into staying put.

"Jax?" Peony pats my arm. Right. She's waiting for my answer.

"I'd like that."

She looks at my face for a moment. I'm not sure what she's searching for, but I doubt she'll find it. I don't have much experience with actual, long-term relationships. My thing has always been quick hookups.

"All right," she says. Her hand swings mine up in a little arc. I'm not sure what she's agreeing to.

We make it back to her camper far too quickly. A quick survey reveals the mother of all puddles in front of the door and a steady mini-deluge from the tarp. A familiar skunk-stink wafts from her neighbor's place.

"Jesus," I growl before I can stop myself. My sister's taught me the value of *silent* protectiveness. I can get away with fixing a lot of things as long as I don't editorialize or comment on what I'm doing.

Peony puffs up and I'd like to kiss the righteous

indignation off her face, but she'd a) punch me in the balls, and b) just go inside this crappy camper that much faster.

I sublimate my feelings for the time it takes to straighten out the tarp and dump the excess water onto the ground. It's not great, but it's better.

When I come back around to the front, she's already got her key in the lock and is working it determinedly. I suspect the lock is as busted as everything else based on how long it takes her to get it open.

And…fuck caution. "This is substandard, Peony."

"It's mine," she says firmly, hopping up onto the first step. "You have a nice day now."

What she really means is *Go away*, but *substandard* is a white lie on my part because I don't actually want to trample her feelings. The truth is that her camper should be condemned.

From the stink eye she's giving me, however, this isn't a battle I can win right now.

Plus, I'd rather kiss her goodbye, and she won't let me do that if she's pissed at me. I don't even try to fight that internal battle. Pleasure wins over ethics.

I swoop in for that kiss, wrapping my arms around her and pulling her into my body. It starts out perfectly PG, my lips pressed against hers. After a moment, she sighs, her mouth parting beneath mine all the invitation I need. My tongue sweeps inside her mouth.

She groans, her hands grabbing my face and angling me so she can kiss me back harder. Not as if I'm gonna protest because once wasn't enough. Twice wasn't enough, either. This girl is my long-term as long as I don't piss her off the wrong way.

I groan when her tongue slides against mine. We're grinding against each other, as if we both need to come one more time right here on the steps of her goddamned RV. Her hands move from my face to my ass, squeezing me over my jeans. My mouth devours hers, hers giving as good as she gets. Never mind that we're outside and on full display, or that the slap of my hand against the RV door makes the whole thing shiver and rock. If we actually did it inside, the place wouldn't be standing.

When she tugs her mouth free, I growl as if I really am the animal she makes me feel like. Her mouth is kiss-swollen and slick, and I want to dive between her pretty thighs and lick her there until we've achieved symmetry.

"No sex on the front steps," she whispers.

I straighten reluctantly. My breath sounds like a freight train, but I know no when I hear it, enough that I don't ask her how she feels about inviting me in.

Instead, I eye her piece of shit rental and run through options in my head. I could track down her landlord and buy her place. Then I could fix it, but I'd a) be officially a slumlord, b) have some serious explaining to do about my finances, and c) worry about things changing between us because she'd be pissed. My sister's explained on multiple occasions that just because I can buy something doesn't mean I should.

The beach cottage we just vacated is a good example. Peony would be mad if she knew I'd bought the place on a whim. The name makes me think of her and it's just up the beach from her. I'm used to founder hounders chasing me, usually naked, so Peony's charming abandon followed by icy reserve is novel. Because I wasn't sure she would call me, did I try to put myself in her path? You bet. Plus, a million-dollar beachfront property—even if it's barely eight hundred square feet—is always a good investment. By this time next week, I'll have already turned a profit.

Peony doesn't invite me inside. The slice of camper that I can see through the open door seems small and eighties-style, with a Formica-topped built-in table with a bench on one side and some dingy faux walnut paneling.

"Bye," she chirps, already shutting the door in my face.

It's a good thing I have a healthy ego.

When she's inside and has things shut up, I tap on the door. "Lock it, Peony."

I press one hand against said door. It's so thin that I can hear her breathing on the other side.

She laughs. "You are so overprotective."

"And you're worth sticking up for." I walk away with a smile on my face. "I'll call you. Pick up, okay?"

CHAPTER TEN

Peony

SECOND-DATE JAX should be illegal.

True to his word, he calls me during the week and announces that he'll be by on Friday night at an unspecified time to collect me for our date. He seems to think this constitutes asking me out—and my accepting—but I sort of don't want to shoot him down. Okay. After a week of self-induced orgasms, I almost call him myself and ask him to come over and help a girl out.

His Friday night arrival is heralded by an almighty bang on the door that has me wondering if the landlord is collecting the rent early, but when I squint through the peephole a previous tenant drilled into the door, it's just Jax. That is kind of like saying *Oh, that's just the Eiffel Tower* or *Hey, look, we're passing the Roman Colosseum.*

He's like a big, inked barbarian and I totally want him to storm my castle. Better yet, when I finish wrestling the door open and get the full Jax picture, I realize he's only half dressed. That makes him half naked and one-hundred-percent hot. Yet another wetsuit covers his lower extremities, cupping his manly bits in impressive fashion and making it perfectly clear the man has legs the size of tree trunks. He's knotted the sleeves around his waist. There's a damp-looking T-shirt tossed over his shoulder and a pair of aviator sunglasses pushed up on top of his head.

His gaze travels down my body. "Are you working?"

Since I'm wearing my usual downtime uniform of cotton shorts and a tank top, I appreciate his vote of confidence. San Francisco is full of work-from-homers glued to their laptops while they build the new Facebook or Tinder one line of code at a time, but my own job skills are less commercial. My most recent stints of employment have included work as a personal assistant, set stager for an Instagram influencer, coffee barista, and—my personal favorite—two months helping a closet design store install thousands of dollars' worth of custom shelving. I love organizing messes.

"As a matter of fact, I just stepped out of the boardroom. I've been schooling the executive team for their lack of foreplay." Oops. Freudian slip. "Foresight. Whatever. You look like you've been making similar inroads on the business community."

I lean against the doorjamb. I'm not wearing underwear because I've just been lounging around completing online surveys for a dollar a pop and checking Craigslist for more lucrative job openings.

He sucks in some air and coughs out a hello.

"Did you want something?"

"Peony." He groans my name like it hurts.

He gets a gold star for not staring at my boobs for longer than it takes to catalog my outfit. To be fair, I'm wearing an old tank top. It's stretched out and the lacy bits barely skim my nipples.

I grin at him. "It's okay to ogle them."

"Uh, what?" He drags his gaze back up to my face.

"The girls. The cupcakes. My twin melons?" I pat the boobs in question. "They like admiration, plus there's no way I'm not going to ogle you since you're half dressed."

"Now I feel like I should have brought them flowers." He sounds slightly dazed, which makes me giggle. I know firsthand, after all, that Jax is Mr. Control, so any opportunity to undo him should be seized. "But I feel the need to say that I'm not expecting sex tonight."

"Oh." I'm not entirely certain what the socially correct response is to that bombshell, so I go with the truth. "That's so weird I can't even plot it on my sexy-times scatter graph."

"What?" He scrubs a hand over the back of his neck.

I want to push his hand away and replace it with mine. I'll bet his skin is warm and soft there. I want to pull him close, kiss him hard, rub him all over me so that when tonight is done, I smell him on my skin. I shouldn't say any of that, though, so instead I explain.

"I don't know if I can promise your virtue is equally safe with me."

He grins. "I'm easy."

"So, fun as this is, why are you here?"

"You agreed to go out with me tonight. Do you want to go surfing?" He points to the ocean, as if his request could possibly need clarifying.

"You may have me confused with someone more coordinated."

He shrugs. "You can always sit on the board and I'll be your Italian gondolier and paddle you up the coast."

"Can you make sweet, sweet love in Italian?"

"Facciomolo adesso." His hands tangle in my hair, his gaze holding mine. *"Voglio di te."*

Holy.

SHIT.

I hold up a finger. "Give me ten minutes."

I shut the door in his face because I'm pretty sure by now that politeness is wasted on Jax. Or worse, he sees it as an open invitation to invade and arrange things the way he'd like them to be. Also, by shutting the door, I have privacy for the little freak-out I indulge in. The man looks like Adonis. He's got muscles on his muscles, while I've carefully concealed mine beneath a layer of fat. It makes me soft and cuddly, but it does not make me particularly athletic and I've just agreed to a swimwear date with him.

I do a quick bikini line inspection and decide things are reasonably okay in the trim and wax department. My red-and-white polka dot bikini is a little smaller than I remember it being, so I do some string adjusting, trying to make it cover more of my ass before I give up. I can stay in here all day, but I'm not going to magically morph into a swimsuit model.

I reinspect my bikini line and make a few repairs. Okay. It's as good as it's getting and he's already thoroughly inspected my business, so I just need to let it go. I pull the tank top and shorts back on, shove my feet into flip-flops, and grab my key. I don't have any reason left to not go outside.

Other, than, you know the big objection, which is that Jax Valentine is six feet four inches of dirty fun and that means I'm going to get into trouble.

I grab a pink Sharpie from my table and scrawl *Remember: This is a bad idea* on my forearm. I should probably enumerate the specific reasons, but my ten minutes are up and I'm chicken.

He grins at me when I come out. "I was about to send in a rescue party."

As we head up the beach together, his hand catches mine, big warm fingers lacing through mine.

"How was your week?" he asks.

"Are we still pretending to be a married couple?" This is new territory for me.

He swings our hands where we're connected. "I like hearing about *you*, Peony."

All righty then.

I run through the events of the week. "I think the highlight was interviewing for a startup in the Mission District. I got off the train, climbed about ninety billion steps to the street level, and then was assaulted by a pigeon that decided to land on my head. I considered turning around and heading back home for a second shower, but I persevered in the interests of gainful employment."

"Very responsible." His fingers squeeze mine gently.

"To get to the interview, I also had to step over a passed-out drunk dude who was taking up the entire sidewalk. It was like a demented obstacle course."

"Did it go well?"

I think it did, but I don't want to jinx it. "I wore my lucky panties."

"You have lucky panties?"

"You bet. It's way easier to sneak panties into an interview than a lucky coffee cup or a rabbit's foot."

He makes a choking noise. "Holy fuck. Are you wearing them or waving them around?"

"Which would make you hire me? Kidding!" I bump his arm with mine. "Wearing. Obviously."

"How was your week?"

He shrugs. "Made some money. Wrote some code. Climbed no mountains."

We get to the part of the beach where he's stashed his board and he starts going over the finer points of surfing.

Surfing is not intuitive. Or easy. Or in any way my thing. This is entirely on me. Jax is a good teacher, but I'm unwilling to stand up on the board because it means falling off and I hate being under water. Plus, I'm less coordinated than the passed-out drunk guy I had to climb over. Eventually, Jax gives up on teaching me surfing mechanics and instead paddles us out until we have a great view of the sunset. We sit together on his board, watching the sun start to set.

I lean my head back against his chest, trusting him to keep me on the board and out of the water. He's big and warm, like my own personal ocean-going armchair.

I peer over his arm at the water. "Do you think there are sharks down there?"

"Maybe." He sounds unconcerned. "It's not really shark season, though."

"Maybe then we should head back in? Is there ever a good time of year to meet a shark face to face?"

He laughs, but points the board at the surf break. This is the opposite of the direction I've requested. He makes a convincing argument, however, that his way will be faster, so I cling to the front of the board while he rides us through a wave toward shore. This isn't Hawaii and the Banzai Pipeline. The top of the wave barely reaches Jax's shoulder, but there's a wall of water and then we're flying, flying, flying toward the beach.

I sort of want to do it again, but it's getting dark and I'm cold.

Since date-night Jax is trying to be a gentleman, he sacrifices his towel to me when we come ashore. I run my hand over it as he tucks it around me, fussing in a way that's kind of cute. The towel is bright blue, like one of those Robin Eggs they sell at Easter, and has InterContinental Bora Bora embroidered on it in gold letters.

"Nice. Did you steal it?"

He assesses his handiwork and retucks an edge. "Maybe I bought it, fair and square. Maybe the hotel gave it to me as a welcome gift, all tied up with some local tropical foliage."

"Really?" I've never stayed somewhere they actually give away the towels.

I rub at my damp arms with the towel. My reminder to not jump Jax Valentine's very fine ass has mostly washed off thanks to the salty Pacific. It's like a sign from above.

"Do you want me to be a felon?" He props his hands on his hips and fakes a glare. "We need to discuss your fantasies, Ms. Peony."

"Well, maybe you just *borrowed* it?"

"Like a pirate?" He gives me a look of mock indignation.

"God, yes. Be a pirate. Please. Better yet, do it naked and let me call you Jack."

His eyes darken. "Run, Firefly."

I consider staying put just on principle, but, oh my God, he's too much fun. I bolt across the sand, shrieking.

My flight to freedom lasts five seconds before big hands snag me and toss me up, up, up.

"You need more cardio." He smacks my ass as he deposits me over his shoulder.

"You have longer legs. I demand a handicap!"

My current position isn't quite as sexy as I'd imagined it would be—his shoulder is rock-hard, which turns out to be a bad thing when it's jabbing into my midsection. It's also not the widest perch in the world. By the time we reach his front porch, I feel like I'm about to slide down his back and face plant in his hydrangeas. You win some, you lose some.

I slap at his porch railings, laugh-shouting, "Safe," and he smacks me playfully on the ass again. My butt's stinging and other related parts of me are on fire.

"This isn't baseball, Firefly." He produces a key and then boots the door open. I promptly forget all the reasons this is a bad idea.

He shifts me until I'm cradled in his arms. This position lets me pepper kisses across his shoulders and lick the little divot at the base of his throat. Muscles working, he somehow manages to simultaneously shove the wet suit down and kiss me. My hands are everywhere because pirating should always be equal opportunity.

"You're my prize," he rumbles, setting me down on my feet. "Savvy?"

"Maybe you're mine." I nip his plush lower lip.

He kisses along the edge of my jaw, his hands holding my face steady as he walks me backward toward the stairs. The upside to his lack of furniture is that we could practically waltz in here if we wanted.

My back hits the wall and he pulls my arms over my head, pinning my wrists with one hand. The other tangles in my hair.

"Ahoy," he says roughly.

"Yeah?" It's not proper pirate speak, but when he kisses me like this, I can't think.

So I just kiss him back.

We're locked together so tight that I can't believe penetration hasn't happened. My bikini bottoms are no match for his enormous, delicious erection. I wrap a leg around his waist and grind on him.

He pulls on the left-hand string and it comes apart. "These are my favorites."

I arch a brow. "Aye?"

"Aye." My bikini bottoms disappear over his shoulder. The man definitely has a thing for tossing my clothing because my top gets the same treatment. His hand descends, tracing my curves and dipping lower.

There's a whole lot of kissing now, more mouth action, our tongues sliding and licking while we try to devour each other. I've never had sex on the stairs before. Despite its popularity in books, it seems uncomfortable.

"Bed," I order. Possibly I whine-groan it, but his mouth has found my boob, his free hand is stroking south, and conversation's never been my strong point.

He scoops me up with a muttered curse and I wrap my legs around his waist and hang on. This could be awkward but Jax doesn't seem to mind my weight. His dick is trapped between us and I get my arms around his waist so I can squeeze his ass. He strides up the stairs and we land on the bed. It's a freaking miracle.

I grind against him, making heavy breathing sounds that are porn-worthy.

He nips my bottom lip. "Yes?"

"I'm naked," I groan, humping his hip. "You're

naked. Yes. Aye. Shiver me timbers but pick up the pace, 'kay?"

A wicked grin tugs at the corner of his mouth. "Firefly, I love hearing you tell me yes."

There's more kissing and shameless grinding on my part, and then, right when I'm ready to beg-demand some more—

He's flipping me over, his hands shaping my ass while he curses and tells me how amazing I look. A strong hand strokes down my back, finding the sensitive, knotted places and pressing firmly. Surfing is hard work.

"God, you have porn star hands."

His hand kneads lower. "And you have an amazing ass."

It's hard to miss my ass, that's for sure. It's always been a little bigger, a little curvier, than most. His mouth follows his hand and I feel the sharp, bright sting of his teeth as he moves lower.

"You're such a kinky bastard," I moan into my pillow.

Touching him like this would require mad yoga skills. I rock back against him to be helpful.

"You like it. You like me." He twists, moving me up the bed as he slides underneath me in what's probably an amazing feat of athletics that I should appreciate more, but his mouth grazes me *right there* and the only sounds I'm making now are greedy ones.

My hips buck and he grabs them, holding me

steady above him. All of his balancing on a board is paying off for me. He licks a scorching path up my center, sucking on me with exquisite gentleness. I'm so slick I can hear the wet sounds, but I'm way past embarrassment. I need more. I need—

Jax is merciless, his tongue stroking, his teeth grazing lightly on sensitive spots I didn't even know I had. His lips brush my clit, teasing, and I press my hips toward his wicked, talented mouth.

"Jax—"

I whimper, tearing at the sheets, reaching for him. He just licks harder, the bastard.

And then he sucks.

Sensation explodes through me. I can't separate what he's doing from what I feel. It's one big maelstrom of white-hot heat and a growing tension as my body tightens, preparing for the big storm. I moan his name.

He pushes one big finger into me and we're both groaning and making sex sounds someone out on the beach could hear. *Yes* and *more* and our names all mixed up with profanities. I think. *Fuck* if I know because I fly apart, coming and coming, squeezing his face with my thighs.

He eases me down because the man's the crowned king of aftercare. He even handles the mechanics of lifting me off his face and finding me a safe landing spot on the bed, which is good because I don't have a functioning bone in my body. I press my burning, sweaty pink face against the cool cotton of the pillow case. He's turned me into the best kind of mess.

He reaches for a condom, tearing the foil packet open. I should help but he's orgasmed me into a useless, happy puddle. I mumble this into his pillow and he laughs.

"I like you this way, Firefly. You stay put."

No problem. I do my best impression of a blissed-out starfish, sprawled on his bed, as he pulls my hips up and presses himself against my entrance. That part of me's apparently an on-ramp to the sexual highway because things speed up fast. He pushes himself inside me in a hard, sure thrust. He works himself into me, one arm braced by the side of my head, his fingers playing with my hair.

I turn my head so I can press stupid little kisses against his inked forearm, licking the sun-bronzed skin just because I can.

"Peony." He groans my name, burying his face buried against my throat. "Is hard and fast okay?"

"Is there a menu? Do I get choices?"

"More like a buffet," he grits out. "You get a little of everything on your plate."

"Okay," I say a little breathlessly.

He pushes himself up on one arm so he can see my face. "Yeah?"

I nod frantically, the heavy breathing starting up again, because the way the muscles in his arm work to hold him is sexy. *Everything* about him is sexy except that his thoughtful check-in has removed his penis from my happy place.

"Come back," I whine.

He groans something and lowers himself against me. It feels so good. He opens me up, driving deeper. "You're amazing, Firefly."

So is he. I claw the bedsheets with one hand and wrap the other around his thick wrist. Each thrust pushes me up the bed and I fight the urge to giggle.

He anchors my hip with his hand, solving that logistical issue, and then there's nothing but the in, in, in as he makes room for himself inside me. Pulling out. Driving in again. I mumble-groan his name.

"Yes?" His mouth finds my cheek.

"Come in me, big guy."

His "You first" is a dark rasp.

He's no gentleman, but his hand reaches around me to find my clit and stroke. My body spontaneously ignites, apparently finding an unexpected burst of energy from somewhere. I don't know. I just grip his arm and moan out compliments because, God, this man knows how to fuck.

My name punctuates the litany of dirty promises that fall from his mouth.

Fuck me, Firefly.

Hold me.

Like that.

I'm gonna...

He comes, I come, and then he collapses on top of me for the briefest of moments before he rolls, pulling me into his side before he can squash me flat. I sound like I just attempted a marathon after a summer of couch sitting.

I don't know what to say, so I say nothing and run my fingers over the arm locking me against him. We were supposed to be playing.

We were supposed to be pirates.

We were supposed to be just fun and games.

At some point, though, we became just Jax and Peony, and now I don't know what the rules are.

CHAPTER ELEVEN

Jax

THE DAYS FLY BY. I've made a point of spending as much time with Peony as I can. Work is crazy as always, but we spend nights and weekends together. For the last ten years, I've worked long hours. It's the price tag of success and I've never regretted it. But now I find myself changing my focus. I'm still chasing new opportunities in the boardroom, but the pace is different. Less intense. It might not be a good thing to admit out loud, but more and more, Peony becomes my focus.

We wander around San Francisco's tourist attractions because Peony is new to the city and hasn't seen much. We ride the cable cars, hike across Golden Gate Bridge, and get lost inside the big museum of modern art that Peony adores and that I will never, ever, get. She insists on going Dutch for dinner, so we also spend hours chilling on the beach, eating cracked crab because "I know a guy who can get it for free" and trading funny work stories without mentioning names. I like that I can complain about my week and let her in on some of my secrets. She shares her own work horror stories, and the teller of the most horrific story gets to choose our Friday night movie.

I know that I should tell her the whole truth—that I'm not just a programmer and that really I own the entire business enchilada. I'm a billionaire CEO and my work stories have been carefully edited so that she doesn't figure out that Mark is the CEO of a major software company and not just an annoying guy down the hall. I should have been honest, but I chose not to be, and that's on me. I keep waiting for the right moment to let her in on my little secret, but it never seems to come.

Tonight, Peony's tucked against my chest, facing outward because otherwise, she claims, I accidentally suffocate her. I'm not sure that's technically possible, but I want her happy and not worried, so this has become our go-to position after sex. I press a kiss against the top of her head, wishing I could see her face.

I love seeing her face.

She mumbles something, shifting restlessly. Peony's a bed hog and a light sleeper. She flails around, kicks the covers off, and gets up at least twice during the night. She usually tries to bug out and go back to her shitty RV after we've had sex, and I always try to convince her to stay. My bed's bigger, better, and right here, so I don't see the point in leaving. Most of the time, I can convince her.

Tonight we played teacher and student. I got to be the teacher because we rock-paper-scissored for it. Peony complained I'd cheated, but I just sent her to stand in the bad girl corner and then things escalated and…we ended up here. Boneless and satisfied.

My brain cells come back online slowly because Peony wrecks me every time. I press a kiss into the hollow where her shoulder meets her throat and roll off the bed so I can take care of the condom. Having sex with her without the latex barrier would be amazing, but it's a big ask. I'm clean, but I'm not sure she's ready to trust me like that yet. When I return, I run my fingers down her back before sliding into bed next to her. Her chin's stacked on her hands as she watches a pair of seagulls battle it out midair. The smaller bird eventually flies off, making indignant sounds.

Peony watches the loser go. Her face is flushed pink from too much sun and her hair is tangled from where I fisted it earlier. She's pulled the throw my sister gave me around her. It's some kind of organic, hippie version of cashmere, and Peony's practically adopted it. She wouldn't take this one, so I ordered three to her RV. She gave me shit about it for a week, but she didn't return them, either. She doesn't expect anything from me except for orgasms, which is something I'd like to change even though my track record with relationships is nonexistent.

If I were like the other guys who've conquered Silicon Valley, I'd tell her who I was. I could spoil her openly then and make sure she was taken care of. I've never had a problem sharing my money. It's more that I want the girl I'm with to see me first and not the dollar signs. Telling Peony that I'm successful should be easy. It's not as if I've gotten rich selling babies on the black market or playing dirty politics, so I think she'll understand.

What I do have is the money to keep her safe and to make her life a little easier. I drag myself up the bed so I can see her sprawled next to me on the mattress. Maybe now is the right time to bring up the complete truth about how I make my money. Mrs. Haverstorm, my kindergarten teacher, always insisted that sharing was caring and important. Didn't make handing over the purple marker any easier, but I'm starting to see her point.

"You wanna talk?" My fingers play with her damp hair, smoothing out the tangled strands. We started in the shower then moved out here. Duvet's halfway across the room, sheets tangled at the bottom of the bed. We're ass-backward anyway since Peony likes to watch the ocean while I fuck her from behind.

"Let's not discuss world peace or anything important until I've recovered from that last orgasm."

"That good?"

I kiss her neck while I knead her shoulders with

my hands. She gives a little groan and wriggles into my hold. "What are you looking at?" I ask.

"They're knocking your neighbor's house down."

"They'll build something new."

There aren't many properties that come up for sale here, and most of the people who buy just knock the existing house down and build from scratch. My Realtor assumed that was what I would do with Our Little Secret, so she was shocked when I just hired a bunch of contractors to give it a quickie fix up.

"I liked that cottage." She makes a face. "And now they'll probably put some multistory glass-and-chrome monstrosity in its place."

"Not a fan of real estate flipping?"

"Not a fan of throwing money around," she says.

"Maybe they've been saving up for a lifetime." I pull her into my side. "Or maybe that particular cottage can't be saved. It could have termites or structural damage. Sometimes knocking things down and starting over is the only option."

"And sometimes people are just assholes." She rolls over and flops off the end of the bed so she can watch the world go by upside-down.

I trace her ribs until she giggles and swats my hand away. "You think all rich people are assholes?"

There's definitely no justification for not telling her I'm a billionaire, but since I'm not a nice guy, I'm going for the intel before I confess.

"No." She thinks about it for a moment. "But my bio dad definitely was."

"He had money?"

She snorts. "Worse. His family used to have it, years ago. When he met my mom, his own bank account was still a work in progress. He had a small trust fund that he was using to bankroll a series of businesses."

I've run into the type. They put everything into stupid ideas without doing their due diligence because their illustrious ancestors made money and good business sense must get passed down in the DNA like blue eyes or brown hair. They usually burn through their cash and then get pissed off about it. "He didn't make a fortune?"

"Blew through one, more like. He could have lived a solid middle-class life if he'd been careful, but he always wanted more. He used to tell us he wanted it for us—the better neighborhood, the vacation home in Martha's Vineyard, the private travel and schools."

"So he wanted to provide for you. That's not a bad thing."

I lie down next to her. We must look ridiculous hanging off the bed, upside down, but I want her to be comfortable. I also don't want her to stop talking because Peony rarely opens up. Her likes and dislikes in regard to sushi, modern art and post-ocean shower sessions are well known to me, but

I know almost nothing about her life before I met her at Liam's party.

She rolls her eyes. "Except he wanted to provide what he wanted to provide. There wasn't a whole lot of consulting going on. My parents would fight about money. Then they'd fight about the house or the car or us. He'd promise that this time he'd got his shit figured out, that our new house and car and life would be for keeps, but then the money would dry up and the bills would start coming in and one day we'd just walk out the door and not come back. After the third time, I stopped decorating my room. The fifth time, my mom took us and told him he was on his own."

"I hate that you had to live like that." I take her hand in mine, lacing our fingers together, and set it on my stomach. There's no good response to hearing her dad was a dick.

"And then one day he got the big house and all the other fancy stuff," she says. "I don't know how he did it, but I don't think it involved felonies or organ sales, so I should have been proud of him, right? Go, Dad—you've made a million bucks. But he acted as if having that money justified the way he'd behaved before, as if he should get a Dad of the Year award because he could pay for cars and college and shit. He wanted to pretend he'd never been an asshole, when now he was just an asshole with money."

Her fingers tighten on mine. I don't think she's done yet.

"So, I wasn't as nice to him as he wanted me to be. I wouldn't pretend we were one, big happy family. My memories weren't for sale. Which, it turned out, was fine with him." She shrugs. "He went and got himself a new wife and kids, ones who fit into his fancy new life better than I ever could have. They're the stars of the Chicago social scene. They're old enough to go to debutante balls and private colleges now, and he sends me a Kate Spade bag every year for my birthday."

"Fuck, Peony."

My thumb's rubbing a groove into her fingers. This is not shit I'm good at. I don't know how to make her believe that she deserves someone way better than her asshole dad.

She sighs. "I like Kate Spade. It's not her fault, and her resale value is awesome. But money changes people, especially when they are chasing the money."

"You want me to find him and hit him where it hurts?"

For a moment, I forget she doesn't know that I'm one of those guys with money. That I have so much that people rush to make things happen for me.

She squeezes my fingers. "Nah. I'm good, but thanks."

"You know I'd do anything for you."

"Murder's a big ask." She flips upright, rolling onto my chest. "I have a better idea."

Her mouth covers mine.

CHAPTER TWELVE

Peony

"Untie me."

I stretch wiggling my wrists at Jax. An hour ago—or two or three—he convinced me that tonight's game should be dirty tie-me-up sex. I offered to tie *him* up so he could see how he liked it, but he refused. Jax prefers to be the one in control, and most of the time I indulge him. He promised I'd like what he did to me, and he was right. I've come so many times that my butt will be sore tomorrow from the clenching.

He brushes a kiss over my throat, and the rasp of his stubble-roughened jaw makes me shiver. "I still have some ideas. Let me show you."

I'm tempted, but that's the problem, isn't it? I'd let Jax do anything and everything. I've given in on our summer living arrangements, and now I basically live with him. He won't take money from me and the series of temp jobs I've worked this summer certainly don't pay enough for me to pay San Francisco rent.

Not for the first time, I wonder what exactly he does with his laptops. Asking seems like a boundary, though. An important one. He disappears during the workweek, like I do, and then we come home to each other, kiss, and fall into bed. We're a bedroom couple, a hookup on repeat. If I ask him about his day, he'll be more than just my fuck buddy. I think we could be friends.

Or something more.

Familiar panic bubbles up in me, freezing my chest in an icy knot. I can't have feelings for him. I can't, I can't, I can't. My lungs tighten on nothing. There's no air in here, just Jax and more Jax. When I breathe, he's everywhere. He's inside me, part of me, inescapable.

"Peony?" His warm mouth brushes my ear, his big fingers covering the ribbons that he's tied me up with, the ribbons I've gift-wrapped myself in for him.

I scramble onto my knees. Jax shifts with me, until he's sitting on the bed. His dark eyes watch me carefully. "What's wrong?"

"I have to go. Away. I've got a thing with my sister this weekend. I promised I'd be there and she needs me."

He processes this for a moment, his dark gaze inscrutable. I've never lied to him before, not directly, and I'm not even doing it well. My story has a million holes, starting with the fact that it's dark o'clock.

"Where do you need to go? I can take you."

"I've got it. It's fine." I tug at the ribbons with my teeth because fuck waiting for him to undo me.

"Let me help." He hesitates, his gaze fixed on the ribbons, but then he cups my hands in his and starts undoing the knots. It's stupid that I want to push him away. I'm sure I look like a rabid animal stuck in a trap or something. It's definitely not good for my teeth and dentistry is one more thing on my Can't Afford list.

When the knot comes undone, he pulls the ribbons off and tosses them away. His expression is tight. "Did I scare you?"

I think about it for a moment. "I'm fine."

It's not an answer, and we both know it. The thing is, he is a big, scary bastard. It's not so much a size-of-his-dick thing, although that part of him is fabulously huge. It's the way he fills up the world around him and takes over effortlessly. People listen when he talks. And then when he finishes speaking, they rush to do what he says. I have, too. Or maybe it just feels that way because when he suggests sex to me my vagina lights up and rolls out the welcome mat. I don't *want* to tell him no.

"I'll fix it." He rubs the faint marks his ribbons have left on my wrists, a frown creasing his forehead.

He'd never hurt me physically because it would hurt him even more. He's a fixer and a watchdog, the kind of man who rushes out onto the battlefield to put himself between you and incoming shit. Some days, it's sweet, but tonight it's suffocating.

"Stop." I place my hand against his chest. I can feel a steady drumbeat beneath my fingertips. Irrationally, I'm pissed off at how calm he is, how always in control.

He stops. That's my safety word, those four letters. He said he'd never play games with me if I used it, that whatever we were doing would end and I could walk away.

"Peony—"

I can't tell what he's thinking. I remind myself I don't care, I can't afford to care. "Do you have to rush off right now, Firefly? It can't wait?"

I stand and make a show of looking at my phone. *See? I have urgent electronic messages of the made-up variety.* I get dressed and debate grabbing the things I've left here over the last few weeks, but they're just things. I don't need them.

"I have to go."

His palm runs down my back, soothing, tracing my skin, the line of my spine, the curve of my bottom. His mouth brushes my hair. "Can I help?"

"No. I have to do this myself."

He exhales roughly, pulling me close for a moment. He feels so good. I want to press my face against his skin, sink into him, and that's a problem. "You say that too much."

"No one likes a clinger."

He grunts something but I won't ask what. He's a shockingly nice guy who thinks he needs to fix everything, but I can't let him fix me.

"You take your shower." I give in to temptation and press a kiss against his shoulder. His skin is like silk against my mouth and yet there's a rock-hard strength under the beautiful surface. "Then you can walk me back."

He watches me for another moment then gives me a brief nod. I watch him right back. This is the last time I'll see him like this and so I drink in the big, hard lines of his body as he gets out of bed. He doesn't bother with his clothes, just stalks to the bathroom all muscled legs, tight ass, broad shoulders.

He pauses in the door. "Do not move from that bed, Firefly."

I hold up two fingers. "Scout's honor."

Liar, liar.

Jax

Peony's face is a billboard for whatever she's feeling. Pleasure, glee and curiosity. Nerves, bravado and sass. The one thing she can't do is lie for shit. It's one of the things I lo—*like*—about her.

At least that's what I thought. When I came out of the bathroom ten minutes after I went in, my stupidity is clear. She's gone. I check the balcony, but no Peony. Dragging on a pair of jeans, I bolt down the stairs. She's not there, either.

Or in the flower-filled front yard.

Or on the beach.

She's nowhere that I can see. How fast did she run away this time to get so far?

I consider sprinting down the sand to catch up with her because she has to be there, just out of sight, hotfooting it back to her derelict, unsafe RV because she knows I'll insist on walking her back. She just needs her space. Some time alone. I tell myself I need to respect her choices. It's not that there's no room for me in her life, just that she has to choose her sister right now. Family always comes first.

I stand there, glaring down the beach, stupidly feeling like I've just lost a chance at something.

I go back inside, opting to text her rather than stalk her.

Don't take chances like that, Peony.

Text me when you're back safe.

She doesn't respond, not now, not an hour later, not two hours. By midnight, I'm concerned. Maybe her phone's died or she's rushed off to be with her sister. There are a dozen perfectly logical reasons why she's not answering, but something feels off.

Tell me you're okay.

Are you okay?

It's not until 1:00 a.m. that I discover the note on my kitchen counter, tucked beneath the bourbon bottle.

Hey Big Guy...
It's been an amazing summer, but I think it's past time for me to move on. I don't relationship well, so I'll just say thank you and see you around sometime. Have you read the Douglas Adams books? The one where his hero is hitchhiking around the galaxy? Anyhow, the dolphins abandon Earth right before it's razed for an intergalactic superhighway and they say so long and thanks for all the fish. *I'll borrow from them and say* so long and thanks for all the orgasms. *P*

What. The. FUCK.
I reread Peony's note because this makes no sense. She's walked out on me without a real goodbye. She hasn't given me a chance to fight for her, for us. I'm apparently just a piece of hot summer

dick and now I'm a memory. Anger's a red tsunami that swallows up the next few minutes of my life. There may be wall-punching involved and some mild trashing of my place. Am I angry at Peony? Yeah, but even more, I'm hurt, and that's a new level of suckitude for me. She wasn't the only relationship virgin.

Reel it in, Valentine. An angry, wall-punching male isn't going to convince her to come back. This isn't my area of expertise, though. Unfortunately, the only thing I'm good at is making money. That is business. So some of that shit has to apply to this. I just have to figure out the common denominator and go from there. It's like a business deal that's made an unexpected left-hand turn. Into oncoming traffic. It's no big deal—I've fixed worse.

Communication seems like an important starting point. I text Peony: Let's talk.

I stare at my phone, willing her to answer, but I've got nothing, not even a fucking *delivered* message from the cell phone provider. Maybe her phone's off. Maybe she's dropped it in the toilet. Maybe she never made it home at all and I should rampage up the beach and rescue her from the ditch or the evil villain or whatever's kept her from realizing she's just made a really horrible mistake.

Three days of silence later, I give up trying to be a nice guy. I'm not and it's killing me. I need her back, so I can figure out why having her in my life matters so much to me. I talk with my sister every day, but she just keeps telling me to give Peony her space and spouting hippie crap like *if you love someone, let them go and they'll come back*. That makes no sense unless you're dating a boomerang or a dog.

It turns out to be a moot point, however, because no matter how long I knock on Peony's door, she doesn't open up. Eventually, her pothead neighbor pops his head out and informs me that Peony moved out the morning after our breakup. Naturally, he didn't bother to ask her where she was going. He's even more of an asshole than I am, although he's way more mellow about it.

I drive up to the bee farm on my bike. It's a great ride—lots of fast road, tight turns and dangerous stretches—but I make it in one piece even though I break all speed laws. Hana's in her front yard, which is really one big, bee-filled meadow. As soon as I kill the bike's engine, the drone of my little sister's bees is deafening.

She launches herself across the yard at me and I catch her in a bear hug. "Are you okay?"

I texted her a picture of Peony's note before heading up here. I hate that she's worried about me. She has better things to be thinking about.

Hana gets right to it. "She hasn't texted you back?"

"No. This feels like fucking grade school," I growl. "I'm not okay with this."

Hana pats my arm. "It sucks."

"She moved out of her place overnight."

Hana's silent for a moment as she processes. Honestly, there's not much she can say, so I barrel ahead and lay it all out. "Not only did Peony break up with me, but she was apparently so afraid or concerned or something that I'd come after her that she ran away from home. The last thing I wanted was for her to feel unsafe."

"You can be overprotective." She shrugs. "And an ass. But you're largely a lovable ass."

"And what do you do, Hana Bear, when I'm up in your space being overprotective?"

She grins. "I tell you to back the fuck off."

"Exactly." I slouch on her porch steps. Jesus. She needs some decent porch furniture. If I buy some, though, she'll howl. She likes to *make her own way*, whereas I'd prefer to spoil her. "You use your words. She knew all she had to say was *stop*."

"Maybe she's not into kinky sex—or thinks she shouldn't be—and you sort of freaked her out?"

I frown. "I don't think we should be discussing this."

"We're not discussing. I'm just touching bases with you and identifying a possible issue so you can come at it from a different angle."

"That almost sounds like you've been reading those business books I bought you."

"Answer the question."

There is no man alive who wants to discuss his sex life with his sister outside of a V. C. Andrews novel.

"You think I'm into kinky shit?"

"You met at a sex party," Hana points out calmly. "I don't want the details, but maybe she's a little more vanilla and you're a little more... I don't know...chocolate chipotle?"

"Maybe." I sound doubtful. What the fuck is wrong with me?

I thought she had a great time.

I thought we were into each other.

I thought we were getting to know each other.

Hana leans her head against my shoulder, wrapping an arm around my waist. She's half my size, but I think she's trying to be supportive.

"Do you want to look for her?"

I do, but Peony's made it clear she's done.

I shake my head. "Can't."

CHAPTER THIRTEEN

Jax

FOR THE FIRST time in months, I feel like myself. It's been three months since Peony ghosted me, and I've spent way too many of those hours moping and resisting the urge to hack into a dozen databases until I find her. Since that would be both felonious and super creepy, I've mostly resisted. My one failure was her landlord. I went through his records, just in case he had any information about where Peony had gone, but I still couldn't find a forwarding address. People who accept crappy campers don't do forwards, apparently.

She also changed her number, as I learned when a random stranger lady answered. She was very nice, but she wasn't Peony, and I apologized for the string of voice mails I'd left on her phone. She had a mister of her own, so she wasn't available, but she said that she thought Peony was a lucky woman and hopefully she'd stop running long enough to realize that.

It would be awesome to run into Peony, or to finally have her reach out to me, but I've sort of accepted that's not happening. I miss holding her, though, and I miss our weird conversations and the way we hung out. What I would like to miss, but am not, is this stupid feeling of being vulnerable. It doesn't matter how hot the sex was, or how amazing she was as a person, because now that I don't have her in my life, I just feel…less.

In the spirit of feeling *more*, I'm in my San Francisco office closing a deal to acquire an internet startup with the unfortunate name of Hotly. When you hear that, you think porn, right? Or hookups or dating apps or some kind of super kinky, dark corner of the cyberworld. You're not even close.

Hotly's a wannabe internet channel that streams Top Ten content 24/7. Right now my laptop's streaming their ten most adorable kitten videos. It's cute and I see how customers could waste a tremendous amount of time, but no one pays for cute felines—they're available for free everywhere you look. Hotly's compounded selling the wrong product with hiring incompetent directors and spending their cash reserves. They've also launched themselves into a dozen different urban markets without a business plan.

It's a total cluster fuck.

The complete hash they've made of their finances is also why I've been able to buy their IP for peanuts. As of an hour ago, I'm the new owner and CEO. For the most part, I just drop in, announce the takeover, and give HR the list of names to ax. If you don't contribute, you don't get paid. If you don't make me money, you're out. Not everyone appreciates that sentiment, which is why I generally don't announce my arrival. I just make a surprise appearance like the Tooth Fairy—or the Grim Reaper.

Since the Grim Reaper is kind of a lurker, I lean against the window and glare ominously at Market Street. I spend as little time as possible in the office, so mine is a corner sliver that looks over the bustling street. There are loads of sweatshirt-wearing tourists, panhandlers, and a steady sea of business suits picking their way past the mayor's bright blue, self-cleaning toilets.

A knock on my door is followed by my lawyer. Thanks to DocuSign, Nina Lake's presence is a bit superfluous, but I appreciate the effort. Ms. Lake has handled my shit for the last five years, ever since I made my first billion. She points out the various legal pitfalls of my actions, and I decide if I care or not. Today she's looking less calm than usual. Her hair looks like she's run her hands through it more than once, there's an actual wrinkle in the front of her skirt, and her suit jacket isn't buttoned.

After shutting my door, she strides across the room and shoves a sheaf of papers at me. "These came in the mail for you."

"Someday you're going to bring me flowers instead of trouble." I take the stack from her.

She looks pissed off, so at least no one's died. "When were you going to tell me that you were married?"

I glance down at my present. "I'm not."

"Those papers say you are. I needed to be informed of this. Did you sign a prenup? For the love of God, tell me you signed a prenup."

I flip through the papers. The top one is a California marriage license. There's some supporting documentation, including the scrap paper Peony and I fake-signed. Peony's signature is round and loopy, sprawling outside the narrow space provided by the form.

"Explain." Lake glares at me. It's clear she thinks I've done this just to mess up her week.

"I went to that sex party Liam hosted." I look down at the license in my hand. "The one that was held on the date of this license. I may have hooked up with someone and we may have been taking turns role-playing our sexual fantasies."

Lake shakes her head. "And yours was getting married?"

"That was hers."

The look Lake gives me makes it clear she thinks I've fallen into a really stupid trap. "And so you just trotted along to a minister with this hookup, said your vows, and thought it was all fine?"

"It was a game. Sexy role play." I hate explaining. "We got 'married' by a ringmaster in a circus costume, Lake. I certainly didn't think it was legally binding."

"And in Nevada you can get married by a guy in a sequined jumpsuit." She waves a hand, dismissing my argument. "You didn't think it was legally binding, but what was Ms. Harding's opinion on the matter?"

"You think Peony set me up?"

"It's a possibility." Lake's mouth tightens.

"It was a spur-of-the-moment game. Fuck, it wasn't even the *point* of the game. That was the wedding night—"

Lake raises her hand. "Stop. Did you tell the officiant that you wanted to get married?"

"Yes."

"And then you said vows to each other in front of him?"

"Yes, but—"

"And you signed something?"

Okay. So I can see how this doesn't look good. "Yes."

"Is your bride at least eighteen?"

I realize I don't know Peony's actual age. For a brief second, I panic that I've done something completely unforgivable, but then my brain kicks back online, reminding me that based on the things she's mentioned, she's of legal age. She's been to college. She's held multiple jobs. She's crisscrossed the country. That would be awfully ambitious for an under-eighteen. "Definitely?"

"Single?"

"Fuck, I hope so. We didn't apply for a license," I point out. "Or show ID. Don't you have to flash a driver's license for this?"

I don't know much about family law, but I'm pretty sure that it requires paperwork. Yes, I scrawled my signature on a scrap of paper as part of our role-play, where we "signed the register," but that seems like thin ground for a legal marriage.

"Walk me through the night. This could be a very expensive mistake, Mr. Valentine."

Reluctantly, I share the details of our "wedding" with my lawyer. She has an excellent poker face, but it's perfectly clear she can't believe I did this on purpose. Or that I got off on doing it. She probably has a nice, vanilla, entirely boring sex life.

Lake blows out a breath. "Are you aware that California is a community property state? And that that means Ms. Harding could make a legal case that she is entitled to half of your earnings since your marriage approximately four months ago? Your marriage is of short duration, so it's unlikely she could successfully argue for spousal maintenance, but it's going to be more cost effective to settle with her."

This bothers me less than I thought it would. I've always fought to protect my financial interests because I've worked hard for my money. It's my castle and moat, my way of keeping the people I love safe, so I don't view claims on it lightly. But this is Peony and I don't mind keeping her safe.

Lake's already moved on, however. After nailing down the more or less exact sequence of events she checks to see if there was copious amounts of alcohol or drugs involved—no—and then tackles the elephant in the room.

"Did you consummate the marriage?"

"Yeah." This is not something I want to think about with Lake in the room.

"Did you live together afterward as man and wife?"

My brow furrows. "Not exactly? We dated. We hung out. We had sex. She spent nights at my place. That lasted about a month, and then she dumped me. I haven't seen her since."

Lake proceeds to reduce my weeks with Peony to a bunch of checkpoints on her yellow legal pad. How often did we see each other? Was there sex? Did Peony know about my net worth?

"Maybe she's a quadrillionaire." If she is, I'm definitely going to be mad about her decision to live in a derelict camper and to put up with shit jobs. Having a ton of money is partly about making sure you have choices, but mostly about *exercising* those choices.

Lake looks up from the pad where she's just jotted something down with neat, precise strokes. I could read her handwriting upside down but I don't. "Do you think that's likely?"

"I don't think she's in this for the money."

She sets her pen down and looks at me. "I hope not."

Lake's eminently practical about these things, so she keeps the rest of her opinions to herself. She would never go to a sex party or fake-marry a hot stranger, because it's a legal liability. She reads every check twice in a restaurant before she signs it. It's a contract, she told me once, when I was giving her shit about it—and before I took it away from her and paid. Peony didn't hesitate before she "signed" our marriage license—she just jumped in and did it.

"You may have to offer her a settlement."

"That's fine." I sort of like the idea that I'm legally entitled to half of her and she gets half of me. It wasn't what I intended, obviously, but it doesn't feel wrong, either. If she takes my money, she'll be safe and she won't have to live in a shitty camper anymore. That's definitely a plus.

Lake stares into the distance, thinking. "Okay. So I'll get the team on this. The real question is whether or not you're legally married. Do you know how to contact Ms. Harding?"

"No," I admit.

Lake nods. Her face is perfectly composed, but I'll bet she's totally judging me inside her head. I had careless, random sex with a stranger with whom I may have accidentally entered into a binding legal contract. And on the surface, that's exactly what happened. I think the Jax in that version of events was pretty stupid, too. But what came afterward didn't feel careless at all. I don't explain that to Lake, though. How do people go to therapists and dig up all their fears and worries? This totally sucks.

"I'll find her?" This comes out as a question, which is also out of character for me, and Lake's head shoots up from her stupid legal pad.

"I'll do that," she says. "Whatever reason the two of you split up, get past it. It will be easier if we can approach her and make an offer." She taps her pen against the pad. "But don't approach her. Anything you say or do with her could be used as leverage by her legal team. I'll get our PI service on it. They can look into her background, as well."

I don't tell her no, even though Peony would hate having someone digging around in her life. No matter what Lake finds, if Peony didn't share it with me, it's not my business. I don't want to turn our sex life into an arms race where each of us tries to dig up dirt on the other and weaponize it. Let Lake do her thing, though. I don't have to read the report or to look at any pictures she commissions or even go to see Peony once I know where she's run off to. I just need a mailing address and a way to communicate with her.

I nod and we exchange the usual brief goodbyes before Lake exits my office and heads off to pry into Peony's past. I know Lake is just doing her job, which is to protect my legal interests, but it feels all wrong.

I find myself staring out my office window at all the people in the street below hurrying to work or to home or to some other place they need to be. A siren blares nearby, but no one looks. For the first time in what feels like forever, I'm not sure what to think or to do. I've avoided relationships and focused on making money instead. I'm as good at the latter as I'm bad at the former.

I don't know what I'm doing here because I've never done it before. Maybe I didn't look as hard for her as I could have because she scared me a little. I've always been a fighter, so I don't like to admit that.

But it's true.

She cracked me open and made me feel things. And the worst part of it is, I'm not sure she realized what she was doing. I haven't been able to walk away from her once, I realize. Not since I pulled her asshole boss off her, not since she wandered up the beach and met me for tacos. She's the one who ended things, otherwise I would probably still be...

Something.

I'm not sure what and I hate that.

Except it would be something with her.

CHAPTER FOURTEEN

Jax

TODAY IS THE kind of work day that's earned me my reputation as a take-no-prisoners barbarian. After learning that I might be married, I spent the rest of yesterday sealing my acquisition of Hotly. I arrive at their front door to start kicking their collective asses up the mountain of profitability. It's as close to raiding and pillaging as I'm legally allowed to get, plus I get the added fun of putting the pieces back together better after I've finished knocking things to bits. Hotly has no idea what's coming.

The startup's in San Francisco's Mission District. The rents tend to be cheaper here than in the financial district or SOMA because the neighborhood is grittier. It's also colorful and the food's amazing. Brightly painted Queen Annes line the streets and there's a cheerful cacophony of languages, people and pigeons. The Mexican markets bustle with weekday shoppers, and vendors with pushcarts sell *agua fresca* and bags of fiery snacks.

I park my bike in front of an old warehouse located three blocks off the main drag. The city's full of these slick, repurposed spaces and I know exactly what I'll find inside: exposed brick, soaring ceilings and enough open space to give an agoraphobic a heart attack. According to the lease, this one is a historic 1865 brick number that's housed any number of businesses since its maritime origins. Fortunately, it's not on any historic registers because that would complicate my job.

The receptionist's eyes widen comically when I identify myself. I decline the offer of an escort party in favor of prowling around my new playground on my own. I have to decide which of my toys I'm keeping and which I'm breaking.

Although it's already past lunchtime, two of the key engineers have not yet showed up; one is passed out at his desk, and since his last code commit has a timestamp of 6:00 a.m., I bypass his sleeping form for now. Hotly keeps the hours of a zoo: officially open for business from eight to five, but the animals are clearly nocturnal.

My solitude doesn't last. It never does. I'm the big, bad boss, so there're plenty of people who decide they'll kiss up to me. Some do it as insurance, some like being near the throne, and others just don't know what to do with themselves unless I tell them.

One of the many VPs of Something Something—they proliferate faster than fruit flies in a kitchen—joins me, launching into what I'm sure he thinks is an amusing story about how my warehouse was a historic place.

I cut him off. "I'm not interested in the past."

And then I walk away. I don't give a shit about their backstory. It's not going to draw subscribers. Also, that VP is on my to-be-axed list. He'll find out in an hour.

Hotly's a weird kind of product. It was pitched to me as an internet TV channel that provides high-quality content to paid subscribers. There's a huge potential upside, but there are also far too many people not pulling their weight. Since Hotly's losing money at an unbelievable rate, my first job is to trim the payroll and fill in any holes in skill sets. My team has made recommendations, but I like to walk the floor first and get a sense for the personalities behind the fancy job titles. Sometimes there's a winner who got hired on for the wrong job.

Hotly's VP No. 10—I've decided to number them rather than learn their names—sidles up, rocking back and forth nervously. He's wearing the standard tech-startup uniform of faded blue jeans, flip-flops and an open button-up over a T-shirt advertising a band I've never heard of. Because I have "ass-kicking" penciled into my planner from ten until noon, I'm wearing a custom-made suit from my personal tailor in London. Taking charge is even easier when I look the part, so I have a closet full of nine-thousand-dollar suits.

No. 10 clears his throat. "Start at the top or at the bottom?"

"Bottom." Going desk to desk makes me feel like a lion hunting deer on the African savannah. They can run, but there's nowhere for them to hide. When you bring someone into a conference room, you lose the element of surprise. Plus, the conference room here is tiny and fishbowl-like. The office-facing side is just a big sheet of glass, a nod to privacy and protecting the engineers coding away in the open floor space from overhearing crap that will take their minds off their next code check-in.

I'll save the engineers for last. I'm mostly keeping them anyhow—they're the brains of this place.

No. 10 points to a metal door beneath an exit sign. "The elevator doesn't go to the basement."

Four months of research, deep dives into code and competitor analysis, and so far Hotly's more of a glorified stair-stepper than an investment. We slam down the stairs, push through another set of doors, and step into a dingy, poorly lit open space where they've hidden the quality assurance team, all one member of it. He's safe, so I push on. It's like a freaking dungeon down here, but without any of the fun, BDSM implications.

"Archives?" No. 10 points to a hand-lettered sign taped to a set of doors on the far side of the room.

"Sign" may be generous. It appears to be a piece of construction paper more appropriate to a kindergarten classroom than a successful company. Someone's printed in all caps The Almighty Archives. The Librarian is IN. The "in" is an orange sticky note; the corresponding OUT note has drifted to the floor. Yeah. She or he is about to be out. Hotly is an internet channel; they don't need a librarian to organize their archival materials.

Female voices filter through a door that's propped partway open with a polar-bear-shaped doorstop. Since it's a fire door, this is a major safety violation.

"He's a bastard," someone inside complains. The VP next to me freezes. "A really hot, completely insufferable prick. He always fires at least half of the staff on his first day."

Well. This is going to be fun.

I slant No. 10 a look. "Shall we beard the lion in his den?"

I don't wait for his response. It doesn't matter. I push the door open and step in.

Rows of metal shelving line the room, each shelf filled with archival boxes. I'll figure out later what Hotly's decided should be stored in the basement of their goddamned building rather than in the cloud or offsite in a fireproof vault. A desk blocks access to the shelving. The desk holds a stack of books and a creepy-looking bobblehead of an old white guy in a dark suit.

My attention lasers in on the two women at the desk. The complainer wears an oversize men's blue Oxford that flaps around her as she waves her arms to underscore my hot bastardy as they continue to discuss the likelihood of my firing them—increasing—and when said firing would occur—imminently. The second female is wearing a bright orange *Hotly* T-shirt and blue jeans.

She nods in response to something Complainette has said and adds, "I don't think we're supposed to tie people up during company meetings."

Holy FUCK. I shoot my VP sidekick a death glare and pad further into the room.

It's only been three months—the longest twelve weeks of my life.

Given her move out, I'd sort of assumed that Peony had abandoned San Francisco. I wouldn't have been surprised to hear she'd moved states or countries even. Considering her behavior, an interstellar move to Mars wouldn't have been a shock.

She looks amazing. Her brown hair is pulled up into a high ponytail that swings back and forth as she punctuates her BDSM-free workplace policy with gestures. Her eyes shine as she bounces up and down in her chair. She hasn't learned how to sit still since I last saw her. I'm not sure if I want her to turn around and see me, or if I just want to stand here and look at her. The full curve of her lower lip, her delighted laugh that she covers with the palm of her hand, the way she leans in, so focused on the person talking with her—I feel like she just stepped out of my life yesterday.

I don't think she feels the same way.

"Ménage is a lot of work. I'm not sure our big bastard boss would be worth the effort," Peony says right as her companion spots us. "You don't agree? It's all the logistics that bother me. You have to figure out where to fit together multiple sets of arms and legs. Unless you were envisioning something more like a spectator sport?"

Peony's companion squeaks and Peony freezes.

I feel like a villain with a freeze-ray gun. No one's moving. There's just a whole lot of eyeballing and side eye happening as my new employees try to figure out how to salvage the situation.

I do what I do best and take charge. "Ladies."

Peony's head snaps around, her wheeled chair pulling an impressive one-eighty, ponytail smacking her cheek. Her eyes round comically. I'm sure she's planning how to run out of the room, the same way she ran out of my place three months ago. Unfortunately for her, I'm bigger, meaner, and blocking the exit. I'm also her employer—and her husband.

The VP dogging my side like a barnacle on a boat's backside decides now would be an excellent time to interject. "Peony, this is—"

"Jax Valentine," she blurts out.

"Your big bastard boss," I growl, prowling closer. "Out."

Peony bounces out of her seat, almost colliding with her friend, who's clearly taken my barked ultimatum to heart and is jogging for the door. She can go. I don't care about her. The VP follows her, and then Peony and I are alone.

I almost laugh at the look on her face. She's seriously considering making a run for the door. I shut it and then, for good measure, I lean against it.

Her gaze flits between my face and the closed door then she makes a face and goes back to her desk. That's as much concession as she'll give me.

"So, you're a billionaire," she says brightly, shoving the shit from the top of her desk into an enormous purse. "And a businessman. I'm not sure how this didn't come up in conversation before, but it's going to take me some time to process that you're not a normal person like the rest of us."

"Peony."

"I'll email my letter of resignation by the end of the day." She finishes clearing off the desk. "Or I can send it from the train. If the WiFi is working and I'm not stuck in a tunnel. Either way, you'll have it and—"

"Firefly." I pinch the bridge of my nose. "You quit too much. You ran out on me. You left a goddamned Post-it note on my kitchen counter. Then you changed your number and moved. I couldn't get in touch with you."

She blinks cautiously. "I didn't think you'd care. We were just a summer thing. Why would you want to talk with me?"

What if I am the only one who felt like we had something more than chemistry? What if she really did mean to be done with me?

Deflect. "I didn't expect to find you here." I lean against her desk. The space is small enough that my knees bump hers.

"So you're not a superstalker. Good to know." She taps my knees. "You're in my personal space, big guy. Pretty sure that's an HR violation."

"Am I doing anything you don't want me to do, Firefly?"

Her fingers brush my knees and I want to rip my expensive suit off, carry her down to her desk and fuck her. She just stares at me, stroking her fingers back and forth. She's gorgeous and here. I told myself I couldn't chase her. She'd made her wishes clear. But she's touching me.

"Peony. I can't do this." She jerks her fingers from my knee. "We need to talk."

"I don't particularly want to."

"You have two choices." I lean down, getting into her space, forcing her to look me in the eye. "We talk now or you can meet me after work tonight for dinner."

"Pass."

"Choose."

"Do you have an evil twin?"

"Pick, or I'll start our conversation now."

"What can you possibly want to talk about?"

"Our marriage."

"That was a game."

"No." I stare at her, not sure how to explain this. "You thought it was. Fuck, I thought it was. But it turns out we're married for real."

"What?"

"I got a wedding certificate in the mail. It seems that we're married."

Her jaw drops almost comically. "No way."

I pull the marriage certificate up on my phone and hold out the device so she can see it for herself. Predictably, she shoots out of her chair, probably headed for Outer Mongolia or Mars. I catch her in my arms, steal her chair, and pull her down onto my lap. I wonder whether she'll ever willingly stay put with me.

I must be a closet sadist because I wrap my arms around her when she starts angry-squirming.

I press my mouth against her ear. "You really want to give me a lap dance right here in the office?"

She smells so familiar. I missed her.

"Let me up." She tugs on my arms. "This is not boss behavior."

"It's not *good* boss behavior." I shrug. "But I'm afraid we've already blurred those lines."

She grumbles something and pries at my arm again. I should let her go—but I can't.

"Talk to me first," I continue. "I don't trust you not to run away." *Again* hangs in the air between us. Tell me what you've been doing. Tell me how your sister is."

She clears her throat and stares down at my forearm. "Yeah, about that. I lied."

"You don't have a sister?"

"She wasn't the reason I left that night."

I tuck her against my chest, resting my chin on the top of her head. "Would you like to explain then why you took off and broke up with me via Post-it note?"

"We weren't a couple, were we? I mean, not really. We hooked up and then we hung out some but…"

"Peony." I growl her name because I missed her but she also drives me nuts. "Let's circle back to that."

"All righty." She fidgets again.

"You found a job." I slide my thumb beneath the edge of her T-shirt, running it over the soft skin. "You're my librarian."

"It seemed like a good opportunity for Peony 2.0. She's supposed to be settling down." Her voice is rueful.

"So you've been here ever since you left?"

"Just about. Yes."

I plan to revisit the *just about* statement later, too. I really, really don't like the idea of her being broke and unemployed and worried about shit, especially since I have more than enough for the two of us.

"Do you like your job?"

"I like organizing stuff and Hotly has some amazing materials, but I've heard the new boss likes to trim the fat. I don't think I'm going to have a job for long."

"Show him what you can do," I suggest. "He doesn't think with his dick. Promise."

"This is so weird." She sighs, letting go of some of her mad. "How did the whole billionaire thing happen? It's not a new thing, right? Because even you couldn't be that scary efficient."

"I've been in software development for ten years."

"I thought you were a surfer who dabbled in code."

My relief at finding her safe and happy, even if it's without me, vanishes. I've been so focused on tracking her down, and maybe demanding to know why she left me, that I forgot she didn't know some of the most important things about me.

I should have told her, but I don't lead with *Hey baby, I'm a billionaire*. That would most definitely make me sound like an asshole, and I generally manage that just fine on my own. So maybe it hadn't mattered when we met at Liam's party, but at some point during the summer, I should have told her that I was more than just a software engineer who preferred surfing to coding. My success is part of who I am—a big part—and I deliberately chose not to share that piece of myself with her. I was so scared she'd look at me differently, that she'd see me as the magical money solution to all life's problems, that my having more money than her would make a difference. And now it has because I wasn't honest.

Although, really…who complains because their boyfriend turns out to *not* be a financial loser?

This time, when Peony shoves at my legs, I move them. She pops to her feet, of course. The woman won't sit still. "Are you really a billionaire?"

"Yeah, although—"

"And you had all that money when we met? You didn't, like, win the lottery or something since then? Inherit a small European country with an inbred fortune?"

"I did and no." I have more now, but that's not going to help my case.

"And now you've bought the company I work for, which makes you my boss?"

"Technically, you don't report to me." Granted, this is because I had every intention of firing the librarian until I discovered she was Peony. I don't share this information, however.

"You're totally my boss." She glares at me, shifting back to anger lightning-fast. "WTF, Jax?"

"I own the company you work for," I say calmly. Okay. The calm is a total front, but if both of us start shouting, we're going to attract an audience.

"And I have a problem with that," she stresses.

She won't be the only one. I can only imagine what Lake will have to say about this. It is never a good idea to bang your employee, and in light of our maybe-marriage, it will look downright bad unless we decide to get married for real.

"Why is my not being a broke bastard an issue?"

Her eyes narrow. "Because you're not who you said you were. You lied to me!"

"And you lied right back." Yes, I'm going to go there. "How's your sister doing again?"

"Are we debating whose lie is worse now?" She throws her hands up and stomps over to a row of metal shelving filled with labeled boxes.

"You ditched me while I was in the shower. You broke up with me by note and you couldn't even be bothered to tell me the truth. I gave you two days to sulk and then I went looking for you and you had *moved out*. You totally freaking ghosted me." I move in for the kill, caging her against the shelves with my arms. There's no way I'll let her go a second time. "I'm not the only one who made mistakes."

"We were a *game*," she snarls, tilting her gorgeous, unhappy face up to mine. "I didn't know who you really were, and you certainly didn't know who I was. And now here you are, crashing into my life once again, and everything is wrong."

"You can get to know me."

"I'm married to my *boss*," she snarls.

Damn straight. I grab her tote bag and rummage

through it until I find her phone. Not only am I technically the boss of her, but I'm bigger and I easily ignore her attempts to grab her stuff. She'll get it back when I'm good and ready. Her phone has migrated to the bottom of the bag, but it's easy enough to locate because it buzzes incessantly.

I hold it out to her. "Unlock it."

"Not a chance," she snaps. Unlike everyone else in this building, she's not scared of me. I like it. I like *her*.

Confrontation is something I excel at. It's also not something I've ever gone out of my way to avoid. Right now, however, I want her to agree to give me a chance, and I don't think that's something I can fight my way to. So I'll be nice.

I capture her hand, press her thumb against her lock screen. I ignore the two thousand texts from people who want to know if she's okay, if she's been fired, if the big bad boss has eaten her—not yet—if someone should pull the fire alarm so she has an excuse to get out of here. Instead, I put my phone number in her Contacts.

"So you can call me," I tell her. She opens her mouth—probably to give me several very loud reasons why she will never, ever, call me again—and I cut her off. I'm still working on that whole nice thing, after all. "We can get a divorce." I slide her phone back into her bag. "Or an annulment. I'm not even sure we really are married because neither of us filed for a marriage license or actually meant to end up married. I'll figure out how to fix this, Peony, but you're going to have to trust me just a little. And while I'm asking you for shit, I'm just going to say that I might want a shot."

She pauses. "What kind of shot?"

I hoist her up onto a nearby table and step between her legs. I'm not feeling nice. The move's not polite and it's definitely not suitable for the workplace. It feels awesome, though. Her legs hug my hips, her crotch pushing against mine.

"I'm going to date you." I press my mouth against the corner of hers. I count it as a win that she doesn't bite. "So well."

She eyes me suspiciously. "Is that a dirty joke?"

"Do you want it to be?"

"I don't want to be Hotly's dirty joke," she says. "And that's what I'll be if you walk around proclaiming me as your Mrs. Valentine. Everyone will think you gave me this job because we're married and you want in my pants."

"I'm insulted you don't think they'll attribute the same motives to you." I run my thumb over her plush lower lip. "Your coworker was willing to jump me."

"With company." Peony makes a face. "Yes, everyone here will think I'm a sucker for a pretty face. And that I'm using you for both your dick and your financial perks. I don't want everyone talking about us."

"And I don't want to be your dirty little secret."
Now it's my turn to get mad. "It's just money, Peony.
You're the one making it out to be such a big deal.
Money comes. Sometimes it goes. I'm not going to
give it all away to a cat sanctuary just because you
don't like it."

Plus, then I'd just make more. I get bored when
I have nothing to do.

"It doesn't matter," she states.

"Then prove it. Spend time with me. Get to know
me. I'm more than just my job."

That may be a lie, but it's not one I'm going to
cop to. Not right now. I've worked my ass off full-
time and then some since I was fifteen and I've done
a lot of shit to claw my way to the top of Silicon Valley. I don't know who I'd be if I hadn't done that, and
I'm damned sure I'm fairly unlikable. Fortunately,
it will take her time to figure this out. My plan is
to distract her with sex and spoiling.

"Give us three months." I nip her lower lip,
drinking in her little gasp. "We'll get to know each
other. If you want to leave when our time is up, I'll
help you do it. If you think my owning Hotly will
fuck up your life, I'll sell it. Fuck, I'll give it to you."

Her mouth drops open and I press my advantage.

"I'm your husband. I'm allowed to give you presents. I think it's part of the job description."

"You can't walk around giving people entire companies." She smacks my chest. "That's ridiculous."

"You're the one who married a billionaire. This is one of the consequences. I distinctly recall you proposing to me, so this was your idea. You volun-told me to be your husband.

"I'm just doing what you asked me to do," I say virtuously.

"Oh my God," she groans. "You're impossible."

"Three months." I kiss her to make my point. "It'll probably take my lawyers that long to sort out all the legalities anyhow, so you might as well enjoy the perks."

"And I suppose you're a perk?"

"I'm the biggest perk of them all."

"You're something," she mutters.

"Yours," I say promptly. "Right now, I'm yours. You should enjoy me."

"I understand now how you got all that money."

"Say yes," I coax.

"I just want it noted that this is crazy," she says. "But okay. Three months. Yes."

CHAPTER FIFTEEN

Peony

I BREATHE A little easier when Jax stalks off to go scare my coworkers. He's intense and he's a big guy. It's not that he scares me so much as it is impossible to ignore the aura of power around him. He's always been the strong dominant type, but I thought that was just a bedroom thing. Apparently, it's a billionaire alpha male thing.

I hooked up with my boss.

I freaking MARRIED him.

At least it's a definite maybe and he's concerned enough about it to bring it up. I guess I should be glad he didn't whip out a checkbook—if real people still use those—or sic a bunch of legal sharks on me.

My mind is busy freaking out, but my body's doing a stupid, happy hum. He's my gorgeous, dirty man. So determined. So sweetly rough. He knew exactly how to bring my fantasies to life and I didn't have to write him an Oscar-worthy script first.

Amazing sex or no, the obvious thing to do is to get up, quit, and go. Boss dating is the worst and it can only end badly. Sure, I'd like to take him for one more ride, play one more game, but it's not worth the price I'll pay. As it is, my phone is blowing up—mostly with texts from Josie, who's convinced that I've either killed our bastard boss—she volunteers to help with the body removal—or that I'm busy tying him up and proving my sexual worth. This is closer to the truth than I care to admit.

I text her a proof-of-life picture and then I pretend to be very, very busy for the rest of the day. Mostly, this takes the form of furious Google searching about Jax. I don't know why it didn't occur to me to search him before, but it didn't.

Jax is not exactly unknown to the internet. Despite—or possibly thanks to—his money and his rough good looks, he's attracted attention mostly for his hardcore partying and for his otherworldly business acumen. Everything the man touches turns to gold; I've apparently married the modern day Midas. He tops the lists of San Francisco's hottest bachelors and evidently he owns real estate in Hawaii, Napa, and San Francisco. There are as many shots of him dating super-pretty women as there are of him attending various charity functions where he writes large checks. It's sort of surreal, honestly, and I can't reconcile that public guy with my beach bum surfer.

Bottom line? We come from totally different worlds. He'll go home tonight to some gold-plated bathroom in an expensive piece of real estate, while I'll take the train—and then two buses and a bike—to the Richmond apartment I rented across the Bay. It's better than the RV in terms of hot water and roofing, but I miss the ocean.

I scroll through his Wikipedia article, looking for clues to who Jax really is. Various online sources claim he was born and raised in Berkeley, the bohemian, leftist paradise across the Bay from San Francisco. There are also rumors that he bankrolled his first investments by participating in illegal fight clubs.

Updates trickle in from the rest of the building throughout the day, like those survivor reports after a natural disaster. Engineering, largely unscathed by his rampaging, nicknames him "The Scythe," while the numerous VPs who head out the door, newly unemployed, provide more unflattering descriptors. Essentially, he stalks around, all dark and broody, barking at people and terminating their jobs, and while he claims there's a reason why some people go while others stay, it's not clear to any of us leftovers.

Josie pops by at 4:55 p.m. Since she's smiling, she must still have a job.

"Drinks?" She bounces up and down. "All of Engineering's going."

If ever a day called for alcohol, it's this one. The

problem is that Jax issued his stay-put order and I have a feeling that he'll come looking for me if I light out. Since Engineering usually drinks one block down from Hotly, I wouldn't be hard to find.

"Not tonight." I pull a face. "I need to go home and convince my nerves I'm not having a break-down."

"Yeah," she says eagerly. "Do you think *he* heard what we were saying? How do you know him? Have you worked for him before? Tim said drinks are on us. He's planning on getting you drunk and pumping you for information."

Tim is the senior architect and he's a great guy. Ordinarily, I'd appreciate his attempts at bribery, but today? Not so much. My phone buzzes with yet another incoming text. This one, however, is from Jax. Dinnertime.

"Pass." Apparently, I'm having dinner with the boss. It's an opportunity, I tell myself, to point out that he's not the boss of me. Except, you know, pos-sibly in his fantasies. That we've reenacted on mul-tiple occasions. Ugh.

Meet you out back, I type after Josie's reluc-tantly departed. By tomorrow, there's going to be a dozen different theories as to how Jax and I know each other. This is precisely why I don't date bosses.

Jax is waiting for me on his motorcycle by the time I make it out back. It's really just dumpster storage and enough room to turn a delivery truck around, which means that none of my coworkers can park here. The ones that didn't walk or take the train are off somewhere down the block—or many, many blocks—recovering their vehicles.

He should look out of place straddling his bike in a suit, but somehow he makes it work. He's shed his tie and his hair's come loose during the day. He looks a little rumpled and yet still completely in charge.

He holds out a helmet to me. "What do you want for dinner?"

"I can have anything?"

He fixes me with that steady stare I remember. "Name it."

I'm tempted for a moment to ask for escargot at the top of the Eiffel Tower because I may never have another chance and surely a billionaire boyfriend/husband/boss should be good for something. I restrain myself—I've never actually eaten snails, I'm ridiculously hungry, and I'd probably end up flicking snail guts all over Jax—and suggest we head down to Fisherman's Wharf instead.

Half an hour later, we're seated at a narrow counter devouring a mountain of fresh-steamed Dungeness crab while a never-ending crowd of tourists pushes past us on the sidewalk. It's loud and smells fishy, the seating jammed so close together that I'm practically sitting on Jax's lap.

"I don't think we should work together." I lick melted butter off my thumb.

He leans forward and gently sucks at my finger, his teeth scraping the pad. It should be gross or cheesy, but it just gets me hot and underscores the problem I'm going to have maintaining the kind of working relationship that doesn't involve dancing like a porn star on his lap.

He sits back. "I know it doesn't look good, me showing up at your work."

"To be fair, you bought it. While my initial reaction was *what the ever-loving fuck*, I'm willing to concede you probably didn't read every single HR file before you…" I pause. "How *do* you buy an entire company?"

"Lots of paperwork, an ironclad contract and a bank wire." He cracks a new crab leg for me. "And your understanding is appreciated."

"So you didn't buy an entire company just to get in my pants." I blame this on my third beer. Crab-meat has proved insufficient to soak up the alcohol. "Not that it would have worked. Or that I should even say that to my boss."

"I wouldn't force you to do anything." He dips the crab and holds it up to my mouth. I chew. "I'm a bastard, yes, but I limit that bastardy to one-hundred-percent legal activities. And some shit's just not okay, even if I was allowed to do it."

"Great." I swallow. "I'm glad we got that cleared

up. Now, tell me how you envision the next three months playing out."

That sounds nice and business-y, right?

"Do you want a contract? Or a postnup?"

I stare at him. "Are you serious?"

I hear the words coming out of his mouth, but they make no sense.

"We could draw up a contract, if you want."

"So… I wouldn't know what to put."

"Then put the things you don't want to do. What are your limits?"

"Like sex stuff?" This feels like one of those deals with the devil, where if you don't spell out your demands super clearly, you end up signing away your immortal soul for a cupcake. "No contracts. I don't usually… I mean it was fun but…"

He shifts, stretching his legs out. His legs bump mine.

"What can't I do in the next three months?"

"We're gonna be an open secret at work, but I'd appreciate it if you didn't do anything that makes people want to whip their phones out. No public sex acts or cute nicknames or anything that makes people think about the two of us being in a relationship. My recognizing you today is a little awkward, but there could be a perfectly good, non-naked reason for that."

He nods. "So you want me to not say anything about our marriage."

"Uh, yeah. That would be great. I mean it's not even a sure thing, right? And I don't need the whole company speculating about our sex life in the middle of a meeting."

"I can do that. You can have nine to five, and then I get five to nine."

I frown. "That's hardly fair."

"You'll have to sleep," he points out. "Plus, it's going to be a lot harder for me to behave myself at work than it is to play with you afterward."

I think he's playing with me now. His eyes are warm and lazy as they move over my face.

"I wouldn't have gone out with you if I'd known you'd end up being my boss."

"And I wouldn't have done it, either. Not that I'm a Boy Scout, but there's some stuff that's off limits, even for me."

"What *would* you do?"

"I'll show you. Later." He leans over the counter and settles up with our crab dealer, then stands. "Come on."

"I should go home." I definitely need to get on the train because it's late and I'm having an attack of the memories. Mostly they're of naked Jax—on his back, on his knees, hand braced against the wall of his shower.

I pull up the bus app on my phone. I can just catch the last bus if I hustle. The train will take over an hour and then I have to sprint off the platform, catch the commuter bus, and hope it makes it to the transfer point before the last regular bus leaves for the night. A Lyft from there will cost a fortune.

"I could take you home," he offers.

It's tempting. I mean it's not as if he can't figure out where I live. It would probably take him all of thirty seconds to call payroll and get my address. My apartment's not in a great part of Richmond, however, and it just underscores the financial differences between us.

"Or," he continues, "you could come back with me. We could start our three months tonight."

"Okay. You still rent that beach cottage?" I love that place.

For the first time today, he looks uncomfortable. "I bought it."

Of course he did.

CHAPTER SIXTEEN

Peony

ON OUR FIRST NOT-DATE, I challenged Jax to name six impossible things that he believed in. In the weeks since I found out that my summer fling is both my boss and my husband, I've made my own list.

1. My big bastard boss has a wicked sense of humor.
2. Not every date has to end in sex.
3. Last night was amazing.
4. Today is even better.
5. Sometimes pretend things feel the most real.
6. I love Jax Valentine.

Jax is super generous, both in the orgasm department and elsewhere. He's also super dirty. Like the whispering filth, fingering me in public, sex-on-the-beach kind of dirty. He has all sorts of ideas about how to get me off and he's definitely a ladies' first kind of man. He likes to surprise me with weird, thoughtful presents. It's kind of awesome. It's also more than a little surreal.

Since we skipped dating and went straight to marriage, Jax decides I deserve make-up dates. So I go to work in Hotly's archives during business hours, and then after hours or on the weekends, Jax shows me around the city. He's happy to take me to all sorts of places and just hang out with me, chatting about the stuff we see or weird crap that's happened at work or on the internet. There are dozens of amazing costume shops in San Francisco and we spend hours browsing through the racks.

It turns out Jax is a dedicated lunch maker. I'm not sure where he got the idea from, but he packs me lunch every day. He has a long way to go before he can quit his day job and become a gourmet chef, but he's really good at Googling recipes. He follows them with laser-like precision, the cutest frown of concentration crinkling the little space between his eyebrows, like he's assembling a barbecue or conducting a killer game of Operation. Mostly, I've ended up with peanut butter and jelly in my cactus-print lunch bag, but the sexy notes he tucks in with my sandwich make up for the lack of variety. My favorite so far is *Have fun with the boss tonight*.

Executive summary? There's a ton of very creative, highly satisfying orgasms because Jax is a giver in that department, too. His favorite is the long, slow fuck, and the man can go forever. Seeing as how I'm a lifelong devotee of the quickie and the hookup, this is a change for me. I'm pretty sure by now that the slow, sweet feel of him deep inside me is literally addictive and his penis releases magic feel-good endorphins directly into my vagina.

Also? My vagina clearly is connected to my heart.

If all the orgasms don't kill me, there's a very real chance that I'll beg Jax for more time after our three months are up. I'm sort of in the mood for forever. And yet…

He hasn't asked me to give up my Richmond apartment. I don't mention it because, hello, *awkward.* I guess I could invite him to move in there with me, but it's a bit of a dump. At first, I make a point of going back there most nights, but it's a two-hour commute, and since Jax makes it his nightly mission to wear me out with orgasms, I tend to pass out in his bed. I'm almost positive that he's doing it intentionally.

Tonight is our date night. At least, that's what Jax calls it. We take turns planning it, but tonight it's his turn. I got a very inappropriate email from him in my Hotly account inviting me to a sexy times masquerade on a private yacht in the San Francisco Bay. He's attached a hand-drawn map of how to get from Hotly to the yacht, which appears to be moored at the Central Waterfront based on the very pornographic penis he's sketched in lieu of the traditional X-marks-the-spot. Since he's offsite today managing one of his other companies, I'm meeting him at said wharf.

Or possibly on the moon.

Or in a sex dungeon.

Drawing is one of the few things Jax absolutely sucks at.

Five minutes after his obscene invitation lands in my inbox, he follows up with a second email.

Dear Ms. Harding, Please respond or send photographic proof of life. I can make suggestions. J.

I'll bet he can. I'm grinning like a loon when I fire off a return email.

Dear Mr. Valentine, This is not an acceptable use of corporate resources ;)

Less than two minutes later, my screen is filled with dancing, purple eggplants.

Dear Mr. Valentine, Don't make me call security.

It's downhill from Hotly to the Central Waterfront, which is a blessing. I can roll if I get too tired. Narrow Victorian-style buildings that have been divided into apartments or pricey condos line the streets, along with more modern glass-and-steel condos, offices, and a few patches of green space. Sure, it's loud, but it's a familiar noise, all car sounds and the Muni buses clattering along the street. A lot of it is postcard-worthy, but there's also a handful of homeless people camped out beneath the trees. I drop a dollar into the coffee cup marked Spare Change for Beer! I know I'm supposed to donate to the programs that offer support services instead of passing out cash, but I can't just walk past.

The wharves jut out into the dark water of the bay like teeth in a jack-o'-lantern. It will be Halloween soon, which is the best holiday ever, so my mind's completely in that headspace. Jax has already promised to dress up as Captain Jack Sparrow and reenact my favorite movie scenes, although this is probably because I had my mouth on his dick when I asked.

The wharf-teeth are lined with boats and the odd sea lion sunning itself. Most of the sea lions hang out by Fisherman's Wharf, so these are clearly the loner seals. I like them already.

Jax is sprawled on the grass, either waiting patiently for me or napping. He's got his eyes closed, his arms stacked beneath his head and his long legs stretched out in front of him. He cracks an eye when I crash land on his chest, his arms coming around me.

"You would not believe the day I had."

"Do tell." He regards me with lazy heat, cupping the back of my head with his hand. His fingers find the sore spots at the top of my neck and press gently.

"My boss came onto me. I had to put him in his place."

He laughs and pulls me down for a kiss. It starts out mostly PG but then I get ideas, or he does, and we're going at each other. There may be some rolling around on the grass and body parts grinding on each other.

"You're never gonna train your boss at this rate," he grumbles when we finally break apart.

I flop onto my back and stare up at the sky. I point at a plane going by overheard leaving a trail of puffy, white exhaust. "Where do you think that one's going? And do you think the people up there are peeping down at us and warning each other 'Cover the children's eyes!'"

"Los Angeles. Vegas." He rolls, shoving to his feet like a big cat. "Tokyo. And yes. You're a bad influence, Mrs. Valentine."

"I blame you, Mr. Harding."

So far, neither of us has won the battle of the last names, but it's shaping up to be epic.

He grabs my hand and pulls me along the wharf. We're waved through a locked gate and then he lays in a course for the big-ass boat moored at the end of the pontoon. Of course he can't own a nice, manageable dinghy. He has to have a big, sleek number that looks like it belongs on the cover of a boating magazine.

"People are going to think you're compensating."

"Take your shoes off." He's already removing his motorcycle boots.

"As you command, oh bossy one."

I plop down on a leather-covered bench and do as ordered. As practical as they are, my sneakers aren't boat-wear.

It turns out that one person is enough to crew Jax's boat, although he presses me into service. I'm promoted to Vice President of Ropes while he gets to be the CEO of the Wheel. Childishly, part of me wants to take issue with his being the self-appointed leader, but I don't know how to drive the boat and he does. He takes us out into the bay, laying in a course for whatever destination he's decided on, while I lean over the side and try to touch the water without falling in. The Bay Bridge looms over us and then we're underneath it, the cars speeding by overhead sounding thunderous as they cross the metal plates.

When we're out the other side and conversation is once again possible, Jax shoots me a look. "Did your boss drive you nuts today?"

"He needs to stop distracting me with sex when I'm trying to work. Plus, what if someone else read that email? Aren't they stored like forever in the cloud or on a server?"

I've read news stories about politicians and celebrities who don't grasp this concept and then their private shit ends up on display for the entire world to enjoy.

Jax fiddles with the boat controls and then holds out a hand to me. I let him pull me into his lap and then wriggle around until I'm as comfortable as a girl can be with a massive hard-on prodding her butt.

"Do you want it?" He secures me with one arm, keeping the other free for what I assume are boat-related emergencies.

"I feel the need to ask you to clarify. We are talking about sex, right?"

He hesitates. "No."

"Jax?"

"You can run Hotly. It'll be yours."

I can feel my jaw drop exactly like in the cartoons. "I'm the freaking archivist. And where will you be?"

His arm tightens around my waist. "You're worried about what people there will think when they find out we're in a relationship. This solves that problem. I'll step back and you'll step up."

"I've never managed a company in my life!"

"You're smart. You've got this."

"People will think you handed Hotly to me because we're boning! Which is the actual truth!"

"Why do you care what other people think?"

"Why wouldn't I care since I have to work with them?"

"I care what *you* think. Just you. Only you."

I twist so I'm straddling his lap. I need to see his face. "Why?"

"Because I fucking love you," he growls. "There's no point in owning Hotly if it doesn't come with you. You like your job and you were there first, so this seems like the best solution. Alternatively, I could shut the whole thing down and then no one would have a job and I wouldn't be the boss of you."

"Wow." I take a minute to process that. "That's—"

"I thought I'd invite you out here, we'd play pirates, and then maybe you could see things my way. I love you. Deal with it."

"That's not very romantic."

He growls some more. There's also kissing. I hope no one is staring out their car window right now or they'll drive off the bridge.

"I don't need your company," I whisper. "I need you."

His mouth devours mine and it's a freaking miracle there are any words getting said. "I want you to stay with me. I want you to have the job you like, the life you like, the future you like. And I want to be a part of those things, and since I get what I want, you can't expect me to start playing fair now."

"I love you, too. But you're not dumping your stupid company on me."

He cups my face in his hands. "How about we figure it out together then?"

CHAPTER SEVENTEEN

Jax

I HAVE AN email from Lake.

The PI's report is in and Lake has attached it for my review. She thinks I should take a look at it as soon as possible. She reemphasizes that I should be careful in how I approach Peony. *In fact, I would advise you to avoid contact entirely. Let your legal team reach out*, she writes.

I didn't tell Lake that I'd found Peony.

She probably knows already because she would never work with a second-rate PI firm.

Peony mumbles something into her pillow. It's early, not yet six o'clock, but I didn't check my phone last night. Thursday night is movie night in the Valentine-Harding household, or so Peony has declared. No phones, no email, no internet distractions. Peony had won movie-choosing rights, and she'd milked it, proposing one chick flick after another. I'd have made her watch World War II documentaries, so it was only fair.

Eventually she'd settled on a Jane Austen movie, *Pride and Prejudice*, that had been every bit as bad as I'd feared. She'd made it up to me by disappearing under the covers while Mr. Darcy was busy screwing up his chances with Elizabeth and droning on. I'd been hard before she ducked under the covers because I love watching her laugh. Her whole face lights up and the silliest sounds come out of her mouth. Peony's all-in when she finds something amusing.

Her mouth on my aching dick had definitely made the movie better. Darcy, that stupid, rich bastard, had still mucked everything up, but I'd come in Peony's mouth and then she'd crawled back up the bed and curled up against me.

She'd given me mischievous side eye as Jane Bennet and her ridiculously impractical sisters had laid marital siege on all of the single men in the neighborhood and I'd pointed out that dancing and dinner parties were the Tinder of the early nineteenth century.

When the credits finally rolled, she'd pinched my side and grinned at me. "Do you feel the want of a wife, Mr. Valentine? Seeing as how you have a fortune?"

I'd tickled her side. "Are you proposing?"

"No," she'd giggle-gasped, trying to throw herself across the bed.

I'd chased her, playing the game, my fingers dancing across her ribs and down her body. "Come here, you."

When she'd been breathless and reaching for me, I'd rolled her beneath me, working her tank top up over her head. Then I'd leaned down and kissed her.

"I'm in want of *you*," I'd said.

She'd called me Mr. Valentine. Over and over. I'd had to resort to kissing her senseless, starting with my favorite spot between her legs.

I look at her, sleeping next to me, taking up more than her fair share of the bed. Her hair's twisted into a messy bun because otherwise, she claims, her hair either tickles her nose all night or gets trapped in her armpits. I have no idea how that would actually work, but I've started keeping a packet of hair ties in the bathroom drawer.

Do I want to know what secrets she's been keeping from me?

You fucking bet I do.

But they're Peony's secrets to share, and this report…well, it feels like cheating. I want her to choose to share her past with me, to let me all the way into her life the way she has let me into her bed. In some ways, I'm far too much like Mr. Darcy. I'm rude; I'm an asshole; I know what's best for everyone around me. But I'd also like to change for Peony.

I fire off a quick response to Lake—*thanks*—and then I delete her message without reading the report.

CHAPTER EIGHTEEN

Peony

NOTHING LASTS. Jax calls me Firefly as a joke, but it's true. Happiness is a spark that lights up the night and then winks out as quick as it came. And the thing about fireflies is that, from a distance, they look gorgeous. Up close, however, they're nothing special.

That's me. You don't want to look too closely at what's making the pretty light because you're going to be turned off. Fireflies aren't anywhere near as pretty in their unlit state; all that winking and flashing is to attract a mate. They're creatures of summer, too. Coming out when it's warm and disappearing when the weather turns colder and harsher.

Today, when we get to work, I'm still cautiously optimistic.

Jax and I are a couple.

We're dating.

Okay, so we're actually married, but he likes to point out that it's perfectly fine that we've done things backward. Put the cart before the horse. Flipped the script. It makes us innovative geniuses, he said right before he tackled me to the floor and had his wicked, bossy way with me. We have a house together. We have a *life*. Maybe this really could work and someday we'll be making up stories to tell our grandkids about how grandpa and grandma met because meeting at a sex party isn't the sort of thing you share publicly.

He stops in front of the building like he always does. He'll drive down the block—and then probably around it a few more times—looking for San Francisco's most elusive unicorn: the public parking space.

I unwrap my arms from around his waist and hop off. I'm tingly in the best possible way from his earlier attempts to convince me to stay in bed and the vibrations of his monster bike.

He snags me by the belt loop when I try to dance away. We do this every weekday morning. "Not escaping, Firefly."

I go willingly into his arms, warming at his teasing tone. "Did you want something, big guy?"

He kisses me, which is expected. His mouth covers mine and I kiss him back, even though Hotly's front door opens and closes while we're locked together. It's not the best kept secret that I'm the boss's wife.

What *is* unexpected is the box he sets in my hand. "Open it."

It's a bright blue Tiffany's box and it's ring-size.

I stare at his face, trying to interpret what I see there. His eyes narrow and his fingers nudge mine. "Open it," he repeats.

I have my suspicions but, sure enough, it's a ring. A big, gorgeous, vintage-looking diamond ring with a matching wedding band. It's also a billboard for Jax's intentions.

"Holy shit." That's me, smooth as butter.

This is supposed to be a normal morning, not a life changer.

The corner of his mouth tugs up. "Put it on for me, Firefly?"

I rub my fingertip over the shiny, shiny surface of the diamond. I totally want to put it on, but am I ready to make this commitment? The last time I tried to settle down a little, it went spectacularly wrong. That time I'd wanted a ring and forever, but it had turned out the guy I'd thought was my one and only hadn't been interested in forever. He'd been my Wickham. Jax isn't my past, though. He just might be my future.

"Too soon?"

"Do you really want to do this here?"

He mutters something, all growly and cranky,

and then his fingers gently close the box in mine. "It's yours, Firefly."

He drops a kiss on my forehead and then goes off to park the bike. I…don't know what to do. I think he just sort of proposed to me for real. Or possibly the third time if you count the sex party and then his gruff declaration that he wanted *a chance at us* when he told me that we might be for-real married. We still don't have an answer about that, although the lawyers' bills are impressive.

I duck inside the building and wave hello to the receptionist on my way to the archives. Jax's rings are hidden in my tote, but I can't stop peeking at the box. No one's ever given me diamonds before. No one's loved me like Jax does.

I think.

I jump when I hear footsteps in the stairwell, but it's not Jax. He knows how I work. That I'll need space to process the rings and to think about what he's really asking from me. He chases and I retreat. Or flat-out run away. It's how we've always worked, and I should be grateful that he gets me.

I need to get over the whole money thing, too. Sure he has a ton of money, the kind of fortune that lands him on lists and makes him a very popular party guest. To be honest, it makes me feel inadequate. What can I really bring to our relationship? Our chemistry in bed is off the charts, but sex won't always be enough. What if he gets bored? What if

I run out of kinky role-playing ideas? It's not as if we stage elaborate scenes every time we have sex, but what if I stopped wanting to do that?

I try not to think about it for the rest of the morning. We're about to launch a new Hotly channel, so there's a palpable energy in the building. The cases of Monster the engineering team has drunk in the last week only adds to the jitters, although someone's ordered in an enormous spread of food that's laid out in the kitchen for anyone who wants it. Mostly it's a nice gesture, although it also cuts down on the need to actually leave the building. Bring in food and your people can work around the clock.

By midmorning I've pulled a selection of scripts and props that were used to create some of Hotly's most popular content. Marketing wants to do a Top Ten for the relaunch, and they've asked to see candidates. I think I've done a kick-ass job of pulling items and I'd kind of like to expand my role. Do more organizing and make it easier for people to find stuff in the archives. San Jose State has an online master's degree in library science that could open some interesting doors for me. Hotly's benefits package comes with a tuition rebate, and that would also help keep my costs down. I don't want to ask Jax to pay for it, although I know he would. Plus, if we stay married, I'll never qualify for financial aid. Ha, ha.

I'm so completely focused on this possible version of my future that I don't see my past coming
for me until I run it down. My rapid flight down
the empty hallway stops abruptly when I plow into
a big guy wearing a dark suit and a spicy cologne
that brings back memories. The box goes flying, its
contents emptying out onto the floor.

Ugh. Go me. I've just assaulted a visitor, probably the "future investor" kind based on the ritzy
suit. I've learned a lot about custom tailoring from
poking around in Jax's closet, and the guy I've just
bounced off of didn't do his shopping in Macy's.
We both sink down on our haunches at the same
time, reaching for a bound script. We're so close
that when my skirt bells out around me, it brushes
his pant leg.

Our shoulders bump, I look up to apologize and
my face freezes. My stomach, on the other hand,
gets that swooping, nauseous feeling. I know this
guy. He's my first bad boss, the one who gaslit me
so smoothly that I didn't realize how he'd made me
doubt myself until it was almost too late.

"Why are you here?" I snatch the script from his
hands and cram it into the box. Nothing good happens when Carter Ren is around. He's usually followed by career carnage, apocalyptic life changes,
and a nauseating level of sleaze because Carter gets
what Carter wants and he thinks almost exclusively
with his dick.

He shoves to his feet, which leaves me crouched on the floor like a pet. It's not the power position I'd choose. I stretch for another script and then have to waddle-crouch for the third. There's nothing dignified about my cleanup and when I glare up at him, it's clear he's enjoying this.

He smirks at me. "Come down in the world, have we?"

"None of your business."

The first time Carter and I met, I was at a disadvantage, too. He was interviewing me for a position as his personal assistant. It wasn't a job I'd held before, but it hadn't sounded particularly hard. Make phone calls and reservations, pick his stuff up, generally organize his life and be his beck-and-call girl. He'd blathered on about slide decks and emails, travel arrangements and his super-important, very busy meal schedule, which apparently starred him, the Bay Area's top-ranked restaurants, and the biggest players in the hedge fund world. He'd had an ego. I hadn't been that blind.

The temp agency had said he could be difficult because he was a perfectionist, but that was why his job offer came with an extremely generous compensation package. I'd taken it and then I'd slowly come to realize that Carter had drunk his own Kool-Aid. In his mind, he was the best player on a vast financial chessboard, and everyone around him should worship at the shrine of Carter.

He'd wanted me to do that worshipping on my knees.

"You're not supposed to be within two hundred yards of me," I remind him.

His smirk deepens. "I'm at a business meeting."

I shove the last script into the box and stand, balancing the carton on my hip. "This is you and me in a hallway. It's not a business meeting."

I mentally flip through the terms of our settlement. He's contractually obligated to keep two hundred yards between us at all times, but there's a list of exceptions and if we suddenly find ourselves sharing oxygen, that list gets longer if it's not a circumstance he should have anticipated. When I signed the agreement, I was just sad that meant he wouldn't have to jump out of a plane at twenty-thousand feet if we were both on the flight. I certainly hadn't thought about what would happen if he showed up at my work.

"I'm getting a feel for the place." He eyes me, taking in my fifties-style skirt and Hotly T-shirt. His gaze lingers far too long on my boobs. Ugh.

"Leave. I have work to do, and a meeting of my own." I try to walk away but he gets up in my space, his shoulder brushing mine. "This isn't two hundred yards."

"Are you sure?"

Carter can be super charming when he wants to be. Usually, this is when he wants to convince you that black is white, a.m. is p.m., or whatever twisted version of the world helps his bottom line the most. His skills in this area are quicksand-like, as I can attest to firsthand. The smartest thing to do is to not engage because one minute you're standing on what looks like a perfectly solid surface and the next moment you're doing some fatal sinking. "I don't have anything to say to you."

His perfect teeth flash. I used to schedule his whitening appointments so I'm pretty much beyond being impressed. "I think you can't. I seem to recall you were paid very, very well to shut up."

That paid silence doesn't sit well with me. At the time, it seemed like the practical thing to do, accepting his money in exchange for keeping quiet. I'd felt like a tree falling in the forest when I'd tried to speak out before: if there was no one around to hear me, did it even matter?

"I do have a business meeting here," he continues. "I'm meeting with Jax Valentine and he's bringing me on board."

I'm seriously tempted to hit him with the box. I just wish one of our props had included a baseball bat. Or a tire iron. "You can't do that."

He smirks at me. "I think you'll find I can."

"We had a settlement agreement that said you wouldn't come near me."

"You set me up. You got a very nice payday for it, but I'm not giving you anything else. I want this deal. Jax Valentine makes a fortune for his team when it comes to startups and this one is going to make him another fortune. I'm getting my piece of it, and you're not going to stop me. How do you think it's going to look when I let it slip that you accused me of sexual harassment and shut up as soon as a check was cut?"

I turn around. I'll go back to my archive. "You were a predatory bastard. You came onto me in the freaking office and told me you were adding sex to my job description."

I'm pretty much vibrating with anger that the karma bus hasn't rolled over this asshole yet. He totally deserves it and yet he's here, threatening my job. He's wearing an expensive suit and a gold Rolex winks from his wrist, so I suspect that he has not been living in a leaky RV or wondering how he'll pay his bills. He's just gotten on with his life as if what he did to me didn't matter at all.

"I'm going to have an ownership stake here by lunchtime," he says, stepping in front of me.

"You can't do that." I've already said that, but WTF is it with this guy?

"You're going to quit this job, like you've quit all the jobs you've held before."

"I left last time, you asshole. That makes it your turn."

"You left with my money. You got paid for sex, so I think we both know what that makes you."

The words hang in the air between us. Objectively, I knew that was what he thought about me. It was what lots of people would think if they knew I'd let him pay me off. It still hurts to hear it, however.

"We had sex twice, and then I realized that I thought we had a relationship, while you thought you had a convenient cum receptacle."

I'd thought we were working on a future together. Dating my boss had given me pause, of course, but it had been true love, or so I'd thought. I'd been so stupid. The work dinners. The little accidental touches. The compliments and conversations. I'd fallen for it all and then I'd paid for it with my career and my self-respect. When I'd tried to break up with my boyfriend, I'd learned that he saw himself as my boss. My boss in the office. My boss in bed.

"If you don't quit," Carter says, "I'll have a conversation with your new boss. I think he'll be very interested to hear about our history."

"It's not like that," I protest.

"It's *exactly* like that." He smirks. "You're fucking your boss. *Again*. How much money do you think you'll walk away with this time?"

Jax

It's almost noon, which means Peony's had the morning to think about the rings. I'm hoping I can convince her to sneak out for tacos. We have a good history with tacos, so it seems like the perfect lunch date to make my case. The receptionist grins at me when I ask if she's seen Peony recently. We're trying to be reasonably professional about our relationship, but people know. It was inevitable.

"I think Peony's downstairs in the archives," she says. "Also, your twelve thirty is here early."

I'm meeting with a potential investor this afternoon, a guy named Carter Ren. I've worked with him once or twice in the past and he's a big-time player at a venture capital firm in Palo Alto. His reputation for backing winners is solid, so I'm interested in bringing him onboard. Unless Peony wants to make a job change, it will be better if someone else finishes spearheading the changes I want to implement here at Hotly, and Ren seems like a good candidate.

Ren's not waiting by the front desk, though, and the receptionist informs me that he's wandering around the hallways "to get the vibe of the place." He was starting in the basement, she adds.

The basement is where the archives and Peony are. Ren's a businessman, and it's not like Hotly is a dating service. But I don't like it.

I feel as if I should go charging after him and either rip his head off or pee on a few walls to mark my territory. I can't work here with Peony, not anymore, not given these caveman urges.

I storm down the stairwell and bang through the

fire doors at the bottom. I have all the subtly of a rampaging dragon. I need to pull back and find my business face, but all I can think about is finding Peony. It's been hours since I dropped her off, so I'm sure there are things that have happened since then that we should share with each other. She could say yes to my proposal.

When I turn the corner—I really need to move the archives to the top floor—I spot Ren. He's wearing an expensive suit, one that he bespoke from my tailor in London. I'm not sure if that's the ultimate kiss-up move or if he just recognizes excellence when he sees it. He's had a few successful deals this year and his net worth is impressive. He likes to flaunt it, though.

Peony's standing next to him. They're so close that their shoes touch. In fact, he towers over her like some villain in a second-rate movie. She's small and he's not, so some of it is just simple biology, but there's something that feels off about the two of them.

That is me overreacting. They don't know each other.

Ren points to me. "Why don't we ask Jax what he thinks?"

"Ask me about what?"

I focus on Peony. She's twitchy, chewing on her lower lip. Something about Ren or her conversation with him is bothering her.

"We can talk about it tonight," she says.

"All right. Tonight, then. It's a date." I brush a kiss over her cheek, ignoring her little indignant look. There's no tongue, so I'm going to argue this in no way breaks our "no workplace nookie" rule. She doesn't stick around to debate me, so Ren's definitely upset her.

"Ren," I snap when she's disappeared into the archives, "you're with me."

I don't know what he said to upset Peony, but I plan on finding out.

Ren falls into step next to me. "So how long have you been hitting that?"

Fuck bringing Ren on board. I stop just outside the conference room where we're meeting with our legal representation. "You don't say shit like that."

"Come on, man. It's not as if it's a secret that you and Peony are doing it." Ren makes an obscene gesture. Apparently, he believes I'm an ass *and* stupid. Punching him would be deeply satisfying, but I'm working on my long game.

"Peony is an employee here. She is entitled to your respect. In fact, no one should have to put up with having his or her sex life discussed at work. It is completely inappropriate."

Peony would have Ren's balls if she knew what he'd just said. There's no amount of excuses that can convince her to put up with anyone's bullshit. It's one of the things I love about her. If I push her, she pushes back. She'd probably give me an endless amount of crap if she ever found out that I'd stepped in to defend her from a creep like Ren. She'd argue that she could take care of him by herself. I don't disagree, but she has me. She can let me take the trash out for her sometimes.

I shove the conference room door open harder than is strictly necessary. Ren crowds in on my heels.

"Lake." I tip my head at my lawyer. "There's been a change in plans. Mr. Ren will not be joining us at Hotly, after all."

Ren puffs up and starts cursing.

Fuck, it's good to be the boss.

CHAPTER NINETEEN

Jax

THE END CATCHES me by surprise. It's like I was enjoying the best movie ever and suddenly it's over in the middle of a scene, the lights go up, and I'm told to get the fuck out of the theater.

It starts when Lake texts me while I'm on my way back to the cottage. Now that I've disposed of Ren's Hotly aspirations, I'm in a hurry to see my girl and find out what's wrong. I have a bag of takeout in one hand and a dozen lavender roses in the other because those are Peony's favorite, even though I've argued her name should make her a fan of her Paeonia namesake.

Look at this. Lake's shared a link to a popular gossip site.

This is the kind of shit my friends text back and forth, but so far Lake has never sent me funny You-Tube links or cat pictures. She generally limits her communications to heart-stoppingly large invoices or dire messages that require equally unpleasant responses from me.

The website Lake sends me to is the kind that posts celebrity gossip. They've got a couple of paparazzi who like to dig up crap on Silicon Valley types. Liam's sex parties are a popular topic, but that doesn't seem to be in play on their main page. I scroll down, looking for whatever's set Lake off. I'm just about to blast off a text asking WTF when I find it.

It's just accurate enough, as these things go, that we're not going to be able to get a take-down order. The writer gleefully announces that yet another Silicon Valley billionaire has bitten the marital bullet thanks to his shenanigans at a notorious sex party. There are a few photos of Peony and me together, along with a copy of our marriage certificate, and the writer has named us both, just in case his audience can't decipher who is who in the photo.

Peony hasn't exactly been open about her past, although I know she's almost pathological about maintaining her privacy. I have to pry personal details out of her. So I'm not expecting the second paragraph in the article—the one that goes on to speculate that Mrs. Valentine neé Harding is particularly talented at parting her bosses from their money and that perhaps our union is something less than a love—or lust—match. There's a bunch of partially blacked-out documents from a lawsuit that Peony apparently brought against a guy a few years ago. I read them, check my texts, and come to a couple of conclusions:

1. Peony successfully sued her former boss for sexual harassment.
2. That boss was Carter Ren.
3. He settled with her for a hundred K.
4. She had Bob Martin in the perfect position to sue.
5. And now she has me.

I skim the website again, hoping I've misunderstood. It's possible that someone's made all of this up, but it's more likely there's some truth and a whole lot of carefully spun elaboration. I can't do anything, however, until I've had a chance to speak with Peony.

By the time I turn onto our block, I've come up with a dozen possible explanations. I don't know which one is true, but one of them has to be. Except that when I reach the cottage, Peony is standing on the porch, looking hunted. There's a guy all up in her face, and I see red.

I toss the takeout and the flowers to the side and charge in, fists flying. The guy hollers, swinging back, and for a few seconds it's mayhem. My knuckles collide with his jaw and then his nose. There's a satisfying crunch, some blood, and a whole lot of cursing. Peony's trying to pull me off the guy—who has zero business being on my property—while the guy yells questions at me and tries to dodge my fists. I can practically feel Lake having an aneurysm.

I suck in a breath. *Step back.* I haven't pummeled the shit out of anyone since I used to earn money fighting in illegal fight rings.

I turn to Peony. "WTF is going on, Peony?"

Fuck. That didn't come out as sensitive and supportive as I meant it to be and the expression on Peony's face confirms that I'm an abject failure in the communications department.

The guy I've been hitting picks this moment to ask if I have any comment on the allegations that my wife set me up for a very lucrative payday.

"No comment," I bark.

Peony's got her back against the wall and looks as if she'd like to add *becoming one with the woodwork* to her list of impossible things to believe in.

A few more punches may be thrown because I am not a fucking saint, not even close, and today has sucked. After dealing with Carter Ren, I have zero restraint left. I only get in half a dozen hits before Peony peels herself off the wall and starts tugging on my arm again. I don't want to hurt her, so I back off.

"Get off my property." My face must look sufficiently scary because reporter dude is almost air-

borne in his haste to get gone. He practically flies
out of my yard.

Unfortunately, it's not a big lot, so this just means
he stands in the street eight feet away from my front
door. I suspect that if we get on the bike, he's just
going to follow us, so I swallow my rage. I need
a better plan than beating the shit out of him, as
tempting as that is.

Peony's key sticks out of the lock; the guy must
have surprised her on her way home. I finish the job
she started and open the door. The clicking sound
from the street warns me that the reporter is now
taking pictures of our home. I'm really not okay
with that.

"Get inside." I try to put myself between Peony
and the reporter, but she's glued to the wall.

"I need to go."

"Inside, Firefly. We can sort this out."

The fucking clicking of the camera is driving me
nuts and I need to find out what Lake's take on all
of this is. Peony looks at the street, clearly weighing
the odds of making it past the reporter to safety. Of
course she's not going to ask me for help. I'm just
her pretty penis and her husband.

Once she's finally inside, I slam the door shut and
lock it. The lock's more symbolic than anything—I
don't think the paparazzo is dumb enough to commit home invasion in my present mood—but I don't
want the outside world to interrupt us.

"What the fuck is going on? Do you know that guy? Are you okay?" I start toward Peony, but she practically sprints across the cottage, putting the kitchen counter between us.

"Do you really want to talk about this?"

"Yeah, I do," I growl. I push my phone at her across the counter. "My lawyer's blowing my phone up telling me to check online because somebody's posted shit about us and then I come home and find that guy harassing you. I can't even kill him because then I'd be locked up in San Quentin rather than anywhere that would actually be helpful. So, yeah. If you know something, I'd like to hear it."

I stalk over to the windows to check out the situation. I've never gotten around to buying curtains, so the paparazzo has a clear shot inside. We might as well be having our discussion on the front porch. Fuck. I stalk around the kitchen counter and Peony's eyes grow wide.

I hate that I make her nervous, but I don't know how to fix that right now. Instead, I sit on the kitchen floor. Loss of dignity aside, we should be safe from prying lenses down here.

God knows what our stalker buddy thinks is happening.

Peony's staring at me as if I've lost it.

"Long-range lens. No curtains."

She mutters a curse and plops down on the floor next to me. I'd rather hold her in my lap and wrap my arms around her, but the expression on her face tells me that she's not looking for that kind of support right now. Even if she might need it.

Peony closes her eyes and leans back against the cupboard. She looks exhausted and I wonder how long that asshole out there was bothering her. We can't stay here—that's clear. I text Lake back and tell her she'd better make goddamned sure none of the pictures the photographer across the street is snapping ever see the light of day.

I'm not the legal expert, but I have my doubts that he can photograph me inside my house without consequences. I skip calling the police and make a quick call instead to a security service I've used before. They promise to send a team out to pick us up and drive us somewhere more secure, and then there's nothing left to do but confront the elephant in the room.

I look over at Peony. "Did you sue your former boss for sexual harassment?"

"Yes." She doesn't open her eyes.

"And that was a different boss at Liam's sex party?"

"Yes, but—"

"And now I'm your boss."

She nods silently.

I wait for her to explain all this to me, but she doesn't add anything more. Two yeses and a head nod aren't going to do it for me. I need to understand what happened between her and Ren so I can... I don't know what. Fix it? Move past it? She doesn't tell me what she wants or what she needs. She doesn't tell me a goddamned thing, including the truth.

"You walked away with a hundred K from Ren?"

"Yes. He didn't want to take it to court, so he settled."

Peony

Jax closes his eyes, rubbing his hands on his thighs. I know he'd never hurt me, but he's still worked up from the fight on the front porch. Tension radiates from his big body and I'm not sure if I want to talk this out or run.

After a long moment, he opens his eyes and looks at me. "We're married. I trusted you. And yet it looks like I was your biggest payday."

"I didn't know you were rich. I certainly didn't know our little game would backfire and we'd end up married for real. We were supposed to be playing." I stare at my hands in my lap, trying to figure out what I should do next. If I get up and leave, will the guy outside follow me?

"Were you planning on telling me?" he asks, his voice calm.

I could lie to him, but I'm so tired of not speaking up. "I don't know."

"Explain it to me," he says.

"I had a temp job working in his office as his executive assistant. He was flattering, smart, successful. I thought he was cute. He was my boss, though, so I didn't want to hop into a relationship with him. But he pursued me and he was charming and sweet and… I fell for it. He said he wanted to be in a relationship with me, that he could see the two of us getting married, making a home together, maybe having a kid or two someday."

I was young and Carter seemed like a generous, doting white knight who wanted to swoop in and carry me off to a fantasy life. I don't say this, though, because there's no point. Jax and I both know how rescue fantasies play out.

"So we started dating on the down low," I continue. "And we didn't tell anybody at work that we were now a couple. We made plans for our future and Carter was talking about a Christmas engagement, and then things starting changing between us."

At first I'd thought it was me. That I wasn't sexy enough, uninhibited enough, creative enough in bed. Carter had started making suggestions, and I'd tried. God, I'd tried. "He said and did some things that made me realize he didn't respect me and that I was pretty much just a convenient booty call. Our relationship was one-sided. It was all me trying to be his partner and his girlfriend, working on our future. I had it out with him when he told me to do something in bed that I didn't want to do. He said I could pretend to like it and it would be fine. And then he wouldn't stop coming onto me at work. He said I'd already given him permission and that it was just a game, a boss and the secretary fantasy."

"He's lucky you didn't kill him," Jax says tightly. "Why the fuck did you go back after the first time? What were you thinking?"

"I had bills. It was a good job. I—" Don't know. Because sometimes when you're scared and your life has been turned upside down and you're having to question everything you believed before, you make decisions that you question later.

Jax mutters a curse. "You took his goddamned money, Peony."

"I did."

I don't tell him that Ren sometimes got what he demanded. That the three weeks I spent working for him after we broke up were hell and that it took me that long to get my head on straight and realize that I needed a lawyer. The money had been an afterthought, something my lawyer had demanded. I'd just wanted someone to listen to me, to agree that what Ren had wanted was not okay.

"Why were you living in a rented RV, for fuck's sake? Someone should have made sure you were taken care of."

"I donated it." I lean my head back against the

cupboard. I can see Jax's surfboard through the kitchen door, leaning up against the fence. "The women's shelter sent Ren a really nice letter thanking him for his generous gift. I didn't think I'd ever see him again. My lawyer included a restraining order in our settlement. I wasn't supposed to talk about him, and he wasn't supposed to come within two hundred yards of me. He was really unhappy to see me today. He told me I had to quit, or he'd tell you all about my gold-digging past. I'm sure you can see now why I didn't want to be dating my boss again. It really hasn't worked out for me before."

Angry crying. I hate that I'm an angry crier. I try not blinking, but it doesn't work and the tears leak down my cheek anyhow. "So now I think you know everything. We can just keep it quiet, handle this how you want. It's all over now."

Jax shakes his head. He doesn't look angry anymore, just tired. "Secret's out, Peony. That guy harassing you on the porch is from the media. There's probably more out there."

He hands me his phone so I can see the website he was looking at. It's all there, for the whole world to see. My relationship with Carter, the settlement, the legal documents where I promised eternal silence in exchange for cash.

I want to bolt from this kitchen and run and run and run, but this hasn't helped me in the past. It's what I did when I thought I'd left Carter behind me.

It's what I've tried to do with Jax, even though he's a good guy and deserves so much better.

"I'll go," I tell him. "You can have that Lake person fix this."

"Peony—" He stops, as if he doesn't know what to say next.

That makes two of us. I swipe away my tears. "I'm sorry. You didn't need to get pulled into this shit."

"Ren's behavior isn't your fault. He made some bad choices of his own. Stay here. I'll figure this out and get back to you, okay?"

Jax shoves to his feet. He keeps his back to the front of the house, though, probably because that asshole reporter is hanging around there, trying for a shot.

"Okay." I should say something else, make a move to keep him here or set him free completely. He's looking out for me, sure, but I suspect it's an instinctive reaction on his part, like putting his fists up when there's a punch headed toward his face or jerking himself out of the way of an oncoming truck. Jax protects. That's who he is. It's what he does. What he needs, however, is to protect himself from me, so I don't stop him when he heads out the door.

CHAPTER TWENTY

Jax

I PULL MYSELF up the rocky face as fast I can. My priorities right now are a) getting to the top and b) getting to the top before Liam does. It's not lunchtime yet, but we've already raced to the top of two different boulders so that I can work out some of my frustration with the whole Peony situation. It's been three weeks since the Carter revelation and I'm starting to suspect I've mishandled things.

Okay. I've definitely mishandled them because I'm alone, no Peony in sight, and I'm not okay with that. I have to fix this. Get Peony back. Preferably make her realize that my silence was a mistake and not a rejection, and that I just want things between us to be like they were before.

I slap my hand on the top of the boulder. "Winner, winner, chicken dinner."

Except my hand meets Liam's fingers instead of

rock. He's beaten me to the top. He swings the rest of his oversize body up on top of the massive boulder and gives me the finger with his other hand. "Loser. Now you have to talk about it."

"I don't have to tell you anything." I flop backward after a quick spider-and-bird-poop inspection.

He tips his head at me. "So let me tell you a few things."

As if I could stop him.

"You hooked up with Peony at my sex party after you went all white knight and kicked the ass of a guy who was accosting her." The corners of his mouth draw down as he lays out my sins. "And then you hooked up some more, she left you, you discovered you were accidentally married, and then you dropped that bombshell on her at her job—along with the happy news that you were her new boss. So then you have all sorts of sex with her and you're convinced it's super special, and she gets the gold star in the world championships of sex acts, right up until you panic because she did some possibly dumb shit in her past and so you push her away."

"Thanks for the unnecessary recap," I snarl.

"Or did she finish with you because you went all Neanderthal and possessive?"

"Does it matter?"

"It does."

"I wasn't a Neanderthal. Much. Peony was just done. Our marriage was a freaking spectacle and her track record with rich bosses is—to be frank—disturbing. I just liked her for her. I loved her."

Liam fiddles with the lines we'll use to drop back down to the beach. "You totally sure she's done with you?"

"As far as I can tell."

"But you're not done with her despite flouncing out the door with her."

"No," I bite out. "I still want this thing with her."

"Thing." Liam snorts. "You need to find some better words. Go channel your inner Mr. Darcy or at least drop the cash for a decent ghost writer to make something up for you. You want me to stand in the shadows and feed you lines? 'Cause I've seen that movie and I'll totally do it for you."

Right. As if he's got a silver tongue and can explain why I need Peony back so badly.

Liam swings over the side of the boulder while I'm still searching for words and I valiantly resist the urge to kick him in the head. The ungrateful bastard still fires a parting shot. "So go after her."

As if I can.

How do you chase after someone who's hit the Eject button on your shared life?

Peony hasn't reached out to me since I left. She has, in fact, officially quit her job at Hotly and she's given Our Little Secret a wide berth. Just to be clear, I thought giving her some space was the mature, husbandly thing to do. Have I screwed things up even more?

I chew on this unwelcome possibility while I climb down to where Liam's waiting for me on the sand. His smirk fades into a pained grimace as he takes in my face. Clearly I should avoid high-stakes poker games and important business negotiations today. Just to be clear, I'm not asking him to fix things or blow smoke up my ass about my chances with Peony.

Even though I'd take it.

He curses and goes for it. "Look. You avoid romantic relationships. You should have been practicing for the last ten years, like everyone else. Somehow we've managed not to kill each other, and your sister thinks you're the best. She claims it's pretty much always been you and her against the world."

If my eyes sting a little, that's because it's allergy season.

"So you totally know how to have a relationship," he continues. "Even if you tend to take the caveman approach."

"She quit working at Hotly yesterday," I tell him. "I haven't checked to see if she's moved out of our cottage, but she never stays put for long."

I wish I could stop worrying about Peony. I wish we were just two normal coworkers who'd met and hit it off, and not a guy with too much money and a girl with too much baggage. I want us to be *us* again.

Liam groans. "I'm only gonna say this once, so listen up. She doesn't need you to take care of her. Jax. She just needs you to care *about* her. Loudly, quietly, publicly, messily, or with your usual god-damned efficiency. Don't turn this into some kind of messed-up-man version of 'if you love someone, set them free.'"

"I wanted her to choose to come back to me."

Liam slaps my back. "The thing about caring for someone is that you have to choose to show up."

CHAPTER TWENTY-ONE

Peony

WOMEN'S MAGAZINES propose fixing your relationship by spicing things up in the bedroom; they publish lists of sexy fantasies you can pick from. But I've already done that. Like so much of my relationship with Jax, I've started from the end and worked toward the beginning. This time I want to start in the right place. I want to end with Jax.

Six maybe-not-impossible things, Peony. That and belief is all it takes to slay the jabberwocky. So I get busy with my pink Sharpie and write:

1. I don't have to leave. I can choose to stay. Fireflies aren't just a flash in the pan.
2. I can find a new job that lets me organize the heck out of other people's stuff. I'm good at it, and people will pay me to do it.
3. I can take care of Jax because even big, bad bosses need TLC sometimes.

4. I can say yes when people want to help me.
5. I don't have to be a world-class surfer. I only
   have to try. And not get eaten by sharks.
6. I can make Jax love me again.

I make Impossible Thing No. 1 happen by moving back into Our Little Secret. It feels like a hundred years ago that Jax and I sat on the kitchen floor together, but it's only been weeks and my key still works. There are no Jax sightings, though. His surfboards decorate the backyard but the fridge is a sad and lonely wasteland. His clothes are gone from the closet, and his bike's not parked in the side yard. He's not here, but I am.

Impossible Thing No. 2 is in progress. I sign up as a temporary librarian with San Francisco county and I promise myself that I'm enrolling in San José State's online library program.

Impossible Thing No. 3. I stalk Jax's corporate website for his Market Street office address. This part is a whole lot less certain than choosing a bedroom or looking for a new job.

Jax has a serious power office.

His company owns the building—naturally—and there's an enormously shiny, chrome-filled lobby full of men and women in sober dark suits and really expensive footwear. I pretend I'm there to deliver an edible bouquet and the security guard in the lobby makes sure I get on the right elevator.

The executive assistant manning the front desk is less easy to persuade, but I flash the monster rock on my ring finger, swallow my pride, and announce that I'm the boss's wife. This means he decides to escort me to Jax's office to wait for my man—and I decide to make a pit stop when we pass a conference room.

Jax is lording it over the suits in the room.

He's sprawled at the head of a long table, legs stretched out in front of him, fiddling on a tablet. His hair is loose around his face and he has shadows under his eyes. He looks like a pissed-off boardroom pirate.

Game on.

I wave at him. Jax has one of those supermodern, fishbowl conference rooms that's all glass on one side, so it's not hard to get his attention. I know exactly when he spots me. He scowls at my assistant buddy and sits up. I knock on the closed door and then push it open.

Come on, big bad wolf. Let me in.

Jax watches me come for him, which means he sits there and glowers.

I smile at our audience. "Ladies and gentlemen, I need to borrow the boss for a minute."

I point to the door, but no one moves. Drat. Bet they're afraid he'll make them walk the plank. I narrow my eyes at Jax.

"Let's take fifteen," he barks.

He stares right back at me while our audience files out.

I'm deliberately dressed for trick or treating, even though it won't officially be Halloween for a few more weeks because costumes and role-playing have been the theme song of our relationship. My black dress is high-necked, long-sleeved, and stops three inches north of my knees. In the interests of not freezing—San Francisco is notoriously cold—I've paired orange-and-black knee socks with my Dr. Martens. It's part sexy dom, part bad ass Goth, so the possibilities are endless.

I thrust the orange plastic pumpkin I'm carrying at him. "I've brought you a treat."

"Thanks," he says dryly. He makes no move to take the pumpkin, so I set it down on the table since it's that or hug it to me like a virgin clutching her pearls.

"And I thought we should talk, instead of me evading and you pouting in your corner. Although it's a really nice corner." I pat him on the shoulder. "If you're going to be all dark and broody, this is a good place to do it."

I give his power chair a little push. Fortunately, it's on wheels or I wouldn't have a hope of moving him. Once I have him positioned to my liking, I hop up on the table.

"What are you doing here, Peony?"

"Fighting for you." I lean forward and try to hook

his chair arm with my foot so I can drag him closer. God, he's gorgeous and I've missed him. "Help me out here, okay?"

He scoots obediently and something inside me melts. "I thought we were done."

"You did walk out on me. Did you mean that?"

If he did, today's plan is going to involve more grovel than I planned on.

He makes some growly sounds and shoves his fingers through his beautiful hair.

"Peony, you don't stick around for relationships and I don't know how to make us work, either. The only relationship glue I'm good at involves cash and sex. That's what I have to offer." He pauses. "That sounds even worse when I say it out loud than when I think it. It was supposed to be a metaphor. Or a simile. Something way less stupid-sounding about how we both need to work at sticking."

His mouth turns down in a frown.

I lean forward so far that I'm practically perched in his lap. "You have a lot to offer, Jax. You've just always started with cash and I've always been afraid to give someone a chance. Now we both have a bad habit we need to work on. Try offering something else. Or let me offer you something. I want to be your go-to person, the one who gets to do stuff for you. The one who's with you.

"I wish I knew what you see when you look at me," I continue. "Because you see a whole lot more than I do when I'm looking in a mirror. I'd like to be that Peony. I like who I am when we're together."

"Peony 2.0 is pretty amazing," he says. There's something in his eyes—hope and nerves, maybe need. Definitely heat.

"I'm not the same without you," I confess. "I totally screwed up by not sharing more earlier. And then I let you walk away when I should have tackled you by the knees and asked you to stay."

His gaze flickers. "I don't want to tie you down if you need to go. I'm not going to be that needy guy."

"I need you," I admit. "Sure, I can make a go of things on my own, and it might even be good, but something would be missing. Some*one*. Everything's better when you're in my life."

Go big, or go home alone. I slide off the table and crash land on his lap. Hopefully, the hallway's cleared out, or they're going to get an eyeful. My arms go around Jax's neck, my fingers tracing the soft, warm skin above the collar of his shirt. I get just one chance at this. I have to be enough.

"I know you're probably angry at me," I say. "I'm angry at me. I should have told you about Carter the Ultimate Asshole Boss. I shouldn't have kept secrets. I know you needed some space, but I definitely should have come after you to explain at some point. Or make you listen. We could have played the tie-me-up game again and it could have been your turn to be it and then I could have explained—"

"That you'd been hurt by too many rich assholes who brought sex and money to the table instead of themselves? Who thought you were looking for a payout?"

"True story," I agree. "Although let's be fair—all that money paints a target on you in some circles. I think those women must be blind. Or something. It's not the money that makes you a prize."

He reaches up and smooths my hair behind my ear. "They don't see me like you do."

"Well—"

"You see me, even when it seems like I might be acting just like all your other asshole bosses."

"You're technically not the boss of me anymore," I point out.

He gives me a slow, sexy smile. "Wanna bet?"

"Maybe I'm the boss of you. Or we could be really revolutionary and take turns."

"Partners," he interrupts.

"Excuse me?" I'm distracted by his fingers stroking the sides of my hips, trying to tug me closer when we're already as close as two fully dressed people not having sex can get.

"We'll be partners. Co-CEOs of the merger of Peony and Jax. We'll make the rules for us together, and the first rule is that we stick together. Always. No more running off. No more silence. Lots of explaining and trust and honesty."

"Total honesty?"

"Always," he says gravely.

"Then I have something to tell you." I peel one hand off him and shove it into the pumpkin where I've stashed my pièce de résistance. It's a Ring Pop, a bright, cherry red with a plastic band. I slide it onto his finger. "I love you. Will you marry me for real, Jax Valentine?"

He yanks me to him, burying his face in my throat. "I missed you," he says thickly. "Yes. I'm sorry I screwed up."

"Me, too. But not all mistakes are bad, right? It turns out sex parties aren't really my thing, but then I met you and you rescued me and now here we are."

"With you rescuing me right back." He kisses me softly.

"Well, taking turns is important. For example, I love you." I press a kiss against his mouth.

He returns my kiss with interest. "And I love you, too. You're my fantasy come true."

"I need a new list of impossible things," I tell him. "Because I definitely didn't see this coming. Say it again."

"I love you, Peony Harding-Valentine," he says, cupping my face with his big, strong hands. My ring looks good on him—cheerful and playful, sweet and yet sticky. "I love you, Mrs. Valentine."

"We may need to work on the last name thing." I may kiss him back because I never really imagined this beautiful man could be mine. He loves me for who I am, not who I can pretend to be. "But I love you, too."

"And in the spirit of total honesty, I have to tell you something, too."

"Okay?"

"It would have been impossible for me not to love you. Impossible for me not to love you yesterday, today, tomorrow, or any other day of the week. I think you need to hear that, and I plan on proving it every day that you'll let me."

"Deal," I say. "I'll hold you to that."

And I do.

* * * * *

SKIN DEEP

LAUREN HAWKEYE

MILLS & BOON

For Patience and Duran Duran

PROLOGUE ONE

Five years ago

FRED VAUGHAN LOVED AMSTERDAM.

It was the last stop on the European trip he and his twin, Frank, had taken to celebrate the end of their undergraduate degrees. In the fall they would both be back at school—Frank for a master's in business, and he to law school—and the trip had been a graduation gift from their parents, albeit a begrudging one on his father's part. Frederick Vaughan Sr., had expected both of his sons to spend the summer working at Vaughan Enterprises, the massive development conglomerate that his own father had started, but he'd been overruled by his wife.

Fred was grateful. As a Vaughan, his future was set in stone, and he'd known that since childhood. He hadn't ever thought he'd minded, either, until he'd had his undergrad diploma in hand and realized that, after four years of killing himself studying while his peers partied, he was about to head right back into the grind. The weight of expectation had started to wrap thin tendrils around him, to tug at his limbs, his skin. Tendrils he thought he could break free of, but the more he pulled against them, the further into the morass he sank.

So really, he would have loved anywhere that wasn't school, or home. Anywhere he felt free. But…he really did love Amsterdam. He loved the history, so rich and old that it made the roots of Boston feel shallow. He loved the beaches and the confidence that the European women wore like a second skin.

He loved the culture, the clubs. And tonight, their last night there, he loved the throb of the dance music in his veins, the rumble of the bass beneath his feet. He loved the icy chill of the beer in his hand and the writhing mass of bodies on the dance floor. He wasn't much of a dancer himself, but he could watch the movement all night. The people. The connections—friends and love and, best of all, lust. People coming together for a moment or an hour or a night.

"You like to watch?"

The voice was husky, pitched lower than the din of the club. He looked down—he and Frank always had to look down, because they were each six feet four inches tall—and found himself on the receiving end of an assessing gaze from a pair of bright blue eyes. Those captivating eyes were set in a fairy-tale princess face, though he had the instant certainty that she wouldn't appreciate the comparison.

Caught by the question and the intensity of those eyes, he took a moment to reply, a single impression working its way through his brain to his mouth. "Is that a Boston accent I hear?"

"Ten points for the pretty boy." She grinned up at him, a saucy curve of full lips painted bright pink, and his eyes tracked the movement. "You expected something else? You sound surprised."

He had been, in fact, and by more than the surprise of finding someone from his faraway hometown here in Amsterdam. Though her face was delicate and feminine enough to have fit in among the pedigreed women he'd left back home in Boston, it was surrounded by long, wild black curls A silver ring pierced her right eyebrow, and thick black eyeliner accentuated that deep blue of her gaze. In short, she looked wild. Untamed. Like she'd sprung from the earth right here in Amsterdam, a magical creature wrought from his wildest dreams.

Looking down into fierce eyes, he felt something stirring inside him. Some kind of primal need awakened, unspooling from a tight knot in his gut, answering her call.

"You're staring," She waved an arm in the air and leaned on the bar to catch the attention of the bartender, who came running the second he caught a glimpse of her lush cleavage. This gave Fred a moment to admire the tattoos that decorated her arms, which were bare, revealed by a simple white tank top. "Didn't your mama ever tell you that's rude?"

He'd never really liked tattoos before. No, that wasn't entirely true—he'd never given them much thought, especially not as applied to women. He was pretty sure he didn't know any women who had one.

"Is it rude if I'm admiring you?" He wasn't sure where the words came from. He did well enough with women, but his brother was the player—a player he'd forgotten was standing right at his elbow.

"Smooth, Fred." Frank grinned at him. Fred scowled as his brother stepped forward, drawing the attention of the ethereal creature in front of them. "Hi, I'm Frank. If you're interested in the looks without the corny lines, I'm your man."

This wasn't a new scene—Frank had been cockblocking him since they'd both hit puberty—but this time Fred felt irritation flickering little fingers into his veins. He was the easygoing twin, and usually he just shrugged it off when his brother swiped a woman out from under his nose. There were plenty of fish in the sea, after all, and he attracted plenty of his own.

This woman, though? He was intrigued. He'd punch his own twin in the face before he let her go with Frank.

The woman had looked from Fred to Frank, her lips curving with amusement.

"Nice to meet you, Frank." The woman smiled up at his twin, that sexy voice curving like smoke around her words. Fred puffed his chest out, about to tell his brother to beat it, but he quickly discovered that there was no need. "Wanna go away now and let me hit on your brother?"

Both twins choked out a startled laugh. Frank looked at Fred, and Fred had a tense moment in which he wondered if his twin was going to push his point. Instead, Frank shrugged before wandering off into the dancing throng of people.

"Are you always so…" He trailed off as he searched for the correct word. She grinned, the smile like lightning in a dark sky.

"Forward? Abrupt? Rude?" She accepted one of the shot glasses the bartender handed her. As she wrapped her fingers around the small glass, Fred noticed that she had a delicate black rose tattooed on the top of each of her four fingers, excluding her thumb.

"Assertive," he countered. He had a sudden vision of that hand, those roses, wrapped around his cock. Heat licked up his spine when she handed him a matching shot glass.

"Generally, yes." She studied the golden liquid in the shot glasses for a moment before shooting him a challenging glance. "Does that offend your delicate sensibilities? Are you one of those men who needs to be in charge?"

He thought about this for a moment. Thought about the men he knew back home. This woman's overt confidence would rub them all the wrong way, he knew that without a doubt. Probably because they didn't have much of their own. They were used to women with good family names, women who'd been raised to support the men in their lives. Women who didn't challenge.

He'd never been overly interested in those women, at least not for longer than one night. Now, as if she'd just appeared, was a woman he found fascinating, and he wasn't interested in anything except being honest.

"I like being in charge." He tapped his shot glass against hers. "I like it even more when a woman knows exactly what she wants."

He watched as something sparked in her eyes, a deep blue glitter. He couldn't hear her sharp inhalation of breath, not over the thundering music, but he saw it. Watched the swells of her high, tight breasts press against the thin fabric of her top.

She wasn't wearing a bra. Through the translucent fabric, he could make out the dusky circles of her areolas, the tight pucker of her nipples, which were hard—hard for him?

He could also see that some kind of jewelry adorned each of those taut buds. He'd never seen anything like it, not in real life, and he felt a sharp, physical ache with the need to touch.

Silently, they each tossed back their shots. Fred's eyes tracked the delicate lines of the woman's throat as she swallowed, then the path of her tongue as she swiped it over her lips to catch the last drop.

"What's your name?" He caught the shot glass from her hands, set it and his aside, using the gesture as an excuse to brush his fingers over hers. He tangled his own large hand in her small one, tugging her closer to him, close enough that the tips of those adorned breasts brushed against his wide chest. He felt fire in the wake of the touch.

"Why?" She rubbed her thumb over his knuckles, looking up at him from beneath long, tangled lashes.

"What do you mean, why?" He frowned. "You know mine."

"Yes." She nodded to punctuate her point. "But what does knowing your name is Fred tell me? Does it tell me what your favorite color is? Does it tell me how your skin smells? Does it tell me what you'll do when I touch you?"

With her free hand, she traced a finger down the center of his chest, awakening nerve endings as she went. He caught it just before she reached his belt, holding it in place.

"Right now, my favorite color is pink. This pink, right here." He lifted his other hand to cup her face, traced his thumb over those pillowy lips. "I'd love to find out what other shades of pink you have."

He felt her exhalation, the damp heat fanning out over his thumb as she spoke. "Pretty words, Boston boy."

"Here are a few more." He leaned forward, felt the heat radiating outward from her body. "Come with me. Somewhere, anywhere. Let me find out."

"Mmm. Tempting." She looked up at him, considering, then shook her head. Before he could feel the punch of disappointment, she pivoted. "Dance with me."

Fred did not dance.

He'd actually never willingly joined a dance floor, not once…well, not unless he counted that time he and Frank had sneaked their father's whiskey into a flask for their cousin Sarah's wedding, which had turned out about as expected.

Still, he let this woman—damn, but he wished he knew her name—lead him onto the dance floor. There, she turned in his arms, her back to his front, and cast an utterly bewitching glance over her shoulder. Enticing him.

Daring him.

When she released his hand, he placed it on her shoulder, tracing the strong curve. He slid it down, following the graceful line of her arm, the swell of her hip, then back up. He grazed the bottom of her tank, then tucked his hand inside, his palm flat on her stomach. Her skin was soft, hot as silk as she pressed into the touch.

It was impossible to stay still with this woman rocking gently back against him, with the sea of people around them swaying. The music vibrated along his skin, through his body, driving the thoughts right out of his mind. Leaving room for him to just experience the moment.

She pressed that tight little body back against him, swaying sinuously. She was tall enough that his pelvis was flush with the curves of her ass, and he felt himself harden as a result of her movements. He felt rather than heard her purr with approval as she noticed, pressing herself back against his growing erection.

He wanted her like he'd never wanted a woman before. Dipping his head, he inhaled the aroma of her hair, something sweet and green and fresh, before pressing his lips to her temple.

Her skin was hot beneath his kiss.

"Come with me." He nipped at the top of her ear, his teeth grazing the pink shell as he whispered hotly.

"Where would you take me?" Turning in his arms, she leaned forward and slowly, deliberately rubbed her breasts against his chest. His cock, already swollen, became rock-hard against the stiff denim of his jeans.

"Wherever you want to go." He was serious. He

and Frank had a room at a hotel nearby—his father had consented to this trip, but no way were his sons staying in some hostel like peons. He could take her there, but a woman might not want to go to a hotel alone with a strange man. A car, a tree in a park, right here, right now—it didn't matter to him, not as long as he could taste her.

She didn't reply. Instead, she sank her teeth into her lower lip and looked up at him through that wild tangle of her long lashes. With one hand, she hooked two fingers into the waistband of his jeans, pulling him close, then closer still, flush against his body.

With the other she slowly, tantalizingly, brushed the tips of her fingers over the rigid length of his erection. Stars exploded in his vision, and he exhaled hard, his warm breath misting over the long coils of her black hair.

"Stop." He caught her hand, stilled it. "This should be about you."

"It is." She arched an eyebrow, expression flirtatious. "This is what I want."

Far be it from him to argue with a determined woman. A groan caught in his throat as she repeated the gesture, brushing her knuckles over his rigid length again, this time more firmly. Without even glancing around to see who was watching, she danced her fingers up, then worked them past the waistband of his jeans, rubbing her thumb over the head of his cock.

In the split second before his brain short-circuited, he thought that they couldn't do this, not here in public. Then he realized that the only reason he cared was if she did, which she clearly did not.

She swiped over the head of his cock again, sampling the bead of moisture there before working down farther. As she gripped him with a firm hand, he imagined those roses inked on her fingers, all brushing against the steel rod of his erection.

He couldn't hold back the growl when she closed her fist around him. Her fingers didn't quite reach— he was lucky enough to be big everywhere—so she clamped tightly around him, creating exquisite friction as she moved her hand up and down with a twist of her wrist.

People rocked in close around them. He didn't know if anyone could see what they were doing, and he didn't particularly care. Emboldened by this realization, he moved one of his hands to cup her breast. She pressed against him with a needy roll of her hips as he sampled the plump mound with his hand, stroking outward to the tip. There he toyed experimentally with the nipple, the bar running through it. He knew he didn't imagine the sharp jerk of response as he tugged on it gently, so he did it again, rolling the tip and the jewelry between his long fingers. In response she worked him faster, harder. He hadn't come from a hand job since he was a teenager, but as the pleasure from her hand coursed through him and his vision started to blur, he knew that he was about to make a mess of himself against the soft white skin of her palm, right here, right now.

It wasn't enough. He didn't want to come in her hand, but in the heated cradle between her long, slim thighs. He wanted her naked and spread before him as he sampled her wet heat. He wanted those pretty nipples, tight as rosebuds in his mouth.

Reaching down, he wrapped his hand around her wrist, slowly pulling her busy fingers out of his pants. Sliding his free hand around to the small of her back, he tugged her against him, hard. His erection thickened even further when he felt her lush curves, right there against him.

When she looked up, sharp need in those blue eyes, he claimed her mouth in a kiss. He'd meant to go in gentle, but she gave way so enthusiastically, lips parting for his tongue, that he couldn't help but accept the gift she'd given. He sipped at her, explored, the kiss somehow as dirty as fucking, and when they broke apart a moment later, both gasping for breath, he couldn't think, only feel.

"Come with me," he said for the second time that night.

This time, she did.

PROLOGUE TWO

Five years ago

AMY MARCHANDE WAS on fire.

She wasn't sure what, exactly, had drawn her to the impossibly tall, lean man in the first place. He wasn't her type at all. She usually found herself drawn to men, and the occasional woman, much like herself—a little bit wild, rough around the edges.

There was nothing rough about this man—Fred, his brother had called him—no matter what image he thought he was projecting. Yeah, she'd caught that. She was an artist, after all, and she had spent a good chunk of her life observing—people, places and things. And before she'd even approached him, she'd noticed that he didn't quite blend in the way she was pretty sure he thought he did. His jeans, for instance—they were distressed, but in a way that suggested they'd come that way from the store, not from wear. His T-shirt was simple, but the fabric was thick, better quality than what could be found at a tourist shop. His sneakers, too, were a brand she knew was expensive.

It was more than what he was wearing, too. There was something about his bearing, the way he carried himself, that spoke of confidence, the kind that came from an upbringing of privilege. This wasn't a man who'd ever wanted for anything, who'd ever found a hill that he couldn't climb. Normally that was a trait that got her back up, but for some reason it didn't with Fred. It was interesting. As was the gut punch of attraction she'd felt when she'd looked across the bar and had seen him standing there, watching the crowd. Observing, like she so often did.

In truth, she hadn't even noticed the twin, not until he'd introduced himself. It said something about chemistry, didn't it, that she'd had two identical men in front of her and only wanted the one?

She hadn't been surprised when he'd led her into the Hotel Paris, a deceptively casual-looking accommodation that she knew cost a lot of money. She'd seen that privilege already, after all. She'd fumbled for a moment in the vast expanse of the marble lobby, when she'd caught the eye of a woman dressed in sleek leather pants and a long trench coat, a wealthy woman who'd looked at her wild hair and tattoos with a sneer. Despite her genuine confidence and bravado, the barb had found purchase in her tender flesh, reminding her that she didn't belong here, that this wasn't her world.

Then Fred had run his hand down her arm possessively, and she remembered that she didn't have to belong here, not if she was only staying for a night. So she'd flashed the woman a cocky grin, then placed her hand on Fred's butt as they waited for the elevator. They'd kissed all the way up, slow and dirty. Now, as he tapped the key card on the lock to his room, she felt anticipation lick along her skin like a flame.

It didn't matter that he was clearly from one world, and she from another. What mattered was this, right here and now, in the moment.

"Lights on or off?" he asked as he guided her into the room, which was worlds apart from the hostel. The space was airy and clean, the kind of place that left little mints on your pillow before bed. She caught the upscale scent of lemongrass hanging in the air, and the slight musk of masculine sweat—of Fred.

She didn't answer. Instead she kicked the door closed behind them, pressing until she heard it latch. She looked up, tracing his dim silhouette with her eyes, then tugged her shirt up and over her head, tossing it to the side.

"Jesus." His voice was hoarse, and she felt his stare like a touch. "Where did you come from?"

"From your dreams." She grinned, leaning back

against the door as she slowly undid the zipper of her jeans, working them down her hips, then to the floor. She stepped out, then stood naked but for the scrap of red satin that made up her thong.

She was gratified by his hoarse intake of breath, but when she expected him to move closer, to cup her breasts in his hands, he did neither. Instead, he reached out for one of her hands, tangling their fingers together loosely and tugging her forward.

"Earlier tonight, you asked if I liked to watch." His smile was just the slightest bit crooked, and she ignored the extra little thud of her heart when she acknowledged to herself how cute she found that. His next words, though, weren't cute at all.

"I'd like to watch right now—to watch you come."

She inhaled, her breath shaky. He had no idea how potent he was, this self-assured man with more depth than anyone expected him to have. She might even have been fooled herself, if she couldn't see the gleam of ruthlessness that had come into his eyes in the last few minutes, the same one she'd seen when his twin had tried to claim her.

She had no doubt that most of the world had been lulled into thinking he was easygoing, but she'd uncovered his secret—once he set his mind on something, he would pursue it until he was triumphant. She was only too happy to give herself over to what she was pretty sure were going to be entirely capable hands.

Silently, she made her way to the bed. Arching her back to give him the best view, she knelt on the bed. Gathering her long black hair, she tied it into a knot to show off the arch of her spine, the muscles of her back. She intended to drop down to all fours, to crawl across the bed and tantalize him, but before she could, he was there, his fully clothed front to her naked back.

Saying nothing, he traced a single finger down her spine. The light touch reverberated outward, waking nerve endings she hadn't known were asleep. Leaning back, she savored the sensation of his hard chest pressed against her, then gasped when he slid both hands around to rest, palm down, on the flat expanse of her belly.

"What do you like?" He held her close as he stilled, so still that she could feel the thump of his heartbeat through his chest. She wiggled impatiently against him, but he remained frozen, holding her in place.

"Less talking, more moving." When he remained immovable, she huffed out a breath of impatience. "I like all kinds of things. Why? What do you like?"

A gasp escaped her as his hands moved to her hips, urging her to bend over. She did, stretching her arms out in front of her, her spine elongated with rear canted into the air. He bent over her, pinning her in place, and she savored the weight of him, pressing her down into the mattress.

"I like sex." The wet heat of his voice fanned out over her ear, and she trembled. "That's what I like."

"Isn't that a given?" She heard the quiver in her voice, fought to smooth it out. "I mean, isn't that why we're here?"

"Maybe I'm not making myself clear." His voice was low, amused, shades darker than it had been before she'd been naked and beneath him. "When it comes to sex, I like everything."

"Nobody likes everything." Her voice was breathless, but there was no room for air, not when everything in her core had gathered low and tight. "What's your favorite position? What's your most wicked fantasy? What do you want me to do right now?"

She gasped when he slowly inched his hands up, smoothing over her flesh until they cupped her breasts. She pressed forward into the touch, aching for more.

"You're being very specific." His breath fanned over the top of her head. "I don't know how to explain it further. Whatever your favorite position is? Right now, that's my favorite, too. Your most wicked fantasy? Also mine."

Squeezing her breasts lightly, he flicked the tips between his forefingers and thumbs, the touch combined with her piercings sending shock waves of need through her.

"And what I want you to do right now?" He

pressed a warm, openmouthed kiss to the base of her skull. Amy had never known that the shallow indent could be an erogenous zone. "I want you to tell me what you want."

"I want…" The words, so vibrant in her head, choked when they hit her tongue.

What was wrong with her? She'd never had trouble telling her partners exactly what she did—and didn't—want. Why couldn't she spit it out right now?

Maybe…maybe because there was something happening here that she couldn't put a name to. Something that went beyond a one-night stand.

"I want…" She tried again, then cleared her throat. She wasn't going to let fear keep her from what she really wanted, right this moment. "I want…you."

"Jesus." Before she could say another word, inhale another breath, she found herself flat on her back. She cried out when he tugged her hips toward the edge of the mattress, then knelt on the floor between her spread legs. He made no secret of the intensity with which he studied her center, sending a warm flush over her skin.

His gaze tracked up over her stomach, her breasts, her neck and face to her eyes. When their eyes met, her pulse skittered. Her brain told her that whatever was about to happen was going to change her, but she couldn't—wouldn't—stop.

His hands clasped her on either side of her waist, then slid down. He traced the outsides of her thighs, down to her knees, then moved over and back up the inner planes. When his fingers brushed her outer lips, she shivered, feeling the burn of his skin right through the satin.

He kept his eyes on her face as he lowered his mouth and pressed it to her mound, over her thong. She tensed, shifted her weight beneath him, desperate for more.

"I think what you want me to do right now is to kiss you right here. Over and over, until you come." She felt his words as vibrations on her sensitized flesh. "That means it's what I want, too."

She wanted to reply, to say something that would break through some of the erotic and emotional tension in the room, but her throat was too dry to speak. Instead she nodded, the movement almost frantic.

She closed her eyes, letting her head fall back on the cool sheets as he hooked a finger in the skimpy strings on either side of her thong. She lifted her hips without being told, letting him tug the fabric over her hips and down. He took the time to rub each ankle, each foot as he unhooked them from the garment, finally tossing it to the floor.

She was naked now, completely so. She'd been naked with others before, but she'd never felt this exposed. When he started to trail a finger in looping lines over the flesh of her inner thigh, she knew that he was tracing the lines of the flowers inked there, a single thorny stem that branched out into two red roses in bloom.

Nobody had ever taken the time to admire her ink like this before, not beyond a question or comment or two. It did something to her, knowing he was taking the time to appreciate something that was so intrinsically part of her.

She just hoped he didn't take the time to admire all her other tattoos, not right now. She had enough that it could take all night, and she was running out of patience fast.

Finally. *Finally* he lowered his head. She opened her eyes long enough to catch the greenfire in his eyes just before he placed his mouth on her naked skin.

She gasped as he kissed her, long and slow and wet. His fingers joined his mouth, holding her open so that he could swipe his tongue through her folds. He worked his way up one side, then down the other. Her fingers fisted in the sheets until finally he focused his attention on her clit. She gasped as he moved his tongue over the swollen nub, over and over until her body clenched with the sheer pleasure of it.

"You like that." He hummed with approval, sending shivers through her sensitive flesh, then returned to the long, slow strokes of his tongue. Pleasure slid through her, slow and sinuous like sun on a warm day. She wanted to bask in it, but heat gathered quickly, low and tight in her core. How had he driven her to the edge so fast? It was like he already knew her body, every place to touch that made her gasp and sigh and pant.

"Good girl." Pulling back for a moment, his face wet with her desire, he grinned up at her. "Give us what we both want."

She made a small sound, deep in her throat, as he returned to his work, swirling his tongue around the center of her pleasure, over and over again. If anyone else had called her a good girl, especially when she'd given him the gift of her submission, she would have had her clothes on and been out the door in the next breath. But when Fred said it, she understood that he was actually demonstrating his appreciation for her giving in to the moment. For her submission, though she felt as though she should chafe at the word.

Fred growled. Grabbing her hips, he yanked her even closer to the edge of the bed. Hooking her legs over his broad shoulders, he licked harder, faster, and within moments she was panting, riding that wicked edge of release. It sliced through her like a razor, leaving her gutted and exposed.

Her thighs trembled as he caught her behind each knee, lowering her pelvis gently back to the mattress. Scrambling up the bed on shaky limbs, she settled back on her elbows as he got to his feet.

"Is it my turn to watch now?" Her voice felt as though it was coming from someone else entirely, someone who hadn't just had the biggest orgasm of her life.

"If that's what you want." His smile was wicked as he moved to stand at the end of the bed. Grabbing at the back of the neck of his T-shirt he slowly, slowly pulled it up and off. When he tossed it to the ground, a sound of pure appreciation purred from her lips.

"Wow." Her mouth went dry, and she swallowed painfully as she took in the view in front of her.

"See something you like?" He stood still, letting her drink in the sight. She'd been attracted to his lean frame from first sight, but she'd had no idea that his sweater had been hiding muscles like these. His shoulders were broad, his chest defined. Ripples of incredibly defined ab muscles led the way to a flat stomach that she wanted to lick.

The thing that really made her drool, though, was the smattering of hair on the tight, flat skin of his lower abdomen. His hipbones were sharply defined, like arrows, and wherever they led was a place she wanted to go.

As she watched, he undid the button at his waistband, giving her another inch. Then came the zipper, and the metallic rasp in the otherwise still air was the sexiest thing she'd ever heard, full of promise.

He worked his jeans down until they hung around his hips. Beneath he wore black boxer briefs, and his swollen cock pressed through the slit in the front.

"More." She swallowed, transfixed by the sneak peek of that rigid flesh. "I want more."

"Good girl," he said for the second time that night, and again, she didn't mind. In fact, when said in this man's decadent voice, she fucking loved it. She *was* a good dirty girl, and she wanted to please him so that he would please her. "I like the way you're looking at me."

"I can't help it." She groaned when he slid his boxers down, too, working everything down to the ground, where he stepped out of his clothes and kicked them aside. "I want you."

"What do you want, exactly?" Eyes still on her, he wrapped his large hand around his equally big erection. She thought she might self-combust when he slid his hand up and down, and then again, fisting himself just for her. "This? Is this what you want?"

"Yes." The word came out on a hiss. She watched as he climbed onto the bed, kneeling overtop of her, one knee on either side of hers. He was still stroking himself, and now that he was closer, she could see the droplet of arousal, shiny against the stretched skin of the head of his cock. Before she knew what she was doing, she'd pushed herself to a sitting position and reached out for him. She ran a thumb through the dampness, then brought it to her lips.

Salt and musk ran over her tongue as she licked the digit, smiling at the curse he muttered in return.

"You little witch." He watched as she fisted her sweaty hands in the cool sheets, restless and desperate, watching as he retrieved a condom from the jeans he'd tossed to the floor. Tearing into the foil with his teeth, he removed the tube of latex. Pinching the tip, he placed the ring over the head of his cock, then rolled it down the thick length. She thought she might stroke out from the sight, and from the fact that he hadn't even asked if she wanted him to use one—he just did it.

Bending at the waist, he prowled over her, forcing her to lie back, her head on the pillows. He braced himself above her, though she was caged in by the defined arms on either side of her head. She arched her hips up to meet his, and they both moaned at the delicious contact.

She expected him to slide inside her then—was desperate for him to do just that. What she was not prepared for was a kiss—and what a kiss it was. Tangling long fingers through the raven-dark ribbons of her dreads, he tugged gently as he took her mouth roughly, awakening nerve endings in both places. She gasped into his mouth as her tongue met his own, as he explored her lips, her teeth, like he might never get the chance to again.

He kissed her until something liquid and golden began to flow through her veins, an ambrosia that mixed with the need that was riding her to become the most exquisite kind of longing she'd ever experienced. She couldn't look away from those brilliant, bottle green eyes when they finally broke the kiss, breathing on her own a strange sensation after inhaling as one.

Reaching between them, he lined up his rigid shaft with her swollen heat, rubbing the tip back and forth through her wetness. One thrust of his hips and he was in, moving slowly but steadily forward until he'd hilted inside her.

"Jesus." She rocked her hips up against him and had the pleasure of watching his eyes cross. "You're big everywhere, aren't you?"

He huffed out a laugh as he lowered his torso over hers. The friction of her pierced nipples against his chest sent a jolt through her system, and she arched up against him, seeking more. Bracing his weight on one arm, he used the other to cup one of her aching breasts, his fingers toying with its tip. She could have stayed like that all night, the twin jolts of pleasure-pain working her to a frenzy, but he shifted inside her. She caught her breath at the new angle.

"That's it," he murmured as she reached up to clutch at his back, her fingers digging into the muscle until he hissed. The dark glittering of his eyes that accompanied the sound told her he liked it, so she did it again, raking her nails down his back as he started to move more insistently inside her. "Come for me."

"I think it's your turn." Still, she clung to him as sensation started to tighten in her core once again. Releasing her breast, he worked his hands between her ass and the bed. He cupped the globes of flesh, pulling her so tightly against him that she gasped, then rolled. His cock inside her touched nerve endings she hadn't even known she had as he settled on his back with her astride him. She felt his hot stare on her breasts like a touch as his hands found her hips.

Wrapping long fingers around each curve, he urged her to move, faster and then faster still. She did with quick movements of her hips that had her clit grazing the flat plane of his pelvis with each thrust.

Her pace quickly became erratic as sparks lit at the tips of her fingers, in her toes and in her center. They heated, bursting into flame as they moved inward, bathing her body with heat. When they reached her core, she shuddered as all the small flames combined to form one, a great fire that roared to life and swallowed her whole.

She shuddered through one orgasm, and when she would have slid off Fred, boneless from release, he found her clit with his thumb, circling quickly and wringing one more wave from her body. This time, as she clenched around him, slick and tight, he let go, too. His hands on her hips urged her on as he thrust up into her heat, a dozen thrusts made sloppy by the drive for release. He shouted as he came, and when she would have closed her eyes, he met her stare with his own. She couldn't look away as their bodies moved in sync, shuddering through the most intense joining she'd ever experienced.

They each stilled, still joined, skin damp with sweat. She still couldn't look away from him, bound by some invisible thread, the same one that had led her to see him across the club, to approach him, to come here to his hotel.

Since her first few relationships, she'd understood that what drew people to one another wasn't always equal. There were a million different shades of attraction, of like and love and lust. She didn't believe in soul mates, either, the notion that there was only one special person out there that could complete her. Instead she thought it likely that there was more than one person in the world who could brighten her life, even if it wasn't forever. She also understood, however, that that kind of connection, the bone-deep pull toward another human, was rare. Incredibly so.

And now here she was, in her early twenties in Amsterdam, on a trip that was supposed to be full of fun and exploration, and one of those bonds had sneaked up to slap her in the face.

She wanted it, craved it and wasn't even a little bit ready for it.

Finally closing her eyes, she broke the physical link, sliding off him to lie down on the bed. She listened to him rise, pad across the floor to dispose of the condom, sip from a bottle of water, then climb back into the bed with her. She kept her eyes averted as he lay on his side, pulling her in close to him, their chests touching.

She wanted to run even as she craved the feel of his skin on hers.

Taking in the bursts of light and sound from the street that cut through the darkness of the room intermittently, she lay there with her pulse pounding. She could feel him watching her but kept her gaze focused on his chest. She didn't want to see her own spinning thoughts staring back at her from someone else's eyes.

That…what they'd just done…that was more than sex. That had been life-changing.

She didn't want her life changed.

"What do you want?" His breath was cool on her damp forehead.

She couldn't bring herself to reply, so she shook her head instead.

"I want something," he started, shifting closer on the bed. She could smell his skin, his sweat, the heady miasma of sex in the air. "I want to know your name. I want to know it more than anything in the world."

How was it possible that he didn't know her name? That he didn't know her birthday, or how many sisters she had? How could he not know all the things that outlined her life, when he'd just looked inside her, down to the rhythm of her heart inside her chest, and had seen everything that made her who she was?

If she gave him her name, it would take this to another level. One she wasn't ready for. Rather than replying, she gave a purposefully sleepy hum and pretended to fall asleep.

She lay still for a long time, savoring the sensation of his skin on hers. When his breathing deepened, the body against hers relaxing into sleep, she slipped out of the bed slowly, carefully, so that she didn't wake him up.

She shivered as she picked up the discarded items of her clothing, the night air cool on skin that had so recently been hot and flushed from sex. She dressed quickly, but after she'd tugged on her boots, she indulged in one final look.

Awake, Fred was a force of nature, charisma coming off him in waves, charming those who came close enough to be tugged inward by his magnetic pull. Asleep, she could focus on the sheer physical perfection of him. That impossibly tall body, leanly muscled, that she'd quivered beneath. The aristocratic planes of his face, the fan of eyelashes on his cheeks, darker than the auburn of his hair. Redheads—gingers—were often the target of jokes in Europe, but as far as Amy was concerned, he couldn't have had any other coloring and been nearly as appealing.

She hadn't bothered donning her ruined thong when she dressed again, and it dangled from her finger as she took one last, lingering glance. If this had been anyone else, any other night of fun sex, she would have left it behind, a sexy little memento to fuel the fantasies of both parties for months to come. She considered this for a moment, then tucked it into her pocket.

Best not to leave any trace. Not this time.

It was time to go. With her hand on the doorknob, though, she paused and turned back. She argued with herself for a long moment, then gave in to her own rampant curiosity. With a quick glance at the bed, she hurried to his suitcase. Her fingers found the luggage tag quickly, even in the dark, and she waited for one of the lights from outside to break through the room so that she could see.

Fred Vaughan. Street address in a fancy part of Boston that she'd never even been to. She'd already known he was from one of those families, the ones that bled blue beneath pampered skin, but seeing it confirmed gave her a little clutch around her heart.

Even if she wanted what had just happened to change her life—and she didn't—this would never work. Not outside the bedroom, no matter how earth-shattering it had been.

Dropping the tag, she swallowed thickly, then

hurried back to the door. This time she didn't allow herself a look back at the man sleeping in the bed behind her, instead opening the door as quietly as she could before slipping through and jogging back to the elevator.

If her heart hurt a little as she left behind a connection she'd never encountered before? Well, that was nobody's fault but her own.

CHAPTER ONE

FRED VAUGHAN HAD walked by Four Sisters Ink a million times, but until now, he'd never been inside. He didn't relish his errand today, and the letter felt hot against the skin of his palm. To his way of thinking, the tenant the letter was intended for didn't deserve it, but he'd drawn the short stick, so here he was.

Despite the letter, he wasn't actually sure what he was about to encounter. He'd never been in one, but when he thought *tattoo parlor*, his brain conjured images of walls covered in graffiti, chairs with naked people getting skulls and broken hearts etched indelibly on their skin. Blaring metal music, drugs and alcohol. Looking down at his seven-hundred-dollar Italian leather shoes, he acknowledged that he was likely going to stick out from the moment he walked in. Rather than the expected metal music, though, soft bells chimed overhead as he entered, brushing the top of his head since he'd forgotten to duck. He paused just inside the door, blinking, as he tried to make expectation merge with reality.

This—the interior of Four Sisters Ink—was a surprise. A shock.

He was familiar with the basic blueprint—every space in the plaza offered similar bones. Four walls, a soaring ceiling, laminate flooring that mimicked hardwood remarkably well and would hold up to traffic far better. Since its opening, he'd been impressed with the way each business had taken the basic space and made it into its own, but this…this struck him as something special.

Each of the four walls was a different soothing color—ivory, soft pink, mauve, creamy orchid. The shifting palette of colors added visual interest yet was simple enough to not take away from the gallery walls. Each wall was hung, floor to ceiling, with elegantly arranged art. With that many frames, he expected them to be plastic, purchased in bulk from some big box store, but when he looked closer, he noted that each slender square was wood, the grain visible through a walnut stain.

Again, he was surprised, and also a little bit impressed, something that wasn't all that easy to do. Not as a member of his family.

Taking a few steps farther inside, he squinted, examining the walls, and saw that the pieces were grouped by type—something he thought was oil paint, watercolor, pastel and ink. Displaying them in homogenous groups was eye-catching in a subtle yet deliberate way, much like the different-colored walls.

Whoever owned Four Sisters Ink knew what she was doing.

Charcoal, dove gray and cream paper lanterns were clustered overhead, with small white fairy lights snaking around them. The fairy lights should have looked cheap, like the interior of a college dorm room, but they were charming instead. A massive bamboo room divider cut the room in half, adding to the bohemian vibe, and the whole place smelled like a spa, some kind of diffuser puffing away in a corner to cover up the very faint scent of rubbing alcohol that he could still detect. The music was quiet but energetic, and after he cocked his head to listen, he recognized an '80s classic by Rick Astley, which shouldn't have worked with the serene space but somehow did.

Against his better judgment, he was impressed. He didn't want to be impressed. It wouldn't help what he was here to do.

"Be with you in a moment!" The female voice was low and husky. Something in it caught his attention, snagged at his memory. Turning toward the back of the shop, he watched the hints of movement behind the latticed room divider. He took a step back, looking around the room at the range of art, which suddenly seemed familiar, too.

This couldn't possibly be what his brain was suddenly insistent that it was. But then the woman came around the corner—a woman he'd never forget.

She blinked, and he saw what he was feeling reflected back at him from her face—for a moment, at least. Then her expression shuttered, and he was left reeling.

"You're Amy Marchande?" He winced as he spoke—he sounded like an idiot. But his mind was whirling, past and present colliding in neon color... at least, until she spoke again.

"What are you doing here?" She frowned, crossing her arms over her chest. He opened his mouth to speak, then closed it again, taking a moment to look at her—just to look.

Her shop might look more like a spa than a tattoo parlor, but she fit his image of a stereotypical tattoo artist perfectly. She was tall and slender, with a slim waist and hips and breasts that he knew damn well fit perfectly in his palms. Her skin, naturally a pale white, was covered in ink, most of it black and white, with the exception of some watercolor flowers. More ink than he remembered.

The biggest difference from past to present was her hair. Last time he'd seen her, she'd worn it in inky-black curls that reached her waist. Now it was a golden color that he suspected was natural, loose curls that barely reached her chin, as though she was growing it out.

As he stared, he noticed two more things. One, she wasn't wearing a bra beneath her thin white cotton tank top. And two, she still had barbells pierced through her nipples. He had a bright flash of memory, of one of those decorations caught in his teeth as she writhed on top of him, and perspiration broke out along his hairline.

"Why are you here?" She arched a thin, groomed eyebrow. Her smirk told him she'd noticed his perusal of her body. He also noticed that she didn't give him one in return. "*How* are you here? Five years is a bit long to wait before you start stalking somebody."

Seeing her again was a vibrant, memory-drenched blow to his solar plexus. Seeing him again, though? She didn't seem fazed at all. Irritated, if anything.

"Uh…" For a moment he was tongue-tied, swallowing against a suddenly dry mouth. He didn't know what to do with himself, and that was unusual for him.

He couldn't say that he cared for it, either.

"I'm assuming this isn't a social call?" She cast him that challenging little curve of her lips again, the one that made him want to give her mouth something better to do.

"What do you mean?" He smiled at her assuredly, the same smile he used in the courtroom. As he did, he slipped the warning letter from Vaughan

Enterprises into the inner pocket of his suit jacket. He hadn't felt great about delivering it before he'd walked in, and he'd be damned if he was going to be the one to give the bad news to the one woman he hadn't been able to get out of his mind since their one night together, five years ago.

He needed to think about this.

"It means that I highly doubt you're here for anything I have to offer." She laced her hands behind her back, then stretched, and it was difficult to keep his mind on the conversation, rather than her breasts and their naughty adornments.

"Why would you assume that?" He frowned, vaguely insulted. "Maybe I am here for a tattoo. Why else would I be here?"

She frowned slightly, and it was his turn to smirk—he'd stumped her. Then she shrugged and pointed at one of her walls with a graceful arm.

"That's the inspiration wall." She smiled benignly as she called his bluff. "Those are ink renderings of the best of the tattoos that I've done. Pick out a few you like and we'll work out a design for you."

"Ah..." He felt his eyes widen as he stumbled over his words. Damn it.

"Unless you already know what you want?" She cocked her head, studying him, clearly amused. She was enjoying this.

"Oh, I know what I want." He slid his hands into

the pockets of his suit pants, then fixed his gaze on her. The cocky set of her lips faded, and unless he was very much mistaken, she exhaled slowly.

"Well, then." She ran a tongue over those full lips, and he was again transported back in time. He remembered looking down at her as those petal-inked curves wrapped around his cock. "Why wait? Let's get you in the chair and get started."

"Don't you already have someone back there?" He looked past Amy to the room divider, saw the movements of someone still back there.

"Oh, Sallie's done for today." Her smile was a swallowed-the-canary smirk. "Lucky for you."

"You know, I need to think about my, ah, design a bit more." He nodded, punctuating his words. Gone was the collected lawyer, the reserved man with roots dating back to the *Mayflower*, just at being around her. How was it that she could still do that?

"Sure you will." She continued to watch him with that unnerving stare, and he felt himself respond, something sparking along his skin. He met her gaze, his own green eyes looking into her blue ones—a deep navy blue, startlingly dark against her porcelain skin.

He sucked in a breath. As he did, he thought he saw her do the same, and he understood. He hadn't seen her—hadn't touched her—in years, but that animal attraction they'd experienced on their first and only night together had transcended time. He wanted her again—still.

"I'll be back," he repeated firmly, and he knew that his meaning was clear. He'd be back not for a tattoo, but for her.

Thoroughly unsettled, he turned on his heel, heading for the door. His entire world had been turned upside down in the space of ten minutes, and he needed to go think on how the hell he was going to manage this.

"Hey." Her voice stopped him with one foot out the door. Melodious brass bells tinkled over his head as he paused, looking back at where she still stood. "The only thing you wanted that night was to know my name. I guess now you do."

"That wasn't the only thing I wanted." He felt the satisfaction of watching her flush, a cloud of pink infusing that porcelain skin. A tendril of triumph snaked through him, letting him edge closer to the control he craved. He scrambled his way back onto solid ground. He winked at her, then exited Four Sisters Ink. Once outside, he exhaled a deep breath he hadn't known he was holding.

He'd gone to serve Four Sisters Ink with an official warning from Vaughan Enterprises Retail Plaza. Other vendors had circulated a petition protesting the presence of a tattoo shop among the luxury stores and upscale restaurants. As the in-house lawyer, it was up to him to inform the proprietor.

That the proprietor was the woman he'd had an epic, nameless (on her side, at least), European one-night stand with years ago? A night he'd never been able to get out of his mind?

Fate was a cruel bitch. And he was absolutely, completely, one hundred percent fucked.

CHAPTER TWO

AMY SAT ON the wicker bench that she'd placed outside the entrance to her shop on the day she'd opened. In her hand was a cold bottle of beer that she'd taken from the minifridge in her back room. Open alcohol wasn't allowed in the open-air plaza, not outside the restaurants, but it was after hours, twilight settling in. Also, she just didn't really care.

The slight buzz allowed her to let go of the tension that had been riding her since her surprise visitor earlier. Her feelings were still a hot tangle, and she didn't know how she would even begin to sort through the snarl.

Fred freaking Vaughan. She'd started her business five years ago out of a cramped room in Boston's Jamaica Plain. She'd sought out a new location because she'd wanted to have a space to display her paper and canvas artwork as well as the designs that she inked onto skin. The fancy seaside shopping plaza had been an unlikely location for a tattoo shop, but she'd known what she wanted and had moved in six months ago. It had been a gamble, but it had paid off in spades. Her clientele now ranged from serious ink junkies to celebrities who booked their time with her months in advance. Her neighbors in the luxury plaza didn't love her presence there, but that wasn't her problem.

What *was* her problem, though? The fact that she apparently leased her space from the one man she'd never been able to get out of her mind.

Vaughan Enterprises. Fred Vaughan. She'd never put that together, but why would she have? Vaughan was a common enough name, and their tryst had occurred an ocean away. The chance that they'd come back into one another's lives was infinitesimally small.

And yet, there he'd been, standing in the entrance to her shop, as commanding as if he owned the place. Which, she supposed, he kinda did.

She'd looked up Vaughan Enterprises after he'd left. It was a family empire that had existed for three generations. They owned retail spaces, mostly malls and shopping plazas, all over the Eastern Seaboard. Fred Vaughan and his twin, Frank, were members of the youngest generation—Fred a high-powered in-house lawyer, and his identical twin some kind of acquisitions wizard.

She'd met them both that long-past night in Europe. It had amazed her that she could be faced with mirror-image faces, matching lean and lanky bodies, and only feel a gut punch of attraction to one.

Sipping her beer, she let her mind wander back to that night, something she rarely allowed herself. She'd been in Amsterdam on a sponsored, six-month tattoo internship. *Sponsored* was a loose term, too—she'd had an online flirtation with the sponsoring artist. He'd invited her to visit, to learn under him in more ways than one. He'd been far more interesting online than in person, however, so she'd broken off the romantic part of their arrangement after a month. She'd stayed on with the artistic side, learning from someone who might have been a crappy lover but was indeed a talented artist.

She'd been poor as hell, living in a hostel down the street from the shop some nights, sleeping on her tattoo chair others. Poor didn't mean miserable, though—she'd loved Amsterdam, the freedom of it, the fact that no one looked at her strangely for being a white girl with dreaded hair, or for having more skin that was inked than not. Nobody cared if she went home with boys or with girls or with both. She'd had the time of her life, exploring who she really was.

This was why she'd been so surprised to find herself in one of her favorite bars, part of a group of people that included, for that evening at least, two American travelers...one of whom caught her eye the way none of the free-spirited locals or Zen backpackers already had. She remembered sidling over to the pair, who were attracting no end of attention with their six-foot-four-inch heights and dark red hair, but there had really only been one for her.

There had only been Fred.

Footsteps sounded, pulling her back from her reminiscing. She took another large gulp of beer before sitting up straight on the bench, anticipation coursing through her veins.

A large herd of men in suits tended to strut by her shop about an hour after the plaza closed for the evening. Her space was near the entrance/exit that was closest to the executive parking lot, and she imagined that they were returning to their leased Mustangs, ready to jet off for dinner with pedigreed fiancées or clandestine town house meetings with mistresses. None of her business, and she'd never before cared.

Not until this afternoon, when it had occurred to her that Fred might be one of these suits. Though if he'd walked past her before, she wasn't sure how she hadn't noticed him.

She cocked her head to listen, her heart in her throat. One set of footprints approached—just one. She held her breath as Fred Vaughan came into view—he was unaccompanied.

Somehow, she'd known he would come. And she'd known he would be alone.

"Open alcohol on plaza premises is a seventy-five-dollar fine." He stopped in front of her, hands in the pockets of his suit pants. At five foot ten, she was a tall woman, but being seated while she looked up at his impressive height made her feel like a dainty fucking flower.

"You going to report me?" Lifting her beer to her lips, she took a large, deliberate swallow. He watched her, and she looked at him, letting her stare rake over him the way she hadn't earlier.

In her memory, he wore worn jeans and a T-shirt an outfit that had let him blend in well enough with everyone else. Now, he was wearing a suit that fit him so well she was certain it was custom-made. And she couldn't deny that he wore the hell out of it.

Her mouth went dry, so she took another sip of her drink. She was surprised—shocked, even—when he reached out and tugged the beer bottle out of her hand.

"Cockblocking my good time." She shook her head in mock exasperation. "Figures."

Rather than pitching it in the nearby trash can, as she expected him to, he merely arched an eyebrow and took a drink himself. She found herself transfixed to see his lips press against the glass where hers had just been. The way the muscles of his throat moved as he swallowed made her mouth water.

Shit. She was in so, so much trouble.

"If I remember correctly, I didn't block your good

time." He handed the bottle back to her, and her skin sizzled when his long fingers brushed against hers. "I made it even better."

Shit.

"You weren't here earlier because you want a tattoo," she blurted out, caught off guard by the punch of unadulterated lust. "I call bullshit."

"You got me." The hand that had been holding her beer reached up, loosening the knot of his tie. He followed up the movement by unbuttoning the top two buttons of his dress shirt, and Amy fought back a whimper.

What the hell was it about him? She'd been with men. She'd been with women. She'd had some good sex and some great sex.

So what was it about this particular man? She wanted him now like she'd wanted him five years ago. And she'd never been particularly good at denying herself the things that she wanted.

"Why were you here, then?" She stood up, trying to gain more control over the situation. Since he still had six inches on her, all it did was bring her right into his kinesphere.

It still made her shiver.

"Five years ago, you kept your name a secret from me." He spoke in slow, measured words, stare on her face. "No matter how much I begged. I think it's my turn to keep a secret."

"The difference being that I won't beg." Amy

heard the breathlessness in her own words, felt promise shiver up her spine as his light green eyes darkened to the color of sea glass. He reached out with one of those massive palms of his, traced a finger along the curve of her jaw.

"I think your memory is failing you." His finger moved over her chin, up to press against her lips. Her tongue darted out, swiping over it, tasting the salt of his skin. It made need tighten in her core. "I've made you beg before. And I promise you, I can make it happen again."

CHAPTER THREE

AMY SET HER beer down on the bench, then took his hand and led him inside Four Sisters. He sniffed for the spa-like scent he'd detected earlier. The diffuser-type thing still puffed away in the corner, but she'd changed the scent to something smokier. Something that made him think of sex.

Who was he kidding? Just being in the same room as her made him think of sex.

His back was to the door. When she turned back to slide the dead bolt on the door home, her chest brushed against him. He thought of those damn barbells in her nipples and was hard in an instant, a fact he couldn't have hidden and didn't want to, the way his pelvis was flush against the flat planes of her stomach.

"Well, well." Her voice was soft and rough, reminding him of the mountains he'd trekked on the same trip where he'd met her. "Looks like I might not be the one doing the begging after all."

"To hell with that." Bending his knees, he cupped the curves of her delectable ass in his hands. She cried out when he lifted her right off her feet. Her legs twined around his waist as he carried her forward through her shop. She groaned, rocking her lithe body against his, and he swore under his breath when he felt her molten core make contact with his rock-solid length.

He carried her past the bamboo room divider, then deposited her in her tattoo chair. It was black leather with a headrest and was already reclined—it couldn't have been more perfect. She landed on her knees, reaching up for him, tugging on the knot of his tie until it came loose. He let it fall to the floor as she reached for the zipper of his suit pants. His eyes crossed when her nimble fingers brushed against the head of his cock.

"Liked that, did you?" Her voice was a self-satisfied hum as she reached into his trousers and wrapped around his erection. "Jesus."

"You can call me that any time you want." He huffed out a breath as she explored his length, working gently up and down.

"I'd say you have a big head." She circled a thumb over his tip, caught the droplet of moisture beading there. "But is it a big head if it's justified?"

"Fuck." He halted his movements for a moment to let her play. Arousal built at the base of his spine as she danced those elegant fingers over his shaft.

Finally he could take it no more and moved back, out of her reach.

"You're playing with fire," he warned her as he undid the buttons of his work shirt. He felt her avid gaze as he worked it over his wide shoulders, then let it fall to the floor. With her eyes on him, he lowered his pants, his underwear until they were around his hips, then wrapped his own hand around the base of his cock. "Undress for me. Now."

"Bossy as ever, aren't you?" Her words were a challenge, but her movements weren't. Still on her knees, she fisted her hands in the hem of her tank top, then lifted it up and over her head, tossing it across the room. He groaned as her breasts filled his vision, those magnificent, adorned breasts that had haunted both his dreams and his nightmares.

"I want to come on those fantastic tits," he promised her, running his hand up and then down his erection. Her avid gaze followed the movements as she cupped her own breasts in her hands, squeezing them together.

"Do it." Her voice was breathless and she climbed from the chair, setting her feet on the floor. In one quick movement, she'd worked her torn jeans down over her hips, all the way down the floor. She stepped out, then stood before him, blissfully naked, her decorated skin open to his gaze.

The piercings through her nipples were something he remembered, but there was a hoop in her navel that was new. He watched her run her hands over her torso, tugged on the barbells, and knew that he wasn't going to last long. Not when the object of every fantasy he'd had for the past five years was here in front of him, tantalizing him in the flesh.

Without speaking, he closed the space between them. Rather than pushing her down into the chair, he sat down himself. Reaching for her slim waist, he tugged her toward him, arranging her knees on either side of his.

"Next time," he promised as he lay back, tugging her astride him until she balanced on her knees, which rested on either side of his hips. "Right now I need you to ride me. Ride my cock until you scream."

She gasped, fire sparking in her blue eyes. Sliding up his body, she took him in her hand, then pressed the head of his arousal against her wet slit. She was wet and hot and he couldn't help himself— he arched his hips upward, his swollen head working its way inside her far enough to make her gasp at the intrusion.

"Fuck." Her voice was a moan. Her head lolled back as she clenched around him. She was tight, even tighter than he remembered, so he dug his fingers into the flesh of her hips and willed himself to be patient.

She shocked the hell out of him when she pressed herself downward. She took three-quarters of his length in with one movement, sending stars spinning in his vision. She bore down, beads of sweat breaking out along her forehead, but seemed stuck until he slid a hand between them, rubbing his large thumb over the center of her pleasure.

She cried out, melting around him, and he seated himself inside her. They froze for a moment, his green eyes looking into her blue, as though neither could believe that this was finally happening, after so many years and so many dirty, filthy dreams.

She seemed at a loss for words, and he understood that this wasn't usual for her. He loved that, loved being the one to make this incredibly strong, mouthy woman lose control.

Circling his thumb over her clit, he watched her eyes blur, then took over all control.

"Move." He surged upward into her and savored the vibration of her gasp. "Move on me."

He expected her to argue, to open that sassy mouth. A delicious thrill skirted down his spine when she did nothing of the sort, instead doing what he'd ordered and feeding into his arousal.

He worked her clit with his thumb until he felt her tighten around him, her knees digging into his sides, her heat holding him tight. He moved faster, harder, and when she clenched around him and cried out, satisfaction that he'd brought her pleasure brought his own arousal soaring sky-high.

Before she could regain her senses, he slid his hands up to her waist and over her rib cage to cup her breasts. Fuck, but he'd dreamed of these fantastic tits of hers. Never in his life had he considered himself even the least bit wild—the Vaughan family didn't do wild—but something about those heavy mounds of flesh, with the silver barbells piercing her taut nipples—it turned him on like nothing he'd ever experienced before.

He couldn't help himself. Catching the adornments in his fingers, he tugged on them and watched her eyes cross as the pleasure-pain swept over her. She shuddered, and he rolled her nipples in his fingers. Without warning, she cried out again, the cleft between her legs contracting and squeezing his cock so tightly that he couldn't hold out anymore.

His orgasm started at the base of his spine, spreading outward until his entire body was caught in the throes of pleasure. He rode the waves with his stare fastened on hers, the two of them shuddering as they came together, each of them ratcheting the other higher with just the memories and fantasies that hovered in the thick, sex-smelling air between them.

Earlier that afternoon, he'd left Four Sisters Ink knowing that he was in trouble.

Now, as he urged the woman of his dreams to ride the last waves of her own pleasure on his cock, milking his own orgasm from his flesh...

He was pretty sure that his life was about to change forever.

CHAPTER FOUR

S<small>HE REMEMBERED NOW.</small>

She remembered why she'd run away from Fred that night so many years ago. She'd gone into the encounter thinking of sex as something fun, a physical release. Sex with Fred, however, had cracked open her rib cage and given him access to her trembling heart. If he'd taken that heart and squeezed it in a fist, she might have been able to tuck her emotions away again, but instead he'd cupped it tenderly, as though it was meant to be treasured.

It had scared the hell out of her and had sent her running away before he could do so much as cajole her name out of her, let alone a phone number. She hadn't thought she'd ever see him again, yet here he was.

Cracking her wide-open yet again. *Nope, nope, nope.*

"That was fun." She slid down off him, not an easy task given the sheer size of him. He propped himself up on his elbows, watching as she gathered her tank top and jeans and started to dress herself, movements brisk. "I've got work to do now, though."

She wasn't looking directly at him—that was rather like looking straight at the sun—but she watched his brow furrow in her peripheral vision. He moved slowly, languidly, as though he was feeling as sleepy and sated as she was.

Turning her head slightly, she watched as he hiked his pants back up to his waist, securing them with a fancy-looking leather belt. His stomach was flat, striped with more abs than a man who wore a suit for a living should have. His chest was also hard, dusted with reddish-gold hair, and the sheer size of everything about him made her mouth water all over again. It also had anxiety coiling in her stomach.

It might have been five years since that first encounter, but she didn't feel any more ready for these feelings than she had back then. So even though she knew it wasn't great manners to kick him out right after sex—a reverse wham, bam, thank you ma'am—she needed some space, and she needed it now.

She opened her mouth to tell him he needed to go, but before she could get out a word, he closed the space between them. With two fingers underneath her chin, he claimed her mouth once again in a kiss, hot and wet and nearly as dirty as sex. Her brain short-circuited, so that when he stepped back, she could only blink up at him with dazed eyes.

"I'll see you soon." It wasn't a question but a statement. He cast her that devastating grin that had once brought her to her knees, then turned on his heel and left her shop. The bells hanging in the doorway tinkled merrily as his head brushed the top of them—good Lord, he was tall.

And then he was gone. Her breath exhaled on a whoosh, and her knees suddenly felt like they could no longer support her. She sank down into her tattoo chair, rising again when something crinkled under her weight.

It was a sealed white envelope, the kind with the little plastic window in the front. Beneath that plastic was her name and the name of her shop, in official type.

She knew the envelope hadn't been there before Fred, so he must have left it, which seemed odd. Still, it had her name on it, so she shrugged and slit the paper open.

It was a letter printed on official Vaughan Enterprises letterhead, and signed, Fred Vaughan—In-House Counsel. She scanned the contents once, then returned to the beginning and read it again more slowly as her teeth started to grind together in irritation. By the time she pulled out her phone to Face-Time her sister Meg, she was ready to breathe fire.

"Uh-oh." Meg's face morphed from a happy smile to instant concern when she saw Amy's expression. "What's wrong?"

"What would you do if you slept with someone and then found a letter from him kicking you out of your business location?"

"Shut up." Meg's gasp was all Amy needed to hear. "Is he still breathing?"

"I didn't find it until after he left." Amy frowned. "I don't think he meant to leave it."

"Hold up." Meg put her phone down for a moment, and Amy heard the low rumble of her sister's boyfriend John's voice. When Meg reappeared, her cheeks were flushed. "Okay, what am I missing?"

"It seems that the mall I leased my space from is owned by the family of a guy I had a one-night stand when I was in Europe." Pushing off from the chair, Amy started to pace. "I had no idea until he came in today. When I recognized him, he said he wanted a tattoo, but I'm guessing he was here to give me this letter."

"Why the hell would he be kicking you out?" Meg's brow furrowed. "You're booked solid. You bring people in."

"Seems the other retailers don't like my *aesthetic*." Amy smiled without mirth. "They signed a petition."

Meg swore, the colorful word echoing Amy's own thoughts. Fred didn't owe her anything, but to find out that he'd had this letter in his pocket when he'd pulled her astride him?

Not. Cool.

"What are you going to do?" Meg sank her teeth into her lower lip as she thought.

"TPing his office seems a bit juvenile, but it might be satisfying." Amy smirked when her oldest sister snorted.

"Getting him drunk and tattooing a penis on his forehead is probably illegal, huh?" Meg rolled her eyes. "All the fun things are."

"I think I need... I need some kind of event. Something that will bring in people, a lot of people, as a reminder of what I bring to this place." Amy pursed her lips as she concentrated. "But also something that gets under his skin. Which shouldn't be hard. He's one of those uptight suits. No offense to John."

"Mmm, those uptight suits are always the best in bed." Meg sighed dreamily, stopping when she caught Amy's pointed glare. "Sorry, kiddo. Thinking cap on. Um...if this was my catering company, I'd probably set something up outside the front door. Like a party, maybe. And advertise to draw people in."

"A party," Amy repeated as the idea took root in her mind. "I think you're on to something. I have to think a bit. But I know one thing for sure."

"What's that?" On the screen, her sister bit into a

cookie, reminding Amy that she hadn't eaten since breakfast herself. She ignored the rumbles of her stomach, though, chasing the tendril of the idea before it floated away.

"He's not going to be able to pretend that this letter doesn't exist anymore."

CHAPTER FIVE

"I STILL DON'T understand why you deleted that waitress's number, man." Andy, one of the new interns at Vaughan Enterprises, shook his head as he and Fred made their way from the parking lot and into the plaza. "She was so hot."

"I wasn't interested," Fred repeated, his teeth grinding together of their own accord. His father, Fred Sr., had tasked Fred with taking his new intern out for lunch to welcome him to the office. Fred hadn't been thrilled, because the new guy grated on his nerves, but hey, it was part of his job.

If Andy—or was it Randy?—didn't shut up about the waitress, or about *hot chicks* in general, though, Fred might just have to give in to the urge to dump the fresh grad into the nearby fountain.

"If you didn't want her, you could have at least given her number to me," Andy-Randy grumbled, flicking his thumb and forefinger together to the beat of music that was steadily growing louder as they walked. Fred recognized the song as Tiffany—

it was going to be stuck in his head all day now. "I could have shown her a good time."

"Are you serious?" Fred stopped in his tracks, looking down at the younger man and not bothering to hide the disgust on his face. "If she'd wanted you to have her number, then she would have given it to you. What is wrong with you?"

Andy-Randy rolled his eyes, then jerked his chin toward the first row of shops. "Hey, what's going on over there?"

Fred followed the direction of his gaze. A long line of people snaked around a corner, some dancing to the music that was now loud and clear. He mentally ran through the list of nearby shops to think who could possibly have generated so much traffic. Not the luggage place, or the one that sold imported perfume and gave him a headache. The cupcakes at the bakery were actually pretty gross, so probably not them, either. Which left…

Amy. It left Amy.

Memories of the night before flooded his mind. The way she'd climbed astride him and taken what she wanted from him was the sexiest thing he'd experienced since…well, since *her*.

He wasn't overly bothered by the way she'd kicked him out immediately after, either. He'd felt it, too—that click between them. He'd felt it five years ago, just a flicker—a spark. Last night that spark had ignited, and he knew he wasn't the only one who'd felt it.

She'd needed some space, and he'd given it to her. But he'd be damned if he was going to let her push him away entirely. Anticipation quickened his steps—every cell in his body perked up at the thought of seeing her.

When they rounded the corner, he saw that the lineup indeed started at Four Sisters Ink. Amy was up to something. What was going on?

With Andy-Randy stuck to his side like a thorn, Fred inched his way toward the front of the line, looking for her. As he neared the front of the line, he noticed that everyone was glued to their phone. Not unusual, but he managed to catch a glimpse over a burly man's shoulder and saw what everyone was flipping through—black-and-white tattoo designs.

The anticipation he'd felt at the opportunity to see Amy was instantly tempered with the sudden flare of impending doom. He was pretty sure that, whatever she was up to, he wasn't going to like it. Trying to hide his wince, he inched forward through the thick throng of people until he saw what everyone was there for—her.

Even with the sudden caution signs blaring in his head, he couldn't help the knee-jerk punch of lust he felt just from looking at her. Today Amy wore a sorry excuse for shorts, the ripped and faded denim not leaving much to the imagination. With it she'd paired a pale pink tank top like the white one she'd had on yesterday and, even from here, he could tell that she was once again not wearing a bra.

He could have groaned out loud at the memory of those silver bars in his mouth, but he thought that was probably frowned upon in public. Or maybe not, because the young dude laid out in the chair she'd inexplicably dragged out front of her shop was clearly ignoring the view. His attention bounced between her gorgeous face, accentuated today with a slash of cherry-red lipstick, and the view he was getting through the front of her shirt as Amy inked something onto his chest. Before he could help himself, Fred had closed the rest of the distance between himself and Amy, leaving Andy-Randy behind.

"What's going on here?" He positioned himself between the crowd and Amy. With his hands, he gestured to her entire sidewalk setup, but he was looking at Amy's lascivious would-be suitor.

"Back of the line, dude." The kid was maybe twenty-two, a hipster wearing skinny jeans and thick, plastic-rimmed glasses. Propping himself up on his elbows, he glared up at Fred, hyped up on the righteous indignation he'd probably picked up at his latest Save the Whales protest.

Arching an eyebrow, Fred looked down at the kid from his full height, smirking as the kid slowly melted back down into the chair. Pivoting, he turned his attention back to Amy...only to find that she hadn't even looked up from her work.

"Amy. What is this?" He was genuinely confused. She has a perfectly nice shop right behind her, so why on earth was she tattooing someone in the middle of the promenade? "Why are all these people here?"

"It's called an event, Mr. Vaughan." Finally, finally she looked up at him, her lips curved into a mocking smile. "It's a tattoo clinic. I posted ten simple designs on Instagram yesterday for a set price. Anyone who preordered one online can come in today and get it done, no matter how long I'm here."

"But…why?" He looked from her to the empty shop behind her, then back.

"I was curious." She looked up at him, and there was something in those deep blue eyes that he couldn't quite identify. "I wanted to see just how many people I could bring in on a whim. Wanted to make sure that I wasn't being a deadbeat tenant—you know, one who can't pull anyone in here to shop."

She jerked her chin across the way to the luxury luggage store to make her point. It was empty of customers, with a bored salesclerk perched on a sleek leather trunk as she tapped away on her phone.

A trickle of unease worked its way through Fred's gut at her words, which seemed like they were directly addressing…something. Slowly, he slid his hand into the pocket inside his suit jacket, feeling for the crinkle of the paper letter he'd been dragging his feet on delivering to her.

Shit. It wasn't there. Had she seen it? Was that what this was about?

He looked down at her, into those blue eyes that seemed to mock him for a long moment. Her expression revealed nothing, and after a minute he told himself that he was paranoid. This woman wasn't one who stood quietly by when she was upset. If she'd read the letter, she would have marched up to his office and slapped it on his desk.

Wouldn't she?

"Something on your mind?" She cocked her head as she looked up at him. That saucy smile made him want to run his thumb over the pillowy curves. "Ready for that tattoo, perhaps?"

"What time will you be done?" He took a step forward, deliberately moving into her space. He watched her chest quiver as she inhaled a quick breath, and he ached to place his mouth on hers... or elsewhere.

"Why do you ask?" Without looking at the young guy in her chair, she patted him on the shoulder to let him know he was done, then stood to face Fred. "Is this where you tell me that staying open after hours is against regulations?"

"It is against regulations," he said quietly, reaching out a single finger to trace over the line of her cheekbone. "But I suspect that you already know that."

"I might." Her look was full of challenge, and it called to him.

"Have dinner with me." He made his words a challenge, too, knowing that if he showed just how much he wanted her—not even the sex, but just to be around her, absorbing her—she'd say no. A challenge, though? He was pretty sure she'd rise to that.

"Dinner?" Reaching for a bottle of water, she lifted it to her lips, and he found himself transfixed at the sight of a water droplet that missed her mouth. "Why would I want to have dinner with you?"

"Are you really going to play this game, Amy?" Lowering his hand, he swiped it through that drop of water, then lifted it to his lips. "You want me. I want you. We both need to eat. What are you afraid of?"

She narrowed her eyes as she finished the bottle of water, then stepped back. She cast a look at the long line of waiting people, as if considering, before turning back to him.

"I don't know when I'll be done." He might have been hearing things, but he was pretty sure he heard a wisp of disappointment in her voice, though she covered it well. "I could be up all night."

"That's okay," he replied, stepping away. Andy-Randy had finally found him and stood off to the side, watching the give and take with confusion on his face. Fred, though? His thoughts were perfectly clear.

"I'm pretty sure you'll be worth waiting for."

CHAPTER SIX

AMY'S ARMS ACHED as she hauled her chair back into her shop. Her wrists were sore, too, her hands numb from the vibration of the needles all day long. She usually worked a full day, but those appointments were for bigger pieces of work. They were longer, with breaks built in.

Today she'd inked images onto small swaths of skin, all of it detail work. It had been a damn successful day, even more than she'd anticipated when she'd thought up the promo. The success, and sizable chunk of change now in her pocket, had been secondary benefits, though. And the fact that she'd demonstrated, quite nicely, just how many people she could draw into the plaza at the snap of her fingers wasn't too shabby, either.

But at its core? The idea for the tattoo clinic had been conceived mostly to irritate Fred. To get under his skin. To kick back, a bit, at the fact that he'd been carrying that stupid letter around and she had no idea what he was planning to do with it.

"What are you afraid of?"

She could hear Fred's words, echoing in her head. Getting under her skin.

She wondered what he would say if she told him the simple truth—that she was afraid of getting hurt. Maybe it was because her father had died when she was young, or maybe the fear had come from watching her sisters get their hearts broken. Rational or not, the panic existed, urging her to keep people at a distance that she filled with sarcasm and flirtation.

The chair was the last piece of equipment in her cleanup. Placing her hands at the small of her back, she arched her spine to relieve the pressure of a day spent hunched over on her stool.

"I've been told I give excellent back rubs."

Amy jumped, clapping a hand to her chest at the sound of Fred's velvety voice in the darkness of her shop. Her front door had still been propped open, so she hadn't heard the usual chime of the bells that she'd strung overhead. She watched, more closely than she would have admitted, as he sauntered into her space, his long body silhouetted by the faint glow of the moon outside.

"What are you doing here?" She frowned, irritated that he'd caught her off guard.

"Don't tell me you've forgotten our date." He moved close enough that she could see the smirk on his lips, even in the dim light. She could also smell the musk of his skin, the end-of-day remnants of his pricey-smelling cologne.

"It's not a date. It's dinner," she replied archly, crossing her arms over her chest. "And it's two in the morning. I had no idea you'd actually stick around that long."

"Then you underestimate me," he said, reaching for where her battered gray leather jacket hung on the wall. Pulling it from its hook, he held it out for her to slide her arms into. Part of her wanted to refuse, just to be difficult, but the rest of her went ahead and did it before she could think it through. "I'm a man of my word."

After helping her into the jacket, he ran his thumbs up the nape of her neck, massaging away her stiffness with small circular movements. She moaned and leaned back into the touch for an instant before abruptly pulling away.

She wasn't into lying to herself, so there was no point in trying to convince herself that there wasn't anything here between them. An electric chemistry that made her want to close the door to her shop and drag him astride her tattoo chair again.

As she adjusted her jacket, though, she felt the crinkle of the letter, tucked into one of the inner pockets. The reminder was enough to have her get a vise-tight grip on her hormones.

They might have great sex, but Amy wasn't into lying, wasn't into pretenses. And Fred had succumbed

to their chemistry and had sex with her knowing full
well what this letter said, and that he was supposed
to give it to her—she assumed, anyway. It was all the
more reason to keep herself walled off.

Why, then, did she find herself closing up her
shop for the night—morning—and following him?

"This way." His fingers found an inch of her
spine between her shoulder blades and pressed
lightly, guiding her farther into the plaza, rather
than toward the parking lot, as she'd expected. She
felt the heat of the touch even through the thick
leather of her jacket.

"Hate to break it to you, but nothing's going to
be open in here." She cast him a sidelong glance.
"Shops close at nine, restaurants at midnight. Plaza
rules, remember?"

"Rules that you broke today. On purpose." He returned her look. She drew herself up straight, prepared to argue, but the look on his face…he didn't
seem mad. He didn't seem anything, really, except
interested.

Interested in her.

"Whatever." *Original, Amy.* She barely hid her
wince. "Still, we're not going to find any food in
here right now, and I'm hungry."

"You did warn me you might be late." He moved
the fingers that had been resting on her upper back,
sliding them slowly down her spine, leaving a trail
of heat in their wake. He guided her around a cor-

ner in the promenade, toward the massive fountain that marked the center of the plaza. "So I worked with it."

"Oh." Amy's breath left her on a whoosh as she took in the scene in front of her. The fountain was usually off at night—at least, she assumed it was, because she'd watched it go still right around midnight one night. Right now, though, it was in full flow, the streams of water jumping and dancing and scenting the air with chlorine.

On the wide marble ledge that ran along the edge of the fountain was a red-and-white-checkered cloth—a picnic blanket. There was a basket, too, a wicker one from which emanated the delicious scents of butter and garlic. There was even a bottle of wine, already open to the air, and two glasses balancing on slender stems.

"I…" Nobody had ever done something like this for her before. Ever. "You didn't have to do this."

"I know that." He cast her a sidelong grin before indicating the place where she should sit. "I wanted to."

"Why?" She wanted—really wanted—to dive into the basket and pull out a big chunk of what she was pretty sure was warm, melty garlic bread, but she refrained. "I mean, yeah, we're good in bed. Or the chair, I guess. But I haven't been very nice to you."

As though he could read her thoughts, he pulled

the foil-wrapped loaf of bread from the basket, peel-
ing back the aluminum and handing her the first
slice. She held it in her hands but didn't bite into it,
her eyes instead fixed on him.

"Why don't we just enjoy this meal? This moment?" He smiled at her, but she noticed that it
didn't completely light up his eyes. "How many
fountain-side Italian feasts have you had, after
all?"

"Oh, a dozen, at least." She offered him a wry
smile before closing her eyes, biting into the garlic
bread and groaning. When she opened them again,
Fred was looking at her with intention written on
his face that made her mouth go dry.

"Make that sound again and we're going to do
some inappropriate things right here, right now,
while Phyllis the security guard could happen along
any minute." The amusement curling up the corners of his lips told her that he might not mind that
overly much. She wouldn't, either, truth be told—
she'd always had an exhibitionist streak. But she
also knew better than to combine sex with the romance on display here.

She didn't want the feelings that might come
along for the ride.

"Guess we need a distraction, then, because if the
rest of the meal is this good, I make no promises."
She bit into the bread again but this time kept her
eyes open and took her time.

"A distraction. Right." Fred swallowed thickly, running a hand through that thick, dark red hair until it stood up on end. "Oh! I forgot the last component to our picnic."

"Last component?" She cocked her head, questioning, as he pulled out his cell and a portable Bluetooth speaker. A moment later, music wafted from the small device, and Amy dropped her bread right into the fountain water.

"'Ordinary World'? Duran Duran?" Her mouth was dry. "This is my favorite song. My absolute favorite song. How on earth did you know?"

"I didn't know it was your favorite." He grinned, and it was the sexiest freaking thing she'd ever seen. "But I noticed that you're always playing '80s music. I, ah, made a playlist. To go with the picnic."

She couldn't do anything but stare. Romance wasn't something that usually came her way. Lots of men—and women—wanted a wild night or two with a woman covered in tattoos and piercings and confidence. They never thought, though, that she might want—need, even—something more.

She didn't often think that she did. And now it was being given to her by the man hiding something from her.

As Fred handed her a second hunk of bread to replace the one now floating in the middle of the fountain, she wondered what the hell she was supposed to do with *that*.

Maybe...maybe she should give him the bene-
fit of the doubt. Maybe he'd never intended to give
her that letter. Or maybe his family had told him to,
but he didn't want to, because it was her. He hadn't
mentioned it, after all, not even when she'd deliberately poked at him this afternoon.

Maybe...maybe she could let down her guard,
just a little bit. They had chemistry. Maybe they
could have more, even just for a little while.

"How's your dinner?" Fred gestured to the paper
carton of fettucine alfredo that was good enough
to make Amy's toes curl. "I wasn't sure what you
liked to eat, but this is from Luigi's. I have lunch
there sometimes, and I just can't understand why
they're not ever busy."

"That's the one by the north entrance?" Amy
twirled her fork in the rich noodles. Fred nodded.
"They're not busier because they just rely on traffic to the plaza."

"What do you mean?" Fred furrowed his brow
and stilled, a forkful of spaghetti noodles frozen in
midair. "The plaza does heavy marketing itself, to
get people in the door. That's why it costs more to
lease a retail space here."

"As someone who pays that higher monthly lease,
I'm well aware," Amy replied dryly. "But a smart
business owner uses that as just a base. If every
shop in the plaza promoted themselves even a little
bit, this place would see double the traffic at least.

It doesn't take much. Social media posts about new items in stock, or contests, or special events. Every little effort to get people through the door helps out every other vendor."

"Events like the one you held today?" Something in his voice had Amy looking up sharply. His face revealed nothing, but something told her she wasn't going to like whatever it was he said next.

"Exactly." Slowly, aware of his eyes on her, she twirled another fork full of noodles and slid them into her mouth, chewed and swallowed. "All I did was send out a newsletter to my mailing list and make a couple of social media posts. It took hardly any effort, but look how many people were here."

"There were a lot of people, and that's great." She heard the *but* before it came out of his mouth. "But I guess I'm wondering why you had it in the promenade, instead of inside your shop?"

Amy was rarely embarrassed, and she rarely second-guessed her decisions. Hearing Fred ask her this simple question in a quiet, level voice, however, made her squirm a bit on the marble bench. She was pretty sure that *because I wanted to annoy the hell out of you* wasn't the right answer.

"Why not?" She shrugged to avoid the question, then set her carton of pasta down, fork sticking out. "Thank you so much for dinner. I'm so full."

"Look, I get that you don't like to play by the rules. It's one of things that fascinated me about you since the first time I saw you." Fred yanked on his tie to loosen it. "But sometimes you need to think about how what you're doing affects others."

"Excuse me?" Amy froze midreach for her wineglass. His words had been mild, but they stung regardless. "What the hell is that supposed to mean?"

"Amy—" he sighed, loosening the tie entirely and pulling it up, over his head and off "—come on. Can't you see why your neighboring stores might not have liked what you did today?"

"You mean by getting some foot traffic into their boring storefronts?" Her cheeks flushed. "They're welcome."

"Right. But you were still the star of the show. The one getting all the attention…while they were the ones following the rules." He pinned her with a stare. "And you know…if it happened over and over again, they might start to resent it. They might want to do something about it."

Amy slowly touched a hand to her side and felt the paper envelope crinkle again beneath her touch. So that's why this lovely little missive had come to exist. Heat blazed along her skin as emotions tangled in her gut—a touch of embarrassment, incredulity and, under it all, a snaking tendril of hurt.

Fred had no way of knowing this yet, but when she got hurt, she kicked back.

"What are you saying here?" She uncrossed her

legs and straightened her spine. "I assume there's a point to the lecture?"

"It's not a lecture." Wasn't it? Amy wasn't sure how else she was supposed to take it. "Just...maybe you should cool it a little. Keep your head down for a bit."

"I see." Her temper snapped like a rubber band stretched to its breaking point. "And is this advice coming from Fred Vaughan, Esquire, part of the mighty Vaughan Enterprises? Or is it coming from the man I've fucked twice who thinks that there's more between us than sex?"

Something flashed in his eyes, so quickly she would have missed it if she hadn't been looking at him so closely. The open man who had so far focused solely on her in their interactions let a new layer slip over his face. She wasn't entirely sure what to make of the steel that made its presence known in the rigid length of his spine, in the posture wearing that expensive suit, and in the lean planes of his face.

She'd gotten what she wanted, finally—she'd worked her way beneath his skin. Rather than satisfaction, though, she was hurt.

How had she let pasta and Duran Duran lure her into opening up, even just a bit? This man might enjoy the chemistry between them, but at his core, he was yet another man who looked at her and saw a fun fling, not someone worthy of anything more.

Which was what she usually wanted too, so why was this bothering her?

The silence had stretched out, thinned, when he finally answered her question. "Can you separate one from the other, when both are who you are?"

"Right." She closed her eyes for a moment, drew in a deep breath, then swallowed down the hurt. Standing abruptly, she pulled the offending letter out of her inner pocket, enjoying the slight widening of his eyes when he saw what she had in her hands. "Look, you must be a fairly intelligent guy to have gotten through law school, and you seem like you can at least muddle your way through a social interaction, so I'm going to just give you a little reminder of something that someone as smart as you should already know."

Tugging up the sleeves of her jacket, envelope still in hand, she ran her hands down her forearms, drawing attention to her sleeves of inked art.

"I'm not the kind of person who is interested in cooling it. I'm not interested in keeping my head down." She ran a hand through her chin-length blond curls as a reminder that they'd been unruly black curls when they'd first met. "I am who I am. And I'm not going to change."

He opened his mouth, then closed it again.

"You should try being open like that." She slapped the now-wrinkled envelope against his chest, where he caught it with one of his massive hands. She tried not to think of the way those hands felt on her body. "We're done here."

Spinning on her heel, she turned and stalked away. If her heart cracked a little bit when he didn't follow…well, nobody knew it but her.

CHAPTER SEVEN

"This is the fourth night in a row that you've worked late."

Fred blinked wearily as his twin appeared in the doorway to his office, propping himself up against the door frame. He blinked again when he saw two of Frank, and again to clear the image.

He'd been staring at his computer all day, and his eyes were shot. He could probably use reading glasses, but that was a problem for another day. For now, he sank back in the chair that was both ergonomic and hideously expensive. This motif was repeated throughout his office, which had been designed for function, and also to not-so-subtly showcase the Vaughan family's wealth. "We can't both be Dad's favorite," he commented. "Some of us have to work for a living."

"I call bullshit." Barging in, Frank flopped himself down in one of the chairs across the desk from Fred. "You've proven yourself to Dad—to this company—a million times over. You don't need to work so hard."

Frank wasn't wrong—he had proven himself to his family, over and over again. What his twin was leaving out, however, was the fact that past efforts didn't count for much in this family. He was only as good as his latest business triumph. Another man might have gotten frustrated by the never-ending weight of expectation that forever draped over his shoulders like a lead blanket, but not Fred… or Frank, for that matter. They'd been raised on a steady diet of family obligation, sprinkled heavily with guilt.

Family came first. Always.

"I'm almost done for the night." Lies. He planned to push himself for at least another hour, after which he would finally head home, hopefully too exhausted to think about Amy's face when she'd handed him the letter he'd been ordered to give to her. Or to dream about her astride him, his cock sunk deep into the heat between her legs as she rode them both to release.

"You haven't just been staying late at work." Frank fixed him with a narrow-eyed stare that Fred was only too familiar with, the assessing gaze of someone who had known him since they'd shared a womb. "You've eaten lunch at your desk every day this week instead of coming out with everyone. You've gone home right after work. And don't think

I didn't notice that you sent me those contracts at two o'clock this morning."

"Don't you have anyone better to stalk?" Fred arched an eyebrow at his brother. "Go follow Randy or Andy or whatever the hell his name is around for a while. Something tells me he'd enjoy it."

"All work and no play makes Fred a dull boy." From his pocket, Frank pulled a silver-plated flask. Unscrewing the lid, he took a large gulp of the contents, then slid it across the desk with a whiff of whiskey.

"I can't believe those words just came out of your mouth." Fred rolled his eyes. "Just like I can't believe you carry this around in your pocket all day. Who are you, Don Draper?"

"Just drink it," Frank ordered. He slapped a hand on Fred's desk, the sound reverberating through the quiet of the otherwise empty office. Fred glared at him but lifted the flask to his lips. The whiskey burned his lips but numbed his throat, and he relaxed for the first time since he'd last seen Amy.

He took another sip for good measure, and his brother nodded with approval.

"Now that you've unclenched, are you going to tell me what's got your panties in a twist?" Frank took the flask back when Fred handed it to him, draining the last sip.

"That's misogynistic," Fred said, and Frank snorted in response.

"Fine. Will you share with me, dear brother, the reason your non-gender-specific underwear is coiled so tightly it is causing you to act so uptight?" Settling back in the chair, he pinned Fred with a stare, waiting for an answer to his question.

Fred hadn't spoken to anyone about Amy, not since she'd come back into his life—or rather, he'd gone tromping into hers. Now, though, his tongue had been loosened by two shots of whiskey. Digging his fingers into the knot at his neck, he loosened his tie and undid the top two buttons of his shirt, then pushed back from his desk.

"Do you remember our trip to Europe after we got our undergrads?" Closing his eyes, he let the images wash over him, the lights and languages, textures and tastes.

"In a hazy sort of way." Frank grinned, but the smile quickly slipped off his face. "The girl. The one in Amsterdam."

"How the hell did you zero in on that so fast?" Fred furrowed his brow at his twin. "She wasn't the only girl on that trip."

"She's the only one who sent you into a funk that lasted six months." Frank looked at him, assessing. "Wanna tell me how the hell some strange girl from Amsterdam has managed to make you depressed again five years later?"

"I'm not depressed," Fred said as his brother eyed him skeptically. "I'm not. It's just…it's complicated."

"I'm waiting." Frank reached reflexively for his flask, frowning when he shook it and found it empty. "Hold that thought. I'm going to go raid Dad's stash. Be right back."

Fred waited as his brother darted out of the room. He wasn't depressed that Amy was probably never going to speak to him again. He *wasn't*.

"Look what I found." Frank burst back into the room, a bottle of amber liquid and two snifters in hand.

"Fifty-year Glenfiddich?" Fred shook his head. "That's his closet stash. Dad will kill you if you drink that."

"Please. He only drinks it because it fits his image." Frank made a great showing of pulling out the cork stopper. "I'll top it up with Maker's Mark and he'll never know the difference."

Fred wasn't so sure of that, but he said nothing as his brother poured generous splashes of the pricey whiskey into two snifters, then handed him one.

"Now talk." Frank picked up his own snifter and settled back down in his chair. "Tell me what's going on with this girl."

"Remember that petition that was circulating among the vendors here?"

"The one to evict the tattoo shop girl?" Frank whistled through his teeth. "Yeah, I remember. Lots of oomph behind it. Too bad, really. She's hot. Looks like she'd be a freak in bed."

"Watch your mouth," Fred snapped, slamming his snifter on the desk with a loud thump. Frank blinked, forehead furrowed as he worked it through.

"Holy shit. Amsterdam girl and tattoo shop girl are the same person." Frank's eyes went wide. "Please tell me she recognized you."

"Her name is Amy." Fred sipped his drink. "And yes, she recognized me, you know, when I went to deliver that eviction notice."

"Shit." Frank sucked a breath in through his teeth. "Awkward."

"You're telling me." Fred sat back, traced a finger over the rim of his glass. "I was so shocked I didn't give it to her."

"Fred." His twin sat up straight at that bit of news. "That's not cool. The tenant has to be notified or we can't legally rent that space to anyone else."

"I'm a lawyer, Frank. I'm well aware," Fred snapped, scrubbing a hand over his face. "There's more."

"Oh, I bet there is." His twin raised his brows, settling in for the story. "And I bet it has to do with the two of you naked."

"Sucker's bet." Fred smiled grimly. "And it was every bit as good as it was that night in Amsterdam."

Fred and his brother had never had that telepathic connection so many sets of twins had reported, but they still knew each other better than anyone else on the face of the planet. Therefore he wasn't surprised that Frank picked up on what he hadn't said.

"You like her." Frank watched his twin, assessing. "That's a plot twist."

"Indeed." Fred grimaced. "Especially when she found the letter anyway."

"Wait a minute. You slept with her *before* she got the letter?" Frank pinned Fred with a withering stare. "Dick move, bro. Even I know that."

"I know that now," Fred snapped in return. "I just...she blindsided me. I lose my mind when I'm with her. Which isn't an excuse, I just... I messed up. And now she's not talking to me and I don't know what to do."

"Well, that's easy." Frank swigged the remaining liquid in his glass, then stole his brother's and polished that off, too.

"Is it?" Fred wasn't surprised that he'd fucked up. But Frank had always been the Superman to Fred's Clark Kent, so he felt a small bud of hope that his brother knew how to get him out of this. "Well? Tell me."

"You're going to forget about her." Frank stood.

"What? Why?" Fred stared up at his brother, who stood just a smidge shorter than Fred's own six foot four. "Surely you've got better advice than that."

"You've already fucked it up. You said so yourself," Frank reminded him. Fred narrowed his eyes and contemplated bringing up that hair's width difference in their height, just to poke at his brother.

"No need to rub it in."

"My point is, maybe she'll forgive you. Maybe, if you work hard enough." Frank's face was set in serious lines. "But I mean…where do you see this going?"

"I…what?" Fred sputtered, taken aback by the question. "I've slept with her twice. I'm not— We're not— I don't know if that's where this is going."

Didn't he, though? Wasn't that the very reason he'd been so down the last few days? In the years since that magical night with her in Amsterdam, he'd almost—almost—managed to convince himself that he'd imagined the heady connection between himself and his gorgeous, tattooed siren. All it had taken was one glance at her again, though, and there it had been, heady and unlike anything he'd felt before or since.

"I swear, watching you work this out is like watching a rat on a wheel." Frank shook his head. "Listen to me. Maybe there would be something there, if you managed to unfuck yourself. But just fast-forward with me for a minute. Where do you see this in six months? In a year? Is she the girl you're going to marry? If not, is it really worth the effort right now?

Panic thickened his throat, making it hard to swallow. *Married?* He barely knew her.

He could see where his brother was going with this, though. His mother and father hadn't been an arranged marriage, not in the strictest sense of the term, but they'd been firmly pushed in each other's direction. Both from wealthy, aristocratic families, their families had been very enthusiastic about the match.

It hadn't been vocalized in so many words. But Fred and Frank had always been very aware that someday they would be expected to do the same.

He was entranced by Amy. Wanted her with a thirst that hadn't even come close to being quenched.

But...could he really see himself bringing her to his parents' house for dinner? He could just picture his mother, sitting there in her silk blouse or cashmere sweater set, arching an incredulous eyebrow at Amy's full sleeves of ink. Or his father barely waiting until she was out the door before making a dirty joke about the nipple adornments that Amy did absolutely nothing to hide.

His thoughts must have shown on his face, because Frank hummed in his throat, apparently pleased that his warning had come across. Lifting the bottle of hideously expensive scotch, he poured another generous measure into each of their glasses, lifting his and holding it out for a toast.

Fred did not feel like toasting, but more than that, he did not feel like explaining why he didn't feel like it. Half-heartedly, he lifted his glass, braced himself for the impact as his brother banged his own into it.

"To common sense," he started before tossing back half the contents in his glass. "And to getting you laid. Let's go."

"What? No." Fred shook his head as Frank slammed his laptop closed. He was not in the mood to go anywhere except his condo, where he would order in some Thai food and then go to bed. He planted his feet when his brother rounded the desk, hauling him up and out of the chair. "I'm not going anywhere except home."

"No way, bro. You're coming out with me. Now." Frank clapped him on the shoulders before handing him his suit jacket. "Listen to your big brother Frankie. The best medicine for getting over one woman is getting under another one. Come on. We'll order a car and go find you someone with big eyes and long legs."

Fred stiffened, his thoughts mutinous. He'd already found someone like that, with blue eyes that saw right through him and legs that felt amazing wrapped around his face. He didn't want some nameless, faceless woman in his bed.

He wanted Amy.

He said nothing, though, instead following his brother as Frank turned off the lights and locked up the office. Said nothing as he climbed into the town car Frank had ordered, and followed him into some new club where the waitresses wore next to nothing and the music was so loud he could taste it in his throat.

He'd thought a night out might help lift his mood. Might take his mind off the woman he'd messed things up with.

Instead, all he could think about was what he could do to make things right.

CHAPTER EIGHT

"HOT GUY. TWO O'CLOCK," Meg yelled over the din of the dim, crowded bar. The place was, frankly, a dive, scarred tables crowded cheek to cheek on sticky floors. When Amy didn't respond, her oldest sister grabbed her face, a palm on each cheek, and turned her head in the direction she'd indicated.

"Dude. Personal space." With a shake of her head, Amy flicked her sister's hands off. When Meg did it again, Amy glared. "Would you stop?"

"Seriously. You'll like this one." Meg smiled so beseechingly that Amy sighed, turning in the direction her sister wanted her to look, then cast Meg some serious side eye.

"That's John." She rolled her eyes when Meg merely grinned, waving at her fiancé from across the bar. "Very funny."

"I was trying to make you smile." Meg nudged Amy's untouched bottle of beer across the table. "Since you won't tell me what's going on."

"Nothing's going on." To prove her point, Amy lifted her beer and took a healthy swallow. "See? Party on, and all that jazz."

"You've been scowling for days." Meg rolled her eyes. "I used to change your diapers, kid. Come on. Fess up."

"It's just work stuff." Amy smiled stiffly and made a big show out of shrugging her shoulders nonchalantly. "Not a big deal."

"If you say so," Meg replied dubiously before waving at John once again. "What is taking him so long?"

Amy peeled a thin strip off the label on her beer bottle as Meg waved like an air traffic controller to get her fiancé to come back to the table. She hadn't lied to Meg; it *was* a work issue that had her down. At least that's what she kept telling herself.

She actually didn't care that much about what the other vendors in the shopping plaza thought about her. She may not have looked like a stereotypical businessperson, but she was shrewd. She knew her value as a business, and she didn't give a flying fruitcake about that petition. If she was evicted for *not fitting in*, which was obtusespeak for being covered in tattoos, then she'd go to the media and raise holy hell.

What she did care about, even though she really didn't want to? The fact that Fred had been the one in charge of delivering her that eviction notice. No, not even that…the fact that he'd hidden it from her. If he'd told her up front, she was pretty sure that they would have wound up in bed together anyway—that was how strong the pull between them was. But he hadn't, and it had…well, it had hurt her feelings.

She never got hurt feelings. She and Fred had a history, however. Even though it had only been one night, it had held meaning for her.

Apparently it hadn't meant nearly as much to him, yet she couldn't bring herself to shake it off and move on. Which was why she was sitting in a bar she didn't want to be in, with a sister who was torturing her for being moody.

As her sister's fiancé finally made his way over to the table, she sneaked a look at her phone to check the time, wondering how quickly she could make an excuse and go home.

"Lucky us, getting the prettiest women in the club." John grinned while he juggled the drinks in his arms. He set a fresh bottle of beer in front of Amy, and she barely held back the wince as she tacked another half hour onto her time estimate.

John slid into the seat nearest Meg and greeted his fiancée with a hand threaded through her hair and a deep kiss.

"Don't mind me," Amy said dryly. The couple continued greeting each other as though she wasn't even there. Focusing her attention on her phone, she started a new game of Candy Crush, wondering if the couple's utter absorption in each other meant she could subtract that half hour back off the time estimate.

A few more minutes of the smooching, and she was done. Meg and John broke apart as she slid out of the booth and got to her feet, stuffing her phone in her pocket.

"Don't leave before you say hi to Theo," John requested, lifting her bottle of beer and frowning when he found it full.

"Theo's here?" Amy looked out across the bar, craning her neck until she saw him. Her sister Jo's live-in boyfriend, and the man she considered the closest thing to an actual brother, was leaning against the bar, holding court in a group conversation.

"He'll be over in a sec," John added as he ran a hand down Meg's bare arm. "He ran into some guys he was friends with in college."

"Maybe you'll wipe that scowl off your face and find one to converse with," Meg suggested pointedly. "Some company might brighten your current dour outlook on life."

"Maybe any man I'd be interested in talking to will appreciate my scowl," Amy replied brightly. Brushing her blond curls out of her face—she should really consider going back to dreads—she leaned back into the booth to grab her small purse. When she straightened back up again, Theo was crossing the room toward their table, and he wasn't alone.

Amy sucked in a deep breath when she saw the men who accompanied Theo. Incredibly tall, well over six feet, with coppery hair and a lanky build.

No. No way.

Then the men were at the table. Theo gathered her in a familiar hug as she frantically tried to compose herself, looking upward into the face of the cause of her angst.

Their eyes met, and damn it, there was that little tug in her gut. Her body didn't seem to care that she was upset with him.

"Jo, this is Fred Vaughan." Theo released her and gestured toward his friend. "I just put two and two together, but his family owns the shopping plaza where your shop is. Small world!"

"Right." Her brain was telling her to play it cool, but the rest of her wasn't listening. She narrowed her eyes at Fred and crossed her arms over her chest. "What are you doing here?"

"Frank dragged me out for a drink." He slid his hands into his pockets. He didn't look all that thrilled to see her, either, which had her temper sparking. What had *she* done, besides giving him crazy good sex?

"Fred and his brother are friends from college." Theo clapped the taller man on the back, grinning widely. Amy could tell that Jo's fiancé had clearly had a drink or three already. "Haven't seen them in years. How cool is this?"

"Uh-huh." Amy could feel Meg's eyes on her, assessing, and struggled not to grind her teeth together. "Where's Jo?"

Her sister Jo had a limited tolerance for the bar scene. A limited tolerance for people, really. If she was here, then they could escape together.

"She's working. On deadline." Theo grinned sheepishly—his significant other worked for him. "Before you get pissed, she's the one imposing the all-nighter, not me. Says she won't have anyone accusing her of sleeping with the boss to get ahead."

"Speaking of getting ahead…" She deliberately turned toward Meg and John, putting her back to Fred as she spoke. "I have a full slate tomorrow. I should get going."

"Fine." Meg heaved a long-suffering sigh. "Don't think you're coming to family dinner tomorrow night with this attitude, though."

"Whatever." Amy rolled her eyes at her sister. "Have fun."

Then she was off, striding into the crowd of the bar without a second glance at Fred. Her spine stiffened when she heard him call after her, his deep voice carrying over the roar of the crowd.

He caught up to her quickly with his long stride, and she paused when she felt his hand on her shoulder. She should have turned around, but she didn't trust herself to remain strong while looking at him, so she remained as she was, facing away.

"Don't touch me," she snapped as he came up close behind her. He dropped his hand from her shoulder, but she could feel the heat of his body, radiating off his lean frame to warm the skin of her back. "I have nothing to say to you."

"Well, I have something to say to you," he replied. If his voice had held anger, she could have pushed away, leaving him standing there alone. She didn't hear any anger, though, just regret, so she remained where she was, silent and still.

"I need to apologize," he continued, dipping his head so that he could place his lips by her ear.

"You think?" she retorted. It took every ounce of willpower that she possessed not to shiver in response to the fan of his breath over the lobe of her ear.

"You have every right to be pissed at me. I fucked up, big-time." He moved in closer so that he could keep speaking over a sudden rise in the noise level. She wanted to moan softly when she felt his hips bump against hers from behind. "Please hear me out. I had no way of knowing that you were Amy Marchande when I walked into your shop with that letter. You never told me your name."

"You shouldn't have been delivering that letter to begin with, to anyone." She spat out the words. "I signed that lease. I pay up every single month. Even if there was a petition against me, you and your brother and whoever the hell else you work with should have shut it down right there."

"I agree with you," he replied mildly, but she could tell she'd struck a nerve. "But I'm not the one in charge. I just happened to draw the short straw."

"And then you walked in, saw someone you might like to fuck again, and decided to tuck it away for another day." Her spine stiffened as she clung to her righteous anger. "Gee, I wonder why I'm upset?"

"Don't twist this around." His hands found her hips, tugging her back against him, and she fought to remain stiff, not to let her body yield to his. "It wasn't like that at all, and you damn well know it. Please let me say I'm sorry."

"Fine." The word burst out of her like a plea, but whether it was for him to let her go or to hold her closer, she had no idea. "Apology accepted. Now, I'm going home to bed."

His fingers clenched on her hips, and she struggled to reach for her self-control as she added, "Alone."

"Let me make it up to you," he murmured in her ear. This time his lips touched the seashell curve, and this time she couldn't hold back her shudder. "Please."

"What did you have in mind?" This, *this* she could handle—flirtation. Lust. "Keep in mind how much you owe me."

He huffed out a laugh, a low sound that did something funny to her insides, then used the hands on her hips to guide her in a half circle. She arched into his touch as he gave her a gentle push back in the direction of their table.

"We're going to go sit down again." His voice was dark, delicious. "Right at that little table, right beside one another."

"Oh?" Her voice was faint; she didn't know how he could still hear her over the music and the crowd. "And what will we do then?"

He laughed again, sounding nothing like the careful lover she remembered from Amsterdam, or the frenzied one she'd ridden in her shop.

"Then we're going to do whatever I want." This was a man in control, so completely unexpected and yet so completely right that the possibilities made her legs quiver. He nudged her forward, and she took a step, her senses suddenly on fire. "Now go."

Swallowing thickly, she did as she was told—in truth, she couldn't imagine refusing. Hyperaware of Fred at her back, she made her way back to the table. When Meg, John, Theo and Fred's twin looked up at them questioningly, she forced her face into a smile, certain that she looked more than a little crazy.

"I think I'm going to stay," she said brightly, reaching for the bottle of beer that was still sitting on the table. "I got a second wind!"

"Great," Meg replied slowly, scrutinizing Amy's flushed cheeks. "We were just about to get up and dance."

"I'm right behind you!" Squeezing into the booth,

Amy hip-checked Theo. Grumbling, he shifted over, making space for her and Fred to sit. Amy clasped her beer like she was clutching a life preserver, waving it in the air for everyone to see. "You guys are three drinks in, though. Let me just catch up and I'll be right there!"

Meg, John and Theo were all regarding her as though she'd grown a third head, and she didn't blame them. She sounded practically perky, not a look she usually wore. Fred's twin, however—was she remembering right that his name was Frank?—was watching her intently, curiosity written all over his face.

He might have been Fred's brother, but the expression made her want to sock him in the nose. It was one she was well familiar with, the look a man gave her when he was thinking about taking a walk on the wild side.

She wasn't here to be any man's tattooed little experiment. If they didn't want her for who she was, then they didn't get any of her, at all.

She willed Frank to head off to the dance floor with the others. He did not; rather, he sat sipping his beer and looking from her to Fred as though there was a puzzle there that he had to solve.

"Dude, what?" Fred reached across the table with his long arm, socking his brother in the bicep. "Stop being a creeper."

"Sorry." To his credit, Frank shook his head, as

though jerking himself out of a trance. Draining his drink, he set the empty bottle on the table and stood. "Another round?"

"No, thank you," Amy and Fred both replied at the same time. Frank furrowed his brow again slightly, as if he couldn't understand what he was seeing, before making his way back to the bar.

"I don't think your brother approves of you hanging around me." Amy turned to Fred with a slight smirk. Here, again, was familiar territory. "Maybe he thinks I'll be a bad influence on you."

"Doesn't matter what he thinks," Fred said as he placed his hand on Amy's knee under the table, giving it a gentle squeeze. "What matters is that you do what I tell you to, right now."

"Oh?" She arched an eyebrow, prepared to tease back, instead losing her breath when he moved his hand steadily up her thigh. Excitement surged through her, gasoline that had been lit on fire. She followed his thought process and understood what he was about to do.

"Drink your beer." He sounded calm while she felt anything but. "Now."

Hand shaking, she picked up the beer. It had gone warm, but she took a sip anyway, not tasting anything because all her attention was focused on Fred's hand and the way it was moving up her thigh with excruciating slowness.

She was wearing tiny cutoffs, the denim so well-worn that it was torn in places and soft as butter in others. Those were layered with a pair of lacy boy shorts, and neither provided the slightest bit of resistance as Fred's questing fingers found the crease where her pelvis met her thigh.

She sucked in a breath, fingers tightening on the bottle. Exhaling slowly, she fought to keep her expression neutral as he tucked one large finger beneath the hem of the shorts, toying with the elastic lace that lay beneath.

"Careful," he whispered, picking up his own drink. "Wouldn't want anyone to look at you and know how wet you are."

"I'm not wet," she retorted. She sank back against the faux leather cushion of the booth back when he delved farther, moving his questing fingers closer to her core by tucking them beneath the lace of her underpants as well. "Shit."

"Don't ever think you can lie to me." His words were cocky, even as she was desperate for him to look at her. He refused, casting his stare steadfastly on the empty table in front of them. "If I slide my fingers inside you, am I going to find you wet?"

"Why don't you try and see?" Her words were staccato, pushed from her torso as she panted for air. "Maybe I am. Maybe I'm not."

"I think you'd like it if I did. If I slid my fingers right up inside you." He rubbed his fingers over her outer folds to punctuate his words, and she struggled to withhold a moan. "I'm right, aren't I, you dirty girl? You'd get off from having my fingers inside you while we're sitting here, out in public where anyone can see."

"*Fred.* Jesus." Amy willed herself not to prove his words true, but as she did, he worked his entire hand into the lace of her boy shorts. That massive hand of his cupped her mound, his thumb stroking over the slit that divided her labia, and it was all she could do to keep from sobbing out loud.

"Shh." This time he leaned in against her, his shoulder bumping against hers companionably. "I know my touch makes you want to scream. But just look…your sister is here. Her fiancé. Theo, and my brother Frank. Do you really want them to see you whimpering from my touch? What would they think, seeing bossy little Amy Marchande melting from the touch of a man?"

"Oh, fuck you." Amy leaned against him, hard, but didn't dare to lift her eyes from the table, to glare at him for withholding what her body so desperately craved. She wanted to look him in the eyes, to lose herself in those pools of pale green and to ask where this thread of dominance came from when it hadn't made an appearance before. She didn't, because she was afraid—afraid of hearing him voice the answer to a question she hadn't asked.

Every single sexual encounter she'd ever had, whether with men or women or beings who identified somewhere in between…with beings who identified as straight or gay or bi… She'd been the one who was in control. She'd always been in charge, the one who had led the encounter, dictating the content and the rules, defining the limits.

When she'd first seen Fred in that bar so many years ago, she'd known only that she wanted him. What had come after had seemed a natural consequence. She'd been the aggressor and had remained in control. Being a woman, of course she had recognized and cherished the fact that he had let her be so, even though his physical body was undeniably so much powerful than hers.

She hadn't realized that she'd internalized that power dynamic until Fred stroked that single finger through her damp folds, searching for proof that she melted at his command. She hadn't anticipated any commands from him at all, and that made her response even hotter.

"See something you like?" She recalled the words he'd once uttered, poised above her in a fancy hotel in a city she'd considered her own, and she melted around his questing fingers.

She'd never thought of Fred as dominant per se. Not since he'd told her that he was turned on by whatever made her melt.

He understood more about her than she'd ever imagined. She didn't consider herself submissive, per se…more that she was happy to assume the role if she happened upon a partner who was dominant.

She'd only slept with this particular man twice, in situations in which he hadn't commanded control, but now she understood. He didn't need to be dominant…unless his partner needed him to step into that role.

In another place, another time, she might have pretended that she was appalled at the bossiness of his words, his voice, his fingers.

Here and now, she felt stripped to the bone. No—to the marrow.

Never in her life had she ever imagined that she was submissive. Quite the opposite, in fact.

Right now, in this public situation in which he demanded her submission? In public, when his brother and her brothers-in-law and sister could return at any moment?

She'd never been so turned on. She'd never been so wet. She'd never imagined that she'd be tempted to flaunt her arousal; no—that she'd be proud of the feelings that this man had coaxed out of her body with his words and his hands. Secretly.

At the moment, as his strong fingers swiped through the slit that divided her lower lips? She didn't care who saw. She didn't care who knew how much she melted at the slightest pressure from this man, and only this one.

Fred's twin, Frank, had reached the bar, never

out of Amy's sight. As her body yearned beneath Fred's expert ministrations, she again pondered the same question that had momentarily perplexed her a handful of years ago in Amsterdam.

Two men. Identical in every aspect that was naked to the visible eye. No discernible differences in grooming, in style, in demeanor.

Yet when she'd looked across that Euro club five years ago, she hadn't seen twins and chosen one of a pair. She'd only seen Fred.

Beneath the table, Fred slid two fingers inside her slick channel. He moved them in a circle, stretching her in the most delicious way. A whimper escaped her lips, and she felt sweat break out all over her skin as she rocked her hips forward, silently begging for more.

"I wonder if anyone in here is watching us." Fred leaned in closer. Wrapping his free arm around her torso so that she was tucked back against his chest, he bent to whisper directly into her ear. "You're so fucking gorgeous, I'm sure that someone is. And I wonder if they know what I'm doing to you? If they know that I have my fingers inside you, right this second."

"I don't care if they do." Her voice was rough and didn't even seem to belong to her. "Let them look."

"I like that answer, dirty girl." Shifting in the booth, he worked his fingers in even farther. He scissored them inside her, and she felt herself contract around him. "I think that even if Frank came back to the table right now, you'd let me keep my hand buried between these pretty legs of yours. That's how much you want what I can give you."

Her breath escaped her lips on a gasp. He was absolutely right—she was too far gone to care who saw. At the same time, his words made her desperate to come before Frank—before anyone—came back.

The fact that they could, though? It was fucking hot.

"I can feel you getting wetter." She could feel the heat of his skin against her back, sealing them together. Her body trembled so hard as he worked his fingers in even farther still that she was glad of the support. "Now let's see if we can make you come before you have to explain your filthy behavior to anyone else."

Before she could breathe, he slid his fingers in the rest of the way. They were thick and they were long, and when he rotated them inside her, it made her squirm in desperation for his cock. As she tried to rock subtly to enhance his movements, he rubbed his thumb over her clit. She jerked against him, teeth sinking into her tongue until she tasted blood.

"If we were alone right now, I bet you'd be screaming." He nipped at her ear, circled his thumb around the bud of her clit, and she felt tension start to gather, low and tight in her belly.

"If we were alone right now, I'd be on top of you."

Her voice sounded like she hadn't had a sip of water in years. "You wouldn't be teasing me like this because you'd have your cock inside me."

This time he was the one who hissed out a breath. She grinned triumphantly, sliding her hand over to his lap. Stroking the firm muscle of his truly impressive thighs, she finally cupped his cock with her palm. It was fully erect, thick and tempting as it pushed against the fabric of his suit pants, begging for release.

"Nope." With a pained groan, he shifted so that she could no longer reach between his legs to stroke, to touch. "This is about you, and the orgasm you're about to have."

"Says you," she challenged, heels drumming on the floor as every single muscle in her body tensed, straining toward release.

"You don't have a choice." He sounded mildly amused, as though she were nothing but a toy he was entertained with right this moment, but she heard the strain in his voice. This whole scene—his bossy hands, the public setting—it was really doing it for both of them. "Now come for me. Try not to be too loud when you do, unless you want every single person in this club to know that you just came all over my hand."

"Oh God." His words were the release valve, as though her body had needed his permission to let go. He rubbed his thumb right over the top of her clit as he spoke, providing the last bit of delicious friction that she'd needed to go over the edge. *"Fred."*

"Good girl." He continued to work on her, pulling a second wave out of her flesh on the heels of the first. "Give me one more."

She shook as pleasure worked its way outward from her core like an earthquake from its epicenter. She was sweating and could feel that her skin had flushed a deep red. Her face was probably contorted, her mouth hanging open, and in that moment she just couldn't have cared less. The only thing that existed in her world was the release Fred had just milked from her hot, slick channel with his clever fingers.

Spent, she melted against him, boneless. A small whimper escaped her as he removed his hand from its cozy space between her thighs, then smoothed her panties and shorts back into place. Tilting her head, she looked up at him, just in time to see him slide those fingers that had just been inside her into his mouth.

"Good Lord, Fred." Reaching for her beer, she took a long swallow, needing to dampen her suddenly dry mouth. "That was…wow."

"I know." He smirked down at her, and she couldn't help but laugh. Damn it. She liked him. This wasn't news, exactly—why else would she have been so hurt by that damn letter—but right now she could no longer pretend.

"I didn't know you had it in you," she admitted, finishing off her beer. "But I have to say... I liked it."

"Oh, Miss Marchande." He leaned in, so close that she could feel the mist of his breath on her face. "I've got moves you've never seen."

"That, my friend, is a quote from *Pretty Woman*." She couldn't hold back the grin as he shrugged, caught out.

"Made you smile, though. Definitely worth it."

"Let's go somewhere." Shifting in her seat, she ran her tongue along her lips and watched his eyes track the motion. "It seems I have a favor to repay."

She'd meant to ask him to come home with her. To let him see the way she lived—in the house she'd grown up in, where she still lived with Mamesie, two of her sisters and a brother-in-law. A house that was shabby and rundown and utterly unlike anything he'd likely experienced in his life.

It would help put some distance back between them again, which would be good.

Right now, though, she didn't want that distance. She wanted to take him to a hotel room, strip them both naked and wring pleasure from their bodies until neither of them could see straight.

"Nope." Fred took a sip of his own drink as she cocked her head, certain she'd heard wrong.

"What do you mean, nope?" Quick as a snake, she rested her palm in the juncture of his thighs to prove her point. Her artist's fingers traced up and down the length of his cock, which was still swollen and needy. "I think your little friend here likes the idea."

"There's nothing little about my friend, and you know it." Fred arched an eyebrow, cast her a crooked grin that was so devastatingly sexy she almost straddled him in his seat, right there and then.

"Then why not?"

"We've tried doing things your way," he reminded her, tapping a finger on her lips. "That involved you sneaking out of a hotel room in Amsterdam without telling me your name. A quickie in your shop before you threw me out. And a temper tantrum exorcised in a public tattoo clinic that violated your lease agreement and could get *you* thrown out."

"It was a publicity stunt, not a temper tantrum." She sat up, straight and prim—her, Amy Marchande, prim—as she refuted his latter claim. She couldn't do the same for the two former.

"We just did a little test run, and you got wetter than you've ever been in your life when you let me take charge." He tapped her on the lips again, and her tongue darted out to run over the tips. She tasted herself, salt and musk, and felt that slow burn between her legs ignite again.

"From here on out, we're going to do things my way. And trust me—you're going to like it."

CHAPTER NINE

"YOU AND AMY looked pretty cozy last night." Theo dropped two massive submarine sandwiches down on the small table in front of Fred before pulling out a chair and sitting down. Even though the small sandwich shop was only a five-minute drive from the plaza, Fred had never been inside. He could already tell he'd be back, and not just for the food, which his nose told him was going to be delicious. He was digging the understated décor, and by understated, he meant non-existent—a bare concrete floor, exposed studs in the walls, and a computer printout held up with masking tape pointing out the route to the washrooms.

"Is this where you pull some big-brother crap and warn me not to touch your sister?" Fred snorted as he peeled the wrapper off his sandwich. Lobster rolls—his favorite. "I'm still not completely understanding why you call the Marchande girls your sisters. Aren't you living with one?"

"One question at a time." Theo held up his index

finger. "When I got back to the table last night, you and Amy looked sweaty and guilty. A year ago, I would have hauled you out of that booth and beat your ass for touching her."

"You could have tried." Fred grinned before taking a big bite of his sandwich, the salty flavors exploding on his tongue. "What changed?"

"Meg punched me in the solar plexus, if you must know." Theo glowered. "When she was hooking up with John. Apparently women don't like it when we tell them who they can sleep with."

"That's very evolved of you," Fred replied dryly. "I don't know her that well yet, but something tells me that if you tried to do the same thing to Amy, you'd wake up with the word *dickhead* tattooed on your forehead."

"You're not wrong." Theo shuddered. "I remember once, back when we were kids. I was over at their house and we were all playing hide-and-seek. I thought it would be funny to hide all her Barbie dolls."

"I'm guessing that didn't go the way you thought it would?" Fred leaned back in his chair, taking a sip of his soft drink.

"She didn't say anything right then, just crossed her arms and looked at me. Like a child of the corn, you know?" Theo snorted out a laugh. "I thought that would be the end of it. Then a week later, I woke up to a freak show in my own damn bedroom. She'd painted all those Barbies that I'd hidden to look like zombies, then hung them all over my room. It was the freakiest shit I've ever seen. When I got all self-righteous about it, she just laughed and laughed. Bet me ten bucks I'd never touch her dolls again."

"Bet she was right." Fred tried to hide his grin but couldn't. "Damn, that's...twisted. And brilliant, really."

"You've just summed up Amy Marchande perfectly." Theo picked up a napkin and wiped his hands.

"How did she get into your room at night, if you were all kids?" Fred swallowed the last bite of his sandwich, then eyed the deli counter, contemplating a second. "Do I want to know?"

"We moved in next door to the Marchandes when we were all kids." Theo crumpled his empty sandwich wrapper into a ball. "We were all friends, though I was closest to Jo. She used to climb the tree outside my room and sneak in my window. That's what Amy did, too."

"And Jo is the one you're now living with?" Fred furrowed his brow. "Isn't that like dating your sister?"

"I've never thought of Jo like my sister." Theo grinned, then pushed himself back from the table with a groan. "Man, I haven't had a lobster roll in years. So good."

"I'll get another if you will." Fred slurped the last of his drink.

"Can't." Theo shook his head.

"A moment on the lips, forever on the hips?" Fred smirked across the table at his friend, enjoying the conversation. He and Frank and Theo had been tight once upon a time, but they'd drifted. It was nice to catch up.

"Hardly." Theo flexed a bicep that was pretty impressive for someone who worked at a desk. "Nah, there's a big family dinner tonight. Meg's cooking—that's what she does, she's a caterer—and she's like a little Ukrainian baba about it. If you don't stuff your face with three servings, her feelings get hurt."

"Family dinner?" Fred sat up straight at the mention.

"Uh-huh." Theo eyed him warily.

"Who will be there?" His voice was all innocence, but he pinned Theo with a charming smile.

"Weird question, bro, but I'll indulge you. Meg and John—you met them last night. Me and Jo. Beth is the sister closest in age to Amy, and her fiancé, Ford. Then Amy, and the girls' mom, Mamesie." Theo arched an eyebrow. "Shall I have Meg fax over the menu for your approval as well?"

"Hey, do you remember that time you hooked up with Janice Richards?" Fred leaned forward, placing his elbows on the table as he smiled beatifically.

"Hard to forget a girl who throws all your clothing down the garbage chute post-hookup."

"Who was it that came to your rescue? Bringing you some sweats so you didn't have to do a naked walk of shame across campus?" Fred looked up expectantly. "Oh… I do believe that was me."

"You want me to get you into the family dinner?" Theo furrowed his brow with confusion. "Why?"

"I…" The words stuck in his throat. "Look. I don't know if there's anything between Amy and me besides sex."

"La, la, la." Theo closed his eyes and waved his hands by his ears. "Not listening."

"But I think there might be." He swallowed the rest of the thought, which was a memory of that thread that had appeared between them the second they'd laid eyes on one another, linking them together. "I want to… I want to woo her."

"You want to *woo* her?" Theo asked incredulously. "Are you a hundred years old? Who says *woo* anymore?"

"I do." Fred drummed his fingers on the table with impatience.

"How does sneaking into a family dinner count as wooing?"

"I'm not sure she even knows it consciously, but she has this attitude like…she expects people to treat her a certain way, because of how she looks." Almost like she was daring people to be jerks to her, just to prove her right. "I think that by giving her things that she doesn't expect, I might catch her off guard enough to sneak past those barriers."

"Interesting." Theo narrowed his dark eyes, considering. "So you're thinking you'll give her a family dinner, maybe some flowers, some romance."

"That's the plan, yeah." Fred swallowed, suddenly nervous. "What do you think?"

"I think it's worth a shot." Theo shrugged, then pulled out his phone. He dropped a pin, then sent Fred the location. "That's where dinner is. And don't get the flowers for Amy, get them for Mamesie."

"Thanks for the tip." The two men stood, clearing their table and tossing their garbage in the bin. As they headed for the door, Fred caught Theo sending him a pitying stare.

"What's with the sad-sack face?"

"Think of it more as a show of solidarity." Theo clapped him on the back as they headed outside. "Taking on one of the Marchande girls is not for the faint of heart."

"Great pep talk, Coach." Fred rolled his eyes. "Any other pearls of wisdom as we head into battle?"

"Yup." Theo sent him a smirk. "May the odds be ever in your favor."

CHAPTER TEN

"DON'T EAT THAT." Meg smacked Amy's hand away from the platter of bruschetta that was resting on the giant island in her industrial kitchen.

"Um, ow." Amy rubbed the skin where her sister had slapped her, frowning. Warned away from the bruschetta, she reached instead for one of the deviled eggs.

Smack. "Don't eat those, either."

"I'm sorry," she offered, voice dripping with sarcasm, "I thought that family dinner involved eating."

"Don't be dramatic." Meg bustled over to the fridge and pulled out two more platters, wrapped in plastic. Balancing one on each hand, she brought them back to the island where Amy was leaning. Placing them on the stainless steel surface, she peeled away the plastic, revealing an assortment of chilled, marinated vegetables. "And don't eat these, either."

"Will I be fed at all this evening," Amy wondered out loud, "or should I head down the street to Taco Bell?"

"Hello!" Beth swept into the large room, arms open and purple hair flying. Right behind her was her fiancé, Ford, who carried an expensive-looking bottle of wine that he handed to Meg. "Jo and Theo are just parking."

Beth picked up a slice of bruschetta from the same platter that Amy had reached for. Amy waited for Meg to smack her hand, too, but nothing happened as Beth sank her teeth into the crusty, tomato and herb–topped bread.

"Yummy." Beth gave Meg an approving nod.

"Try this one." Meg sliced a chunk off a home-made loaf and topped it with something from a jar before handing it to Ford, who lifted it to his lips. "This one is eggplant."

"Have I done something to piss you off lately?" Amy planted her hands on her hips. "Why do they get to eat and I don't?"

"They're choosing the appetizers for their wedding dinner." Meg shared an exasperated glance with Beth. "I need to make sure they try everything so they can choose."

"You've made enough food to feed an army," Amy pointed out. "And don't you want my input, too?"

"You? The woman who announced that just because all three of her sisters are heading to the altar didn't mean she wanted to wallow in wedding details all the time?" Jo and Theo entered the kitchen, the door slamming behind them. They made a bee-line for the food as Jo spoke. "Oh, are these the ap-petizers for Beth and Ford?"

John entered the kitchen then, swinging by the island to grab Meg around the waist and press a kiss into her neck. The oven timer went off, and Meg looked over her shoulder at Amy. "Can you grab those from the oven for me, Ames?"

Grumbling to herself, Amy did as she was asked. She grabbed a purple hot mitt from the counter. She pulled the steaming baking sheet of savory pastries from the hot depths of the oven, then placed them on the stainless steel counter. Turning around again, she tugged the oven mitt back off.

The three couples were clustered around the is-land, two by two. All were talking excitedly and laughing as they sampled the various things that Meg had prepared. Nobody asked for her opinion, or even looked to include her in the conversation at all.

For the first time in her entire life, Amy felt like an outsider among her own family.

Stung, she tossed the oven mitt back onto the counter. Prickles gathered behind her eyes, at the top of her nose, so she silently slid from the room. Grabbing her messenger bag from where she'd hung it, she slipped out the front door, settling herself on the top tier of the concrete steps.

The early evening air was cool and helped the tears that had threatened to retreat. Amy wasn't a big crier—she actually couldn't remember the last time she'd given in to tears—and she was embarrassed that she almost had inside. Sucking in big breaths of the crisp Boston air, she willed herself to calm down.

She and her sisters were close. They always had been. She knew them all well enough to know that none of them meant to make her feel excluded. The fact remained that she did, and she was tempted to jog down the street, catch the next bus and head on home. That way she wouldn't have to listen to hours of wedding babble that would inevitably make her feel even more left behind. Or the inevitable jokes about each of her three sisters tossing their bouquets straight to her, because there would be no one else.

If she did that, though, she'd have to explain herself when the rest of the crew got home—the perils of still living at home. Instead, she loosened the ties of her bag and tugged out her sketchbook, then rooted around the bottom of her bag for a pencil.

Drawing was the one thing that soothed her when all else had failed. When she drew, she became so utterly absorbed in what she was doing that the here and now—the anxiety and hurt—faded away and she could just be.

She hadn't been to Meg's workspace for a few weeks, and in that time, the bower of cherry trees in the park across the street had bloomed. With her pencil, she outlined the tree branches as they reached up toward the evening sky as if in prayer, then shaded in the trunks. She contemplated penciling in the blossoms, so fluffy and full of promise, but decided she didn't want the gray of the pencil lead to detract from the beauty of the blooms. Eyes still on the trees, she rummaged blindly through her bag for her pencil case, where she knew she had a pastel the exact lavender-pink shade of the silky petals.

Balancing the pastel in her fingers, she pressed it to the paper of her sketchpad, adding the blossoms with light, feathery strokes. Her fingers flew expertly across the page, ignoring the approaching footsteps until someone moved directly in front of her, blocking her light.

"Do you mind?" she asked irritably, expecting one of Meg's employees, or someone else who rented part of the industrial space. When a familiar hand moved into her line of sight, plucking the pastel from her fingers and nudging her hand to the side, her pulse quickened in her throat.

"Has anyone told you lately how good you are?" Amy looked up, unsurprised to find Fred standing in front of her. He was balanced on one of the lower steps, leaning on the wrought iron railing with his free hand tucked in his pocket.

"Not in the last hour or so." Her throat went dry as she took him in. He was dressed down for the first time since he'd come back into her life, in jeans and a light sweater, with polished leather shoes. Her eye for detail told her that any one of those pieces had probably cost ten times what she'd spent on her entire outfit—a denim miniskirt and vintage concert tee she'd scored at a thrift store. Still, it suited him. In truth, it took her right back to the first time she'd ever seen him, in that dingy bar— the guy who'd tried to fit in but hadn't quite been able to hide the layer of polish that came from his very pores.

"May I?" Rather than snatch the sketchpad from her lap, as people often felt was their right to do, he extended a hand in question. She looked at him silently for a moment, then placed it in his hand. He whistled softly as he looked from her quick sketch, then back to her face. "You did this just now? In a couple of minutes?"

"Well, yeah." She shrugged under the weight of his admiration, not something she was used to. "It's not something I'd hang in my gallery or anything. I was just blowing off some steam."

"I love it." He looked her in the eye, and she saw that his words were true. He ruffled the corners of the pad with her fingertips, as though itching to look at the rest of her work, and she snatched it back before he could.

She made a show of tearing the cherry tree piece from the perforated edge. She hoped it would distract him from the urge to see more work, because

he'd only have to go back another ten or so pages
to see sketches she'd done of him after she'd ridden
him in her tattoo chair. She had no qualms about
the fact that she'd drawn him in the nude—he had
a fantastic body, after all.

What she didn't want him to see was the emo-
tion that might have leaked from her fingers to the
page. She wasn't ready to show that to anyone yet,
not even herself.

Silently, she handed over the piece of paper on
which she'd sketched the cherry tree. "You can have
it if you want."

He was silent for a moment as he studied the
paper. Finally, he dragged his stare back up to her
face, then placed the paper back in her lap.

"Going to sign it for me?"

The tension stretched out between them, thick
and as delicious as it had been the night before. She
could still feel the echoes of pleasure his fingers had
pulled from between her legs.

And she was still more than a bit nervous about
what he'd meant when he'd said that this time,
they'd do things his way. It was in her nature to
poke, though, so she went with her gut. Rather than
scribble her name in the corner of the paper to sign
it, she pressed it to her lips. A moment later she
pulled away, a round, red-lipsticked kiss in place
of a signature.

She looked at him as she handed it back and saw

the same flicker of heat that had ignited low in her belly. She sucked in a deep breath, smelled expensive cologne and laundry detergent, and knew she was in trouble.

"What are you doing here?" She closed her sketchbook, tucking it back in her bag. Rubbing her hands over her skirt to rid them of the pastel dust, she finally noticed the market bag and bouquet that he'd set on the steps beside her when he'd approached. "What's this?"

"Bribery." He grinned sheepishly before swinging himself down to sit beside her. "I thought I'd bring out the big guns, since I might have guilt-tripped Theo into letting me crash your family dinner."

"Bribery?" Her brow furrowed as she grabbed the bag from him and riffled through it. She huffed out a breath when she felt its heft. Fingers crinkling cellophane, she removed a gift bag, whistling when she lifted it up to eye its contents. "If this is for Meg, you've got her number. If you're not careful, actually, she'll dump John and marry you."

"Pink salt, capers, kalamata olives, sun-dried tomatoes and a whole bunch of cheese." Amy made a face, genuinely impressed. "Excellent choices for the food-loving chef. You're observant."

"I had some help," he offered, shrugging off her compliment. "I, ah, asked my parents' chef for some recommendations."

"Your parents have a chef?" She wasn't shocked by this—she'd grown up close to Theo, and when his Brazilian mother hadn't been in the kitchen, they'd been known to hire the job out. Still, it was a little thorn on the stem of this moment, the reminder of just how different they were.

"Don't do that," he said, placing a hand on her knee. Warmth radiated out from the touch, and she wanted to nuzzle into his arms like a kitten, which was part of the problem. "Don't pull away. Here, let me distract you."

He thrust his other parcel into her face. The blossoms of the bouquet tickled her nose and she laughed.

"They're beautiful," she admitted, admiring the multicolored roses—she didn't stop to count, but there had to be at least two dozen.

"Don't get any ideas, now." He bumped her shoulder with his own companionably. "Those are for your mom."

He'd brought flowers for Mamesie? And had taken the time to select the perfect hostess gift for Meg? Against her better judgment, her heart did a funny little quiver in her chest as she realized the lengths he'd gone to here…just for her.

"She'll love them." She tried to keep her voice light. "Roses are her favorite."

"How about you?" He took the bouquet back, sniffing at the flowers. "What's your favorite?"

"I like roses, too." She was a little disappointed, in the most irrational of ways, that the flowers weren't for her after all. "Not red, though. There's this orangey-pink color of them you see sometimes. Those are the ones I like."

"Damn it. I was so close." When he set Mamesie's bouquet down, she saw that he'd had not one bundle of flowers, but two. The second was much smaller, a single rose with a spray of greenery, and this he handed over with another one of those sexy-as-sin smiles of his. "I guessed orange. Now I know."

"I—what?" She looked from the blossom in her lap to Fred, then back to the flower. It was perfect, a true, sugary-soda orange, and smelled like nectarines. "This is for me?"

"Why do you look so surprised?" He reached out to toy with his fingers. "Haven't you ever gotten flowers before?"

She hadn't, but if she told him that, she'd be admitting the significance of this moment. Instead she pushed abruptly to her feet. Turning, she stood between his spread thighs, placing her hands on his shoulders for balance.

"I know you said we're going to do things your way," she started, arching an eyebrow, "but is it possible that your way might involve getting out of here?"

Placing his hands on her hips, he tugged her

closer, then brushed his lips over the swells of her breasts, through the thin cotton of her T-shirt. She shivered as he dipped his thumbs beneath the waistband of her skirt and rubbed gently.

"Ever been on a bike?"

"Like…a community cruiser?" She was confused. "Not how I pictured you getting around."

"Like a motorcycle, brat." He ran those thumbs over her belly to meet in the middle, where he toyed with the button of her skirt. "Ever ridden one of those?"

"What kind of stereotypical tattoo shop owner would I be if I hadn't?" She grinned at him, then gestured to her skirt. "I'm not exactly dressed for it, though. We might have to get up close and… personal."

She yelped when he stood abruptly. Lifting her with him, he slung her over his shoulder and jogged down the steps.

"I'm counting on it." She laughed like a loon as he carried her halfway down the block, leaving his packages behind on the front steps of Meg's kitchen. When they reached his bike, he slid her slowly back down his body, and the journey down all those hard planes stole her breath.

Placing her back on her feet, he slid his hands up under the hem of her skirt to cup her ass. The street was quiet, though not deserted, but she didn't care who saw as he massaged her skin, bared by a lacy thong.

His eyes on her, and hers on him, she hiked her skirt up to her hips before straddling the bike. She could feel his stare like a touch as it raked over her bare legs from ankle to hip, a sexy smirk tugging at the corners of his lips.

"See something you like?" She deliberately echoed the words he'd once spoken to her, and his quick intake of breath told her he remembered. He closed the space between them, and she expected him to swing one of those long legs over the bike, to straddle it in front of her. Instead he opened a compartment and pulled out two helmets. Placing one on his head, he pulled out his phone, swiping and tapping, before dressing her in the matching one.

The one-hit wonder by '80s music icon Tiffany flooded her ears through the helmet, and Amy laughed out loud with delight. She couldn't see Fred's mouth, but the crinkles around his eyes told her that he was smiling, too, as he climbed onto the bike in front of her. Reaching behind him, he took her hands and urged her to wrap her arms around his waist. She did, squeezing him tightly as he started the bike.

They were from different worlds. This could never last.

That didn't mean she couldn't enjoy it while it did.

CHAPTER ELEVEN

"WANT ME TO take you home?" Fred used the speaker function so that Amy would be able to hear him inside her own helmet. She didn't reply with words, but he could feel her shaking her head. Rather than stopping the bike to ask where she wanted to go, he took a chance and navigated them to his apartment building.

He parked the bike in the underground garage and cut the engine. He climbed off, removed his helmet, then took Amy's off for her. Her blond curls were slightly flattened, her cheeks red from the wind, her signature red lipstick long gone.

He thought she was beautiful.

"How was that?" He grinned at her as he helped her climb off the bike. Her arms were icy cold, and he ran his hands up and down them to help her warm them. "Everything you dreamed of?"

"Best thing I've ridden today." Deliberately, she adjusted her tiny skirt, but not before giving him a sneak peek of the pretty pink folds barely covered by that excuse for her underwear.

"Should I take that as a challenge?" He hooked a finger in the front of her T-shirt, tugging her against him. When she was close enough, he slid his palm down, through the valley between her breasts, over her flat belly and beneath the hem of her skirt. Tucking his hand between her legs, he nudged past her thong and slid two fingers inside, without resistance. "That's what I thought. You're fucking soaked."

"I can't imagine why." She widened her legs, whimpering when he pulled out, then thrust back in. "I just spent the last two hours riding a giant vibrator, pressed up against this."

She reached around his torso, hands stroking over the curves of his ass. The flash of her pretty pussy as she'd climbed off the bike had brought him to half-mast, and now, with her hands on him, and her liquid heat bathing his fingers, he felt his cock fill.

She moved her hands, heading for his erection like a homing beacon, but he caught her around the wrists. He walked backward, pulling her along with him toward the elevator.

"Is this your building?" Those big eyes of hers took in the sleek, modern lines of the elevator, as well as the fact that he didn't have to press buttons for any floors, merely tap a key card for the elevator to start moving upward. He wasn't nervous for her to see his place, not exactly, but…okay, yeah. He was apprehensive. He didn't care about the wealth disparity between them at all, but he knew that insisting she not care, either, would just be a display of his privilege.

She was quiet as they rode up, and silent as the elevator opened right into his apartment. Each floor in this building only had one unit—his brother, Frank, lived two floors beneath him. He followed her out, heard the hiss of the doors closing behind them as they stepped into his place, and he looked over the hardwood and massive windows of his living room, tensely waiting for her reaction.

She wandered to the window, which was a floor-to-ceiling span of glass. He joined her, standing shoulder to shoulder as they looked out over the city of Boston at nighttime. She pressed the fingertips of one hand to the glass, as if testing its thickness.

"Nice view," she commented, and the knot of nerves in his gut relaxed.

"It's why I settled on this building."

"Can I sit here and draw sometime?"

Her question surprised him.

"Of course." He turned to her, but she was still looking out into the night. "Anytime."

"Thanks." Pressing her fingers to the glass again, she tapped, a bit harder than before. "I bet this is pretty sturdy, huh?"

"Two sheets thick. Heat strengthened and shatterproof." He cocked his head at the question. "Random curiosity?"

"Not at all." Turning, she met his stare, then fisted her hands in the hem of her T-shirt. Before he could even suck in a breath, she'd pulled the shirt over her head and tossed it away. She did the same with her skirt, wiggling it down and stepping out. "I was wondering if it would hold up to you fucking me against it."

"Jesus Christ, Amy." Sweat broke out along his hairline as she ran her hands through her hair, tousling the curls. She stroked her own palms down her body, stroking the side of her neck, cupping her breasts, sliding her hands between her legs. He caught one of them, pressing her hand to his erection, already hard before they'd gotten into the elevator, swelling even more now with her standing in front of him, almost naked. "The things that come out of your mouth."

"You don't like the things that come out of my mouth?" Smiling wickedly, she dropped to her knees in front of him and reached for the buckle of his belt. "Maybe you're more interested in putting something into it, instead."

He looked down, watching her pretty blond head as she made quick work of his belt and the fastenings of his jeans. He helped her tug his jeans down around his hips and pulled off his own sweater. When she rose halfway, placing her hands on his hips for balance, he slid both hands into her hair, tugging gently.

She gasped, then licked her lips. Their eyes met, and he felt a surge of power—not power over her, but power that she was choosing to give him the gift of herself. It made him want to give her what she wanted, everything she wanted, so he tugged on her hair again, not as gently this time, and savored the resultant gasp.

The connection stretched between them as always, velvety and full of promise, but this time it held a whisper of darkness. Something about seeing Amy here, on her knees before him… He'd touched her eagerly, and he'd touched her carefully. Right now? He wanted to give in to the restless storm brewing between them, to combine his thunder with her lightning.

The navy glitter in her eyes told him she wanted that, too.

With his free hand, he grasped the full length of his erection. He stroked his hand up the shaft, slid over the head and back, a handful of times as Amy watched with greedy eyes. With the hand tangled in her hair, he guided her head until her lips touched the swollen tip of his cock.

"I'm not going to be able to keep things gentle this time," he told her, his voice dark, so rough he almost couldn't recognize it. "If anything is too much, just say so. Or if you can't, just do something three times. Got it? Blink, or hit me, or whatever. Three times, and I'll stop. Okay?"

"Okay." Her breath warmed his shaft, damp and warm. Anticipation was a drug, sliding through his veins and making him high. "But I'll tell you now… I won't."

Before he could speak, she parted her lips and took him into her mouth. Her tongue explored the weight of his arousal, stroking the underside of his shaft with practiced motions that made him see stars. She kept her eyes open, watching him as she worked on him with her warm, wet mouth.

Following an instinct he hadn't known he had, he sank the hand that had been holding his shaft into her tousled blond curls as well. He saw her eyes widen when he used his grip, which was still gentle enough, to hold her in place.

She hummed around him, the vibration working through his flesh, and his fingers flexed against the flaxen silk of her hair, working her forward on his cock. When he would have eased off, she placed her palms on his thighs to steady herself, the tips of her fingers digging into the muscle while her blue gaze brightened.

She'd liked that, having that bit of control taken away from her. And if it was what she wanted, then he wanted to give it to her.

"You were right," he started, using his grip to pull her back slightly, then move her forward again, taking charge of her movements on his cock. "I do like it when you put things into your mouth."

She swallowed around him, and he groaned. She liked that, too, that bit of dirty talk, so he closed his eyes for a moment, then let what he was thinking, feeling, spill off his tongue without censure.

"I wonder if you like it as much as I do," he pondered out loud as vibrant colors swirled behind his closed eyelids. She moaned around him, and he parted his lashes to look at her again. "Your skin is flushed such a pretty pink from sucking me, I think you do. But I wonder if I can make you like it even more."

Bending slightly from the waist, he cupped a gorgeous breast in each hand, felt the sensation of another of her inarticulate cries muffled by his cock in her mouth. Squeezing softly, he stroked his thumbs over the tips of her nipples, felt her body jerk in response.

"I've been fascinated by these little bits of jewelry since the first time I saw you, standing there in that bar, your shirt so sheer that I could see them, plain as day." Her sucking faltered, and he stopped in his ministrations until she understood her error and resumed. "But we're always in a hurry, aren't we? I've never had nearly enough time to play with these gorgeous tits as I'd like to."

She whimpered when he released her, but he only did so long enough to wet his fingers in his mouth.

He returned his hands to those soft, creamy mounds, this time catching each nipple between a thumb and forefinger, rolling and teasing to see what elicited a response.

The rosy peaks were already puckered from his touch, but when he gave a light tug to each silver bar, Amy's body bucked, as though he had stroked a finger right over her clit. Fascinated, he did it again and felt her nipples contract and harden, crinkled beneath his fingers.

First the gentle hair pull, now the pinches on her breasts. It seemed that Amy liked a bit of pain with her sex, or at least that she wanted it right now. Fred had never really been into pain play, not anything beyond a bout of rough sex, but something about these responses from this woman reached inside him and turned his blood to lava.

Catching the silver bars in his fingers, he pulled again, and again she moaned and writhed with a whole-body response. He did it again, adding a twist, and her lips parted, his swollen cock falling from her tongue as she panted, hands digging into his muscles.

"Fuck, yes. Fred." Her spine arched as she tried to press herself more firmly into his touch, her entire body begging for more. "More."

He did, adding a squeeze to the soft, fleshy mounds as well, and she closed her eyes. Again moving on instinct, as though he'd been possessed by a darker self with more taboo desires, he took his hands from her breasts and caught her chin in one hand.

"Did I say you could stop sucking me?" His whole body stilled, a stark contrast to the quivering of the woman on her knees. He caught a flicker of apprehension in her eyes, but it was twined with debauched delight.

They were on.

"No." She exhaled the word, her smoky voice like a siren's. "You should probably punish me."

Punish her?

He should have been revolted. Turned off. Instead he saw that this was what she wanted, what her body craved, and he knew he'd do anything to give it to her. He didn't care what her kinks were, so long as she let him give her what she needed.

"Damn straight, I should." He cocked his head as he took in the eagerness in her body. "I want you to sit on your heels, hands in your lap. Do not move."

She hummed under her breath, a soft sound of satisfaction. It was physically painful for him to move away from her, but he needed something from his bedroom for what he had planned next.

In his bedroom, he pulled a bottle of lube from his bedside drawer, and a silver strip of condoms as well. These items in hand, he returned to the living room and found Amy exactly as he'd left her, but for one difference—her busy fingers were buried between her thighs, one hand stroking in and out, and the other circling her clit.

"Oh no, you don't." Bending, he caught her by the wrists, forced her to stop touching herself. She laughed, a breathy sound meant to bait him. When she saw the answering smirk on his own face, the amusement faded from hers, replaced with that hint of anxiety again, as well as an undeniable streak of need.

"If you need something to occupy your hands, then I have just the job." He let the corner of his mouth curl up just slightly and heard her needy sigh. "But I have to get you ready first."

Pulling open the lid to the bottle of lube, he poured a generous pool into the palm of one hand. Setting the bottle down, he rubbed his hands together, warming the liquid before again cupping her breasts.

"Fuck," Amy hissed as he massaged the cream-colored mounds. She pushed into his touch when he glanced his fingers over the turgid tips, but he focused his attention on making her breasts, and the crevice in between them, deliciously slick.

"Lie down." He traced a single finger over one silver bar before picking up the bottle of lube again. She did as he said, propping herself up on her elbows to watch as he took another generous palmful of the lubricant, this time applying it to his swollen length.

"I love your cock." Her voice was rough, as though she hadn't spoken in a week. He felt himself thicken at the words, but otherwise ignored them, instead straddling her hips.

"Doesn't matter if you love it or not," he informed her, sliding his hand up and down his engorged shaft, feeling the pleasure sparking along the nerves left in the wake of the touch. "You're going to do what I want with it, anyway."

"Yes," she replied on a hiss, dropping to a fully supine position on the carpet. Bending her knees, opening wide, she cupped her breasts in her own hands, panting with excitement. "Is this what you had in mind?"

"I guess we'll see." He smirked again before ranging himself over her body. He longed to use her parted thighs to cradle his pelvis, to slide himself home and fill her over and over and over again.

Instead he moved farther up her body. Bracing his weight with an arm on either side of her head, he slid the tip of his erection between her breasts, his eyes almost crossing from the pleasure.

"Can you reach your nipples?" He slid forward just a bit, savoring the sensation of her snug flesh around him. She nodded, breathless, and he worked forward the rest of the way. "Good. Play with them while I fuck your tits."

Another harsh sound from her, and then she did as he asked. Her artist's palms cupped her breasts, holding them together as he worked his cock back and forth in the slippery space between them. At the same time, she used her talented fingers to pluck at her nipples, much harder than he would have dared.

He could sense her arousal reaching a fever pitch. Her hips bucked beneath him, and she craned her neck so that she could swipe a warm tongue over the swollen head of his erection as he thrust. Swearing, he pulled out of the warm hollow, the sudden cool air on his engorged shaft making him crazy. She cried out as he flipped her over to her belly, using bossy hands to pull her hips up while she remained bent over.

"You keep trying to take control," he chastised her, placing a hand on the small of her back, pinning her in place. He was in his role now, the one she'd wanted him to take on, and enjoying every second of it. "Every time you do, it's just going to postpone what you really want."

"How do you know what I really want?" Her words were meant to taunt but quivered with arousal. With need.

"Because you told me." With his free hand, he pulled back, then swatted her across one side of her ass. She gasped, that tight, delicious body jolting forward on the carpet. Her pale skin reddened, and he knew he should feel bad about that, but truthfully...

Truthfully, seeing it glow scarlet, watching the

mark from his hand on her skin? It did it for him, dug a hook into some primal part of himself and pulled it forward into the light.

His biggest kink was, and always would be, giving his partner—giving Amy—what she wanted.

But this?

This was really fucking hot.

Bending over her, he delivered a second swat, this time to the other cheek. Again she cried out, a wordless jumble of sound, and when he massaged the heated skin, she rubbed her thighs together as if searching for a friction that would give her some relief.

"Please." She canted her behind in the air, the pretty pink peeking out from between her legs making his mouth go dry. He swatted her sharply again, then delivered a rapid succession of lighter blows that rained down over her flesh, which elicited a series of whimpers, gasps and moans. "Fred. I can't wait any longer."

"You'll wait as long as I tell you to wait." He swiped two questing fingers between her folds. She was soaked, hot and wet, and his cock ached to slide inside. Tamping down the urge, he worked those fingers into her slick channel. "Lucky for you, this is where I want to be. I want to be here so badly it hurts."

Climbing to his feet, he worked his jeans the rest of the way off, taking his underwear with them.

Tearing into one of the little foil packets he'd retrieved from his bedside table, he rolled the ring of latex down his shaft, then turned his attention back to her.

His dick was already at attention, rigid and swollen with the need to be inside her. But as he looked at her there, on the floor of his apartment, he felt something flutter around his heart. She was beautiful, sure—the graceful arch of her spine, the riot of skulls and wildflowers inked into the smooth skin of her back, the heart shape of her ass—but it was more than that.

After a lifetime constrained in a little box made of the expectations of others, he was free to be who he wanted with this woman. More than that—she expected it from him. Demanded it.

He never wanted to let her go.

"Up." He held out a hand to help her off the floor. She stood on shaky legs, and he spun her until they were face-to-face, where he could claim her mouth in a kiss. Dipping his head to hers, he coaxed his tongue between her lips as he lifted her off her feet. She wrapped her legs around his waist as he carried her to the window. They both groaned at the friction of skin on skin as he set her back down on her feet, his cock pressing into the flat surface of her belly.

"Turn around." His hands skimmed her body as she followed his order. A gasp escaped her lips at the discovery that she was an inch from the floor-to-ceiling window of glass, thirty floors above the streets of Boston. "Is this still what you want?"

"Yes." She shivered.

"You're not afraid of heights?" He spanned her waist, his grip promising to catch her if she fell. Rather than push back into his touch, she closed that last ribbon of space between herself and the window.

"No." She settled her smooth cheek against the cool glass. "I love them."

"Good." Taking his cock in hand, he rubbed the tip through her wetness, then worked it up and down, through the crevice that divided her buttocks. Bending his knees slightly, he placed the head at her opening, working the tip into her swollen tissues. She squeezed around him, and he groaned.

He wanted to surge forward, to seat himself inside her, but forced himself to slow down and savor the moment. Dipping his head, he inhaled the spicy scent of her shampoo, then pressed a kiss to the top of her head. She sighed, a soft little sound of contentment that reached right through his rib cage and grabbed his heart in a tight fist. He needed to get closer to her; he wasn't sure he could get close enough.

Pressing a palm to the window to brace himself, he began to move, filling her at a slow but steady pace. She gasped once he was sheathed inside her to the root, her greedy center clenching around him.

Pleasure tightened in his core, and he pressed his forehead to the chilled glass, trying to get himself under control. He wanted this to last.

Amy had other ideas. Pressing her own hands to the glass, she arched back against him. Bending at the waist to allow him to slide in just a little bit farther, she gave a delicious little wiggle of her hips.

"In a hurry?" Fred's voice was amused. "Got a hot date I don't know about?"

"I'm so sorry," she replied, her voice thick with arousal and dripping with saccharine sweetness, "but I thought you said you wanted to give me what I wanted. And what I want is to get fucked."

Heat shot through him like he'd touched a live wire, a single sizzle from head to foot, and he growled. Clasping her by the hips, he dug the tips of his fingers into her soft flesh. "Then I'd suggest you hold on."

Using her as his anchor, he began to move. Slow, punishing thrusts at first, as deep inside her as he could go. They both made incoherent sounds every time his hips met the curves of her behind; both exhaled when he pulled back. The deep thrusts quickly gave way to shorter ones, harder ones. His pace quickened until he could hear their flesh slapping together, a sound that shouldn't have been erotic and yet was the dirtiest thing he'd ever heard.

"Fuck, yes." Her hands, damp with sweat, slipped on the glass. He wrapped his arms around her waist to anchor her, continuing to move inside her as his entire world narrowed to the place where her soft pink flesh squeezed around the steel rod of his erection. "Please, Fred. I can't wait any longer."

"Come for me." Dipping his head, he nipped at the delicate curve where her shoulder became her neck. She growled, a purely animal sound, so he did it again, this time giving her a sharp bite since he already knew she liked a bit of pain with her pleasure. Her pussy tightened around him, and her body stiffened, hot and tight beneath him. "Now. Come now."

He watched her shudder, felt the vibrations through his flesh, and then she screamed, the cry bouncing off the smooth glass. He moved through it all, her pleasure spurring on his own. His arousal starting to barrel through his body like a runaway train, and finally he could hold back no more. One thrust, two and three and four, and he poured himself inside her, pleasure causing stars to dance behind his eyes.

They were both out of breath, panting hard enough to create mist on the glass. Heat had sealed them together, and as they both laughingly tried to catch their breath, Fred realized that he could quite happily stay like this, right here with this woman, for the rest of his life.

The realization should have been terrifying. It should have had him easing out of her body and running for the door, never mind the fact that this was his apartment. Instead, he found that it felt… well, it felt right.

He knew he had to pull out, but he resented it, even as the slow drag through her tissues sparked pleasure yet again. Carefully, he eased them to the ground, sitting with his legs apart, and Amy between them.

"Think anybody saw us?" Amy murmured, nestling back against him, her back to his front. They were looking out the window they'd just been pressed against, watching the bright lights of Boston at nighttime, twinkling thirty floors beneath him. "Whatever would your neighbors think?"

"They'd be jealous," he replied with certainty. "They'd look at this incredibly hot woman, writhing on my dick, and wonder what I'd done to get so fucking lucky."

She laughed, and he liked the husky sound. They were silent for a moment, and Fred held his breath. This was the point at which she usually withdrew, or ran, or otherwise broke their connection.

When she twisted around to give him a soft kiss, he found that he could exhale again. She wasn't running. He could relax.

He wouldn't, though. Not until he'd figured out a way to make her see how right this was, this thing between them. Not until he figured out a way to make her stay.

CHAPTER TWELVE

THE NEXT DAY, Amy was sore. Deliciously so, her every movement a reminder of the ways Fred had used her body—the ways they'd used each other.

Several times today, a dirty memory from the night before had flashed before her eyes, as vivid as a summer day. Her on her knees at his feet, his cock heavy on her tongue as he fucked her mouth with bossy thrusts of his hips. Her on hands and knees, face pressed to the plush carpet as he spanked her ass, leaving wicked heat in the wake of his blows. The strange, exciting sensation of cold, slick glass pressed to her breasts, her belly, her cheek as he claimed her from behind.

This morning, the searching tenderness in those green eyes of his when he'd pulled up in front of the house she'd grown up in, where she still lived. He might not have known what a big step that was for her, letting him see the old brown house that was so much shabbier than its newer, fancier neighbors, but she'd wanted to do it—wanted to give him a little piece of herself.

That alone told her how much trouble she was in. It was like she was on board a train that had been set into motion five years ago, one that kept going faster and faster and was bound to crash, to end in a giant, fiery explosion, but she couldn't get off— didn't *want* to get off—because the speed of the ride felt so damn good.

After sending her midmorning client out the door overjoyed with their new ink, she stretched to loosen her tight muscles as she stood behind her front counter, contemplating her lunch choices. She had no plans for that evening and found herself wondering what Fred was up to. Picking up her phone, she thought to send him a text asking just that, but stopped herself.

This—these floaty, good-sex feelings, the emotional buzz—this smacked of a relationship.

Was it a relationship?

If it was…would that be so bad?

The chiming of the bells hanging in her doorway took her attention from her phone. Her stomach clenched with excitement when she spotted the familiar ginger head brushing against the copper of the bells because of his height.

"I was just thinking of texting…" Her voice trailed off when the man stopped just inside the entrance of her shop, looking around. "You're not Fred."

"Guilty as charged." The man held out his hands, palms facing her, with a self-deprecating smile. It was a familiar expression, one that she'd seen on Fred's own lips, but while she found it sexy on her Vaughan twin, on this one it just seemed contrived. "I don't think we've ever actually been formally introduced. I'm Frank."

Closing the space between them, he offered her his hand. She shook it, though she arched an eyebrow as she did. "Trying to steal me away from your twin brother at a crappy club in Amsterdam doesn't count as an intro in your world, then?"

He laughed, and she experienced a discordant moment. He looked so much like Fred that parts of her assumed he would sound like Fred, and he did a bit. The tone of his voice was a slightly higher pitch, though, and the inflections in his words a little different.

Given the thoughts she'd been having about this man's identical twin all morning, this was just... weird.

"Did you do all this yourself?" Tucking his hands into the pockets of his suit pants, Frank rocked back on his heels, making a show of looking around her space.

"The art, you mean? Or the wall painting and

light fixtures?" Her brow furrowed as she watched him. Why was he here?

"Both, I suppose." Nodding, he cast her an approving glance. "Good job. It's very different than I thought it would be. It's really nice."

That's a hell of a backhanded compliment. It was on the tip of her tongue to say just that, but something had her biting her tongue. She was pretty sure that something was Fred, and the fact that she didn't know where they stood exactly. Still, she wasn't pleased that Frank seemed oblivious to the fact that she didn't need or want his approval, and it made her tongue slightly sharper than it would be with the ordinary lookie-loo. "Can I help you with something? Would you like to see some designs?"

"Some tattoo designs?" He looked at her with amazement. "For me? Oh, I don't think so."

She caught what he wasn't saying—that tattoos weren't for people like him, they were for people like her. Her temper flared—she and all three of her sisters had more than their fair share of it—but the bells in her doorway jingled again, distracting her.

"Hello." The six-foot-four-inch man with auburn hair who entered her shop this time was the right one. As Fred approached the desk, she thought she could actually feel her body vibrate with excitement. He looked at Frank, then cast Amy a quizzical glance, to which she shrugged. "What are you doing here, Frank?"

"Just giving her a second chance to choose the right twin," Frank countered, grinning slickly at his brother. He winked at Amy and seemed a bit startled when she frowned in return.

"Good luck with that." Fred winked at Amy, too, and while she had not appreciated the gesture from Frank, from Fred it made butterflies flutter in her belly. She expected him to make some kind of bro-type comment, like the fact that he'd proven he was enough man for her, but when he continued, she realized that she was coloring her expectations with past experiences. "She's a woman who knows what she wants."

And there, right there, she knew that she was falling head over heels in love with him. Mouth suddenly dry, she groped blindly for the bottle of water she knew was sitting somewhere on her desk.

"Well, if there's no hope, then…" Frank rolled his eyes at his twin, then nodded at Amy with a small smile. "I guess I'll take my leave. Looking forward to speaking more with you later."

What did that mean? She didn't have time to ponder, because she was still grappling with the realization that she'd gone and fallen in love with the man standing in front of her. The one who was looking at her strangely as she stood there with crazy eyes, frantically flailing about for her water bottle.

"Are you okay?" He cocked his head, moved in closer. "You look…warm."

"Water," she croaked, gesturing to her desk. With deft movements he grabbed her water bottle—it had been literally right in front of her, because of course it had—unscrewing the cap before handing it to her. She took a long sip, both to quench her thirst and to give herself a moment in which to compose herself.

"Better?" He didn't give her a moment. Instead, he nipped the bottle from her hand once she was done drinking, setting it back on the desk. He studied her with a small smile that made her knees quiver. "Hmm, I'm thirsty, too. Wanna share?"

Before she could suck in another breath, his lips were on hers, his tongue stealing away the droplets of moisture that remained. What started as a light, teasing kiss quickly deepened, pulling her under to a place she never wanted to surface from again.

"I like the way you say hello," she gasped when he finally released her. He grinned, grabbing her around the waist and tugging her against him. He dipped his head to nibble at the lobe of her ear, and she felt dampness pool between her thighs. "Didn't you get your fill last night?"

"Never." He spoke with such certainty, looking into her eyes, that her heart skipped a painful beat. She didn't know what to do with these feelings— didn't know if she was ready for them—so she tried to lighten the current passing between them.

"What are you doing tonight, then?" Sex, she thought. Bring it back to sex—back to familiar territory. Rising onto her toes, she rocked her hips against his, felt the first stirrings of his desire as she pressed a finger to his lips. She sucked in a quick breath when his tongue darted out for a taste. "Maybe you can *fill me* some more."

"Dirty girl." He sank his teeth into the tip of her finger, then licked again to soothe the sting. "That's why I stopped by, actually. To see if you had plans tonight."

"I don't." She let her finger slide from his lips, down his chin, his solid chest, down until she could hook it in the leather of his belt. She felt the flat plane of his belly quiver in response. "Unless you can think of something I should do?"

He hissed out a swear when her fingers dipped into the waistband of his dress pants, dancing over the head of his cock. He grabbed her by the hips, squeezed, pulled her tighter.

"I can think of lots of things you can do. Things that you will do," he started, grinding his pelvis lightly against her. "But before that... I'm hoping I can convince you to join me for dinner."

"I like to eat," she replied lightly, rising on her toes to nip at the line of his jaw. "Bet you can think of something I'd really like to put in my mouth."

"Woman." With his grip on her hips, he pulled back, huffing out a pained laugh. "Stay with me here. I mean real dinner. With food. A nice meal. And…company."

"Company?" She stilled her hands as she looked up at him. "Your company, I presume?"

"Mine," he agreed, watching her carefully, "and my family's."

"What?" Startled, Amy pulled back from him completely. "Why on earth would you want me to have dinner with your family?"

She looked into his face, searching for a sign that he was kidding. He was not.

"I was under the impression that there's something between us, here. Something bigger than I've ever felt before." He narrowed his eyes. "I want my family to meet you."

"Fred. You can't be serious." She shook her head as panic bubbled up in her gut.

"Of course I'm serious." He seemed taken aback by her reaction, and frustration followed her panic. "Why would I joke about this?"

"Your family owns this mall," she reminded him, planting her hands on her hips. "They're the ones trying to kick me out."

"Hey, hey, it's okay." Reaching out, he rubbed his hands up and down her upper arms. "That won't come up tonight. You'll be there strictly as my… my…"

"Your what?" Temper heated her words. She was getting whiplash from her own emotions. "The woman you were supposed to tell to shape up or ship out? The one you also happen to be fucking? Do they know that, by the way? Is that why Frank was in here? To keep an eye on me?"

"That's not fair." His voice was quiet. "I was a part of my family before I ever met you. Part of being a Vaughan means participating in the family business. Of course I said I'd deliver that letter. I had no idea I was supposed to deliver it to you."

"Well, now you know." She tapped a foot on the floor, trying to release some of her pent-up energy. "And I assume they do, too. What do you think will happen tonight? I show up to dinner, and they're going to think I'm sleeping with you to keep my retail space. Or worse. They'll think I'm a gold digger."

"Amy." His voice was filled with frustration. "I get that it's not an ideal situation, but that's part of the reason I want them to meet you, to spend some time with you. I know once they get to know you, they'll see that that petition was ridiculous. That you should stay."

"I'm not going to beg them." A dart of hurt burrowed its way into her chest. "If they can't see what I bring, then they don't deserve to have me."

"No one expects you to beg." This time his voice dripped with frustration. "Give me a break here, would you? I want you to come to dinner so that my family can meet you, end of story. Come have a nice meal and let them meet the woman in my life. I'm sure they're going to be as wowed by you as I am. And if that affects their thoughts on that petition, that's just a bonus. Okay?"

Amy sucked a breath in through her nose, her temper still sharp. She was under no delusions here.

That petition was essentially a piece of paper that the other vendors of the plaza had signed to say that Amy didn't fit in and they didn't want her there. Not nice, but also not surprising—Amy had never fit in anywhere, and usually she was fine with that. What had surprised her about this whole nonsense was the fact that Vaughan Enterprises—the company made up of Fred's family—had looked at what was essentially an opinion and had acted on it. They'd issued her a warning telling her to conform, to toe the line, while ignoring the fact that she had just as much right to be there as anyone else. More, if they'd stopped to examine just what she brought to the table.

This meant that the company, and Fred's family, was very concerned with image. She looked down at her right hand, with the four roses tattooed along her knuckles, and knew that she did not fit their aesthetic. She never would.

She shouldn't go. It would only end in heartbreak.

"Please?" Closing the distance between them again, Fred squeezed her shoulders gently as he looked down at her beseechingly. "It would mean a lot to me. Okay?"

After a long pause, she nodded once, a jerk of her chin. The moment she did, she knew that she was going to regret it, but Fred's smile chased away the chill.

Fine. She'd go have dinner with his parents. But she wasn't going to pretend to be anyone but herself.

Four hours later, Amy drummed her fingers on the gold-flecked vinyl countertop in the bathroom she shared with Jo.

"Stop fidgeting," Meg insisted as she wound another lock of Amy's fine hair around the barrel of her curling iron. "You're going to get burned."

"Sorry." Amy slid her hands beneath her butt to keep them still. She was seated on the closed lid of the toilet as her eldest sister worked on her hair. "Better?"

"It would be better if you told me why you were so nervous." Finished with the curling iron, Meg set it on a silicone mat on the counter, then picked up an aerosol can of hairspray. "Close your eyes."

Amy did, waiting for Meg to finish spraying before she spoke again. "I'm not nervous."

"Pants on fire," Meg replied around the bobby pin in her mouth. "I just watched you brush your teeth for the third time because you forgot you'd already done it twice."

Amy scowled as Meg ran her fingers through the curls she'd just created, then pinned a piece back with the bobby pin. "I'm not... It's not that I'm scared to meet them, exactly."

"Close your eyes." Satisfied with the hair, Meg waved a mascara wand in the air. "What is it, then?"

"I already know there's a really good chance that they're not going to like me. I'm not their kind of person." Amy held perfectly still, felt Meg brushing the liquid onto her eyelashes as she tried to put it into words. "That doesn't bother me, much. It's more that... shit. I don't know how to say it."

"It's because you actually care about this guy." Setting the mascara aside, Meg dusted powder over the apples of Amy's cheeks. "And you're afraid that he's going to start seeing you through his family's eyes."

Amy opened her eyes, squinting narrowly up at her sister. "There's a terrifying thought. Thank you ever so much for putting it into my head."

"You're welcome." Meg smiled beatifically. "You're done."

Meg moved back, clapping her hands together to remove the remnants of face dust that clung. Amy craned her head around to the mirror to see. She frowned. "You didn't do what I asked you to."

She'd told Meg to...well, to tone her down a bit. Pink lipstick instead of her signature red. Easy on the eye makeup and the contouring.

Instead, her sister had taken her usual look and classed it up, for lack of a better word. Her lips were painted red, but it was a deep crimson rather than her usual scarlet. Her eyes had been accentuated with a set of smoky browns, her cheekbones emphasized with a tawny shade.

She looked like herself. And she looked like she could kick some ass.

"It works," she told Meg, nodding with approval. "Even though you went off book."

"You wanted me to go off book," her sister replied with a shake of her head. "You wanted me to make you look like someone you're not. Like someone you think these people will be happy to meet."

"That's not true," Amy replied, but even as she did, she knew it was a lie.

"It most certainly is." With a wide smile, Meg handed Amy her bottle of signature perfume, indicating with a pinch of her fingers to go easy on it. "But that's not who Fred invited to dinner. Family or not, I have to think he wants you to be you."

"I guess we'll see." Sucking in a deep breath, Amy placed a hand on her stomach in an attempt to quiet the nerves rolling around in it. "Still totally not nervous."

"Right." Meg rolled her eyes as she handed Amy a small makeup bag that she'd stuffed with the essentials for touch-ups. "Look. I get that you care about this guy, and that changes things. Believe me, I understand."

Meg had gone through her share of strife with her own love, John, so Amy knew this to be true.

"Here's the thing, though. If he's worth it, really worth it? He won't expect you to change a thing. More than that? He'll fight to keep you, just the way you are."

"Right." This wasn't news—it was a truth Amy lived her life by. She'd never before cared enough, one way or another, if someone she'd been seeing came up lacking.

This time? If Fred proved himself unworthy tonight...she wasn't sure she could recover.

CHAPTER THIRTEEN

"Wow." THE LOOK on Fred's face when he opened the front door to his parents' house was worth every second that Amy had let Meg layer her face in makeup. He looked her up and down, appreciation evident in his features. "Hi."

"You're staring." She smirked at him as she hitched her purse up higher on her shoulder. Her wallet stuck out the top, and she took a moment to tuck it back into the bag—she'd splurged on an Uber to get here. Fred had wanted to come pick her up, but she'd wanted her own means of escape, just in case.

"You're worth staring at." He gestured with his hand for her to turn around. She did, laughing, letting him get a full view. "Let me use some of the many words I've learned over my life to say, *damn*."

She knew he hadn't expected her to show up for dinner in her habitual torn cutoffs and tank top, but he'd never seen her in anything else. She was vain enough to enjoy the hell out of the way he was looking at her, and she knew she deserved it. It had been a bit of work, but damn it, she looked good.

A sleek, satiny, plum-colored dress clung to her curves from throat to knee. It was Meg's dress, and where it hit midcalf on her sister, it ended just above the knee for her. She'd paired it with spiky-heeled black boots that made the most of her legs. She'd added a thin black sweater that covered her shoulders and arms but was fitted enough not to distract from the lines of the dress.

The look had been chosen with care. She wasn't ashamed of who she was, or the ink that she'd chosen to mark indelibly on her body. That said, she also wasn't so naive that she thought any set of parents would be thrilled to be introduced to a girlfriend with as many tattoos as she had. She and Meg had chosen this dress because the high neckline covered the black stars on her neck, and the sweater because it took the attention away from her full tattoo sleeves.

She left her legs bare, the ink there open to view, as well as the four roses that adorned her right hand. And she still felt like herself, but like…well, like a grown-up version. Like a woman who was ready to meet the parents of a boyfriend.

She'd done a lot of things in her life, but she'd never done that.

"You're drooling already? I haven't even shown you the whole dress." Her words were teasing.

Shrugging her sweater down her arms, she turned away from him so that he could see the back of her dress—or rather, the lack thereof.

She heard him suck in a breath when he saw the way the high collar of the dress circled her neck, and then the naked skin that continued to the base of her spine.

She felt him move closer, trailing a finger down her spine. She shivered as he traced her shoulder blades, the muscles of her back, the delicate stripes of her rib cage.

"Let's just leave now," he announced, moving his finger to stroke over the side of her breast. A small sound of arousal escaped her mouth. "Dinner is overrated."

Closing her eyes for a moment, she sucked in a deep breath to center herself.

"No way." Stepping forward, out of his reach, she slid her cardigan back into place and turned, fixing him with an arched eyebrow. "This was your idea. Into the belly of the beast we go."

"The belly of the beast?" She'd thought that he might be insulted by the description, but instead he sounded amused. "Amy, it's just my family. The people who raised me. It's going to be fine."

Shaking away the sense of foreboding, she resisted the urge to tell him that she was pretty sure it wouldn't be. Either way, she was here and she was going to see this through. Maybe she was a mas-ochist, but she knew that she had to do it.

She wanted Fred, and he came with a family. A family business. She knew that he expected them to just accept her, but she also knew that wasn't how it worked. She had to know, though—had to know if she would be accepted as part of Fred's life.

If she wasn't, then it would be better to get out now, before her heart could be broken any further.

"Amy, you dazzle me." Reaching out, he took her hand, pulling her through the door and into the house. "You'll dazzle them, too."

The Vaughan family was arranged artfully around what she would call a living room, were it not for the ornately carved mahogany bar at one end. They looked like a painting, four people posed beautifully throughout a decorative room, four faces turned toward her and Fred with curiosity written into their features.

"Hello!" Fred helped her down the steps into the sunken room, waving to the room at large. Amy quickly checked her shoes to make sure she wasn't tracking mud or wet onto the expensive-looking woven rug that covered a large portion of the gleam-ing hardwood floors.

She could feel eyes on her. Normally this wouldn't faze her in the slightest—nobody pre-sented themselves the way she did if they didn't enjoy attention. The fact that she desperately wanted the people these eyes belonged to to like her, though, or at least tolerate her?

She cast a quick, desperate glance to the bar. She could use some liquid courage right now.

An older man she recognized from the Vaughan Enterprises website that she'd studied earlier this week was standing at the bar, a cocktail shaker in hand. Well over six feet himself, with a rangy build, he looked like an older version of the twins, though the way he carried himself suggested Frank more than Fred. Setting the cocktail shaker down on the bar, he opened his arms in a gesture of welcome as he looked her over.

She saw the exact moment he noticed the tattoos on her legs, his smile freezing in place.

Here we go. She tried not to grimace.

"I was beginning to think your, ah, friend was going to stand us up, Frederick." Frederick Sr. looked her over top to bottom again, a wrinkle in his forehead demonstrating that he was perplexed. "What is your name again, dear?"

"Dad, this is Amy." At the introduction, Amy extended a hand—not the one with the four rose tattoos. "Amy, this is my dad, Frederick Vaughan Sr."

"Lovely to meet you." Amy smiled brightly. Frederick Sr. seemed slightly taken aback by the wattage, as though he'd been expecting her to glower.

"Ah, hello." Frederick, Sr. belatedly set down the cocktail shaker and took Amy's hand. Though he seemed slightly taken aback by her bright smile, his icy reserve seemed to thaw just a bit under the brilliant wattage. "Welcome to our home."

"Dad, I'd like one of whatever you're mixing there." Fred smiled pointedly at his father to move things along. "Amy? Would you like a drink?"

"Wine would be lovely." Her voice caught in her throat—nerves. "If you have it. If not, anything is fine."

"Oh, we have it." Fred rolled his eyes. Reaching over the bar, he grabbed a stemmed wineglass that looked as light as air. "My parents are wine snobs. Red or white?"

"Really, Fred." This came from the only other woman in the room, who stood, dusted off her skirt and crossed to the bar as well. "The correct term is *collector*."

"Yeah, yeah." Fred grinned at the woman, who was as short as her sons and husband were tall, with chin-length red hair and a face full of fine-boned features. "Hi, Mom."

"Nice of you to make time for your parents," the woman replied wryly. "Are you going to introduce me to your friend?"

"Mom, this is Amy." Fred smiled down at her, rubbing the small square of her back where his hand rested. "Amy, this is my mother, Rosemary. The wine *collector*."

"That's it. None of the good stuff for you." Rosemary rounded the bar, snatching the glass Fred had retrieved and replacing it with a shorter goblet that had a shallower cup. "I'll send someone out to Discount Depot, shall I? Now Amy, tonight we've opened a Chevalier-Montrachet we purchased several years ago in France. It has hints of citrus and some spice notes, when served in the correct glass. Does that sound appealing to you?"

"It sounds lovely." Amy smiled mildly. The wine she usually drank came from the aforementioned Discount Depot, usually for about seven dollars a bottle. She was sure she'd like whatever they gave her just fine.

Rosemary filled a glass precisely one-third of the way, then handed it to Amy as if bestowing her with a glass of liquid gold. Amy quickly lifted it to her lips and sipped. When she lowered it, everyone in the room was staring at her, aghast, except for Fred.

"It's...very nice." What? What had she done? From the corner of her eye, she watched Frederick Sr. pick up his own glass. Holding it beneath his nose, he sniffed at it as though he was starring in a commercial for men's body spray. He then took a tiny sip, rolling it around his lips before nodding and, finally, swallowing.

Amy was put in mind of the time her brother-in-law Theo had taken them all to a fancy restaurant— one that wasn't too far from this house, actually. Theo had ordered the wine, so the waiter...no, not the waiter, but the sommelier…had initiated something similar. He'd poured a swallow of the wine into a glass and handed it to Theo, who had sniffed and tasted, approved, and then promptly been called a pompous ass by Jo.

So apparently rich people drank their wine a certain way. Duly noted. She sniffed awkwardly at her glass, sipped again and received a thin smile, but a smile regardless from Frederick Sr.

"How's that cocktail coming, Dad?" Sensing her discomfort, Fred cast his father a look. With light pressure in the fingers that rested at the small of her back, he quickly and smoothly steered her across the room, stopping in front of his twin. Amy's fingers clutched the stem of her wineglass tightly as Fred clapped his brother on the shoulder, then shook the second man's hand.

"Amy, you know Frank." Still put off by Frank's backhanded comments that afternoon, Amy didn't offer a hand. "This is his boyfriend, Mark."

So Frank was bisexual, or pansexual. Not something that would normally have her even raising an eyebrow, but she did wonder what the very proper Frederick Sr. and Rosemary thought of it, when her own reception had been so very lukewarm. Of course, clad in a pricey-looking blue button-down, navy blazer and well-cut charcoal trousers, Mark gave off a very different vibe than she did.

A bead of cold sweat rolled down her spine. She

couldn't remember the last time she'd been so uncomfortable. Why was she doing this again?

Fred chose that moment to press a light kiss to
the silky gold curls on her head. An absentminded
gesture, but it sent warmth streaming throughout
her entire body.

This. This was why she was here, at this dinner
where she didn't feel entirely welcome. And maybe
it would all be okay.

"You know Frank as well? How interesting."
With her own glass of wine in hand now, Rosemary
settled herself back on the sofa. An amused smile
curled her lips. "How did you come to meet my
boys? Neither of them seems the type for tattoos."

Another subtle zinger from a Vaughan. Lovely.

"Well, I lease a space in the newest Vaughan Enterprises property," Amy started. She stood tall, trying to draw confidence from her core. Fred pressed
his hand more firmly against her back, so she continued. "But I actually met them both in Europe,
five years ago."

"The infamous postgrad Europe trip." Mark el-
bowed his boyfriend lightly, careful not to let his
martini slosh over the edge. "You were there? I have
so many questions."

"All in due time," Frederick Sr. started, "but I
can see Margaret waving from the kitchen. Let us
adjourn to the dining room, shall we?"

Wrapping an arm around her waist, Fred steered

Amy toward the attached room, with its long mahogany table and velvet-cushioned chairs. As he pulled out her chair for her, he bent to whisper into her ear. "You're doing great."

"Liar, liar, pants on fire," she replied through a bright, fake smile. He rolled his eyes.

"Amy." Settling himself into the chair next to her, he ran a finger along the line of her jaw, just one quick movement. "I don't want you to pretend to be who you think they want you to be, okay? Just be yourself. Be the woman I lo—the woman I know."

The woman he *what*?

"What did you just say?" Amy turned fully in her chair to face him, but then the woman she assumed was Margaret, a young woman with pale blond hair, was there. She took the crisp cloth napkin from the table in front of Amy, flicking it through the air before laying it gently in her lap. She repeated the action for every person at the table, then disappeared into what Amy assumed was the kitchen. She returned with a tray, placing small bowls of soup in front of each of them. Amy dragged her attention back to the table. She reached for a spoon, then froze.

In front of her was a place setting more intricate than anything she'd come across before. Could all this really be for her? A quick glance around the table showed her the same setting at every place.

Unlike her, however, no one else seemed intimidated by it.

The central feature was a plate, shiny gold and larger than a dinner plate. The napkin now on her lap had been resting on top of it. Arranged precisely around the plate were four different forks, two spoons, two knives, another napkin, a bread plate and four glasses. She looked from all of it to the soup and back again. Which one was she supposed to use?

"Work from the outside in," Fred leaned in toward her and whispered. He nodded slightly toward the correct spoon. Amy picked it up, hoping nobody had noticed, but a quick glance showed her that Rosemary had noted her hesitation.

Well, whatever. So she didn't come from a household where they used four forks per meal. Whatever.

There was silence for a moment, spoons and china clinking as everyone worked on their soup. Once Frederick Sr. was done, he sat back, eyeing her again.

"Let's circle back to our earlier discussion. How did you meet the boys?" He took a large sip of wine, which Amy noticed had been topped up, in a fresh glass. She thought briefly of the extra washing involved with all this excess and couldn't quite wrap her head around it.

She didn't like it. And while she wasn't quite ready to give up on the evening just yet, she decided there and then that she wasn't going to feel bad for not fitting in.

"I met both Fred and Frank in a club in Amsterdam." She continued to eat her soup.

"And you've kept in contact with them?" Rosemary set down her spoon. "I must say, neither of them has ever mentioned your name."

Zing.

"That would be difficult, as neither of them knew it." Amy took another polite spoonful of soup. "This soup is lovely. My compliments to the chef."

"I don't imagine you've ever had lobster bisque." Frederick Sr. nodded at her down the table. "I believe the next course is beef Wellington. This meal should be a treat for you."

His words weren't meant to be cruel, but Amy caught what he hadn't said out loud. That he assumed she didn't eat meals like this because he couldn't imagine she could afford it.

Her temper flared. Setting down her spoon, she placed her hand on Fred's knee and squeezed once, hard, to let him know she wasn't feeling this. He cast her a quick, worried glance.

"Actually, Amy's sister Meg is a chef," Fred interjected. Reaching for the bottle of wine, he refilled Amy's glass, though everyone else had signaled Margaret to do the refilling. Amy was sure that didn't go unnoticed. "She owns a catering company."

"Interesting," Mark interjected. "What kind of cuisine?"

"Is it gourmet," Rosemary wondered out loud, "or is it one of those food truck situations?"

Food truck situations?

This time Fred squeezed her knee, and she swallowed the vinegar on her tongue.

"The type of cuisine is dependent on the needs of the client," Amy replied. "She can do anything, though. For my last birthday, actually, one of the things she made was lobster bisque, as it's one of my favorites."

"Do you have any other siblings?" This was Frank. He cast her a quick smile of apology, and Amy thawed toward him, just the slightest bit.

"I have three sisters." Amy thought of them each in turn, of how they'd react in this particular situation. None of them, she knew, would put up with these passive-aggressive putdowns, especially not for a guy. She sat up straighter in her seat, calmly sipping her own glass of wine. "Meg is the oldest. She's the caterer. Next is Jo, a writer. Then Beth. She's a mechanic. And then me. The tattoo artist."

Frederick Sr. furrowed his brow as though something had just occurred to him, but Fred spoke before his father could.

"Do either of you remember Theo Lawrence? That friend Frank and I had in college?" Fred eased back in his chair as Margaret served the next course. "He's engaged to Amy's sister Jo. And Dad, I recall you used to golf with someone named Lassiter? His son, Ford, is married to Beth."

"Theo Lawrence? And Ford Lassiter?" Rosemary turned to look at Amy, calculating. "It seems your sisters have made good marriages."

They'd made good marriages? Who talked like that?

"Is your sister Meg engaged as well?" Rosemary continued.

"She is." Amy's smile was tight. "To a very wealthy businessman named John Brooke. In fact, all my sisters are going to be rich as hell once they get married."

Rosemary's upper lip curled with distaste, pre-sumably at the fact that Amy had actually spoken out loud of wealth. "I see. One might think it was your turn. How lucky that you kept in contact with a suitable candidate. Two of them, in fact."

"Mom!" Fred sat up straight, glaring at his mother. "Why are you being so rude?"

"Protecting my son from people more interested in his bank account than his personality isn't rude, son." Rosemary sniffed, pushing away the plate that held her portion of beef Wellington with a nose in the air. "It's called being prudent."

"Tattoo artist. In our plaza." Frederick Sr. scowled at her over the edge of his wineglass. "You're that

Marchande woman that the other tenants signed the petition against."

"What?" Rosemary looked between her sons and her husband, clearly eager for ammunition. Amy wasn't overly insulted, because she understood now that this woman had been prejudiced against her since before she had even walked through the door. Rosemary wouldn't have been polite to anyone she didn't consider a suitable match for Fred—it was nothing against Amy personally. "I must say, I'm not surprised. The plaza was conceived to create a luxury shopping experience for the wealthy Bostonian, you see. It requires a certain…aesthetic."

"Mom." Fred pulled his napkin from his lap and slapped it down on the table, right overtop of his beef Wellington. "That is *enough*."

"Your mother isn't wrong." Frederick Sr. nodded into his wine. "Who approved the lease for a tattoo shop in the first place? Might have a word with them. Unsavory elements can decrease sales over the entire plaza. And traffic. Not surprised they formed that petition."

Amy didn't want to spend even one more moment around these people. These people, who couldn't see past her choice of career, what she looked like, who her family was.

Had she really expected anything different?

She had not. In fact, she had come prepared. Following Fred's example, she removed her nap-

kin from her lap, placing it delicately over the con-
gealing gravy of her entrée. Lifting her glass of
what she was sure was hideously expensive wine,
she lifted it to her lips and drank…and drank…and
drank. Once it was empty, she handed it off to Fred,
who took it with what she thought was a nod of appreciation. Then she stood, pushing her chair back
so abruptly that it wobbled.

"I might not have grown up in a rich area of the
city. I might not have a big house, or a huge business, or ties to the *Mayflower*." She pasted a fierce
smile on her lips and looked at Frederick Sr., then
at his wife. "But I have a hell of a lot more class."

"Class?" Rosemary made an unpleasant sound.
"You run a tattoo parlor, dear. I'm surprised you
know the word, and I don't understand why you're
taking such offense at the truth."

Beside her, Fred slammed his palms on the table,
starting to rise from his chair. He stopped when she
shook her head.

She didn't need a knight in shining armor to
come save her. She could do this all by herself.

"I did not keep in contact with either of your
sons in hopes that one day I'd marry one of them.
In fact, I never thought I'd see Fred again until he
came wandering into my shop this week, claiming
he wanted a tattoo to hide the fact that he'd been
ordered to deliver a warning letter he didn't agree
with. So really, you have yourself to thank that he

got reacquainted with me." She glared at Frederick Sr., then turned her attention to Rosemary. "By the way, your sons might be twins, but they are not interchangeable, at least not to me. It's only ever been Fred I wanted. I'm not the least bit attracted to Frank. No offense."

She nodded across the table to Fred's twin, who looked shocked and not a little delighted at the drama. As she looked, Frank shrugged, then wrapped an arm around Mark. "None taken. As you can see, it's worked out all right for me."

"I never—" Rosemary started, but Amy wasn't done.

"As for who approved my lease, that would be you, Mr. Vaughan." Reaching into one of the hidden pockets of her sleek dress, she removed a thumb drive and tossed it at him. It fell into his plate of beef Wellington. "Perhaps you allowed it because, in addition to offering works of art that use skin as a canvas, it is a gallery. Both of your sons have agreed that its aesthetics go above and beyond most tenants in the plaza."

Frederick Sr. blustered, but he actually stopped when Amy held up a hand to indicate she wasn't done.

"On that thumb drive, you'll find a copy of the lease agreement, with your signature, in case you disbelieve your own role in events." From the corner of her eye, she saw Fred rise to stand with her.

"You'll also find letters from every single tenant who signed that petition, recanting their signature."

"How did you manage that?" Across the table, Frank whistled. "Some of those tenants have iron rods up their bums."

"It wasn't difficult." Amy smirked at him, and he grinned back. Okay, he was growing on her. "I merely did some statistical work. I researched traffic into and out of the plaza on a random sampling of days. Conversion of that traffic to sales, and where they shopped. Compared the numbers to the likelihood that these shoppers had been drawn into the plaza due to any given piece of advertising, be it the plaza's, another tenant's or my own. And guess what? Since the day the plaza opened, Four Sisters Ink has been the reason that twenty-eight percent of shoppers have entered the plaza. And in case you've forgotten, there are two hundred and twelve storefronts, so let's please dispense with the notion that I am an unsavory element scaring people off."

"Fascinating," Frank muttered, drumming his fingers on the table. Beside Amy, Fred stood still. She couldn't see his face, couldn't bring herself to look. Was he proud of her? In disbelief? Angry?

It didn't matter. She'd wanted to impress his family, but at the end of the day, all she could be was herself.

"How did you get them all to back off from the

petition, though?" Frank continued, speaking over
the inarticulate sounds his parents were making.

"I wrote out a case study about my own marketing methods, and the percentages by which each
tactic had increased my business. I broke it down
into ideas that other businesses in the plaza could
apply to themselves." She sucked in a breath. "They
all backed down, and most apologized on the spot
for judging me on the nature of my business. The
petition you drafted the warning in response to is
now null and void, I would think, so unless you have
some other problem with my business being in the
plaza, I think we're done here."

"But…" Frederick Sr.'s face was scrunched so
tightly that he resembled a bulldog. "How do I know
your numbers are true? That you didn't just make
them up to get yourself out of trouble?"

"I guess you don't." Amy pinched her lips together as she looked at Frederick Sr., then at Rosemary. "But before you continue with your judgment,
I'll tell you that I have a business degree. It's from
a community college rather than an Ivy League
school, but let me assure you, I'm as savvy as I am
artistic."

There—she'd had her say. She'd expected to feel
relieved, triumphant, even. Instead, as she turned
to Fred, still standing silent beside her, she only
felt empty.

"I'm sorry. I can't do this." The words were heavy

on her lip. He'd risen to stand beside her, but she couldn't quite read the expression on his face. He was silent, too, and she didn't know if it was because he was proud of her for standing up for herself, or because he was loyal to his family and Vaughan Enterprises, to the end.

She supposed it didn't matter, really. No matter what she'd thought had sprouted between them, it would shrivel and die with the way his family felt about her. She looked up at him, into the eyes of the only man who had ever made her want more, and she took a single, painful step back. Something hot stung at the backs of her eyes.

She would *not* cry in front of these people. Not ever. So she went with the only other option available to her in that moment—she decided to leave. Spinning on her heel, she crossed the dining room, her steps loud on the marble floor. Just before she passed through the archway that led back to the sitting room, she paused, looking back over her shoulder.

"By the way," she started, catching Rosemary's eye and winking, "I have a frequent shopper card at Discount Depot. I think I'm almost at a free bottle on my stamp card. When I drink it, I'll make sure to think of you."

CHAPTER FOURTEEN

FRED HEARD THE front door slam, and before he could even think about what he was going to do, he was halfway across the room, following her.

"Frederick!" His father used a tone that Fred was well familiar with, conditioned to, and he turned around even though every cell in his body called out for him to follow Amy.

"Explain yourselves." Fred couldn't remember ever being this angry. He looked into the faces of the people he'd thought he'd known so well, the people who had raised him, and wondered how he could have been so wrong.

"I beg your pardon?" Placing his napkin very deliberately on the table, Frederick Sr. rose to a standing position. "Watch your tone, young man. When you are under this roof, you will show some respect."

"That's the thing, though, Dad. You've always taught us that respect is earned, not automatically given." Fred flexed his fingers, surprised to find that his hands were actually shaking with rage. "Why would I show you respect when you just treated the woman I love so horribly?"

"Love?" Rosemary gasped, clutching her short pearl necklace to her throat. "Oh, surely not, Fred!"

"Fred." His father tried a placating tone now, one Fred had heard him use on investors when they became antsy. "Look. I must admit that your young woman has, ah, spirit. A certain resourcefulness and business acumen that I hadn't expected someone like her to have."

"Someone like her. What does that mean, exactly?" Fred shifted his weight, itching to go after Amy but understanding that this conversation had to happen. "Are you referring to the fact that she's a tattoo artist? To the way she looks? To the fact that you don't know her family? Which is it, exactly? Please, enlighten me."

"That's enough." Frederick Sr. waved a hand in the air, gesturing for Fred to stop talking. "As I was saying. I suppose I can see the appeal as you sow your oats, or whatever this attraction is. But even if the Lawrences and the Lassiters have approved matches with girls in this family, you are a Vaughan. Blood is thicker than water, and this is not the girl for you."

Fred stared at his father for a long moment, silent. He'd convinced himself that introducing Amy to his parents would be fine, but now that the words had been spoken, he wondered if he hadn't expected this the whole time. Expected it, and wanted it.

Being with a woman who was so true to herself had made him understand things about himself that he'd never before been brave enough to acknowledge. And one of them, the biggest one, perhaps, was that while he would always love his family, and be grateful to them for the opportunities they'd provided, he was no longer interested in being associated with the way they handled business. The way they treated people, on the most basic level of human decency.

He was done.

He looked at his father, shook his head. Eyed his mother with disappointment. Caught his twin's eye and gave a nod to indicate that they would speak later.

Then he turned on his heel to follow the path Amy had taken out of the dining room and to the door.

"Frederick!" His father's voice thundered through the room, at a decibel that would have made Fred tremble in the past. Now he paused but didn't deign to look back over his shoulder as he spoke.

"Yes?"

"If you walk out that door right now, you can consider your participation in Vaughan Enterprises over." Did his father know how smug he sounded, how utterly certain that Fred would fall into line with what he'd demanded, simply because he wished it so?

There was so much privilege in that. As a wealthy white man from a prominent family, Fred knew that he possessed much privilege as well, but he'd just discovered a huge difference between himself and his father.

Frederick Sr. was content to let his privilege continue to serve him. Demanded that it did, even.

Fred, though? Maybe he'd felt that way, too, once upon a time. But being with Amy, with a woman who followed her own passions, had shown him that he'd rather use his position to make some kind of a difference.

He understood exactly what he was doing by walking away, but he did it anyway. Where was he going?

He needed to go find Amy.

CHAPTER FIFTEEN

"How DID YOU get in here?"

Paintbrush in the air, Amy stilled, just for a moment, before continuing on. On the sawhorse beside her was an artist's palette that she'd brought up from her shop, fully loaded with pools of oil paint. Alizarin crimson, cadmium yellow, Prussian blue and zinc white.

Dabbing the tip of her brush—a dagger, this one was called—into the crimson, she swept it across her canvas, leaving a deliberate streak behind. Her canvas in this case was the plain white wall of the single empty retail space in the plaza. Well, formerly white—it now featured the outline of a giant orange rose, the beginning of a mural she'd sketched out to work through her anger.

"It wasn't hard." She shrugged as she examined her palette, still facing away from Fred. She wasn't surprised that he'd found her, and in fact, she'd wanted to be found. "I know security is up to each tenant, but all you had protecting this empty space was a door with a thumb lock. I was prepared to try to pick it with a hairpin, but it opened with one hard twist."

One hard twist that had broken it, but that was neither here nor there. She expected him to sigh heavily, to remind her that if she wanted to stay here, she needed to back down. That she should go apologize to his parents, grovel on her knees for not being who they wanted her to be.

"All *they* had protecting this place," he corrected, as she geared herself up to argue with him.

"I'm not going to…" Her voice trailed off as she processed what he'd said. Turning slowly on bare feet, she found him standing a few feet behind her, hip propped up on the dusty sawhorse she was using as a table. He was watching her calmly, hungrily, and unless she was very much mistaken, he wasn't in the mood to argue with her. "What did you say?"

"I think you heard me." A sexy grin curved his lips, and Amy felt something tighten in her chest, a fist clutching her heart. "It seems that I'm no longer part of Vaughan Enterprises. Which I suppose means that we're both trespassing, but I think Phyllis will give us a pass if she happens by."

Amy was pretty sure that security guard Phyllis read Harlequin romance novels on her phone when things were quiet, so she was pretty sure that Fred was right. With no possibility of interruption, though, it meant that there was no more wasting time—it was time to have the hard conversation.

She ran a dry tongue over cracked lips, then tried to swallow. She opened her mouth to speak, but Fred beat her to it.

"I'm sorry I insisted on dinner with my family. I should have known better."

"How could you have known?" Setting down her paintbrush, she crossed her arms over her chest. "Have you brought home other tattoo artists that you met in Amsterdam that your parents hated?"

"No." The corner of his mouth quirked up with amusement. "I met the best of the lot right out the gate. Didn't need to go looking anymore."

"Maybe you shouldn't say things like that." Her voice was faint. She cleared her throat, tried to speak more firmly. "It will only make things harder."

"What things, exactly?" He moved in closer, and she could feel the heat emanating from his skin. She wanted to touch.

"You know." She swallowed again, wishing desperately for a glass of ice water. Warm water. Anything to wet her throat with. "Things between…us."

"Amy." Reaching out with one hand, he cupped her cheek. She couldn't help herself; she pressed into the warmth of his touch.

"You didn't follow me." Her breath hitched; her cheeks flushed with embarrassment. "When I left. You stayed. That says something."

"I stayed because I had some things to say." He dipped his head, brushed his lips over her forehead. "Things that have been fermenting for years. Things that could no longer wait to be said."

"I think my feelings about your family are pretty obvious at this point." Restless, she shifted her weight from one foot to the other. "But…well, they're still your family. I'm not sorry for what I said to them. They were awful. But I… I don't… I mean. I understand that you're trapped in between a rock and a hard place."

"I see things differently now that I'm with you." He stroked her cheek with his thumb, absentmindedly. "And you know what? I'm not trapped at all."

"What…what are you saying?" Her pulse stuttered.

"I'm saying that…if you hadn't come back into my life, I might have been content enough to stay on with the family business. To float along, meeting the status quo and living a shell of a life." He sucked in a deep breath. "But you showed me that it's okay to want something different. To be who you really are. To love who you love."

"What did you say?" Her knees trembled. She looked up at him with wide eyes, her heart on her sleeve. "Don't say it unless you mean it."

"Amy." Curling his free arm around her waist, Fred pulled her in closer to him. Her breath was unsteady as she looked up into his eyes. "I love you.

I love everything about you. Don't you know that by now?"

She closed her eyes, inhaled deeply, let the anxiety wash away. She'd known this somehow, on some level, but even knowing that, she hadn't been certain that love would be enough for him to defy his family.

Was he defying his family? Squeezing one eye open, she looked up at him with suspicion.

"How does this work with your job? Your... legacy?" She gestured wide with her arms, indicating the empty space. "I don't think your dad is going to be pleased for you to keep seeing me."

"I don't care." Fred's smile was so quick, lighter than she'd ever seen it. "As of right now, I'm no longer an employee of Vaughan Enterprises. And you know what? I've never felt so free."

"What?" A siren rang in her ears. "Fred, Boston is expensive. What are you going to do?"

"I'll be fine, I promise." He laughed lightly. "I went to law school at Harvard, and even if I've been disowned, the Vaughan name carries weight. I'll have plenty of opportunities...if I want them."

"What else would you do?"

"I don't know." He turned to study the unfinished mural on the wall. It was a shame that it would inevitably be painted over once tenants were found. It was some of her best work. "Maybe I'll become a tattoo artist."

She had a quick, bright mental picture of Fred, tattooed up as he bent over someone lying in his tattoo chair, and snorted. He raised an eyebrow, but he was smiling.

"What? You don't think I could do it?"

"I think perhaps you should leave it to the professionals." Biting her lower lip, she reached around him for a brush. Swirling it through the yellow, she turned back to the wall, considering where to place the bristles. "It's an art form, you know?"

"I'm aware." Plucking the paintbrush back out of her hand, he set it back down on her palette at the same time he turned her around. Catching her chin in his hand, he held her still while looking her over. "You have paint on your dress."

"I make a mess when I paint mad." She smoothed a hand over the purple satin skirt and grimaced. "I'll have to buy Meg a new one."

"Hmm, I think it's salvageable." The hand at her chin moved down, stroking over the delicate curve of her throat. "But you should probably take it off right now. So you don't get anything else on it, you know."

"I see." She eyed him, momentarily uncertain. "Is this a good idea? Not to overthink sex, but right now…might it not complicate things that you need to think on?"

She gasped when one of his hands slid right into the side of her dress, cupping her breast, which pebbled against his palm. Fire in her belly ignited, she inhaled deeply, waiting to see what he would do next.

"The only thing I need to think about," he replied, delivering a sharp pinch to her nipple that made her gasp, "is how many spanks you're about to receive for questioning my desire to be with you. Understood?"

"Understood," she gasped, pressing into his touch. He plucked at the silver barbell, and her need became a sharp ache, traveling quickly from her breast to the space between her legs.

She'd loved it when Fred had taken control the night before but had imagined that it was a one-off, a kinky game he'd indulged in to appease her. Hearing the rough edge in his voice right now, and having a better understanding of the dynamics to which he'd been born, told her that this dominant streak of his likely ran deeper than she'd anticipated.

She fucking loved it. Even more, after the way the evening had gone, she was more than happy to hand over the reins to someone who wanted to take control—her control.

"Do you still want me to take my dress off?" A taunting note in her voice, she did a slow spin. She'd removed her sweater and shoes when she'd broken into this space, so her naked back was revealed. She paused facing away, to give him a good look.

"No." Closing the space between them, he

quickly undid the hook and eye closure that held
the neck in place. Amy gasped at the kiss of cool
air on her naked skin when the top of the dress
fell down around her waist. She moaned when she
felt him reach around her from behind to cup her
breasts, working the tips insistently until she was a
panting mess, pushing back against him.

She groaned when he released the soft flesh. Trying to steady her breath, she felt him fist his hands
in the hem of her skirt, slowly pulling it up to her
waist. He tucked it into the waistband of the fallen
bodice.

"You create beautiful art." His voice was rough,
harsh in the quiet air of the dusky room. "But I
don't think I'll ever see anything more beautiful
than this."

She was wearing full-bottomed panties, but they
were sheer and black. Without warning, he slapped
his palm over the crease that divided them once,
then twice. Heat pooled between her legs, and she
felt herself pushing back toward him, desperate for
more.

Rather than delivering another blow, he gathered
the waistband of the panties in his long fingers and
ripped. Amy gasped again when she heard them
tear, felt his questing fingers explore the opening
he'd just made.

"I want to take my time with you, but I don't
think I can." Reaching between her legs, he swiped

his fingers through her wet heat, then traced them back, along the crease that divided the cheeks of her behind. "I'm feeling a bit primal tonight. I need you, Amy. I need to claim you. If you're not okay with this, please say so now. I'm afraid I'm going to lose control."

His clever fingers found the pucker of her rear entrance. Her body bucked, and she cried out her response.

"Take me." She barely recognized her own voice. "However you want to, but take me now."

He snarled—that was the only word for it. With a palm flat on her back, he bent her over the sawhorse, then ground his pelvis against her naked behind.

"Hold on to this." He delivered one more quick blow as she did as she was told, fingers digging into the rough wood on either side of her body. When she closed her eyes, she could hear the metallic rasp of his zipper being undone, the soft sound of fabric dragging on flesh, the metallic crinkle of a condom wrapper. She inhaled, and he pressed the head of his cock to her soaking-wet entrance; she didn't have enough coherent thought left to be embarrassed by her shameless state.

With a grunt and a single hard thrust of his hips, he was inside her, all the way inside her; the way she was bent over the sawhorse left her open, inviting him deeper inside than he'd been before. She gasped for air as he pulled back, fingers digging into the wood. When he worked his way back in, he pressed a finger to the hidden rosette of her rear, shocking her body into sensations she'd never experienced before.

Working his finger past the tight ring of muscle, he filled her in two places, and she couldn't hold back the scream. One thrust, two, and then she came, his bossy fingers ordering that she take her pleasure. She did, clenching around him like a vise. Behind her, she felt him shudder, his muscles tighten. His movements shortened, because a short series of sloppy thrusts as he pursued his own pleasure, and then he came, his shout mingling with her hoarse cries as she continued to come, around his finger and around his cock.

The force of his release made Amy shake, pushing her up and through one more of her own. Her body resisted it for a moment, overly sensitive at this point and not sure it could handle more, but Fred had told her he was going to claim her. Her body knew that this wasn't her decision, so when he thrust into her roughly again, and again, and again, she fell, spiraling through the glittering dark in a way that should have been terrifying. Should have been, but wasn't…because Fred was there to catch her.

EPILOGUE

"NICE DIGS."

Fred looked up from the cardboard box he was unpacking to find his twin in the doorway. While Fred was dressed down in his new daily uniform of khakis and a crisp button-down shirt, Frank was, as always, wearing a perfectly fitted custom suit. He looked, Fred thought, much as he himself had, only a month before.

"Thanks for signing off on the lease." Pushing the box away with one foot, Fred lowered himself to his new office chair, which still had a layer of plastic on it that squeaked beneath his weight. He gestured to the equally new chair that sat on the other side of his box-store desk.

"There wasn't much to think about." His twin shrugged as he lowered himself into the chair that Fred had indicated. "The space was sitting empty, and a law office is a good fit."

"It's not a law office." Fred scowled at his brother.

"Jesus, Frank, didn't you read the paperwork? If this doesn't pan out because you—"

"Chill." Frank rolled his eyes, then placed the long, slender box he'd been carrying onto the desk—fifty-year-old Glenfiddich. Nice. "Have a drink before you have an aneurysm. Yes, I read it, but 'legal counsel for the Boston Underprivileged Housing Authority' is a bit of a mouthful to say every time."

"As long as it's legit." Fred eyed his brother again, then reached into the box he'd been unpacking. From it he withdrew two mugs, both with Amy's artwork on them, a new item she was offering in her shop. Frank nodded at his approvingly before reaching for the scotch.

"It's legit." Fred watched as his twin opened the box. Removing the heavy bottle, he uncorked it, then poured a generous measure into each mug. "You did have the upper hand, though. No one else wants to lease a space with a giant mural on the wall."

"That mural is fine art, I'll have you know." Picking up his mug, Fred inhaled the peaty aroma, then took a careful sip. "Did you buy this or steal it from Dad again?"

"I didn't steal it," Frank replied, indignant. "I told him I was heading over here, and he took it out of his desk and handed it to me. Told me to bring it."

"Interesting." Fred paused with the mug at his

lips again, considering. He and his family had reached a détente of sorts when he'd applied to lease this space, but he and Amy still wouldn't be heading over there for dinner any time soon. He wanted an apology for the things they'd said about her—to her—and thus far they hadn't offered one. The scotch was a small step forward, but there were a lot more steps to take.

Fred held on to the hope that they would be taken, at some point. And if they didn't, that was okay, too, as long as he had Amy.

"I have to get back to the office." Frank nodded to his brother as he stood. "Anything you want me to tell Dad?"

"Tell him thanks for the scotch." Fred pondered saying more, but he just wasn't ready. Lifting his mug, he saluted his brother. "Thanks for being the go-between."

"I don't work for free, you know." Frank drained the last sip of his drink, then held the mug up to the light for inspection. "Can I have this mug? It's cool."

"Sure you can. For twenty bucks." Frank rolled his eyes, and Fred gestured widely with his palms. "Hey, I just work here."

"Uh-huh." His twin made a big show out of pulling a money clip from his pocket and extracting a twenty. With exaggerated gestures, he moved to lay it on the desk, then snatched it back. "I suppose I should go downstairs and leave this with Amy, then?"

Fred grinned as he tried to come up with a snarky comeback, which he knew his twin would then inevitably try to top. Happiness was a warm glow in his chest, spreading outward as he leaned back in his chair and looked at the gigantic orange rose that stretched the length of the wall in his new office space.

Life wasn't perfect, but he no longer thought it was supposed to be. And with his twin still in his life, a new job that ignited fire in his gut and, most of all, the woman he loved at his side during the day and in his bed at night?

He might not be part of his family legacy anymore. But you know what? He was doing just fine anyway.

* * * * *

MILLS & BOON

THE HEART OF ROMANCE

A ROMANCE FOR EVERY KIND OF READER

MODERN

Prepare to be swept off your feet by sophisticated, sexy and seductive heroes, in some of the world's most glamourous and romantic locations, where power and passion collide.
8 stories per month.

HISTORICAL

Escape with historical heroes from time gone by. Whether your passion is for wicked Regency Rakes, muscled Vikings or rugged Highlanders, awaken the romance of the past.
6 stories per month.

MEDICAL

Set your pulse racing with dedicated, delectable doctors in the high-pressure world of medicine, where emotions run high and passion, comfort and love are the best medicine.
6 stories per month.

True Love

Celebrate true love with tender stories of heartfelt romance, from the rush of falling in love to the joy a new baby can bring, and a focus on the emotional heart of a relationship.
8 stories per month.

Desire

Indulge in secrets and scandal, intense drama and plenty of sizzling hot action with powerful and passionate heroes who have it all: wealth, status, good looks…everything but the right woman.
6 stories per month.

HEROES

Experience all the excitement of a gripping thriller, with an intense romance at its heart. Resourceful, true-to-life women and strong, fearless men face danger and desire - a killer combination!
8 stories per month.

DARE

Sensual love stories featuring smart, sassy heroines you'd want as a best friend, and compelling intense heroes who are worthy of them.
4 stories per month.

To see which titles are coming soon, please visit

millsandboon.co.uk/nextmonth